Saga

Dead Men Walking

Dead Men in Winter

Book II of the Snowflakes Trilogy

Joshua E. B. Smith

Publisher: Joshua E. B. Smith
Cover Illustration: Peggy J. Smith
sagadmw@gmail.com

DEDICATION

I cannot begin to thank everyone involved in getting Dead Men in Winter to print – for that matter, I can't begin to thank everyone involved in helping with Snowflakes in Summer, either.

I can, however, call out a few notable names.

Randy Zinn, Sarah Zinn, and Adam Hill all provided direct support with the GoFundMe campaign I ran in early 2017 to help cover the initial setup fees to register ISBN numbers and to pay for book setup fees through my publishing agency. Jennifer Staley provided a huge stack of business cards, and I absolutely have no way to count the number of times that Renee Haugh, Josh Snider, Sara Gainer, Travis and Tracey Berry, Megan Whitehair, Sage Edwards, Deanna Jones and so many others helped me share posts, advertise, or otherwise drum up business and get the word out.

I'd also be doing a huge disservice if I didn't give a 'Thank you' to Peggy Smith (hi mom!), Rose Beck (hi sweetie!), Heather Smith, Alecia Gulley, Erin Schweri, Bill Kane, Tony Workman, and Jeff Jones for all the times that I needed a place to sell copies of Snowflakes, to talk about gaping plot holes, or to generally give me a kick in the ass to get in the right direction. An extra bonus call goes out to Erin and Kristen Corwin for doing beta-reader work on the final draft of Dead Men in Winter.

From the bottom of my heart, thank you.

And now...
Time to make you question if all that help was worth it. ;)

~Josh

CONTENTS

DEAD MEN IN WINTER

Arin-Goliaths.

*Commonly known to as 'nesting wraiths,' these lost souls
are a strange breed, even amongst the rank and file of the damned.
They are a plurality of spirits, all anchored around a single essence.
One is many, many is one.
Their personalities are absorbed each in turn, but fractured
and disjointed to the point that each spirit believes it is the same entity.*

*They are rare in the waking world.
Not unheard of, but rare – rarer still to be more than a pest.
Often you'll find them hiding under cities or encamped
in ruins where civilizations once stood.*

*Over time, they siphon energy off from the world,
consume any souls that enter their territory.
Over time, they grow. Slowly but steadily,
they will grow. It is their nature.*

*Even after they grow in strength for years, they are never
much of a threat. Expulse them one at a time.
Banish them, purge them, condemn them. One at a time.
In the end, the core will remain – and then you banish it too.*

*How... unfortunate... that the one that named itself Daringol
found more power than just what was natural to the land.
It drank and drank from a well of wild magic unfettered, effectively
giving it centuries of strength in a scant handful of years.*

*And... this one had minions.
Two pit-hounds, purged by my student and returned to the Abyss.
Another, a true-blood demon, a sentient beast that could have only
come from the Lower Plane of Elemental Ice.*

*That thing – that creature by the name of Makolichi – that thing?
Oh I've no doubt that the first
Battle of Coldstone's Summit wounded it severely.*

My student almost gave as good as he got.
Akaran almost destroyed him.
Akaran almost beat him on his own.

Almost.

I watched him fall to that beast.

Now if I could only find where he went
after he died...

~Paladin-Commander Steelhom

I. HEATWAVE

Mirah-Anne had died and gone to the Abyss.

All about were fields of lava and insufferable heat. Souls wailed in the distance as an all-consuming cloud of pure darkness descended upon her. The only thing she could do was watch in abject horror and scream silently in her mind. There wasn't any escape, there was no place to go. She was trapped, hopeless, and knew it was only a matter of time before her very essence was crushed beneath the heel of the demonic legions soon to come.

In the midst of this, there was one man; her personal tormentor. His hair was a dark chocolate brown with streaks of gray through it. He was easily forty-five years old — a rough forty-five, at that. He had haunting white eyes with no iris to be seen at all. She would have thought him blind if he didn't seem to be able to see everything perfectly clearly. He bore a scar on his lips, which appeared to be ever-turned to a frown.

He had sized her up the moment he had come into her room, and the apprentice alchemist felt like a bug before him. The events of the last few hours had her in shock still. Demons had descended on Toniki, her home, leaving bodies and ruin in their wake. Two hounds almost as tall as fawns and as wide as boars had ravaged everyone they could catch, while a skeletal monstrosity in a shell made of frozen black brine destroyed homes and eviscerated almost everyone that tried to help.

A handful of lost souls came behind them, creatures of inky fog and countless tentacles that flung themselves into any corpse that they could find. Each body shook and buckled as the lost souls took them over, claiming new homes. She had seen fallen friends launch themselves into the air with haunting cries as the wraiths twisted and tore at their essences from the inside out.

As she sat there under this man's unwavering gaze, he held a book in his hand; a journal left behind by the man that had been sent days before to try to protect them. Once the carnage outside had been organized and brought under his control, the journal had been the very first thing he had demanded to see. She had watched him read it and had watched his face darken with every single page until he reached the end of it.

That's when the inquiry, and her personal torture, began.

"So then. Allow me to make sure I understand what happened here," Sir Steelhom intoned. "Stop me if I seem to have gotten any of this wrong."

Mariah cleared her throat and looked up at the Paladin-Commander and nervously swallowed. "Ye... yes... sir..." she stammered. It would have been funny, if he wasn't towering over her. They both sat in the Rutting Goat with the fireplace burning brightly behind them and a flagon of foul ale burning into her stomach.

It wasn't really the Abyss, and he wasn't really a demon, but *damn* did it feel like it.

"This village has been suffering a winter that has had no end in the last four years. The bulk of the people here have long moved away. The ones left are either too stupid to know that they should or too poor to be able to. There's no more than twenty, maybe thirty of the Queen's citizens left here?"

"Yes... yes sir, that's correct. Though I'd not call them stupid..."

"I would," he snapped. "Those two pit-hounds my protege left smoldering outside have been hunting anyone that left the city walls and they ate a patrol from the local garrison. You don't know how many they've killed, in total, other than 'a lot.' They've been supported by that foul demon in that brine-and-ice shell. Makolichi, you said?"

Her only response was a hesitant nod.

"To join those three monsters you apparently have a cadre of wraiths that have manifested as floating masses of tentacles, arms, faces, and a black fog. Oh, and they *love* to take over bodies and animate them for their own use. Animals, specifically, but they don't seem to be too picky."

Since the first nod worked, she gave him a second one.

Steelhom clenched his jaw and continued to stare at her. "Akaran also discovered some kind of obscura - a masking spell - that has kept the work of some local wizard a secret, and it's allowed the Abyssians to operate here freely without running afoul of the Order's attention. Is that correct?"

"That's what he said... um, sir. Don't think he ever called it an 'obscura,' though..."

"He should have. So. He also declared that whatever's left of that fountain out by the shrine is tapped into a font of wild magic. He used that magic to keep himself alive and it's in a very large part of why he was able to last so long against this... Makolichi... and the dogs."

The alchemist's apprentice swallowed another gulp of the rancid ale and tried not to gag on it. Little desperate thoughts of *Please work please work please knock me out*, echoed in the back of her mind. "That's what he said. I don't know. I'm no mage."

"But this village, as small as it is, seems to be full of them. Your mentor is not just an alchemist but is also a former druid in service to the Goddess of Nature – and she lied to him about her magical aptitude in violation of Queen's Law. There's the wizard, Usaic, that Akaran surmised was behind this wretched mess. My student believes he is an outcast of the Granalchi Academy with a focus on elemental-ice spellwork, isn't that right?"

"Ye... yes, sir."

"You've had a Civan spy living here for years; Rmaci, isn't that her name? Oh, and *she* ran off, leaving assorted headaches behind? That Illiya-blessed blade being one of them?"

She nodded slowly. "I can't speak for the weapon, but yeah, the bitch left more headaches than happiness. Can blame a lot of people on her."

"You've had bodies up and moving around outside *but* your people opted against calling up on the Order to come put them down. Let me not forget the medic from the garrison that lied until he was blue in the face about being able to use magic of his own, magic my student attributed to the Goddess of Purity."

Mariah tried to hide another meek little tremble of fear into her mug. The dogs had scared her. The wraiths had frightened her. That damn goat was more disgusting than horrifying. The pale-skinned elemental that he hadn't brought up yet was powerful but not really scary. That monster in the frozen suit of armor? Makolichi was **terrifying**.

This guy?

This fire-breathing monster from the furthest reaches of all of the most unholy would be enough to give any of those Abyssian nightmares a dozen times over and she didn't blame them one bit. "Yes, sir, yes to all of those."

"Is it safe for me to assume that he has already asked the lot of you how you all could be so blessedly stupid?"

"I believe he said 'fisking idiots,' sir."

"At least I don't have to repeat it then. Good to know he did that much right."

She cringed and refused to meet his burning stare. "He saved my life..."

That didn't impress him. Not even remotely. "Ah yes, the lives he 'saved.' Let's count them down. Vestranis, the blacksmith. One of the hounds took him. Tornias, the medic; the other hound, by your accounts. The Civan spy – who helped run this very inn, alongside her husband – accounted for not just the stablemaster Mowiat, but also Ronlin, your town elder, and probably Yothargi, her husband. There was also that orphan... what was his name?"

"Julianos, sir. Tornias sent him to the graveyard and Makolichi went there and -"

"Ah yes. Julianos. A child."

Running her hands through her blonde hair, the girl blinked back tears at the full list of the dead. "The hounds killed Surchi too, when they attacked. I... I don't think Akaran had ever met her..."

Neither of them knew (or ever would know) that Yothargi had provided the killing blow to Ronlin. He had been egged on and set up by his lovely traitor of a wife, Rmaci, but he had the last bit of blood on his hands. Not that it saved him from when she drained the blood from his heart after the fact...

With a small pause, he looked back at the journal and flipped a few pages away from the end of it. "Oh. And one more. It seems there's another creature that manifested as a young girl with pale eyes and brown hair, 'skin as soft as ivory,' he wrote, who had a 'chill to her touch but one not unpleasant.' He claims she has a significant level of magical ability and assuredly is *not* at all human. He seemed to think that she is in no way Abyss-touched although *completely* a creature not of this world."

"Yes. She called herself Eos'eno. I've never seen her, ever, not until after he arrived here in Toniki."

"I assume that she is also the creature that absconded with him after the battle was over?"

When the last attack came, there wasn't much warning. The dogs had come first and had made it towards the edge of the village where the Shrine to the Order of Light stood. The mana-font that Akaran had discovered was out in front of it; the dogs seemingly had wanted it. Or they had wanted the exorcist that had been vexing them; since he had been sleeping inside the shrine, it could have gone either way.

The fight was bloody from the very start. The hounds tore apart everyone that came near the shrine with ecstatic glee. Akaran put up a great showing against both of the dogs before Makolichi intervened. He had used every trick in his book to batter down the hounds and the demon at the same time while other people joined the pile of corpses.

Then the corpses started to animate themselves with the help of Daringol. When the wraith intervened, everything went south. There wasn't time to expect them; let alone time to deal with them.

Hirshma had entered the fray at one point, and eventually Eos'eno did too. The three of them were able to kill both hounds and badly wound Makolichi. When the corpses entered the fight, they had offered enough of a distraction to let the demon in ice mortally wound Akaran with a spear of frozen brine that cut through his stomach and out his back.

Steelhom unexpectedly arrived at the end and salvaged the battle (and savaged the monsters). He put down the animated corpses and forced Makolichi to flee. Before he could reach his student though, Eos'eno had shoved him away and vanished with him in a sudden cloud of pure snow and perfectly clear crystal.

That was just a few hours ago, just after the crack of dawn. It was now mid-day.

It felt like it had happened more than a year ago.

"Sir?"

"Yes?"

Trying to ignore the screaming butterflies in her stomach that should have kept her from opening her mouth, the blonde asked the one thing that had been nagging at her since the interrogation had. "Why are you here? Why are you asking me all these questions? Why not my miss?"

"Your miss? The town alchemist? The woman that – again – admittedly intentionally mislead my student, refused to cooperate with an inquisition, withheld pertinent knowledge of the disaster as it stands, and apparently is able to control aspects of nature magic?"

It was impossible to refute any of that. "Yes, that's Hirshma. I wish I could say otherwise."

"Oh I bet you do."

"But... there are others...?"

Steelhom shrugged his shoulders. "I saw that you carried out the execution of two of the risen bodies. I saw your face when that elemental-kin absconded with my student. If you like him that much then I assume you can be trusted."

"I don't like him. I can barely stand him."

"Then you are still doing better than most. Not just most of the people in your village, but... most, as a whole. You also accounted for a sizable portion of his journal entries; if *he* likes you that much, one of two things has occurred."

Mariah's eyes widened. "He did? I was?"

"Either he has become infatuated with you and seeks to bed you, or he believes he can trust you." He paused and looked her up and down with a raised eyebrow – and she immediately blushed a shade of bright crimson. "I will assume the latter."

It took a minute for that to sink in, and her blush flickered to cheeks full of rosy-red rage. "HEY! Now you wait a damn minute - !"

Ignoring her outburst, the paladin pushed on. "Now, this leads me to my next question, and girl, please do allow me to *stress* that I *need* a very helpful answer."

Oh shit.

"Where did that creature take Akaran? What in the name of the Heavens did he *do* that you aren't telling me?"

There were few ways to transport someone from one point or another by magic. All of them took a great deal of effort and no small level of discomfort. Throughout most of the Kingdoms, the wizards of the Granalchi Academy had a near-monopoly on the ability. They were expensive and their aim, at times, truly left a lot to be desired.

They shoved your body fully into the ether, in a magical pocket that they forced to come into being between worlds. A second wizard would pop open the bubble from somewhere else to drop you back into reality safely. Or if time was at a premium, the bubble could be configured in a way to allow for it to re-open on its own; though it was a decidedly more expensive (and risky) option.

Disorienting, disturbing, and occasionally terrifying, it worked. Most people surmised that the only reason that the Granalchi hadn't used that magic (and their other tricks) to take over the world was only because they didn't want to be burdened with the paperwork (and nausea from traveling through that many portals) world domination would entail.

It was a small comfort to those with an innate distrust of magic.

What Eos'eno did, on the other hand, was something else entirely.

The exorcist saw things as they traveled. He had glimpses of mountains of nothing more than ice and frozen lakes that were crystal clear through and through. There were spires built upon spires of crystals in colors he never thought possible. Blues, greens, even soft purple and gold. He didn't think he could be impressed by anything else after those brief flashes.

He was wrong. Wonderfully wrong.

When he saw the creatures that inhabited the fascinating landscape he could barely comprehend it. He watched as mammoths the size of castles trundled through the snow-covered landscape. Floating masses of icy shards spun about in the sky, dancing with each other in ways that defied all manner of the Laws of Normality. His ability to hold onto his sanity nearly left him entirely when he saw a mountain began to take steps of its own on legs of flowing quicksilver.

Akaran caught sight of the girl that had his hand in a death grip. Her hair billowed everywhere around her. She was lit up with a pale white glow that was just short of heavenly. Crystals ebbed and flowed over and under her skin. Icicles sprouted up and down her arms and chest. Her clothes vanished as her very body shed the humanity that barely contained it. She was filled with such joy that it was nearly blinding.

Briefly, very briefly, he thought he saw the face of a woman the size of an island look up at them from beneath a frozen sea. The universe and all of time everlasting was reflected in those eternal eyes. She blinked, once, as Her mouth began to form into a *[Who?]*

There was no way he should have seen Her.

He really wasn't meant to.

He'd have to answer for it later.

The most important (or if not *the* most important) thing that he felt wasn't the soothing chill or the comfortable feeling of the snow on his back as Eos laid him down on the ground. It was pain. Nothing but raw, searing, horrific pain. He could almost still see the spear of ice that Makolichi had thrown as clearly as if it was right in front of him.

They fought in the middle of the courtyard outside of the shrine at Toniki. The two hounds were dead and in smoking heaps nearby. The demon, encased in his shell of toxic, brine-like ice, disgorged a shard of ice as long as Akaran's sword from his arm. The shard shot through the air like it had been fired from a cannon.

It hit him in his stomach and ripped itself through the other side.

There was no reason that he should have been drawing breath right now and he knew it.

That was another issue – there was no air here to breathe. Try as he might, nothing filled his lungs when he gasped or struggled to inhale. His body didn't care, or at least, didn't seem to. His chest burned from the toxic mass in his gut but it didn't feel like it was being deprived of air. In fact, if it wasn't for the pain, he wouldn't have felt that anything was wrong at all.

"No die, won't die. Can't die. Ice preserves, cold secures. Life and time changes but ice is slow and sure. Rest and be at ease, Guardian of Winters. You've no fears no worries here," she quietly crooned.

Reeling from pain, he looked up at her and saw her for what she was. Golden caramel hair danced of its own accord across her shoulders and down her back. A web of soft white crystals covered her naked body from head to toe, each one glinting with a sheen from the extra-planar sun that hung somewhere above. Her eyes were larger than a human's, with no iris to be seen – just a pale blue that spilled light freely.

Her true beauty was a far cry from the waifish girl in a ratty patchwork cloak she had first appeared as on that first fateful night in Toniki. Not that she wasn't pretty then, but now... now it was obvious that her form was the work of a Goddess, and not some mere human mother. There was more to it though, a hint that Istalla hadn't simply pulled her from the elemental plane and sent her to the mortal world.

There also a gash in her side that he could almost see through to the other side. Makolichi had swung his claws at her and ripped a chunk of flesh the size of Akaran's head out of her ribs. She didn't bleed red – but she *did* bleed, and bled silvery slush freely from the hole. It was impossible to tell if it was a mortal wound on her, but if it had been on him?

The damage was so extensive, he would have been dead.

As it stood, he was convinced he already was.

"Won't die. Won't let you die. Ice preserves, cold secures. Do you hear, do you understand? Be at peace, rest and hold your head low. Mother's home will protect you. It is what ice is to do."

It was debatable as to if her soothing words helped. When his trembling hands found the hole that the demon had left behind, that question was quickly answered. "Hurts," he croaked, specks of blood spitting out between his lips. "Hurts so much. Let me... let me see the Goddess..."

"No! Mother will not see you. Mother should *not* see you," Eos chastised. "She may be quite annoyed if She finds you, living among Her children. Ice will preserve and protect you but Mother may choose to leave you preserved longer than either of us wish."

Her warning went unheeded. "Not... yours. Mine. Niasmis..."

"Niasmis will not be welcome to enter the home of Istalla without an invitation. For invitation, Mother must first know you are here. Guardian of Winters must not have listened. Mother should not know you are here. Thus, She will not issue an invitation to Niasmis. Thus, you will not see your Lady. Not today."

Painfully, he pushed himself up and looked down at the ruined mass that made up his stomach and tried not to throw up (not that he could, even if he had wanted) from the sight of it. *In shock, must be shock, must be dying, must be seeing things...*

Eos'eno sighed and the beautiful crystals that covered her skin seemed to flatten down like the ears of an irritated cat. "In shock? No. Seeing things? You see me, you see the glory of the realm of Istalla. You need not try to speak. I hear your thoughts as plain as day, Guardian."

"Hurts! Hurts so much please let me go please stop calling me that please...!"

"Does not hurt. No pain here. Pain in your head nothing more nothing else. Rest easy."

Akaran shook his head rapidly and pulled the wound open again. Makolichi and the dogs had attacked before he could so much as to slip a tunic on, let alone any armor. If he had had some on, it might have made a difference. Then again, with the size of the hole left behind? Probably not. "No, please... it hurts, hurts so much."

"There should be no hurt and no pain, not here, not while here. Magic of Istalla will heal your wound. Guardian of Winters will be healed. Rest and be patient, be calm. Ice preserves, cold secures." Her tone was that of a mother scolding and comforting a whining child. Any other time, he would've felt insulted.

"You don't understand, please!" He steeled himself for the worst and plunged two fingers into his stomach. She grabbed at his hand but he fought her off, and miraculously, it didn't hurt at all when he did. Not until his fingers found what he was searching for and pulled it free. The black crystal shard turned from a piece of solid ice to a squirming mass of shadows and tentacles the moment that it hit the 'air.'

Eos'eno hissed sharply and batted the living piece of corruption out of his hand. When it hit the ground it sizzled and boiled in the snow. For a brief moment, it billowed to life and swelled up. That particular display came to an end when a dozen-dozen pieces of pure crystal erupted in the air itself and lanced through it in every direction imaginable.

Any sort of calm demeanor that the elemental-kin possessed vanished on the spot. "Brine's blood. Yes, Brine's blood, I see. Hurt it must. It seeks to grow in here the corruption seeks to..."

Groaning in pain, he dropped his head back down against the side of the snowy hill she had set him on and closed his eye. "It hurts Goddess it hurts can't feel Her to pull strength to purge..."

"Purge. Yes, a purge shall do," Eos whispered. Without giving his comfort a moment's thought, she pushed her hand – her entire right hand and almost halfway way to her elbow – into his wound. Akaran screamed. There was no mistaking it; he *screamed*.

A pulse of total cold poured into his every fiber, his every vein, his every bone. It hurt worse than the bloody tunnel that Makolichi had left in his wake, though at the same time, it felt wonderful. All thoughts of pain turned to sudden revulsion as he felt a *thing* get forced into his stomach and up his throat.

Nausea replaced pain as his reeling mind realized what was coming up – and that lead his body to help her magic do its work. His back arched and his chest heaved and he vomited blood and something horrible all over his lap. He felt the scrambling tentacles push themselves up out of his throat and felt the toxic bile slide over his teeth and between his lips.

A cloud of Daringol's essence rolled out of his mouth and down his goatee. It tumbled down his body and lurched into the snow beside him. He had time to make out a face twisted in joy and terror in the middle of the shifting black mass for a moment before the inherent magic of Tundrala gave the wraith's spawn the same treatment it had given the shard of Makolichi's corruption.

The moment that it was gone the pain in his body ceased. The cold feeling of misery faded as she slipped her bloody hand out of his gut, leaving him feeling nothing more than just... simple relief. "There. The purge. Guardian, do you feel better? Does it hurt so still?"

Weakly, he shook his head.

Then as he watched, his stomach began to mend with streamers of silver ice. Skin turned blue and white as it sealed the wound. A chill erupted deep inside his soul as her magic pulled flesh and bone back into shape. It defied understanding, even familiar as he was with medicinal spellwork. Even with what little he knew, there was no doubt that this was above and beyond *anything* mere mortals could manage.

"Good. But not so."

"Not... not so?" the exorcist croaked.

"Not so," she reaffirmed. She pushed herself away and stood up, looking at something far in the distance across the rolling snowy hills, and back towards where she had seen the walking mountain minutes before. "Now She'll know. Mother will be displeased. Mother will be most displeased. The taint of the Lower will catch the eye of the *episturine*. Their eyes will be Her eyes. Her eyes will be most annoyed. With you. With me."

Akaran sat up, slowly, but it didn't hurt as he did. "*Episturine?*"

If a creature of ice and snow could sigh, Eos'eno surely gave it her best effort. "Humans. Think you know all. Know so very little of the things all about your world. The *episturine* watch the River of Souls from your world and the Waters of Eternity from the High Mount. They ensure there is no corruption no darkness of any kind no souls not of Tundrala that pass into this realm. They will sense the pollution that the other left behind in you. They will then see you. They will be displeased. Displeased like Mother."

"River of Souls... Waters of Eternity?" That was when he looked – *really looked* – and realized that no, he hadn't been seeing things. "Where am I? Where did you take me?"

"A place once safe. A place not safe anymore." With what could only be described as a frustrated huff that made the small canyon they were in flex in response, Eos'eno took his hand in hers and gave him a foul look (like any of this was *his* fault). "We leave. Work to be done. Work you need to do."

Any other questions died on his lips as the plane seemingly collapsed all around them.

With that, they left for the mortal realm and the work she was desperate to have him do.

✳ ✳ ✳

Sir Steelhom had replaced Mariah with Hirshma, Moulborke, Romazalin and Peoran – the last four citizens of the village that mattered much to anyone. There was a bar wench in the background that had called herself Ipteria between mugs of ale – and she was so drunk that nobody listened to a thing she mumbled. Talaoc was somewhere out in the village doing who knows what.

The paladin was not in any way impressed by the remaining village elders. Romazalin owned the largest farm on the mountain, and while all she grew was wheat, potatoes, and cabbage, it made her important. Or at least, it had before the winter set in and devastated her crops. Her fiancee had been murdered by the Civan spy days prior – Mowiat had been in the wrong place at the wrong time.

Moulborke and Peora were the only two that hadn't lost anyone near and dear to them in the last few days. The pudgy woodsman and lanky trapper (respectively) hadn't made it through unscathed in the recent memory; one lost a brother and the other lost a livelihood. Moulborke hadn't stopped drinking since his brother went missing (although after seeing what happened in the village with the goat, he'd recently decided to try sobriety with the hope he'd live longer and hopefully avoid the Abyss). Peoran simply sulked in his cabin, cold and alone, with no courage to risk harvesting nature's scarce bounty in the woodlands.

Hirshma, on the other hand? Her brother, her position, and the trust the village had in her? And now, as it was discovered, her former lover is the same wizard everyone blamed for this mess of epic proportions?

She'd lost it all.

She was also easily the most outspoken of the lot. "So. While that stupid boy you sent here has been getting battered and broken, you've been what? Camped outside the walls? Watching him? Letting more of us die? To what end?"

"I did not know people were dying. I did not sense that magic was being used. I could not sense the Abyss. I assumed he was simply taking his sweet time and delaying returning home."

"You couldn't tell? Aren't you some kind of battlemage? Some sort of instructor at the Grand Temple?" Hirshma growled, a red flush creeping up her chest and across her cheeks.

Steelhom shook his head. "There was no aura to be felt of anything. There still isn't. Even a few scant feet away from that mana-font, there's nothing in the air to give clue to the disturbance."

Tiredly hanging her head and staring at her fingers, Romazalin tried to choke back tears. "You could've saved my Mowiat. You were there, right out there, you could've... You just call it a *disturbance?!*"

"Vestranis too," Peoran added. "And Surchi, when the dogs first charged in. And the others."

"And I would like to know why that is, for certain," the paladin-commander replied, a deep apology next on his lips. "I am so sorry, so very sorry, so much ill befell you while I waited for word from my student."

Hirshma kept her burning gaze locked on his face. "You're *sorry?* What good is your *sorry?* You've yet to say why you were sitting out there instead of being in the walls providing aid!"

He couldn't argue the validity of her question. "Every neophyte is sent on a mission to determine if their skills are suitable to serve the Order, upon graduation from the Temple. They are sent supervised, though they do not know it. If they fail, their... mistakes... are corrected."

"So you really were just watching, letting people die," she snapped.

"Watching, yes. People dying? Madam, there was no taint in the ether. Now I understand why. He discovered a masking spell. One so strong... this is as infuriating to me as it must be to you."

Way off to the side, Ipteria belched. "Doubt it!"

Giving her a glare out of the side of his eye, his response was as cold as Hirshma's displeasure. "Doubt what you will. Had I known I would have come inside much earlier. I give my word about that."

Hirshma kept her own glare fixated on him. "Your word don't matter much to us."

"I don't care. I may be too late to save your dead, and may be too late to save him, but once I realized that he was being overwhelmed..."

"Oh. You 'realized' it. What a wonder," Moulborke grunted. "What clued you in?"

Steelhom picked up a small sack sitting behind him and dumped the contents out on the table with a sickening thud. All of them blanched and pushed away from it. The woodsman looked like he was going to vomit. "This."

It was hard for any of them to say if the head had been decaying out in the wild or if it naturally looked that ugly. It had a slightly angular skull with an elongated trio of jaws that parted open and shut like a flower's wilting petals. It had neither eyes nor ears; just slits for where a nose should be.

"In the name of Kora what is *that?!*" the alchemist all-but shouted.

Curling his lip, the paladin looked down at the festering mass and gave a calm, measured reply. "This is the head of a *shiriak* demon. A lesser creature. More pest than demon. A scavenger. Drawn to battlefields, scenes of slaughter, and places where magic runs rampant."

"Such as here," Peoran grunted. "So you found a magic-hunting goblin."

"A goblin? You've no such luck. Goblins, at the *very* least, do not smell this foul. This thing shouldn't be anywhere near this place. Not without far stronger magic being used than what I can feel. I intended to drag the head back in here and feed it to Akaran for not finding it before it found me – then I felt his magic at work once I stepped inside your walls."

"Oh so you came here to scold the boy. Not to protect us, but to scold your student," Hirshma grumbled.

Steelhom put his hand on top of the head and forced divine magic into it. They all jumped back when it caught fire and burned to white ash in a matter of heartbeats. All of them except for Ipteria, who cheered and crowed for him to do it again. "At first, yes. Then to intervene on the Goddesses' behalf when I realized the strength of his magic – and to discover how a neophyte could command so much of it."

"Well so now you know," Moulborke half-growled half-snarled. "You get accosted by a demon so you come barging in expecting to lord over everyone. You really are the man that trained the exorcist, aren't you?"

Before Steelhom could respond, Hirshma cut them both off. "So. You're here. What exactly is it you plan on doing next?"

"I leave. I have little doubt that the elemental-kin will take my student to where the masking spell is being generated. I read his journal; he seems to think it's located at... Teboria Lake, isn't that right? In some invisible floating tower? Even if he isn't there, destroying that spell is my immediate priority. Once it's gone, the Sisters will discover it and send more assets to bear on this infestation."

"An *infestation?* Isn't that a wonderfully calm phrase to use," Hirshma said, a look of disgust on her face. "Nice to know you consider our losses nothing more than an inconvenience, just rats in the barn."

The paladin slapped his hand on the table. "*I* consider this a disaster. *I* consider your people dying to be an inexcusable result of inaction from everyone involved. Myself included. *I* will bear this guilt for as long as *I* live because *I* could have stopped it before *you* lost anyone else. And now *I've* lost my 'boy' as you call him, my student, my charge, my task, my *friend*. He's likely dead and buried under a mountain of snow right now because *I* didn't intervene when *I* could have. Would you like to doubt my resolve further or are we quite good without all of this fisking *bullshit?*"

"I can see where he got his mouth, too!" Ipteria giggled.

"Would you shut up already?" Peoran snarled back at her.

She just laughed.

"Now I will tell you what you are going to do," he spat, glowering at all four of them. "I understand he gave you orders to leave. I am rescinding them. If there are *shiriak* present, it is hard to guess what else is roaming the woods. I'll not have more of you dying on my watch and at least now the hounds are dead. I'll place enough wards to keep any more wraiths from popping in and I can assure you that *mine* are stronger than *his*. Or are you going to argue the point with me like he described in his journal – at length and in detail – like you did with him?"

That was far from the response any of them expected. They sat in silence until Moulborke spoke up. "So what do you want us to do instead? If we can't leave... what do we do?"

"Burn, then bury your dead," he answered.

"And don't join them."

II. FROSTBORN

The cabin hadn't changed any since his last visit, except that – like everything else – it was colder. Because of course it was. It wasn't like it was going to get any warmer. That would just be spiffy, and spiffy just wasn't an option.

(The sad thing was, at some point in his semi-near future, he'd regret his hatred for the chill and would wish for snow. He wouldn't get it, but he'd wish for it. Hindsight...)

He knew he was in Usaic's cabin right as he came to on the bed; the hounds may have been destroyed but their sulfuric stench still lingered in the winter air. Combined with the general must and dust in the house, it made for a not-so-delightful assault on his senses.

The rest of those senses were abusing him equally on every other possible level.

His body didn't just ache now; it *hurt*. His stomach was 'healed,' but there was a thick scab where slightly-blue blood seeped out. The gash on his shoulder and chest only looked slightly better. He could feel a lump on the back of his head and something was making his thigh burn like someone was holding a candle to it.

There was a really unpleasant taste of blood and brine in his mouth and his teeth had a gritty texture against his tongue. If he thought he could have mustered the energy to do it, the idea of retching all over the floor would have been a wonderful one. As it was, it was nearly impossible to do more than just open his eye and try to figure out what was going on now.

Eos'eno must have seen him start to move – and he could feel the sigh of relief that washed out of her. "Awake finally, takes you too long. Should have been up, should have been moving."

"Moving...? I... I thought I died? I... died and ended up... in ice?" Groggily, he started to sit up and felt every cut every stab every bruise in his body as he swung his legs out and sat up. "I'm not dead? I'm... here? I died and went to... Tundrala? If I'm not dead... Why did you bring me here?"

"Of course you are not dead. Ice preserves. Ice protects. It is what ice does. You do now what you do." She gave him an irritated look. "Oft I've said this. Do you not listen?"

"If... if I'm not dead... Makolichi. Where... is he? Did you destroy him?"

Shaking her head softly, Eos'eno ran her fingers across his cheek. "No, no Guardian of Winters, Makolichi still lives."

"Then we have to find... he'll be coming back to finish what..." he groaned while he tried to push himself out of bed.

"Guardian. He is gone. He is gone. He is not here. Ice protected you. You are safe. You are safe here. It will be some time, time before he comes back as how he was."

Grimacing as he tried to stand up, it was all he could do to grab her for balance before he fell over. "How do you know? And where is here? And... *why* am I here?"

"Your wards, I have seen them. I know them. Please, I beg you. Please put one here," she asked, pointing to an otherwise vacant spot on the far wall, "and another, the steps. Please."

It was an odd request for sure. "Why? I don't even know what it is you are. You've saved my life twice now, I... think. But... *why?*"

"Questions, must you ask questions? Time is short. The souls from the brine are hurried. You are the Guardian of Winters. You must know you must act against them. Spells, please?"

He was starting to warm up a bit to the title, if nothing else. Still, there was appreciation – and then there was trust. "Eos... if I don't know what you are, the wards I use may harm you." That was a half-truth and she didn't need to know the difference.

"Oh! So you seek to guard me as you guard the winter. I understand. I am of the winters. I am of Tundrala."

"You've said. But you haven't said *what* you are or... why you're here."

Eos took a nervous breath and looked at him. He suddenly realized that her wound hadn't healed up. Her blood was the color of quicksilver and it was still streaming down her side. She was also gliding – no, floating – with her feet not even touching the ground. The same couldn't be said for the small puddle of slush under her. "I was gifted to my lord. The Queen on the Glacial Throne knew he needed companionship. A warmth for the cold, a soul to serve as he did Her work. He has no care for Her or the Lower, but They have care for master and his work."

"You... you're an elemental?"

She gave a short shake of her head. "No. I know of the creatures you mean, what it is you mean by their name. My lord has broached a dialogue with them in the past. I have seen them in my home, my first home. They are most odd. Most odd indeed." Her hand roamed over the stone wall, fingers deftly stroking between the cracks. "I am a shard of the eternal ice, placed into a body bereft of life. You... your people may know mine as a wisps. We float free, we live free, we are one with all of cold, and with of the cold of all."

That didn't give a lot of room to think around. A spirit from the elemental plane of ice, gifted to a wizard to aid him and provide his 'comfort.' One sent to him by, supposedly, the Goddess of Ice Herself. A hybrid of elemental magic and physical will of a Goddess? *This just gets better and better.*

A few questions popped into his head at once. If her words were true, then it solved most of his problems with her – starting and ending with why his magic wouldn't touch her. "A wisp. Blessed be, never thought I would ever see one in my life. Let alone see one in the flesh. Or... not in the flesh, really, I guess."

"I am in the flesh. I am in her flesh, this flesh." The girl wasn't dead and she wasn't Abyssian. There wasn't much he had that would put her down if it came to it. That wasn't a reassuring thought. *Maybe burning her alive? Beheading? That usually works for most things. But...* He suddenly realized that there was absolutely no malice in her plans for him. It was all making a weird kind of sense.

Except for one small nagging issue.

"The body. Where did it come from?" This part was going to answer if he tried to take her head off now and hoped for the best or if he let her stay in this world (and to still continue to hope for the best).

Nervously, she started to cringe away, floating back into a corner. Any bravado she once had was completely gone. "He... a companion, he had. She died, she passed. Off to the snow-crested hills; to those hills in my home. His grief, so strong. The Queen of Ice sent me to him, after. He bound me to this body. I preserved her. He preserved her body with my chill."

It was quite possibly the last thing he expected to hear. "A companion? What were you to him?"

"I... I have been, as I will always be, many things to him. There is a place, a shrine to her. It broke his heart when she passed. The eternal ice feared he would never resume. Resume his work. Work towards the goal of the Queen. Complete his task. That's why they sent me. I helped his shrine. Made it so he could grieve." Her voice quivered a little after saying it. "Then I... I was more to him."

The exorcist stood there and looked at her, just *looked* at her. *That is disturbing on a whole new special level. His companion died, so he made a deal... with a Goddess... to make a shrine for his companion... and She sent a wisp to our world to fill his companion's body to use as... Okay, that's just **distressing**.* "What is it you're doing here? The dogs wanted you dead. The wraith in the mines cursed something called a 'half-breed.' That's you, isn't it?"

"Yes. Yes, they seek to destroy me. I am too quick. They are not fast enough. They are not strong enough when they come one at a time. But I hide, I have to hide at times. You have my gratitude, time eternal, for sending so many of them from this world." Eos gave him a pleading look. "Your wards. Please, place them please? They will come soon. They will, unless they are not here now."

Her desperation was telling. It was also unnerving. He didn't doubt it in the least. Just because those infernal dogs were dead didn't mean that Makolichi was gone. Or that he'd seen the last of Daringol. And now was *not* the time he wanted to risk seeing any of them again. "Why?"

"Why? What need does a dog turned rabid have need to answer a why? What need does a soul unhappy need to seek harm to others? I have no wish for them to spread, thus they have no wish for I to continue."

Well. That makes as much as sense as anything else so far. Wards it is. "I need chalk, ink, or cinder. A dagger would work too, or a chisel."

Her hair whipped through the air as she moved away from the wall and to a cabinet bolted to the side of the stairway. Eos had a piece of ages-old charcoal in her hand before he could even start to think of the next thing to ask her. For a moment, he didn't say anything more than a whispered "Thanks."

21

After he finished drawing the ward in the center of the floor, he hazarded a guess about what had been going on. "You're not the cause of this weather, you're just trying to protect the village. Or is it that you're trying to protect something or someone here?"

"There are things... things that won't let us be! It haunts my master and serves my master's haunter! Have done what I could do chase them away from the people but snow does not dissuade them and ice does not harm them! Only slow them down. It is what I can do and that itself is not enough to make them go away!"

"So you've been protecting them," Akaran finally was able to say. "At the cost of your own peace."

"M...m...m...my master would have wanted it that way!" she stuttered. "I meant no harm! They will surely kill me if I return to save him. I can't, not alone! You were sent to aid me! But you wanted my head too? Why didn't the ice tell you? It told *me!*"

Akaran looked up at the wisp. "What help did you think was coming?"

"The help that was promised," she answered.

"By who?"

"The wind of Tundrala! The ice!"

'*A simple haunting,*' the Sisters said, '*it'll be over soon,*' they said. "I'm not who you expected, am I?"

With a well-deserved look of trepidation, Eos'eno answered honestly. "I... no. Not of your kind. One of the ice. Or many of the ice. I did what I could to save them. There was so little I could do for them. Blessed that I could do so much for you. You were not what was expected. Your presence makes this all worse."

Trying to process that, he walked to the wall and began drawing the same set of interlocking symbols and runes where she had touched. "So you hinted. What made this worse? What did I do?"

"You have done as is your nature. They shall do as is theirs. I shall do as is mine. We must all. Ice has a purpose. We have a purpose. No, no more time. I will show you your answers. Soon. Your wards. They seem ready?"

Akaran looked them over and gave a small nod. "Yes. Why did you need me to...?"

"No, no time to tell. Time to show. They will come soon. Your magic? That will make them come."

"Them who? Them *what?* The wraiths? More dogs? *What?* Why do you keep saying that they're doing this because of me? I mean, I suspected, but..."

Eos didn't answer. Instead, she floated to the far wall, well away from everything else in the basement, and started to chant something under her breath. It was some kind of spell, but the purpose? It didn't sound like anything he knew.

And for good reason. As soon as she finished it, a huge part of the wall crumbled away, revealing a doorway to... a cave? What he could see of it, it was nothing more than a tunnel of gleaming white ice. The floor was covered with a carpet of shining snow. It took a sharp curve almost immediately so there wasn't much he *could* see.

It was just a tunnel hidden below a cabin, owned by a wizard, protected by a wisp from Tundrala.

There was nothing in that statement that gave him confidence.

Least of all the growing pain in his stomach and leg.

Neither Steelhom nor Akaran realized how close the two of them were to each other. Actually, Akaran didn't even know that his mentor was in play; the paladin-commander didn't realize that his student was being tossed in and out of Tundrala like some sort of depressed metaphysical yo-yo. What Steelhom *did* know was that Akaran's wards covered enough of the village that there was no reason that *any* demon should have been able to walk past the vines without alerting every priest from every Order from Toniki to the Queen's castle.

That wasn't much of an exaggeration, either. But since they didn't do the trick, they were reinforced. In excess. He was able to make his pass and lock things down much faster than his student, barely taking a quarter of the time. While Akaran slumbered after Eos'eno dropped him unconscious into Usaic's cabin, Steelhom finished setting up a divine barrier that would be enough to keep anything short of an Abyssian Lord from breaking through.

It wasn't like one of them was out and about.

Hopefully.

The mana font was another story entirely. Hirshma had been conscripted into service after he saw the ruins of it. Under his intense scrutiny and supervision, she used her piddling excuse for magic to push brambles out of the ground in a wall that encompassed it. It was a slightly risky proposition but he came to the same conclusion that Akaran had – the waters could supercharge anything magical that touched it.

The net result was a dome of thorns that was at least three feet deep and seven high. It even sprouted pretty little red roses all along the vines. It was also the first vibrant green growth anyone in Toniki had seen in the last three years.

There was a downside for the old woman though. It wasn't just that using her magic drained her (it did). Nor was it that Steelhom's next edict was that she was to attempt to 'reconnect' to her former Goddess (either through an act of contrition or forgiveness or simply begging Kora'thi to bring her back into the fold). That was bad enough, but...

It was that every villager that had gone to bed hungry, every person that had watched their children grow more and more destitute, and every person that had lost someone to sickness that was exasperated by near-starvation realized that at any time, she could have willed the land to bring forth fruit. Vegetables. Edible leaves. A few wondered if the stories about druids were true and that some could even call for the animals of the land to appear with a call.

Hirshma's arrogance and rejection of her faith had caused people to suffer. *Nobody* was going to forget or forgive her for that. A few had demanded — even threatened — to stake her out in the woods if she didn't make things grow right then right now to feed the masses.

Steelhom had been the only thing that had stopped them from getting their wish. He insisted that she needed to rest and start to find her path back to the righteous. He argued that if she didn't, she'd have a harder time explaining to people why she had the *ability* but not the *providence* to work magic that would convince them that they should keep her around the village.

And not hanging by a noose on the gate.

Although to be honest he didn't have much hope they'd listen to him while he was gone.

Once all was said and done, he left the village with directions to find the cabin. His student had left a bit of a trail behind him on the way to follow, though the terrain hadn't improved any. Neither had the wildlife. He also shared many of the same opinions about the cold that Akaran had expressed in perpetuity.

Usaic's cabin was off to the northwest of the village. While it was only a walk that took it a scant few hours away in the spring in summer months, the landscape was a deterrent in and of itself for most. Rumors and tales about the wizard — and a general distaste for anything magic — kept most people from heading up his direction even in the best of times.

As this was not the best of times, the only people that had gone this direction were the daring that sought to find the source of the creatures that were terrorizing the countryside, and then the soldiers that went after the daring who had never returned. Before then, the only people that even traveled to the north were trappers and the occasional secretive young couple that sought a hidden rendezvous with a lover (or child that sought a private rendezvous with a flask of the awful swill they called ale in these parts). After all – though this part of the Province was ignored, the Queen had other interests nearby.

Those interests were overseen by an interesting, delightful, and terrifying Maiden: Piata.

This particular portion of the Waschali Provincial Region was known for pine trees and shrubbery, with plenty of rocks, errant streams, and... and that was it. It didn't have much else to offer and honestly, hardly anyone cared. It was so far out of the way from just about anything anyone gave a damn about that even bandits were rare. It had exactly one and only one notable aspect to it, and that was a sylverine mine off to the east.

In other words, it was just about perfect for a wizard with secretive plans to set up shop. Although while Steelhom had to feel his way up the mountainside using the only path (and it was a stretch to call it a path) leading to the cabin and the lake it was nearby, there was one thing that made the place *not* entirely perfect.

It made it incredibly terrifying that Usaic's base was able to remain undetected by the Maiden that called Waschali her home. If she had caught a whiff, *any* whiff, of what had been going on? Usaic would have had a very long time to wish for death. The ignorant fools that called Toniki home had no idea how lucky they were that the Garrison Commander trusted the Order of Love enough to send for an exorcist instead of sending for the her Consort.

Then again, it was entirely possible that Piata considered this haunting below her station.

Rubble, rocks, and frozen trees? Hardly worth dealing with. He could see her dismissing the chronic cold to nothing more than an aberration of the local weather. Mountains get cold. Villages along the treeline of the Equallin Mountains have to deal with snow. That was life and nature. Word probably already had reached her.

It would not be a stretch for her to think that the local garrison could handle it, whatever 'it' was, if the situation got dire enough for these stubborn fools to ask for help. I'm an idiot myself if I think that she didn't know that the area is in trouble even before the garrison got involved. It wouldn't take much...

They have no idea how lucky they are that this didn't catch her interest.

I can see why the Queen has quit sending her people to the area. Nothing more than crumbling rocks and sad trees. I can't even say that the history of the place is worth noting. I understand that this was one of the few places that sylverine can be mined, which excuses the first generation of settlers from staking a claim on the mountain. But once that mine closed? There's no reason for anyone to want to live this far out on the frontier.

Before he had left the Temple to supervise Akaran from a distance, they had been nice enough to send him a pile of literature on the history of not just Toniki, but the entirety of the Province. You couldn't say it made for interesting reading. For that matter, you could hardly say it made for reading.

Waschali. The north-easternmost territory under the Queen's eye, and one of the few regions that directly includes the Equallin Mountains in their borders. Known for access to Anthor's Pass - leading travelers through the mountains and directly into territory owned by the Midlands war-tribes. From there, it's just a short hop to territory owned by the Civan Empire. Tactically it represents a troublesome chink in the Kingdom's armor; one that the Queen wants reinforced at all costs. She will be even less happy to hear of this infestation than her Maiden will be.

His thoughts were interrupted by the discovery of Akaran's work at the small bridge leading northward. The boy's journal noted that he had encountered and disposed of the pathetic remains of a garrison soldier while it tried to crawl out of a frigid stream. He didn't expect anything to come back from the ashes, though he would have been remiss if he didn't double check the expulsion.

Everything is fine here. Feels the same taint as the possessions at the village. So far so good.

The Queen doesn't like chinks in her armor. The Pass is under command of one of the most vile of her Maidens. They call Piata 'The Madwoman' for a reason; the rest of her Consort is little better. More than a thousand soldiers are encamped at the pass at any given time, including Paladin-Commander Hitrio and Consort-Blade Brandolin. Piata lives there, but her Betrothed exercises his Governorship from Lador, in the middle of the province.

It does not fill me with confidence that they were unable to detect *this nightmare so close. I will **not** be the messenger that goes and reports this failure to her. I won't let Akaran do it either, if he's still alive. I don't imagine she'll be happy with him for failing to resolve it quickly or quietly. Maybe I'll make that alchemist do it. That would be fitting.*

Now what to do with those villagers? The closest city is the town of Gonta, and the people here have said that it's essentially a refuge camp for Toniki now. It's the second-largest in the Province, excluding Piata's Manor and the city that sprung up around it. With luck, they can handle a few more. With greater luck, the corruption here won't have spread that far south yet.

Like student like tutor, the paladin was going to see his hopes dashed in a painful way.

❄ ❄ ❄

The wisp of a girl (said very literally) waved him forward. Without trying to question her again (he didn't think it would do any good) he followed along, suddenly wishing he had his sword. Or at least a walking stick. Thankfully the tunnel had enough grit to give him some bit of balance. She vanished past the curve as he got closer.

There wasn't much to say about the cave; it was tall and wide enough to be comfortable to walk through. He saw small pathways leading elsewhere interspersed at odd intervals. Sometimes they had entrances blocked by crystalline stalactites and stalagmites. Others just branched off to Goddess-knows-where chambers and more hallways. It was cold – but it didn't *feel* cold enough to keep the ice from melting. How it stayed intact boggled his mind.

Or maybe her magic had done more for his body than he had given her credit for.

They limped around for maybe a quarter candle-mark before she paused and said another spell at the dead end they eventually ran into. That wall melted away as the words were said and brought them to their destination. That archway opened up to a huge domed cavern with a pale blue statue – more than twice his own height – dead in the center. White flowers and a cornucopia of crystal food covered the ground at her feet.

Her entire platform was in the center of a small pool of pure, still water. She was very plain on the surface, though there was just something about her that made her look beautiful if you let your gaze linger long enough. In truth, she was almost as pretty as some of the golden busts of Niasmis that decorated the Temple halls. Long white strands of white ice hung from her head and fell to her hips, and she

27

had a smile that could have brightened the entire mountain.

She also looked young. Very young. Younger than he felt comfortable with until it clicked. He didn't quite know what made it make sense, but it was right there for his naked eye to see. "That's not a 'companion.' He has a daughter... had a daughter."

"Yes, man of Love, yes. His daughter. I was given the body of her to serve the Goddess and to serve his needs. Bring him back to the path. He spent so much time making it. I feared he would never return to his work. But see this, this he had to see. He had to see every time he walked this path. This is the path to his ice, our ice, to our home in the cold. We made it together. As one, for both. For all."

Akaran didn't see or sense a damn thing that might have been a problem, and thankfully, nothing from the statue. "You don't look like she does though. You are... different."

"The body was not perfect. It did not fit me. I had to stretch it and change it. Master helped me in this. It made me one with her body." She hesitated as she looked up at the edifice. "He truly loved her. I am a pale imitation."

Mayabille. Oh Goddess. We have gone from heartbreaking to disturbing to... horrid. If Hirshma finds out about this it'll kill her. What in the name of all was Usaic **thinking***? For that matter, what was the* **Goddess of Ice** *thinking?*

While he looked at Eos'eno and chewed on the thought, something else in the chamber started to leave a foul taste in his mouth. Something *stank*. It was subtle, but the longer he was there, the worse it got. He didn't just smell it. He *felt* it. *I'm standing where this wizard dedicated a statue to his dead daughter, and I didn't think to check...? **Goddess** this pain is killing me*, he seethed to himself as he reached down and clutched at his thigh.

"Eos'eno. Wait."

She turned to look at him and shook her head. "Wait? Why wait? I've waited for too long too far as it is."

"You wanted me here, we play by my rules." The wisp looked as if she wanted to say something. The conviction in his voice made her stop. He gave another look around the chamber, then closed his eye and whispered the same spell that had tracked the first few undead to the mine. "*Illuminate.*"

It didn't do anything at first. No light erupted from the shadows, nothing caught fire. The only thing that happened – at first – was that the air grew still. You could hear the drip from the girl's wound and even

Akaran's heartbeat.

At first.

A flicker of light began to pulse around the statue. One flicker turned to three; then the flicker turned into a rapid strobe. A lump of rubble laying on the far side of the pool started to stir – then stood up. Chunks of desiccated flesh and unidentifiable bits of meat tumbled off of the body as it stood up. There wasn't much to be said about it. Whomever it had served was a question lost to time, though pieces of steel plate held on by rotting leather straps gave away its former profession.

"Every soldier eventually loses one fight or another," he muttered.

While it turned to focus on the exorcist, pale purple tendrils started to unravel out of hollow holes where its eyes used to be. A larger one rolled out of its slack-jawed mouth like some kind of grotesque parody of a tongue. It tilted its head off to the side while it somehow looked at Akaran, but when it saw Eos'eno, a haunting angry wail escaped its lips.

She gave it a look in return that was equal parts offended and disgusted. The wisp opened her mouth to retort the wordless condemnation, and nearly did. The priest did not approve of being ignored by the zombie.

A quiet Word set his right hand ablaze with pale lavender light. A second Word made a length of silvery, ethereal chains manifest on his left arm from elbow to fingertips. Just as the corpse took a few short and shambling steps towards Eos'eno, Akaran jerked his arm in the air and whipped the chain around the monster's bony leg.

One solid jerk and yank later, the dead thing was on its back with the lower part of the limb sliding across the room. Limping over to it, he watched it try to haltingly scramble away with a scornful sneer. The ground was a little too smooth and the corpse was a little too damp for it to find much purchase. The spirit inside it was too desperate to hold onto a shell for it to even think about abandoning the body for the sake of safety.

It should've. He knelt down and put his knee on its chest to hold it in place, and wrapped his left hand around its throat. Unlike the others, it didn't try to talk to him. The tentacles just coiled and snapped in the air, black light radiated out from what used to be eyes. He covered its face with his right hand and whispered a simple, single Word.

"*Expulse,*" made the back of the zombie's head wetly explode all over the cavern floor.

Victory was not something he could claim for long.

Moments later, and he could see a steady shimmer in the air on the other side of the cavern. First one, then another. Then he could feel a pull leading that direction. It started small. It grew stronger. A lot stronger. A lot faster. There was so much of it somewhere beyond the cavern that it made his stomach churn anew. There was so much of it that he barely realized that some of it was coming from *him*.

There wasn't any time to think about before the wailing started.

Two wraiths manifested in the air around the statue's head. Eos'eno answered them with a screeching cry of her own that reverberated in the ocean-blue cave of wonder at the sight of them. They were exactly the same kind as the ones before, down to the wicked tentacles that snapped around and out of their mouths. The young exorcist lifted his blade up and locked his gaze on the closest of the two.

They charged him. His chains twisted around his fist while his leg started to buckle. A Word hovered on his lips – but it wasn't needed.

Out of the corner of his eye, a pale silver shimmer took form just below the chamber's roof. A hazy little creature bounded out of the glimmering smoke – just a small pale gray mote barely the size of a tiny rabbit. It was next to impossible to tell what it was, just that it had four legs, no neck, and a grinning maw under bright ruby-red eyes.

What it did was infinitely more important than what it looked like. It jumped onto the top of the statue, then jumped through the farthest wraith. The spirit shattered like someone had fired a cannonball at it, and just as quickly, it fell in upon itself and vanished. The moment that the mote hit the ground it jumped back up and lanced through the second one before coming to a stop on the statue's shoulder.

While the other wraith was sucked into non-existence, the mote looked down at Akaran and gave a chittering laugh before it spoke. "[I watched/I waited! I knew/I know!]"

The priest whipped his chains up at the mote, and cursed under his breath when the little beast danced away free and clear. "What in the name of...?!"

It kept chittering and laughing. "[I watched/I waited! I knew/I know! Was right/Was here!]"

"Oh what fresh headache did that wizard make..."

Eos'eno didn't appreciate the blame and quickly said as much. "Not one of masters! That one is not one of his!"

"[Oh no/Not one! Not one/Not them! Not like them/Not at all! I am my own/But owned by another!]" Its horrid laughter took on a darker, more insidious chuckle as it scrambled across the top of the statue.

"Then what is it?"

"You ask if I know? Exorcist, you must know, not I! This is what you do? This is what you fight, yes?"

It reared up on its hind legs and pawed at the air with its front claws. "[Knew if I waited and watched I'd see/Find a source a cause a why for! Found you/Found more! Exorcist here?/Exorcist knows! Exorcist knows?/Humans know! Humans know?/Heavens know! Not out of sight from above now/Never ever been out of sight below!]"

Akaran tensed his arm back up and raked his chains soundlessly across the cavern floor. "What are you? What do you want? Are you an enemy of Daringol? Or of mine?"

"[What am I/What are you? You haunt things like me/I mock things like you! Enemy of souls en-mass?/Enemy of *you* solo!]"

"I can work with the enemy. Whatever you are, in the name of the Goddess, I —"

It bounced down into the pool and splashed cold water everywhere. "[Name of *Goddess*?/Name of *worthless*. Shells of souls the *abogin* and hounds!/Things you seek and hunt and slay! Rishinobia cares not for these/Rishinobia felt magic's exquisite pull!]

Eos'eno slipped through the hair to circle around behind it as it continued its mad conversation with the priest. "Rishinobia? Is that a name, your name?"

"[Tell Rishinobia if it matters?/Your name is worthless too! This is a warning now/Heed it well or not!]"

"A warning? Of what? Don't test me, damned thing. It hasn't been that fun of a week."

The mote jumped up and did a flip in the air, laughing all the while. "[Week of fun?/Maybe Rishinobia wrong. Maybe exorcist a kindred soul!/Maybe exorcist a dark heart? Matters not here not now/What matters is to come! Rishinobia brings no harm to girl/Rishinobia brings message to priest!]

Akaran backed away slightly and twisted his ethereal chain tighter around his fist. "Then tell me what it is. I'm *not* in the mood for games."

"[Not in the mood for a game?/Know all of this is a game! You know/I know! Gods know/Abyss knows! We know you hide this powerful magic from us all/We know your prey is too weak to take it!]"

"**We** know? Oh, *shit*," he groaned as it started to dawn on him.

"[Yes you know!/Now you know!]"

"That's your message? The Abyss knows?"

"[Boy priest is now finally right!/*Corpsuals arin-goliaths* the *abogin* and *gitia!* Sad pale weak pathetic things that congregate here!/Could not cannot harness the magic of the hereafter! Rishinobia **can't**/Priest **can't**! Rishinobia master **can**/Rishinobia master **comes**!]"

"Your master? What are you...?"

The mote did another jump for joy and screamed out laughter. "[Man of the Red Death/Man that watches knows all! This fresh clean magic/Untainted pure wild magic? This is magic Red Man will want/This is magic Red Man will have!]"

Eos bristled and hissed at the ugly little mote. "Your master, your liege, it seeks the magic of my master? The magic is not his to claim! It is of the heavens; the pits have no right to claim to hold sway!"

"[To Rishinobia the right is here!/Keep the magic if you can! A mess you've made/A mess others made! Man of Red will tolerate no mess/Man of Red sends acolytes to search!]"

Akaran gave it a grim little smile and tensed up. Another few heartbeats... "Then I suppose it would be in my best interest to be rid of his messenger."

His attack whipped out and almost hit the cretin – but only almost. It jumped away faster than he could blink and faster than Eos'eno could fling frozen shards at it. "[So close so far too slow!/You won't win this fight today! Abyss knows by now see?/Now Abyss knows you know! Work yourself faster now!/Work faster fight more! Think this is only one?/So many more than one! Two of small/Two of large! Two of upper/Two of elsewhere!]"

The only answer that the exorcist gave was an angry growl and another attempt to lash at the demon with his chains. All it did was laugh at him again – then it jumped back into the shimmering air over the statue and vanished from sight.

"DAMMIT you son of a bitch! Get back here!"

The... thing... must have heard him. It popped back into the chamber and gave him one last haughty, fang-filled smile. "[The light touches the land from the sky ten times/The dark touches the land from the sky just nine! After ten and nine/The magic the font? Is his/And mine.]"

That final warning delivered, the more jumped back into the portal and vanished again. Akaran staggered towards the spot and cast murmured spell after murmured spell. All of them confirmed it: whatever it had been, it wasn't on this plane anymore.

"FISK. Oh this is... FISK!"

Eos cringed at the profanity and floated backward until she could put the statue between her and her (possibly temporary) ally. "That creature was not of this world. That thing was not one of masters! I promise I swear I didn't know it was here. Please do not be angry with me, holy man, please don't be angry with me."

It took him a few moments to regain his composure and a few moments more to swallow the lump in his throat. "I'm not, I believe you... oh fisk, just... so much fisking... Well, at least they're giving us a warning."

"Who what? Do you know what that creature was or why here? Why it was waiting here?"

"I knew if we didn't get this under control bigger things than Makolichi would find out. I just... didn't think it would be this sudden. Then again, this has been going on for years and nobody apparently noticed before now so... small bloody blessing."

The wisp floated back over to him while he started to sink down to his knees. A hand on his shoulder helped him stay upright (even as badly he wished that she would have just let him fall). "It was just a messenger? Why would a creature of the pit send a messenger? Why not simply come forth and conquer?"

Akaran shook his head and sighed. "I don't know. But it did. That's the important part. We have to get this fixed and *soon* or we're going to be up to our neck in the damned. Ten days. If it wasn't lying, ten days. I have to reach the Order. They have to know."

"The Order? Your Order? What can they seek to accomplish in ten days that I have not been able to do in years three?"

"A lot... a lot more than just me." He looked down and ran his hand over his upper thigh and gave it a squeeze, wincing. "Abogin... corpusals? Arin-Goliaths... that's what that wraith is... nesting wraith... fisk. Why do I feel like that creature just... gave away the game?"

Eos floated a few feet away from him, confusion blossoming on her face. "A game? You think this is a game? A thing that people play, for enjoyment, for laughs?"

"No, not... that kind of game." No matter how hard he tried to hide it, there was pain creeping into his voice. That she didn't pick up on it was both a testament to his efforts to pretend everything was okay – and a glaring example of her own inhumanity. "No, I'm... why did you bring me here?"

"They seek shelter. They seek power. They seek, they are drawn, to both. The greater the power the more that they seek it the closer it is. You. Your power. They're here for it now. You and your kin have placed everyone in danger. You are not what help the ice spoke to me of. Had I known I'd have spirited you away when first you arrived but you know nothing. I can still, spirit you, take you from here. It would make the people safer now, now that the hounds are gone, now that Makolichi is hurt."

"You're hurt too." Akaran let his sword fall to the ground as he clutched at the throbbing wound in his thigh. "Then why did you bring me here... if I'm making this worse? I want to help... and those things have to be banished."

With a frustrated sigh, the wisp took his hand in hers. "Because I need from you what the snow cannot give. I tried, you will see. I watched you. Saw you do the things you did. I did what you did but they don't work."

"*WHAT* doesn't work?"

"Follow. Again, follow. Ice is slow to travel but even it moves faster than you."

It took just about every ounce of *his* patience to keep from telling her where she could take her moving ice and... and the rest of that thought was best left unstated. He didn't resist her attempts to drag him away, as sorely as he wanted to. She pulled him along behind her to the other side of the chamber and at the entrance to another tunnel leading to Goddess-only-knows-where.

Then he saw what she had done, and suddenly why she brought him here made perfect sense. Eos started to gesture wildly at the ground and the tunnel entrance. "Those things, the monsters, the worst of them. They cannot pass from master's home to master's cottage to the village through the walls of the cave. It was made with magic too powerful. It is the only way to master's home, their home, where they have stolen home."

The young priest sank down to his knees to get a closer look at what she had made on the floor. For a moment, taking his weight off of his leg made it feel much better (if only for a moment). "For the love of the Goddess. You tried."

She nodded emphatically. "I did. Copied, made ice of your marks. Made the words in the frost. Same words, your words, your symbols, your constructs. But they, I, I am a pale imitation, even of you. Of the Queen of Frost and master and master's daughter and master's mate and even of you. Of you of your work and to make this work I need you and your work."

A sudden (and way too sharp) stab of pain in his leg took his breath away. Still, he had to be impressed. Every single symbol was perfectly carved into the floor and walls. At first he was confused – why would she need him if the job was already done? Then the realization hit him. "You need a touch of the Goddess to activate the spell... my Goddess. You've got the words but... but not the connection. Blessed be... you poor creature." He kept staring at it while he played with his goatee, eye tracing over each and every mark she'd left behind. "You know what I did but you didn't have the blessing to power it."

"Yes! The blessing. The catalyst. The sudden crack of sound that warns of an avalanche. The wind that blows and takes water and makes it pure and eternal when it falls again! I need what it is that will work! The dogs are gone now and in your debt now and for all and ever I am. But the wraiths. The spirits. They, they are as grave of a threat. Your wards. I feel the light from them. None of them can so easily cross their path. This point, at this point, they have to travel."

At this point, he wasn't even going to try to understand all of her logic or reasoning (though for now, it made an odd type of sense). All he could do was operate on two different, yet poignant, assumptions. Activating defensive wards here might save lives, and it might buy him time to think. It also might buy him time to recover. Against half of his rational judgment, that's exactly what he decided to do.

He bent down, lips almost touching the largest of the wards she had so meticulously made. "*Celiouso et-vas balintin lumin,*" he whispered to the ground. Translated, it simply meant 'Circle of warding, provide a bastion of light.' As he spoke the incantation, the symbols on the ground and around the cavern door began to light up. One after another, each rune began to glow a soothing pale lavender mixed with streaks of blue.

Right about then was when he realized that the wards stretched all the way from the mouth of the tunnel all the way to the statue and the pond it was set in. For that matter, a massive ward stretched around the edifice – and the water within it was the same extra-planar mana font that was the source of all this madness.

When it activated, he felt the bottom of his stomach fall out and a surge of energy course back up through him from the soles of his feet to the top of his head. The world spun around him and he started to pitch forward. He had a brief moment to panic as fresh bile and blood pulsed up out of his throat and hit the back of his teeth – a very brief moment.

Beside him, the wisp spun around in the air with a smile and a laugh that filled the cave with warmth that it hadn't felt in a long time. "You did! Condemned, secured, locked away! Time, now we have time!"

As she spoke, Akaran muttered something behind her.

She couldn't tell what, and right that moment, it hardly mattered. "Now they won't, they can't, be drawn to you! You may leave; I shall send you home! Then the ones that the ice said would come will come and master's work will be saved and master's home will be ours again!" The wisp dove into the tunnel and spun again, laughing all the while.

The exorcist said something else. She still couldn't tell. It really didn't matter to her.

"No more shadows in the woods! No more worry to villagers! Master's wishes are made! You did all, resolved all. May the cold forever give you comfort!" She clapped her hands in joy and danced around the cave with excited exuberance before she noticed that he had quit trying to tell her something. "Exorcist, exorcist, aren't you as happy as I? Your job your time with us is done and you may leave and..."

When she turned to look at him, the words died in her throat. Akaran was on the ground, passed out and laying on his face. A steady pool of blood seeping from his leg was turning the snowy ground bright red. She couldn't even tell if he was breathing. But as bad as all of that was?

There was acrid steam rising where his leg – and his blood – touched the ward. She needn't have worried. She couldn't hear the whisper on the wind, but amazingly, he did.

{Rest now. I will not let you die here. I will send you My peace.}
{So you may send My wrath.}

❄ ❄ ❄

Her wrath wasn't too far behind as it was.

"*EXPULSE!!*"

Coming from Steelhom, the Word had a bit more kick to it. Coming from Steelhom, the *kick* had more kick to it. The head of the *shiriak* bounced off of the cabin door as his spell reduced the rest of it to bubbling slime. Beside it, one of the Daringol wraiths desperately tried to escape into the ether.

It didn't work. Steelhom strode through the ice and snow like an unstoppable juggernaut. Finding the cabin wasn't difficult. He followed the trail Akaran and Rmaci had left behind on the ground, barely more than two days prior, and followed the trail of curious spirits that had begun to cluster around the woods.

His staff made short work of the spirit when it finally turned to face him. Specifically, his staff went through the spirits' face when it turned, and made a 'thunk' against the wooden wall behind it. The paladin didn't even bother to check to see if it was completely gone before he pushed his way inside the hut.

A cursory search turned up nothing – but finding the ward at the mouth of the formerly-hidden tunnel let him know he was on the right path. He closed his eyes and touched the runes, focusing his efforts on Akaran's spellwork.

"These are fresh...? **Akaran**, by the name of the Goddess, *what* are you doing?"

And how are you still alive?

That wasn't the best of ideas. His skin prickled up for a brief heartbeat before a tsunami of magic washed through the tunnel and over him. Focused and in tune, there wasn't much to protect his head when his student activated the wards deeper underground.

The feedback wasn't pleasant. When he could get his vision to focus again, he stumbled through the tunnels, using his staff as a cane. It didn't take him anywhere near as long to travel through the cave that Usaic had meticulously carved out before he reached Mayabille's statue.

Unlike his student, Steelhom didn't have a clue who it was.

Also unlike his student, Steelhom recognized that she was the anchor point for the wellspring of magic that flowed freely through the village. *No blessed wonder that whatever Akaran just did knocked me on my ass. His journal was wrong. **That's** the font. **That's** the source. That statue is a crack into another world...*

He carefully scooted around the runes he could see all over the floor and made his way to the base of the statue. He didn't need to touch it to confirm that the mana was seeping out of Tundrala. He did anyways. The cool chill enveloped his arm and began to war with the warmth of Love in his soul.

Nobody should be exposed to this. Nobody human. If you weren't used to it or tapped into it it would rip you apart and you wouldn't even notice it until it was too... His stomach cramped up while a grim realization hit him. *And he's had wards all around it, spells cast in the middle of it, and as uncharacteristically unbalanced as his magic feels, I bet he's been drinking it.*

Goddess. If that fool isn't dead yet he's going to be.

Even if I have to do it myself.

It didn't take more than a minute to get a picture of what happened in the cave, though he couldn't put a finger on what had left behind a smell of rancid butter. He did, unfortunately, find the still-sizzling blood on the far side of the chamber. He did not, fortunately, find any sign of his student in the short passageway beyond.

*That creature teleports. So where did she go **now**?*

He didn't have to wait for an answer. Angry shouts echoed back from the way he came and a small pulse in the air around him got his attention. Without giving the portal a second thought, Steelhom turned around and ran back to the cabin.

The door to the village's field hospital did not provide any defense against a panicked wisp. In her desperation, the winds that preceded her ripped the door off of its hinges and sent conscripted villagers (and Hirshma) scattering like leaves. At first sight, she looked like a monstrosity covered in spikes and ratty clothes with streamers of silver steam billowing out of her side... and bright red blood covering her front.

"Aid please! I beg aid, I beg it now!"

Bewildered, Mariah-Anne was the first person to manage to get a response out. "Aid? Aid *you?*"

"Yes, me, aid! Aid me, aid him!"

Roaring in anger, Hirshma didn't hold back. "If you think for a moment that anyone in this village is going to aid you so help me all you demon, I will aid you in a trip back to the pits for what you've done!"

"Lady please, he needs you I need you we need you, the frost needs you," the wisp pleaded. Right then was when Mariah noticed that it was all that Eos'eno could do to hold herself upright. Her legs were buckling, and her right arm quaked with tremors. The silver steam that radiated from her seeped from a gash in her side that had begun to cause radiant cracks to spread out from the hole and up her nearly-naked body.

"NEEDS?! NEEDS?! I *know* you, I know what you are! I *know* you took my daughter's body, you monstrous thing! Leave us be! You've claimed enough lives, haven't you!?"

Mariah wrapped her hand around her mentor's arm and slipped between them. "Mistress, no. Look at her. *Look* at her. She's hurt. She's hurt badly."

The elder snarled and reached for a knife sitting on a table next to them. "Not hurt enough, not hurt anywhere *near* enough."

Eos hung back away and kept her right hand on the door-frame. "One, only one, only claimed one life. Not claimed, no truly. Given, after the fact. I beg you to come with me to keep from another being taken away, wherever away may be!"

The younger girl took a few steps forward. "Help who? If you want our help, who do you want it for? You?"

Shaking her head, the wisp continued to beg, the glow from her wide eyes flickering with each word. "I need help to help me to save the boy!"

"Save the boy? You *took him* from us! I'm not so daft that I didn't see the shape he was in! You don't heal from mortal wounds! He's dead!" the alchemist shouted back at her. Her voice boomed in the barn, and if she hit that note again, the rest of the township would be crowding in to see what was going on.

Eos tried to calm herself but she couldn't do much about the shards of crystalline ice that were forming along her arms. Hirshma thought that she was getting ready to attack. The truth was anything but. "I took him to save *you*. He is the problem and the solution but now *his* problem is more than what I can fix and *he* is hurt and *he* needs more and he needs *you* now to save *him* so I can save *master* so he can save *you!*"

"He's not dead? Akaran isn't dead?" Mariah pressed, stepping (nervously) closer, hands at her sides and nervously flexing.

"No, not dead! Healed him what I could, thought to save him. I cannot. I cannot save him. I do not know what, *ice preserves, ice protects*, it is what it does! Ice... ice *can't* preserve him! *Ice* failed, *I* failed!"

Hirshma stormed forward, pushing past her student. "You've done more than fail. You've done so much more than fail, you monster!"

"MISS! *Listen* to her. Just... shut up and *listen!*"

"Speak to me that way and again and -"

Mariah ignored her. "Eos'eno. That's your name, right? Eos'eno?"

"Yes, my name. Why does it matter? I don't need names, I need *help*."

"The boy. That's Akaran, yes? The one you want us to help?"

Nodding fervently, the wisp took her attention off of the elder and began to plead with her student instead. "Akaran, yes. I rescued him from here. I aided him, helped him. He helped me. He helped me and now he can't stand he can't wake up I can't wake him up like I couldn't wake up master!"

Even Hirshma had to give pause at that. "He's alive? You really mean it?"

"YES! How many times must I say it? He lives, he's alive!"

"Alive and you're turning him into... whatever *thing* you are, you mean," she snapped back.

39

Mariah grabbed her again and made the older woman turn to face her. "Miss! If he's alive, we have to go help. We *have* to."

"I have to do nothing I -"

"He sacrificed himself for us. I saw what that demon did to him. If he's alive, we *have* to go help him. Either you go or I do."

The wisp stumbled closer, with what looked like tears streaming down her face. "He is. He lives. I swear to Mother that he lives. He does not live for longer without help. If you do not come for me, come for him. He... he would, for you. I feel it I know it, he would. For you, if not for him."

Hirshma looked back away from Mariah and affixed Eos with a hateful stare. "You could have left him here. I'd have had him back on his feet by now," the alchemist snapped.

"I couldn't. She couldn't. You couldn't. Only ice could. And I needed. I needed him then now I need you."

"You need to let my daughter go find peace," the alchemist seethed. "If you expect my help for anything, you can go fisk yourself until you let my daughter go."

Eos'eno straightened herself up and matched the angry glare with one of her own. The crystal scales that covered her from her neck to her feet rippled up and over each other. "I am no daughter of yours. Not of yours. No daughter of any but Istalla. Your child your girl is not with me, I am not with her, I am simply one with her form, as Mother bade me, as master made me."

"I do not care who made you or what they made you, if you think for one instant -"

"I'll do it. I'll go," Mariah interrupted. "Take me."

The wisp flicked that glowing blue gaze at the younger girl and blinked. "You? No. Not you. You've no magic. No magic, no help. No ability *to* help! Need magic, need *her*!"

Indignant, Maria pushed her way past Hirshma to stare the wisp down. "No help? You are going to demand help then look at me and say -"

Frustrated past the point of words, the Eos'eno bit down on her lip as she considered her options. With a flurry of movement, she darted past the apprentice alchemist and took the older woman by her wrist. Startled, Hirshma didn't have time to pull away. The last thing any of them heard was a very pointed, very uncharacteristic remark from her lips.

"Ice is constant, ice is slow, and ice is patient. *I* am no longer," she nearly snarled – and then vanished with the village elder in a small blizzard.

Mariah stood there, almost entirely alone, fists balled up and a dead shout on her open lips. When she could finally process that she was just blown off by something not even from this plane, she did not take the rejection well. "No magic? No *magic?* And that makes me somehow less?"

Off to the side and in the back of the barn, Ipteria gave an uncharacteristic frown before smoothing her features and offering her own two coins over it. "I bet the priest thinks you're magical."

"Oh, just shut up."

III. THE THAW

Words. Images. They popped in and out of his mind like little bubbles.

"Get your hands away from the boy! NOW!"

"I didn't want to be here any more than you! Send me back home, *you* can deal with him!"

"Send *you* to the gallows, and with the will of the Goddess behind me, I will send that wisp right along after you! *GET AWAY FROM HIM NOW.*"

Eos slipped between them, the cracks around her ribs looking far, far worse from the back. "Look and watch! Look, see! Brought her here to help, brought her here to *help!*"

"Look at him! There's no help you can give him! Step away from the boy, *now!*" The tip of a quarterstaff punched through the air where the wisp had just been standing, missing her completely while more shouting picked up through the cabin. He felt something move in his leg and then there was a scream that came from nowhere and everywhere at once.

He briefly realized it was coming from him before everything faded back out again.

※ ※ ※

He was thrashing on the bed. He could feel Eos'eno holding him down by his shoulders, and heard Steelhom chanting a prayer beside him. It was a Word, the same Word over and over and over. "*Bonds, bonds, bonds, bonds, bonds,*" again and again.

Other hands were ripping his chausses off, and the owner of those

42

hands were saying words that would have spoiled milk. "Goddess of the World, piss, simply the *World*... I've never... I've never seen..."

"*AID!* I told you! Needed you to provide aid for him! Must I say it again?! I failed ice I failed him I failed the winter!"

"Either explain what you did or quiet yourself girl, or he is going to die," Steelhom snapped, interrupting his chants for the scathing reply.

"Look at those blisters on his thigh... I've never... and what is that seeping out of his stomach?"

"I do not know! That's not how it looked when I reached inside and placed it within him!"

Hirshma's voice wavered a moment while she dipped the end of her finger into the hole in his gut. "Placed *what* inside?"

A lot of pain blossomed around her questing finger, and he remembered hearing another scream.

"Must I say it again? *The ICE!*"

"He's a living breathing man! He's not made to have ice stuffed into his every bloody hole!"

"*SHIT*, Steelhom, stop fighting with her! You got it wrong, *he's not breathing!*"

The paladin dropped his hands and ending the binding spell he was focused on, and then he grabbed the quarterstaff a second time. "Neither is that!"

Hirshma ducked his swing just in time for the world to go black again.

❄ ❄ ❄

"Eos'eno... wisp, girl, whatever... there is only so much raw mana that a man can withstand... he isn't a construct from your Goddess, he isn't a native to your plane... I can see what you did but..."

"Men are hardly native to this one! The elemental planes gave them birth at the dawn of time and now Ice seeks to help this man when no other help was soon to come! You could have helped you could have but you denied your own magic for so long and hurt master as you did!"

Hirshma snarled at her. "I hurt *him...?! I* hurt that son of a bitch?!"

Steelhom bent over Akaran's head and felt his cheek for a fever. "Your histories don't matter. Not now. It'll be only by the grace of the Goddess if he wakes back up. Tell me that neither of you gave him the foolish idea to drink from the mana font? Or... I am assuming, all but bathe in it?"

"His stupid ideas were all his stupid ideas. We kept telling him to go back to his shitty little Temple and get real help."

"I *am* the real help from his 'shitty little Temple,' Hirshma, and your shitty little town still awaits my edict to see if you get to keep it or if I decide that the Order is moving in."

"Even I know your Order moves from home to home! Mother always said that -"

Glancing at the wisp, Steelhom shut her down. "*YOU* have an even *less* tenuous grasp on the immediate future, *inhuman*. That you kept him alive after that demon ripped his stomach in half is the only reason that you still stand there now."

Meekly, Eos'eno quieted down and slipped off into a corner.

"Just as well you take her head for wearing my daughter's skin. That monster has no reason to be allowed to live!"

"I am no monster! I had no choice, the choice was not mine! Mother sent me here to aid master, master made me as I am! All him, not I, not Her! I've done naught to you in this world! Naught!"

"You are -" she started.

Steelhom finished. "- trying *my* patience. Now *both of you* sit down and *shut up*. I think I removed the last of the toxin in him. Neither he nor I can rest if I have to make plans to have you both put to death."

Wisely, the two of them shut up.

And not a moment too soon, he blacked back out.

Looking down at the bed, Sir Steelhom pulled off his bloody gloves and sighed tiredly. "Well. He is stable, I believe. There's little more we can do for him now other than hope and pray. If he survives, it is only through the will of the Goddess."

"Will of your Goddess. Little good that it's brought us."

Steelhom glanced aside at the alchemist and snorted in derision. "Far more good than your abandonment of yours."

"I brought Mother's will to him. The Divine have smiled upon him as he has fought for your people. Fought for me, fought for master, he has done so much and been infused with so much," Eos'eno softly whispered from the foot of his bed.

That earned another snort of derision. "Yes. Infused. *Infused* being the correct word."

"Are you sure the boy will live?"

"No. Although I am sure that it is no longer in our hands," the paladin sighed.

She didn't look any better than Steelhom did – her hands were slick with blood, and some strange metallic substance had been smeared

44

over her chest and stomach. Thoughtfully, she gave him a reply that he didn't think she had in her. "Thank you, Sir Steelhom." Before he could answer though, she did something else he didn't think she had in him. Grabbing a knife at the side of Akaran's bed, she lunged after the wisp in the corner with a scream on her lips. "YOU! MONSTER!"

Eos'eno flung her hands up protectively and suffered a deep cut to her wrist as she tried to fight Hirshma off. "Attack me?! Strike me why?! I did what I could did the best I could!"

"THE BEST YOU COULD? YOU'RE WEARING HER SKIN! IS THAT YOUR BEST? LET HER GO, LET MY DAUGHTER GO!"

The wisp let out a cry as crystals and pale blue slush splashed on the bed along Akaran's head and on the walls beside them. The wind began to pick up all around them inside the cabin while Hirshma desperately tried to stab her in the face. That came to an abrupt end with a Word and a swing of a staff. "**DESIST!**"

Billowing at the two of them, Steelhom flicked the end of his staff between them both, pushing them away from the side of the bed. His Word not only stopped the winds from picking up, it also served to stun them both and shoved them apart from each other. "What is WRONG with you people?! My student is *right there,* nearly dead, and you think now is a time to attack each other?"

"My daughter IS dead, and that... THING is wearing her body! Wearing it like... like...!"

"That *thing* saved his life, regardless as to if I care for it or not! You will stand down or be taken down, alchemist; I will not give you that warning twice."

Tears flowed down her face as she desperately tried to plead her case. "That's my daughter! You can't ask me, you can't... she's demonic! She has to be! Do your job and excise her!"

"Please! Please trust and believe I meant no harm I did no harm! Please I had no knowing that it would cause so much hurt to be seen! Master was right to have me hide!"

Steelhom didn't care about what either of them had to say. "HIRSHMA. Stay your hand!"

"You daft fool, you can't say you trust her! She's not human!"

He looked over at his student and barely kept his voice in check answering. "Neither are cats. We still let them live with us."

"She's pitspawn! Do your duty and excise it!"

"*No*, she *isn't.* OUTSIDE. NOW."

Eos'eno hadn't done more than cowering in the corner, hands up defensively still. "Master told me told me again and again if you of all saw me you of all would hate me and I knew you should know once he told me of you but he hurt me *please* don't hurt me like he hurt me!"

Hirshma shrieked back at her. "He knew did he?! He knew I'd **hate** you? Oh, *hate* isn't a strong enough word!"

That was enough for the paladin. He lunged for the wisp and grabbed her by her wrist. Ignoring every single one of her protests, he pulled the ethereal woman out the door – while shoving Hirshma out ahead of him. "I SAID OUT!"

"Get your hands off of me you bastard priest, and do your damn job!"

With a hearty shove that nearly knocked them both on the dirty snow, he sharply cracked his staff on the ground. "You have both earned a pass, brief as it otherwise is, for aiding in keeping Akaran alive. I know he's already passed judgment on you, alchemist; you've given me no reason to consider otherwise. *For now.*"

"You can't be taking the side of that... that monster! That thing!"

"*I'm not finished*. You. Wisp. You're trying to show that you're an ally but my trust only goes so far and we are now at the end of it. You stole her daughter's body? Does her soul reside with you still?"

Bleeding freely down her arms, and bleeding all over again from the gash in her side, Eos looked up at him with eyes full of frosty tears. "Stole? Not stole! Given! Master gave me this body as Mother gave me to him!"

"Does her soul still reside in that flesh with you? Answer me, or I will let Hirshma have you."

"No! No, her soul is not with me. Her soul is wherever her soul is. I do not know her I do not feel her I do not! Please, please believe me!"

"I am a paladin of the Goddess of Love. I don't believe *anyone* that begs for me to believe them." He whipped his staff to her and pressed the tip to her forehead as he pressed his two fingers to his right eye. With a whisper, he saw what he needed to see. "*Unmask.*"

A thin ripple of air coursed down his staff and touched her, and where it went, her form shimmered in and out of phase. She was just a vortex of swirling snow wrapped around a core of quicksilver and pure, untainted light. Hirshma couldn't see it, but if there had been any way for any kind of doubt to remain in Steelhom's mind?

There wasn't now.

"She's inhuman! Of course she lies!"

There was more to it, though. The hole in her flesh was worse on the inside. While snow and crystals and light were filling and spinning most of her body, her side was dull gray, splotchy, sluggish and cracking. It was the same toxic mess that they had just spent hours pulling out of Akaran's stomach and legs.

"*Enough,* you old crone. She's not lying. There's no... human soul. Just... energy. Just the wisp. And she... you don't have a lot of time left, do you? You need help."

Slowly shaking her head in agreement, her voice was as broken as her aura. "Time, no, no time. It hurts. Ice protects and endures but even ice melts in the sun and..."

"You're still not human. You're still an aberration in this world. Convince me to give you aid."

"Give her aid...?! Are you -"

The paladin snapped his head around to look at her and pointed the end of his staff at her face. "Goddess above. I'm surprised Akaran didn't beat you to death within a day, and I am less patient than he. *Let the girl talk.*"

Kneeling on the ground in supplication, Eos'eno looked up at the two of them. "Many years, many times back, my master discovered a passway from your world, this world, to mine. I know not where. I know that it was imperfect. It was flawed. It did not last long, as they are not meant to be. What he saw within it inspired him, changed him.

"I do not know what he had been like before this. I do not know what his goals were or how he found a tunnel into the Eternal Tundra. I know only that before, he had been... what it is you call an adept? An Adept, he said, of the Grand Library. I can only say what it was he told me of that time, that is all I can now or only or ever."

"A Granalchi," Steelhom clarified, the name bringing a sneer and a twitch to his eye. "How quaint."

Ignoring him, the wisp went on. "After, he devoted his studies to the magic of ice. And ice and snow and cold is magic, it is magical, it has a nature. It is nature. And he grew obsessed with it. He began to experiment with powers too great for his ability, for a time.

"One day, his teachers expelled him. His attempts to create a being of pure ice caused pain, suffering. So much of both. He was wracked with guilt. He never told me what truly happened that day. Only that others suffered for it. He never forgot them. He never forgot what he had done.

"Distraught, exiled, condemned, he fled. He once made allusions to assassins that sought to end his life. So he fled, far, and far away. I know not how long he must have traveled or how many years he hid before he came here. Only that he did."

The paladin shook his head. "If the Granalchi wanted him dead, he would be dead. They just didn't care about your master. I am willing to concede that may have been an error on their part."

"They wouldn't care? How can you say to know? They are fools, and blind, and monsters, and hateful! He warned that he had to hide himself away so they would never find him!"

"Because if the Academy thought he had gone rouge, they would have sent one of their Collectors for him. He'd be dead, his work would be locked in a box in the bottom of the ocean, and you would be rotting in a jar on a shelf somewhere."

Eos'eno didn't know what to say to that, so she simply moved on. "Whoever sent them, they sent. So he hid. So he made his way here. But he was obsessed. Too obsessed. He couldn't stop. He had no way to.

"Over time, my Queen, the Queen of all Frost, she noticed his efforts. She watched him, She was entertained by him. After a time, his work changed. He realized that to create a being of pure ice, one must have the essence of such.

"What he knew was that such an item did not exist in this world. He turned to attempts to create a way to bring forth something of my home to this home. His home. Only it was not to be. His home grew lonely and cold, a cold not born of nature. A cold born of a loss of the thing your Lady grants so freely and recklessly.

"He once found a woman, a maiden, someone he soon discovered feelings for. He had no intention to stay in this place. He only decided to after he met her. In time, his affection for her grew. Soon after..."

Hirshma took a ragged breath and blinked away an angry tear. "Soon after, I gave birth to Mayabille. You know that because you stole her body from me."

It was Eos's turn to nod her head. "Yes. A daughter. But she and her mother were taken away from him. Incensed over this outsider, this man that had defiled his descendant, the one that laid claim to the people of Toniki demanded him to leave. He demanded it, and was prepared to kill for it. Sergibon, elder of Toniki, and priest of my Mother's Mother, the Lady of all Growth, Kora'thi."

"He was a druid as well? It seems magic runs in your family," Steelhom dryly observed.

Hirshma couldn't help but retort, even as upset as she was. "Not my brother. Only magic that man had was with whores."

Eos'eno ran a hand over her side and resumed her story. "He would not have been able to do so. But my master had no wish to make the people suffer. His heart ached and bled for his loss but he knew, he did. He knew that if he stayed or if he fought in the ways that he knew how, many would suffer. They should not be made to feel pain because he was wracked with it.

"The village exiled him as the Academy had. Only this time, he did not travel far away. He traveled here. To this cabin, in these woods. Furious over his loss, he plunged into his work and gave no thought nor care to anything else around him.

"All he could do was wish for his baby to see him and to grow strong like him. Perhaps with him. You humans, your ways of spawning new of your own are so strange. You do not craft them and make them. You throw your bodies together and hope for the best. So strange. Odd so wet, so... unpleasantly damp."

Steelhom just shrugged. "There are worse ways to bring life into this world. I've seen enough of them."

Undaunted, the wisp continued on. "The daughter was perhaps a decade old in your ways to tell time. A blink in mine. But a decade she was when the torrid affair between master and... you, master and you, was exposed once again. I know he met you many times since he was banished for having you, and for you having his.

"It was a visit, one of those trips, that fate turned against him yet once again. The elder sought to be sure that master's bastard creation did not return from her trip. He told me this, he told me of this tale. There was a plot; a scheme. It was more than just an action. An action born of shame and rage and disgust and hate and demand for control. He set after the bastard daughter one day as she played in the woods near his cabin."

Hirshma took a few steps towards her, stopping only when Steelhom lifted the point of his staff again. "Set after her? Mayabille died when one of our wolves attacked her! We had the pair; Hunsri and Zenifer! Hunsri got sick; a frothing disease, made her mad. The scar from where she was bit is on your shoulder!"

"Like daughter, like mother, like father. The father, your father, held sway over nature, the land. She was an abomination to him, an abomination like you see me. He used that sway to change nature. To make nature do as *his* nature wished."

The alchemist balled her fists. "What exactly is that supposed to mean, you bitch?"

"That dogs do as their master wishes," she quietly replied. "A dog will bring ruin to an abomination, should it be told."

"An abomination to him...? What are you trying to say? That my father made Hunsri sick? That he made her attack my daughter? That's insanity!"

Face crestfallen, Eos'eno told her a truth that the alchemist did not want to hear. "Those that speak for nature control many aspects of such. Disease is nature as much as growth. The elemental nature is always of dual-faces, of good and ill, and disease may grow and flourish as much as a baby grows to an adult or a sprig grows to a mighty oak. He spoke that you sought to counter the disease, to cure your daughter, but you couldn't. The growth in her was too strong, spreading too fast, for you to bring divinity against."

She didn't take it well. "I... no, I couldn't... it set in faster than I've ever seen, Hunsri's bite... it had to have gone deeper than I saw, that was all it... it couldn't have been..."

"It was not the fault of the wolf. Divinity had been brought and guided and given, then knowledge of that divinity was twisted and turned and changed to be stronger than what someone... what you... could do to cure. Her fate was sealed; master knew this to be true the moment that he saw her. The father of her mother, your father, tapped into magic that you do not could not dare not call upon..."

Hirshma's face crumbled and she sank back in her chair. She looked like a mountain had just been placed on her shoulders. "No... oh, no. Please. It was an accident... Father wouldn't have ever... he couldn't have... spreading disease, decay, that is not what a priestess of Kora'thi does! Under no circumstance, for no reason! We push for growth; we push for life!"

"Kora'thi does. Neph'kor does not," Steelhom quietly grumbled. The very idea of what the wisp was hinting at was beginning to give him a sick feeling in the pit of his stomach. He could only imagine what the alchemist felt.

"The God of Decay does not, the other face of growth, the face that all come to in death or life both," Eos added. "No. No, it was no accident. Whatever it was that was told to the people of Toniki, it was no accident. Your father could have slid a blade to her neck and been more kind; he was pleased with her suffering, to punish my master. Master knew that he delighted in it, that he was full of joy for making master suffer as his daughter suffered.

"Soon after, master did something that none knew. He recovered the body of his child from the grave dug and entombed her. He protected her, he gave her immortality in ice. He gave her a home, a proper home, for her body to stay as pure and pristine as it had been in her life. He wished to tell his lover but he never could. She... you... never gave him the chance."

The older woman's shoulders fell, tears poured from her eyes, and she sagged to her own knees. "That... that bastard... all... of them, bastards... all... no... no, you said... he even *dug her up?!*"

"One day, he watched you leave her village. He nearly ran to you, he said, he nearly came to you and told you all, but he couldn't. He was stopped by a voice, a man, *that* man, he heard, he didn't see. He heard him laughing, and happy, and joyful for some small thing. It was more than master could... Master needed one thing more than to tell you everything. He needed to be sure that his lover's father would not ever, ever harm him nor you again. Never again."

Everything was so crystal clear at this point that Steelhom almost stopped the story. "Grief gives action to the lost."

"No. NO! You can't say it! He fell from the bridge over...! A freak storm! A gust of wind!"

Eos swallowed nervously, and a small breeze spun into existence around her knees. Little errant snowflakes were kicked up into the light wind around her. "Yes. Sergibon fell, and fell far. Master can cause the raw air to turn into a solid mass of ice. He can coax snowflakes from streams and extinguish flame with a wave of his hand. A man that can move his tower and protect it under the waves with but days of planning... you do not think that master can control a simple gust of wind?"

"NO! He didn't! HE **COULDN'T!**"

Shrugging, the priest was hard-pressed to disagree with Usaic's motives. "He realized your father killed his daughter. I've ordered heretics to the gallows for less."

Hirshma looked like she was going to lunge at him, weapon be damned. "You're as bad as Usaic! Monsters, both of you, and you're attempting to defend the existence of *THIS* monster!"

"I am a *paladin* in service to the Goddess of Love, and a *paladin* in service to the Queen of Dawnfire. I am no monster, but I *am* a man of law."

"And... you believe her? *Why?*"

"Because I can see the truth in her words. She's not done with those words yet though, is she? You still haven't explained how it is that you came to be."

The breeze started to subside, but her own tears did not. "The suffering, the hurt, the loss. It made him lose his way. He spent years trying to find it again. He spent years hating himself and terrorizing himself and doing so many things to himself and to his creations.

"Through that, through all of that, he began to discover the nature of pure ice. He began to find ways to make it manifest. It took so much power and energy that he could not bring it to this world on his own. Not without help. So he threw his angst-wracked mind into his new task.

"I do know that even through his pain, he tried so hard. But without a companion, what was he to be? What way was his work to finish? Would he ever? Could he ever? The Queen of Ice did not believe so. As you know, what you know, you do know what happened next."

He did. "That's when she sent you."

"Yes. It was. She did, I did. She gave me this body, her body, the daughter. Thus, I came to be."

The name that Hirshma choked out made Steelhom's heart break for her. "Mayabille..."

"Yes."

"He gave... he gave our daughter to a monster? What right... what possible *thing* do you think you are worth to... have her? What...?"

"His work! His work is key, his work is worth all!"

The alchemist suddenly reared up, grabbing for Steelhom's halberd. "You MONSTER!"

It was all that the paladin could do to hold onto it. "She had no control over it! It wasn't her doing! The blame for this lays with Usaic!"

Furious in her new-found grief, the older woman slapped him across his cheek hard enough to leave a bright mark behind. He saw it coming but didn't stop it. It wouldn't have done any good. "YOU! You KILL things that do what she's done! KILL HER!"

"Not yet. Hold!"

"You see a creature that has no right to be in our world living in the skin of my daughter! My Mayabille!" she screamed, sobbing all the while.

The wisp made a cry of her own that drowned out both of the mere mortals. "I harmed none!"

"YOU TOOK HER! AND HE TOOK MY FATHER!"

Eos returned her shout with conviction and pain and loss to match. *"He* took *me!* He spoke of me of this world and your ways and your people and touched me and showed me so much of you. I was of ice then and I am of ice now but master made me his! He made me *his!* He made me what you used to be!"

Steelhom's head whipped to the crying girl and his eyes went wide. "He what?"

The implications of the statement were both sudden and staggering. It was almost more than the alchemist could bear – and her own cries stopped instantly. Neither of them took it better than Akaran had, and in his defense, he was half-dead at the time. "Usaic... did... what?"

Shrinking in on herself, the wisp answered as clearly as she could. "He still loved you. Loved you with all his heart. He left here, time and time as he could. He brought aid to your people. He attempted to pay a penance for a sin only he and I knew. He wished that one day you could forgive him for what you knew he had done and to never find out the things you didn't."

Hirshma had to put a hand out to steady herself against a nearby tree as the awful revelations kept coming. "So... all those times that he came to us, after father... those times he came to just... help..."

"If you had extended even but a flicker of kindness back to him, he would have given you the world. A world of beauty and shapes and clarity and a feeling so cool that your soul would be forever adrift in its current."

"He came to find absolution. That sick, sick man..."

The paladin shook his head. "He took you? As his? As his what, exactly? I cannot possibly be right with my thoughts."

The wisp answered with her eyes downcast. "Yes. As time grew long and his world grew older. He showed me how a human provides warmth. I... I provided what I could, as I could."

"In the body of his daughter," he whispered as his voice started to waver in disgust.

"In a body that I had to grow to survive in. Yes. In this body and this form. I became his."

Too many emotions raged through the alchemist at once. Revulsion, horror, anger, loss, and in some distant part of her, pity. "Oh... oh child," she whispered. "What madman did I give myself to..."

Exceedingly cautiously and with far more bravery than most would have had, Eos floated a little towards her and reached for her hand. It was an innocent enough gesture; and for one brief moment, the alchemist took it and then just as quickly jerked away. "The man that loved me as a companion loved you as more. He did not grow to be mad while in your company, lady. I swear this on pain of my own ice. He did not grow to be mad at all!"

"Not mad? He... he's... done all this, and you don't think he is... mad?"

"No! Not at all! Consumed by his work, consumed by the need for his work! I was there to aid his work, to provide him with comforts so he may continue to do his work! Mother wished it!"

Steelhom cleared his throat to interrupt, and when they didn't work, he rapped his staff on the snowy ground. "What, exactly, is this all-important work that you keep referencing?"

The wisp took a deep breath, and you could tell that there was a war waging in her heart as to if she should answer or not. Eventually, she caved. "Five of your years ago, master was able to discover the formula to not just bring an object from my home to this, but to keep it. To let it power itself. To anchor it into your world of flesh and blood so that it would be forever. No other spells no rituals no guidance. A thing from my world placed firmly in yours. One spell, one expenditure of magic, and no more needed."

The implications of her reply gave Steelhom his own opportunity to debate if he was going to cry or throw up. A nasty little voice in the back of his head remarked that it was only fair that he should have his turn too. "What... *thing* would this be? What is its nature?"

She took a deep breath and started to elaborate. "He named it the 'coldstone.' He found a way to have it forged through both sides of Mother's will. He... he believed that it could render a person immune to flame, or allow a man to create vast fields of ice at will... to stop a flood with power channeled through it; to end an inferno. To preserve stores of food, to preserve a person until aid could be given to heal them. The possibilities within it are endless. The power in this world would be so vast, so vast to any that could hold it."

"Immunity to flame." He stood there, jaw clenching and grinding audibly. "There would be a war to end all wars for that... for us to keep it and the Civans to take it... this... rock... that would tip the scale of power for generations..."

"Tip the scales? What is that supposed to mean? What does it matter? Ice is... it's not difficult magic to work. Even I know as much."

The paladin shook his head. "You aren't seeing the big picture."

"A big picture? Isn't this? Isn't this *big* enough for you?"

"No. Listen to me. The Kingdom of Dawnfire has been at war off and on with the Civan Empire for decades. Centuries. Longer than even the Hardening. You know that. Their entire society is built around the worship of the Goddess of Flame. This coldstone? The knowledge of how to make it could give the Queen an edge that the Civans might not be able to overcome if she can use it to stop the Knights of Flame and the Disciples of the Grand Inferno in their tracks."

"Politics?! A time like now, with that thing here, pretending to be on our side? *Politics* is where your thoughts lead?!"

"Hirshma, see past your anger. If word gets out, no, *when* word gets out, this is the type of magic that people will slaughter each other for. That spy in your village should be enough to prove that point! If she's started her run to the Empire – and I am *sure* that she did – then... that assumes they don't already know. They would have had to even know to send her. **Shit.**"

Flinching back, the older woman's jaw fell open. "Are you to tell me that the Civian Empire will risk a war with the Queen to get this stupid little rock the bastard was working on? That they'll destroy the village?"

"The *village?* Empress Bimaria would see this *mountain* burned to ash if she found out what he was doing. I swear to you on the name of the Goddess, if she were to find out that it had been completed? Ash. There would be little more than ash, everywhere. Do you understand? This isn't simply a matter of a few demons; this is a matter of the start of the next Imperium War sitting around waiting for someone to claim it. That spy that has been so casually misplaced? If she has reached any kind of safe harbor, she has already begun the process to end the world as this portion of the Kingdom knows it."

"She already did, damn you. She murdered my brother. Did it because of what Usaic made. That bastard... he's... not just responsible for this... *thing* here! He murdered my father, cost me my daughter, and now... now I can blame him for Ronlin as well? And... everyone else that's fallen to these demons?"

"So it would appear," Steelhom grumbled. "At least now we know what the prize everyone is battling for. Civans and Abyssians both. And now us. This is more than troubling. I hope you can see it."

Hirshma stumbled over her tongue while his words started to make far too much sense. "I... can. That doesn't excuse that creature! She is still an affront to everything!"

It was hard to disagree with her. "She may be, she may be not. Girl?"

"Ye... yes?"

"Why have you been helping us?"

Eos'eno gave a trembling smile. "Master bade me to. He made me promise that I would give aid. That if anything did not work as it should, if his magic failed, he bade me to protect the village... protect his lover, no matter... no matter what."

"Protect *me?!* He defiled Mayabille's body, and tasked you to protect *me?!* The *gall* of that man!"

"Yes. You. You. The people of Toniki. He knew there was a risk, a chance, that things would not go well. But ice preserves, and as long as he is preserved, his work is still intact! His other help... his other help... does not feel the same towards master or his wishes as do I."

Steelhom clenched his jaw again. "Usaic made the demon as well then, did he?"

"He did not make him. He needed a servant from not just Tundrala, but Frosel. He needed a balance of light, of dark, to bring the coldstone into this world. He was granted the understanding to bring forth an ally... I was given that knowledge, to give to him... it was one of my tasks."

"Helped him? You told him how to summon that monstrosity? YOU?" the alchemist all-but shouted. She picked up a loose branch and started to make her way to the wisp when Steelhom stopped her with a flick of his staff.

"It wants the coldstone. It doesn't care who gets hurt, but it wants the power for itself."

"Yes. Makolichi does. He does, the wraith does, they seek it together. They are not in concert. Makolichi uses the wraith to do what he can not; grow stronger, grow bigger, to break the spells master worked on his work to unlock it."

Steelhom grumbled an obscenity and glanced at the cabin. "How fisking quaint."

"I've tried to hold them back as long as I could but they are too strong together for me to banish, they are... I've held them away for as long as I could. I swear that I have! I saved as many of your people as I could but... they are too strong for me. They simply are."

The paladin gave a long, drawn-out sigh in response. "No wonder the boy nearly got himself killed. This is a mess."

"A mess? Is that what you call it? That all you can call it, Steelhom?"

"I can call this a great many things. Disaster, a royal cock-up. A nightmare. A bastardization of even the most base of the Laws of Normality. The precursor to the next Imperium War. Or, yes, *a bloody fisking mess."*

Eyes slowly drooping, Eos clutched at her side. The subject of their discussion looked up at him and then shied away again. "The ice says he's a murderer, not a boy..." She spoke so softly that neither of them heard her. They would have ignored her anyways.

Hirshma's glare said it all. "It doesn't matter what you call it. I don't believe her, I don't believe a word she said. She stole a body. She's not human. She's not mortal. She doesn't belong here. Do your job, or I will, I promise you."

"Believe or not! They won't move on until they have master's work! I can't recover it and protect his tower and watch your people! Should they claim the stone, they would come rip and rend and then the ice would be bad and...! No telling what would come of things then!"

He looked back at her for a moment and shook his head one last time. "No. I won't. She may not be mortal, she may not belong in this world, but she is not evil. There is no cause for me to bring her to judgment," he decided. "For now."

"There isn't?! You're going to get us killed!"

"Look at her!" he snapped, patience finally at an end. "She is *terrified* of *you.* I can see what you can't. I can *feel* the loss and sadness in her. Your lover made her like this, and... I cannot believe that being with him, this girl, this creature... he abused her. He abused her badly. And she still loves him and has put her own life at risk saving yours. Saving Akaran's. Saving... everyone that she could. In her own way, but, saving."

"There was no abuse, none! I did what I did because I was made to, because I had to! Because he wanted, and because he wanted I wanted, because that is what a companion does!"

Hirshma wiped tears from her eyes and tried so very hard to reign in her grief. "Then you're no better than a mule. They only do what they're made to do as well. You're... less than a mule, a mule is natural, a mule is *real.*"

Shaking, the wisp knelt down to the ground and hung her head. "I did what I could, I helped how I could, I was all I could. I never meant to hurt a soul, hurt a person. I was only here to provide comfort and aid in the snow to master, so many years ago. I've loved him longer than any! For twenty of your years, for twenty! You loved him for how many? How many seasons passed, how many winters came and went? A mere four, a mere five?"

"I loved him because I am not a *thing!* I loved him because I am a *woman*, a *human!* YOU can't imagine that! You can't *be* that! Even a mule can love her owner," the older woman argued. "You... you won't excise her, will you, Steelhom? You're not going to give my daughter peace?"

Steelhom glared at her, and then knelt down next to Eos'eno. "Wherever your daughter is, she isn't here. I'll entertain no more grief from you on the subject. Wisp..."

"Yes... yes, man of Love?"

"You do not belong in this world. You will have to return to your home, where you belong, when this is over. I will not destroy you; I will not condemn you... but you will *have* to return to your world when it is time."

She blinked away tears of her own. "Please, send me back to Mother. Now. Please. I will go. I've hurt too many, caused too much pain, to be allowed to stay. I cannot... I cannot serve and aid and rescue master from where he is when I am... when I hurt the other mother... when I hurt the mother of this body so."

"Not today. You saved my student. You've earned a reprieve. For your abuse, you've earned a pass on penance. You do know you do not belong in this world, yes?"

"I... I do. Please believe. I do. I... I want to go home. You... you will not let me go home, will you?"

The paladin looked to Hirshma, and kept his voice level. "You are going nowhere yet. And 'the mother of your body' will not attempt to harm you again. Will she?"

"Don't ask me to accept that... thing, don't you dare, don't you expect me to -"

"I expect you to follow my command. I would hope and pray that you can believe that you are not the only person who has been wronged by this wizard. I hope you can see that this creature has lost... she has lost. It will suffice to simply say that."

Hirshma blinked away her tears and let loose an epithet that could have set the world afire if she had the power to make it manifest. "Usaic. He dies."

"Kill? No! Master you can't no! NO!" Eos pushed herself off the ground and shards of ice sprouted from her skin like jagged teeth. "NO! I will not allow you will not I care not YOU WILL NOT!" she shouted in a rush.

Steelhom intervened again, this time with a hand on her bleeding arm. The barbs dug into his gauntlet almost enough to draw blood.

"Your master has done incalculable harm. He has a *great deal* to atone for. You may not like it but you *will* abide by the verdict of the Goddess or *my* verdict on you will be revised."

"You will slay me to slay him?! You expect me, a creature, a thing you keep saying is not of your world to accept the death of my master for your laws? I am not of this world! I am not to be here! Why should I honor your laws? Your rules? I should care for your wishes *why* if my presence, my life, my existence is such a horrific thing?!"

"Because he is out of control! Because he has murdered a man, because he has caused more than one demon to wander unchecked! Because he has brought pain and suffering and death and apparently even rape to this world and his life and *yes*, he *will* be brought before judgment. *He will.*"

Eos tried to jerk away and free herself from his grip. She couldn't. No matter how hard she tried, she didn't have the strength to get away. "You want to undo him! Undo his work!"

"I want to keep his work from being used to hurt more people! I am here because it already has! You're proof of that yourself! You are not daft and you are not a fool and *you* of all the things in this world are in a unique position to understand *all* of that!"

"I understand much! I understand that you want his work for your own needs! You are no different than Daringol, no different than Makolichi! You're no different than any and all, and what of his work when you have it? What of his work then? Your queen, your people? Your Order? I am made to ensure that his work is used for the sake of nature, not for the whims of man or beast!"

With a hard shake, Steelhom pulled her close and let his lip turn to a snarl that almost matched Hirshma's. "What I will do is risk my life and my soul to do the same as you. To make sure that his work *does not* fall into the hands of warmongers or the damned."

"You admit! Your own Queen, she wants his work! She would use his work to wage war on her enemies! This is why he hid, this is why he kept his work away! Because he knew!"

"If the Queen is willing to kill for it, if the Empress has ordered people to kill for it, if the demons *have been* killing for it, then it's too late for that. More people are going to die until the stone is destroyed or it's secured."

Weeping, Eos slapped him, drawing a welt across his cheek. The blood on her hand left a cool tingle on his cheek, and he showed remarkable restraint in not hitting her back. "End his work, end the reason for me, end why I was even made. You don't care, none of you care! The Guardian of Winters cares! Awaken him, let him decide!"

"His work has come with a price that must be and *will be* paid in full. Hirshma is correct. He dies."

The alchemist's voice crackled behind him. "Steelhom you... you won't have to," Hirshma finally interrupted, giving him the same tear-streaked stare Eos had when she had looked up from the ground at him. "He's dead."

"Dead? No! Master isn't dead! Master is protected entombed, secured by ice! *Ice preserves!*"

He didn't let go of the wisp, but he did spare the alchemist a moment. "How do you know?"

"What... what's the one thing that Usaic has done? He... he kept control. You don't know the man as I did. He would never let his spell go wild or unchecked. He wouldn't let a raindrop fall out of place. The only way he could, or would fail to keep this to his chest... is if he died."

With a small shove, Steelhom pushed Eos'eno back a little bit. Crystal scales fell off of her arms, and more of the quicksilver-colored blood splashed to the snow from her side. "He died casting the spell."

"No! He didn't die! He's not dead! The coldstone caught him saved him preserved him!"

"If he's not dead... do you think the magic could have done it? Preserved him?"

"Or turned him into a block of ice," she answered.

Looking back at the wisp, Steelhom gave a long thought to what he was about to say. "If he's alive, and agrees to surrender the work, I'll spare him death. If he doesn't, even if he survives me, you know that others will not be so kind as to render him the option. I will, at least, be quick."

"You... I see why you say, I see why you think of him so, but you cannot ask me to be willing to give you help if it will end in his demise!"

Before the paladin could answer, Hirshma did. "I hate you. I hate everything about you, and I will always hate him for what he's done. You keep saying he's so brilliant, and that he told you to protect the village. Is that true?"

Wrapping her arms around her midriff, Eos agreed wholeheartedly. "It is! He is! His mind is as perfect and sharp as a human mind can be!"

"Then he knew that someone would come to recover his work if he died."

"Yes! He knew, the Ice knew!"

Stepping forward again, half-trembling in disgust (and half-shaking from the cold), the older woman sized up the otherworldly girl and let out a long breath through clenched teeth. "Then he accepted the risk that the people that come may not be pleased with his efforts. He knew that you would protect it until someone came to help. The paladin is here to help. The exorcist. They're not pleased. He understood that risk. He's not so stupid to think that he would be rewarded if something went wrong."

Eos crumbled again as her words hit home. Hirshma had just won this argument, and everybody knew it. "He... he pleaded that I convince anyone that came to... to save his work... I can't, who can I help when..."

"You can because he wanted you to. It might not be what he wanted, but he knew that if something horrible happened? He could count on you to make sure that the people were protected. That was his instruction. To keep the people safe. It's his work that they need to be protected *from*."

The wisp didn't answer. She couldn't. Steelhom knelt down to her, and did what the alchemist couldn't (and wouldn't). He carefully, slowly, reached for the girl and brought her head to his chest. "It must be done, Eos. It must. We have to recover his work before it wreaks any more havoc. Will you help us, please?"

She didn't answer.

She couldn't.

Steelhom shook her, and when he did, she slumped to the ground on her side. Her eyes were closed and she didn't move no matter how hard he tried to wake her. His swearing didn't help either, and as he tried to do *anything* to get her to awaken and respond, it was Hirshma who intervened.

She bent down and wrapped her arms around the wisp and started to pick her up. When the paladin asked her what she was doing, her response was succinct. "We need her so I can see Usaic hang, just in case he isn't dead already."

"There's a statue underground. It's the source of the water from Tundrala. Or, at least, *a* source. I am no longer convinced it is the only one. Still, it might be enough to help her recover. She took a beating as badly as my student did."

"Then what are you waiting for? Get her inside."

❄ ❄ ❄

On a beach, far away – farther away than he realized – Akaran woke up.

The sand felt wonderful under him. So warm, so inviting. So soft, even as it nestled into every crevice on his body. It didn't even feel uncomfortable in the places it should have felt uncomfortable. It just felt...

It felt like he was at home.

A little girl was hovering over him, and her voice was insistent in his ears. She didn't look like she was more than six years old, if that. She had little curly blonde tresses and a simple white dress on. Her eyes shone with golden warmth and delight, and he could hear giggles off in the distance behind him.

It was wonderful – until he realized he was naked... and until he realized that his stomach felt like it was on fire all over again. "Oh Goddess, no, it felt better, it..."

Cheerfully chirping, the girl finally got his attention. "...hello!!! Hey! There, you, hello!"

Blearily blinking and looking up at her, he did his best to focus on her face. "Hurts... I hurt..."

"Not surprised," she answered, a cheerful perky tilt to her voice. "That's an awful gash you've got going on down there. Not a worry. We'll get that fixed."

"Get it... fixed? It was fixed..."

The girl giggled at him again. "Was fixed? Oh no, not at all. Looks like someone tried to patch it together using spit and shit. No wonder you made it up here." She gave a little frown and poked at his stomach before she complained a little more. "Cold spit, too. That's a little gross. We'll fix that."

It felt so warm here, so calm, so peaceful, that he didn't even object when she kept stabbing at his wound. "Where am... this isn't Toniki..."

"Toniki? What's...? OH. There's a village called Toniki. Isn't there? Awful little place. Uncomfortable and damp and cold and just... No, you're not there. Didn't think any of us were over there. Not for, say going on twenty, thirty of years in the Lowland before now. Of course, the ones before that too but they were so long ago. Back in the Troubles."

"Lowland? One of... us? One of who?"

"You know, the Lowlands. Well, that's what we call it. 'Cause, you know, you're so far down there."

Struggling to sit up, he realized that he was resting with his back against a knotted piece of driftwood. In front of him, a crystal-blue ocean lapped against the sandy shores. It looked like it went on forever.

"So far down...? One of us? One of who?"

"Well, yes. You know. Followers?"

"Followers...?"

The little girl sat back on her heels and smiled at him. "You know! *Followers.* That's a silly question. Silly boy. But no, you *can't* be from Toniki. We keep close watch on all of Her people, and we only sent two of you and you're too young to be... to be... you're not..." Her smile vanished as she realized something that was simply too terrible for her to stand. "Oh... oh no. No no no."

Akaran managed to scoot up the rest of the way and started to turn his head to look over his shoulder. She grabbed his face before he could see anything past the beach and wrenched his head around. "Hey! Let go of me! What's going on? Who are you?"

"One eye... deep scar on your chest, two in your bicep... goatee... you look like you've been trying to cover fresh scratches with fresher scars... how is that even possible? What *have* you been doing...? Oh dear. Oh no, this won't stand. Nope. Not at all," she muttered, poking and prodding at every spot as she mentioned it.

"Let me go or so help me I'll -"

"So help you is right," she continued to mutter. "Who put a rune of the Frostmaiden on your neck?" Looking aghast, she recoiled slightly. "You didn't... *disavow* Her, did you?"

"Disavow? What? Who...? *Who are you?*"

Quickly shaking the thought off, the girl started to pace around him. She was so tiny and petulant; it was adorable, if not infuriating. Every time he tried to look around, she grabbed his jaw and made him focus on her. "I'm someone that's about to kick your ass out of here. You're not supposed to be here yet. You're not. There's rules. There's things that have to be done first. You should know that."

"I am... so tired of these questions... please, let me go to sleep or let me hurt something... just... Rules? Who's rules...? What rules...? What's going on?"

"*Her* rules. Far be it from us to question Her choice in men but you really are an idiot. The rest of us have always said that. Since the day She picked you. Why him? Why the brother of a dead man, son of a madman? Do you have any idea how upset She is going to be if She finds you here?"

Frustrated and giving up on getting answers, he sighed and closed his eye, nodding off a little bit. "You know what? I don't care. I hurt, I am tired, I have been bitten, cut, and thrown around and... I can't keep doing this..."

"Oh no. No no no. Don't you fall asleep. Don't dare. She'll kill us both. Redundant in your case but I just know She'll find a way to do it and do it again a few times over. You don't know Her like I do."

"Are you... are you insane? It's so nice here... please go away, let me..."

"Am *I* insane? Am *I* insane? Coming from *you*? You of all of *us*? So questions Her fiancee. Nope. You can't be Her fiancee yet. You're not even a grown man yet. Boys can't be a fiancee! Can't be a husband! Not allowed. We won't let it. *SOMEONE* has to speak for sanity when She's lost Hers."

Her chaotic ramblings were having less of an impact the longer she kept at it. "Please stop talking... it's warm here... I haven't been warm since I left the Temple... I'm going to take a nap now."

The little girl growled under her breath. "You haven't been warm because you've been off pissing around in the snow. Nap? Nope. You can't stay here. If you go to sleep here you'll stay here. Snow'll be the least of your worries if you do. It'll be the least of mine. Goddess only knows where She'd send the both of us. Can't have that, can't do that. Though suppose that's redundant. Of course She'd know if She's the one doing it."

"Worries are for the awake... I'm tired of being awake..."

Growling still, the girl leaned closer to him. "Oh blessed Goddess. Get this in your head, you beaten and befuddled twit. You sleep, you're dead. Not a little dead. A *lot* dead. You die, **I'm** dead. That's not going to be fun because I *can't* die. I suppose if you got to this state you're listening to all the wrong people. Oh you stupid person, bloody stupid boy."

"Everyone is so fisking rude, it's... they don't want me... I don't want them..."

"You do, you just don't know it yet. You're gonna want a few of them actually. Well. One. No... two... no. No, that's not right. You're gonna want several as you grow up. Or have you already met her yet? The blonde? Young one? Likes women as much as men? Can't blame her. Can't fathom why anyone would stay with men. Is that... now? No?"

Akaran tried to croak out a response, but nothing came out that made any more sense than she did.

"Oh, right. No, now's the other blonde. The one-eyed wench. Always the blondes with you. At least it's not the redhead yet. *Or* that dreadful lady with the claws. *Goddess* that one is going to be a nightmare to watch. I don't even want to know what all you're going to offer Mother to get her to quit trying to kill you... and you won't even know it's her when she's doing it! How sad is that?"

He tried to push her back with no luck at all. "Please, let me sleep..."

The kid didn't budge. "You'll sleep when you're dead. Well. Dead-er. More than you're close to now. Which if She has Her way about it won't be for a while yet. You do not want to get in Her way either, I'll warn you now." Akaran could just *feel* the irritation coming off of her in waves. "Gonna have to fix that pain in your head, too, all that... ain't just a headache from magic. Looks like your brain got all bounced around in that thick skull of yours. Do the people that worked on you know that you'd otherwise have more in common with a vegetable if you ever woke up *without* Our intervention?"

"One eye? Claws? Vegetable? Are... are you mad?" he whimpered. "Am I?"

"Yes. You are," she chided before running her hands over his wounds again. "Blessed *be* what did you *do*. You reek of... just... you *reek*. Ugh. So much stuff in your system in the Lowlands that it's made a mess of your soul. Guess there's not much of a surprise you landed on the beach. At least Pristi was nice enough to let you go through the damn gate and didn't send you through a tumble in the sands first. Saved you *that* miserable and desolate slog. She's thrown people out for less, you know.

"Honestly. More of a surprise you haven't turned into a puddle on the inside after the kind of week you've had. Truly remarkable. If I could tell anyone about this encounter I'd be heaping praises about your constitution. Suppose it's not your mind She's after, not with that kind of stamina. But you're not supposed to be here so I can't and *that's* just gonna take a lot of the fun out of it for me because if anyone finds out I'm gonna be cleaning *sephilal* droppings off of the beach with my lips. Guess She really did build you right."

"Do you... do you have to ramble on with all that... inane chatter? You... said you'd fix my head, fix my eye, too?"

With a very deep and pained sigh, the little girl placed a finger on his chest and looked him dead in the eye. "Oh honey, I can patch up your soul, but there's *no* fixing your head." With that, everything drifted into darkness, and he didn't hear anything for a while yet to come.

❄ ❄ ❄

Later, in the dark, he heard a voice.

"Akaran, please, wake up. I didn't know how bad it was here. You fought hard, but you can't rest forever. I should have given aid earlier... I should have. I will forever owe you a debt of apology if you wake up. Please. You're almost a... You're you. So... please. Please, wake up, my boy."

❋ ❋ ❋

And later still, another.

"Alright you little shit, you've had your nap. Can't fault you for taking one but it's time to wake up now. Don't like your breathing none. Don't think that that gent from your temple is gonna be none to happy with me if you don't get up off your ass soon. Mariah will probably throw a monster of a fit too. Wake up. Just... do it, and wake up."

❋ ❋ ❋

There was no way to tell when the third one touched his ear.

"Ice protects... you protected Ice... Ice protects you. Istalla promises."

❋ ❋ ❋

It was much later, hours later, when the final whisper reached him — one carried on the wind.

[**There you are.** *Gauntlet to My fist, you still nap? You've slept long enough.* **Wake up.** *You have work to do and I grow weary of watching you piss about in the snow.* **AWAKEN** *and channel My annoyance!*]

❋ ❋ ❋

Morning came with blood on his lips, and was soon joined by vomit on the floor. It took a few minutes worth of coughing, retching, and whimpering before he was able to get his bearings. Not that getting his bearings improved his mood any. "Goddess..."

"Figures that you're too damn stubborn to be dead," Hirshma said from across the room.

Blinking and looking up at her, he gingerly shook his head. "I think I was."

"You were. You got better."

"Doesn't... feel like it. I... what happened? I... I remember flashes, remembering hearing... Brother Steelhom, but... he's in the capitol..."

She stood up and walked over to him. She looked like she hadn't slept in a week, with deep circles under her eyes and fresh wrinkles across her forehead. "He's here. He was watching your work. Got as blindsided as the rest of us."

Her answer caught him by surprise as he tried to get his vision to focus. "He's here? When? How long?"

"Since you got here, I suppose. He ran into the same snag as you." She tried to push him back onto the bed without much luck and settled for dragging a ratty blanket up over his shoulders instead. "Couldn't sense the magic on these mountains 'till he was right on top of it. He saved your life."

He fought it off and started running his hands up and down the bloody bandages that covered him from just below his neck to just over his hip. "Goddess... where is he? I need... I need to talk to him."

Hirshma shook her head and swatted his hands away. "Quit fidgeting. He's in the cave. Securing the statue with... that *creature*."

"Creature?"

"The... girl."

"Oh. Eos'eno... of course she's here. Is she in one piece? Did he attempt to excise her?"

She shook her head and sighed tiredly. "No, and no. He felt we were all better off if she was alive. The fool."

"He did? That's... okay. At least he agreed with me." He slowly, painfully, stood up... and sat right back down again. His ribs, his stomach, and his left leg felt like they had been burnt from the inside out. "What happened to me? Why do I feel like I've been under a boulder?"

While some bird with more courage than sense chirped away maddeningly outside, Hirshma's answer jarred him into focus. "What happened? Boy, you died. Every inch of your body was pumped full of just about every essence of mana on the mountain. You've been out cold for the last day. Bit longer."

"I was half-kidding. I didn't die, I'm still right..."

"You died. You drank down a barrel's worth of the water from the font, that bitch tried to hold your stomach together with even more magic snow, and one of those wraiths had a hold of you when we got our hands on you. What did you *think* was gonna happen?"

He looked down at the bandages and poked at the older ones around his wrist. "A wraith...? I thought I was purged..."

Hirshma wasn't done with him. "There's also the toxins that demon and those dogs covered you with on the outside. And *none* of that touches on the fact that Makolichi ripped your gut half-open. The *only* reason you've stayed alive is because all that magic kept your body humming along."

"Oh."

"Oh. You go through all that and *oh* is all you can say? Blessed be, you *should* have been dead ten times over!"

Akaran quietly sagged his head and tried to remember anything of the last half-day and gave up trying to piece together bits of things in the fog of his mind. "The eleventh'll be the charm..." Carefully, he stood up a second time and gave himself a quiet pat on the back for making it. "If it's that bad... how am I able to..."

"Stand up? Talk? *Breathe?* Boy, it took the three of us *four hours* to purge you of the bad and patch up the good. Even I don't understand it. Growth can heal and repair and fix, and I think the only way that we were able to stitch you back together is that the magic that that damn wisp shoved into you jump-started the healing process somehow."

All of that made the pain in his chest and stomach feel somehow well-deserved. "Why do I think that Brother Steelhom is going to have different words for it?"

She snorted in half-derision-half-laughter. "Oh he had plenty. So, no. Don't ask me how you're still alive. Don't ask me how you're *awake*. If I needed rock-solid proof that there's a divine being out there that watches over children and fools, that we're even having this conversation right now is all the evidence I'd need."

"Well... Goddess, it does hurt a lot, have... to say that." Groaning, he tried to straighten up and regretted it immediately. He did it anyways and held the position for a few long heartbeats before he had to bend back forward again. "Alright. Enough. Where's Steelhom? The statue, you said?"

Crossing her arms and standing up, she confirmed it. "I did. I'll go get him."

"No. I'll go."

The alchemist stopped him with a hand on the bandage around his chest. "No, boy, you won't. His orders and mine both. You leave this bed and there's no promise you won't be spurting blood from every hole in your body before you get a yard and a half away."

"I can -"

This time she was far more insistent about it. "You *can* and *will* stay right there, you bloody fool child."

There wasn't any way he was going to win the argument. With a sigh, he relented. "Fine." Then, with a second one, he put his hand on her shoulder as she started to walk away. "Hirshma?"

"What now?"

"Thank you."

Hirshma gave her own sigh and gave him the shortest hug in the history of every hug ever given. "Thank you, too. Most of us are still alive right now because of you. Hate... hate to say it but you were right. We needed your people long before now. Weren't for you, we'd all be dead. Either by now or... later."

Stunned by the (however brief) act of kindness, he just stood there and mumbled a reply. "I'm sorry I couldn't do more."

"You did more than most would've. I'll be back soon."

Down in the tunnels, things hadn't improved much. Steelhom was on his knees, head bowed in supplicant prayer. The ice along the walls and in the roof of the cave glistened and shone with star-like lights. Sneaking in behind Hirshma, Akaran heard the other priest talking before he saw him.

"He's awake? Already? I'll be up to talk to him in a moment."

Clearing his throat, he scooted into the small room and leaned back against the wall. "How about now?"

Hirshma's growl of disapproval echoed through the chamber. "Dammit, I told you to stay in bed."

"You've told me a lot of things I haven't wanted to do."

Steelhom lifted himself up off of his knees and gave a deep growl of his own. "No more bickering. I've had enough of it. From *everyone*."

His student smiled a little at him, then sagged against the rock-face. "That makes two of us. Goddess be my witness I am so glad to see you."

Walking over to him and giving him a hug that was far longer and closer than the one the alchemist had, Steelhom held the younger man as close as he could. "And I you, my friend. Even if you should be laying in bed. There's nothing to do now that won't take time. You've taken the biggest of the threats off of the table."

"They're not... No. I haven't. But... first? Why are you here? Not that I'm ungrateful..."

"The last test. I was supposed to make sure you dispelled the haunting. Safely."

Akaran looked up and pulled away slightly. "Last test? What do you mean...? You've been here all along?"

Nodding slightly, the paladin had to admit to it. "Near. I didn't know about the concealment spell. I should have intervened earlier. I am sorry. So sorry. This wasn't supposed to be..."

"...a pile of dragon scat?"

"Yes. Succinctly put."

Grunting, the exorcist cradled his head in his hands. "It gets worse."

The look on Steelhom's face slowly went from delighted and relieved to irritated and coldly frustrated. "Oh, does it? How does your leg feel?" As he spoke, he walked back to the statue and picked up his staff.

Akaran followed along behind him, limping, but following. "Like a dog clawed it open."

"So, it still hurts?" he asked

"Yes."

"Good." The paladin-commander gave him a formal nod, then without giving him or Hirshma a chance to realize what he planned on doing, he flicked his staff out and caught the exorcist on the inside of his thigh with the bottom tip.

The impact drove Akaran down to one knee with a thundering wave of pain bursting out of it. "GODDESS!"

"Good that you invoke Her. I imagine She is as displeased with you as I am."

"What in the... pits... was that for!?"

"Many reasons. Oh, and those are just mine. I am *sure* that the Goddess has words for you as well. I sensed that there was an undercurrent of irritation when we attempted to heal you. I believe that the magic felt like She... is a tad agitated with you. Care to confess your sins?"

Swearing under his breath, he held onto his thigh for what felt like dear life. "Pissed at me, maybe. Yeah. She's pissed alright."

Steelhom began to pace in a circle around him. "Do elaborate. Why, do you believe, is She pissed at you?"

"A few impolite prayers... may have – *ow* - left blood in Tundrala... and there was this weird little girl when I was sleeping..."

The look on the paladin's face was absolutely delightful... if one enjoyed seeing terror, disbelief, and stunned shock. "You... traveled... to Tundrala?"

Standing slowly, Akaran kept his voice to a low mutter. "Not by choice. The wisp took me." Steelhom didn't approve, and gave his thigh another whack with his staff. The impact knocked him back down to his knee. "DO YOU MIND?"

"Did you forget you are nothing more than a man? A mortal, a human? We are forbidden, not just by the Goddess, but by the rules of mortality, to never trek outside of this plane! That is power that is not for us!"

"Getting reminded of it right now..."

His mentor wasn't done. "*Humans* cannot *wallow* in wild magic! You are not made for it, you – *of anyone* – are not *attuned* for it, and in all of my years to come I am *sure* that I will *never* understand your reasoning to *drink* it!"

Half-smirking, Hirshma spoke up. "Maybe I like you after all."

Steelhom cast her a sideways glare. "Do not test me, woman."

"Goddess, brother, that fisking *hurt*."

"*Goddess?* Maybe I should ask you which one." Fuming, the paladin couldn't even see straight. "*Tundrala?* Care to explain that, neophyte?"

Akaran shook his head. "Not... really. Wasn't like I had much of a choice."

Pointing at the girl floating in the pool behind them, Steelhom replied with a grow. "Such as the choice you had to banish her?"

He looked over at her and tried to discern how badly she was hurt, or if she was even still alive. "Is she... dead?"

"No."

"Then can I stand up or do you plan on hitting me again?"

Still glaring, his mentor relented a little. "Yes."

"Which?"

The older priest shrugged. "You will have to find out. Do go on."

"Wonderful. Don't end her. She saved my life."

Hirshma cleared her throat and interrupted. "Prolonged. Not saved."

Casting a quick glance at her, Akaran gave a little shrug. "Same thing."

Steelhom did *not* agree. "Far from it. It turned you into a powder-keg. The only thing that kept you from burning to ash was that wraith. It fed off of whatever she filled you with."

"A wraith?" His eye went wide as he looked down at his leg. "I was infected? Again?"

"Again? **AGAIN**? Again implies more than once!"

The exorcist glared at him as he stood up. "I've had a really shitty week."

"Oh you've had a shitty week? Is that what you want to call it? Suppose you want a treat for not getting killed? Well, for not staying dead?"

Both Akaran and Steelhom scolded her at the same time. "**ENOUGH**."

She quieted, and the exorcist started to hobble over to the fountain. "Eos. If we're done playing lecture the neophyte, what of her?"

"We are far, far from done with your lecture. Tundrala. You... *we* are not, *humans* are not to leave this world! We defend against that! We do not belong any place but *here!* Not in any of the other worlds. We belong in this one!"

"We belong where we are sent. We all end up in the next world eventually. Besides. The Granalchi send people through the ether all the time."

The paladin rapped his staff on the cold cavern floor. "Being sent along the outskirts of the Veil is not the same thing as barging through it and stopping on the other side for a snack! There are repercussions to face, if you're not suffering some of them already!"

"When it's time to pay I will."

Steelhom wasn't convinced. "It may not be you that has to pay."

"I've said it before, boy. Magic has a price," Hirshma interrupted. "It always has a price."

"For once, the shrew and I agree."

"A *shrew?* Did you just -"

"I did. Akaran, do you disagree?"

This, at least, he had some confidence in answering. "No."

"Then it's settled. You. Are. A. Shrew."

It was all the alchemist could do to keep from sputtering her reply. "I will have you know, I -"

Ignoring her, Akaran looked at the girl in the pool and back to his mentor. "Steelhom... is she okay? Eos'eno... is she okay?"

Sighing under his breath, the paladin shook his head. "She is... recovering."

"What happened?"

"It would appear she nearly destroyed herself keeping you alive. The fight against Makolichi left her nearly as injured as it did you."

"Damn," he sighed, going over to her to look at her up close. "Will she be okay?"

Steelhom didn't have much of an answer. "Truthfully? I do not know. Her very existence is more a matter for the Granalchi than it is us. We don't study the extra-planar; we banish it. I set her to rest in the font after she collapsed just after we worked on you."

"So much for not wallowing in it."

His mentor tried to ignore the sarcasm. "She is not bound by the same mortal constraints as you, my student. I am unsure if she is made for it either, but she is leagues more attuned to it."

"Damn. We need her," he said, rubbing his leg again and muttering a short bit of profanity under his breath. "We need her soon. Trouble is coming."

"Trouble? I have no idea what you mean. An untold number of wraiths in the woods? The arrival of scavenger demons? Or that... Makolichi... thing?"

Akaran looked back to him. "Worse is coming." Then, with a slow blink, he realized what else he had said and paused. "There's scavengers?"

"*Shiriak*," he answered with a dismissive flip of his hand. "What do you mean worse?"

He pursed his lips and crossed his arms. "Well damn."

Steelhom pressed on. "Worse?"

The exorcist sighed and spilled the beans. "When Eos brought me here, there was a thing here. Don't know what it was. Abyssian. Said it was putting us on notice. Ten days."

"Ten days? Ten days until what?"

"We're getting company. 'The Man of the Red Death' is going to show up."

The paladin's jaw clenched in vague annoyance. "Pretentious."

Hirshma looked at the two of them like they had both grown an extra head. "Some new demon in the fold and all you can say is 'pretentious'?"

Steelhom answered while he strummed his fingers on his staff. "Abyssians that swing around titles like young men swinging swollen cocks tend not to have powers to back those titles up."

"So much like overly-pompous priests?"

Ignoring her, he focused on his student. "Akaran. What did it say, exactly?"

"That it had been waiting for the Divine to know about this crack into Tundrala. That we had a mess here and we needed to clean it up soon, or this Red Death will."

"*This* crack?"

The exorcist winced. "It implied there was more than one. Four. Two of them... not to Tundrala. It wasn't happy about it."

"This much, it and I are in agreement of. Did it say anything else?"

Akaran actually had an answer to that one. "Called itself Rishinobia, implied it was the acolyte of this 'Man.'"

Steelhom thought about it long and hard for a few moments. "I... hm. I don't know the name. I will look into my journal at once. Did it say anything more?"

"It said four other names that... I don't know them. *Corpsuals, arin-goliath, abogin*, and *gitia*. I know what the *arin* is Daringol."

"Oh blessed all. Are you *sure* it said *'abogin'*? You've been in pain. Think as clearly as you can."

Nodding a little as he answered, Akaran looked at him confused. "I'm sure it did. What is it?"

The reply was educational, if not positive. "*'What are they,'* you mean. These are the Abyssian names of the things you've been fighting. *Corpusals* are the zombies... *giata*, the hounds. An *abogin*? You'd know it better as a revenant. You truly did sleep through the lectures on names of power and classification, didn't you?"

His head slowly fell back as he closed his eye and groaned. "Oh... piss."

"I have to agree. Piss, indeed."

Totally lost, the alchemist interrupted them again. "If you two are done speaking in tongues, do you care to share what these made up words are?"

The exorcist shrugged. "Doesn't matter. I *told* you worse would come, Hirshma. This is the worse."

Glaring at him, she crossed her arms. "You still didn't say what a revenant is."

"Oh, would you... Dazzle her with your knowledge, Akaran."

His student obliged. "A creature that can and will regenerate again and again until you can find – and destroy – the foci it's bound to. They won't stay dead, in other words."

Steelhom added a little more. "You can banish one every minute of every hour, but they will return just as quickly."

"He's probably pissed at me, too."

Hirshma did her best to try to process all of it. "Well then. Some egotistical unknown that just goes by a title and an unstoppable monster are now fisking around in my yard? You boys know how to warm an 'old shrew's' heart."

"That's... dammit... not discounting the wraith... the cause of all this. Were you two able to figure out anything...?"

Looking up at the statue, the paladin rubbed his eyes. "We did. It isn't good."

"Share?"

Steelhom took a deep breath and slowly started to go over everything they've learned while Akaran sat on the edge of the pool next to the wisp. He didn't say a word until his teacher finished and Hirshma added her own tidbit at the end. "All of it... Usaic. His arrogance..."

"Don't... forget. One more thing," the youngest of them slowly interrupted.

"One more? Is this not enough?"

Akaran shrugged a little "The army. Local garrison regiment will be here soon. How many days have I been out?"

"Just the one. We've split our rations while we watched over you."

That made him sit up straight. "You've not been back to Toniki? With all the shit wandering around in the woods? We need to hurry back, we -"

Steelhom raised his hand to quiet him. "My wards have held. I can feel them intact."

"Doesn't matter, these things don't seem to give a damn about the wards."

"Maybe not yours. They do not care to tangle with mine. If you live long enough, you may just learn how to reinforce their abilities."

Akaran's dirty look spoke volumes. "Yeah. If. So... what's next?"

Still floating, Eos slowly opened her eyes and looked up at him. "Next, Guardian of Winters, next we must enter master's tower. There is no other way."

The alchemist looked surprised that the girl was able to say a word. "You're awake."

Slowly – just as slowly as Akaran had – the wisp moved to the edge of the pool and sat up on the ledge around it. "Yes, mother of flesh. I am awake. Guardian... oh, Guardian. I've given my thoughts to them, but now I give them to you. You have served the ice well, and I failed to serve you. My heart, my apologies, are to you, and my thanks, my many thanks."

"I'm... I'm just glad you're okay. You kept me alive... you've no apologies to make."

Steelhom didn't bother to hide his irritation. "That's very much up to debate."

"I've kept the mountain safe as long as I could. Your magic, all the magic, all the spells. Makolichi cannot afford to let this continue... he will be back."

Hirshma couldn't either. "Safe? You kept it *safe*?"

"Maybe not true, not entirely, no," their inhuman host reluctantly sighed. "This place has been safe until you and the watcher came to be.

I couldn't keep the eyes of the unholy away from it after you did."

Akaran bit his lip while the crone barked a laugh. "Oh? You think that you've done such a great job keeping things away? What about our restless? That doesn't seem like you 'kept their eyes' off of us."

"But I did! His dogs never came near the homes, your homes. The wraiths in the wind, yes, they did, but they only cared to find homes of their own. Your homes aren't their homes. They had no need no use for anything here. No power was great enough to catch their eyes." Then she let her gaze linger on the exorcist. "Until he and the watcher arrived."

"What watcher?" Either of them could have asked the question. Akaran took the honor.

"There are eyes in the storm, things in the wind. This place has been under the watch of many for years long come. Now there's one more. What is one more for me to care about in the snow? It is such a beautiful thing, eyes always come to see it."

Disinterested in waiting for her to clarify, Steelhom pushed to the next topic. "We're ignoring something of importance."

"What?"

"What exactly is in that damn tower?"

Eos'eno looked around the cave and hung her head, almost guiltily. "Things..."

That didn't work for the paladin. "I am certain I threatened to banish you. That still stands as an option," he snapped. "What else is in there?"

"Daringol." The elemental-kin took a deep breath and looked like she was warring with herself over what she could say, should say, or wanted to say. After enduring a withering glare that lasted for far longer than it should have, the spirit cracked. "I know very little of the beast. Lord Usaic said it was a creature lost many years past. It approached our home time and time again. He always drove it back. It had no strength of its own, none that I could feel."

Akaran nodded a little. "We know what it is. Is it after the coldstone, or is Makolichi?"

"Both, them both. The aura is unmistakable. So chaotic. Speaks like so many winds at once. I do not think it is of one mind."

Steelhom stared at her. "And it took over the tower?"

She crossed her arms and turned to the window, refusing to meet his stare. "Yes. It came into the tower. It took our home after master became still. It brought bodies. They broke in... it pushed inside... it fed, it grew as it got close to his work. The... bodies, they serve it."

"More zombies," Hirshma muttered. "This thing has a lust for a body, doesn't it."

"They don't serve it. They are it," the paladin grunted.

Akaran scratched at his goatee. "Well, it's... I mean, there's not a lot of people in this region. That isn't too bad... not that many for it to feed on... or whatever it's doing with them."

That was when the alchemist pointed out how stupid of a thought that was. "My grandmother settled on this mountain. Travelers come by every season for potions and herbs. They have for a long time. She told me that caravans went up and through and around these parts for a great deal longer than you or I could imagine."

Eos chimed in. "The ice says it has claimed many. Some old. Some new. Surely enough to bury the village, should they get loose."

That sick feeling in his stomach started to come back. "Um... how many did it reanimate?"

"As many sheens of light upon a lake of ice by quarters, I have seen the minions of this creature."

He cleared his throat. "Numbers, girl. Real numbers."

"Oh..." she lingered at the thought, fingers twisting in the air before her. "I have seen far more than twenty. Many more."

"That's... a problem," he muttered.

The alchemist cleared her throat. "She means she's seen closer to fifty. Haven't you?"

"Yes..."

"Oh." He stood there with a stupid look on his face. "That's not a small problem. That's a lot. A big problem. I don't like it being a lot. Wait, how did you know?"

She shrugged. "The sun rises in the sky, approaches the mid-day point. It travels a half circle over the world before darkness claims it. One hundred eighty degrees, by the Rules of Normality. A quarter of those is but forty-five." Dumbfounded – and at a total loss for what she meant – Akaran looked at her with his mouth hanging open. "The tangible world has rules. I learned them. You *temple* people would do yourselves a wonder if you did as well."

Steelhom looked bored. "Finally, she shows knowledge that's useful."

"I thought we asked for the commentary to stop?"

Ignoring their banter, the girl with the winter hair continued on. "I did all I could to bury them in the ice. My best efforts only have sealed them inside. I dare not try to destroy them again. Every time I approached, I have suffered."

"That makes two of us," Akaran muttered.

Eos sighed, a little tuft of snow passing from her lips as she did. "You will like this less," she went on, pointing down the passageway on the opposite end of the cavern. "That is the way to the tower when it is submerged. I feared that the unholy would march through it, so I sealed it with ice."

"Just ice? That seems to be a thing that shouldn't be difficult for you to overcome. You were the one to cast it," Steelhom interrupted.

Shaking her head, she went on to the less-than-ideal news. "The water I sealed with? I did not know, was in too much of a haste to realize so, that it was infused with Tundrala. I fear I have made it impenetrable, even by me. The tower will have to rise for us to find a way inside to confront the *arin*, regardless as to if you or I or him or her wish it otherwise."

"Speaking of suffering," Hirshma said, looking at the neophyte. "You thought it was bad now."

"More of my luck. *Dammit.*"

"You have to do *something*, we all must, " she said, scolding.

The wisp agreed. "Yes. You must. They see you now. Another source of power. Light always attracts dark. They will come for you as long as you stay here. Longer, mayhaps, if more of them break free of the tower."

That sick feeling in his stomach was starting to make his throat burn. "Oh *good.* Why do I suddenly feel like we're being hunted?"

"You are," she answered.

"Because you're not as much of a fool as you act?" Hirshma added.

Eos turned to look at him and offered an apologetic half smile. "For what it can do, I will lend my ice to you, should it help. I've no desire to see you die."

"Neither do I," the alchemist offered with a shrug to go with it.

He didn't believe it. "You don't care if I get killed or not."

"Well..." Akaran just looked at her, his face totally blank, before she shrugged. "Okay that's true. But win or lose, you can't stay here. Not if they are going to continue to come to you, after you. You personally, I mean. You have to do something or leave."

For some reason, that even rankled the denizen of Tundrala. "That is no way to be kind to a man offering to help."

Akaran pointed to Eos'eno. "The creature inhabiting a corpse is being nicer than you are."

"She has cause to be. I don't. Don't dare speak of my daughter's body as just 'a corpse,' boy."

He started to ball his hand into a fist and was about to say things he wasn't going to feel at all bad about when it hit him. "How many spirits could it be? Fifty bodies, but nesting wraiths multiply... Eos may have sealed the corpusals in the tower, but the wraiths are still getting out of the lake. Or the ones that had made it out before have figured out a way to spread without the central body being needed. *That's a* thought worth revisiting, if it turns out to be true."

That burning in his throat took another turn for the worse. "How many people do you think the mountain has claimed?" Steelhom asked with a frown.

The alchemist suddenly looked very uncomfortable. "I don't like you."

"*I* don't like me."

The paladin-commander pursed his lips. "Quantity may not matter. As it feasts, it will be growing. In due course, it could be enough to take over the mountain on its own, with no aid from others."

"Master could be held by one of those things! One creature or many. How does one dispose of such an abomination?"

"A simple exorcism," Steelhom answered. "Well. Not exactly 'a' simple exorcism. It will take... numerous ones. If not by one of us, then by both. At its core, it *is* just a wraith – and wraiths are easy enough to deal with, regardless of size."

"The numbers are going to be a chore though. And the revenant. That won't be so simple," Akaran sighed. "Steelhom... he has to be first. We need to draw him out, and bind him until we can find his foci. Once we have him under control, we can work on exposing the tower and getting this done."

Eos'eno slipped over to him and looked down at him, half-puzzled. "Draw him? He is not here, he has not returned since the battle. You drove him off."

"Drove him where?" the alchemist asked.

"I... I do not know. I oft have seen Makolichi looking down to the valley many of your miles from here. I have seen him stare at that city of mud and things pushed into mud many a time, many a time after we have brawled."

Hirshma answered with a half-smirk. "City of mud, you say? Well then. That's as an apt description of Gonta if I've ever heard one."

"Gonta? Why would it be interested in someplace so far away from here?" Steelhom asked while he crossed his arms. "This is his source of power."

The younger priest had an answer for that that nobody liked. "His source of power, sure. What if his foci is hidden down there?"

Frowning, Steelhom reluctantly agreed. "Well. How wonderful. We cannot leave the area unsecured long enough to go hunting on a *maybe*. If you haven't forgotten, *you* can't fight and *I* can't abandon this portal."

"There's a third option."

"What?"

"Send me after Makolichi anyways."

Hirshma looked down at him with her mouth agape. "After all the effort we just put in to keep you alive, you're rushing off to get killed? You've a death wish."

Akaran shook his head. "Hear me out. I'm weak, but he's just as. If he's making a play for his foci, we may never get a chance to get it again. Steelhom, there's something watching us. Please brother, do not be offended, but if this has gotten the attention of the *wrong* thing..."

Steelhom clenched his jaw and looked at the statue. "You assume that this demon isn't simply trying to manipulate us. Amuse itself with our follies?"

"It's a demon. I'm sure it is. But if you're asking me to pick between the two? An emissary of some unknown entity that just threatened us to clean up this mess or it will do it for us? Evil things gravitate towards power; they don't warn that they plan to re-establish order."

"No. They do not. That *is* an odd thing for one of the damned to claim to do."

"What was it you always said about the 'odd things' that demons tended to do?"

His mentor glowered at him. "You paid attention to *that* lecture, at least. Yes, I see your point. When confronted by odd behavior, assume there is a reason, and treat it seriously."

"Yeap. So, do I wait around for the unknown, or go or hunting down a revenant that we *know* has a body-count attached to it?"

"You have a point, much as I hate to admit it. You understand that this may well kill you."

Shrugging, there wasn't a way to argue that. He went with an honest assessment instead. "There are no old exorcists. I believe you yourself said as much."

Annoyed having his words thrown back at him, the paladin gave him a murderous glare. "That doesn't mean you have to rush headlong into it."

"Yes it does. That's what I am. That's what we do. We don't sit around on the sidelines. We hunt demons, damn them back to the pit, and we don't always win. I've already lost my chance once so far. I *know* it's gonna be hard but I don't see another choice."

"We have no way of knowing where he went. Without a way to scry through this... fog... tracking him is going to be neigh-impossible. If the Sisters couldn't, what makes you think that we could?"

Akaran chewed on it for a minute. "How far does the masking go?"

"It was far enough to obscure this portal and Toniki."

"But you *could* feel the magic I was using when you were closer to the city walls, yes?"

"I could."

Hirshma slowly walked over to the wisp of a girl in the water, and sat down at the edge of the pool while they prattled on. "I couldn't feel anything at Teboria. If Usaic has a tower *in* the lake, that's a lot of magic that was in my face."

"Master does, he does. I've lived there many a year under the lake and hidden from -"

Akaran interrupted him as a new thought popped into his head. "Let's say the epicenter is the lake. Or even right here. It loses strength over distance. It's been getting steadily stronger since Usaic worked his magic but let's assume that it hasn't spread down the mountain. If it *had*, someone down there would have probably noticed by now and would have been raising a fit."

Biting his bottom lip, Steelhom gave that plenty of thought. "You're putting a lot of assumptions in play, my student. How do you know that Makolichi cannot hide himself on his own? You already told me that he has some magic of his own."

It barely even took a second for the idea to spring to life in the back of his mind. "I did, didn't I? We can find him because we have something that belongs to him."

"We do?"

With a little huff, Hirshma continued to stare down at Eos as she floated in the pool. "And he accuses me of having secrets, the nerve."

"Would you just... follow us outside? Bring the girl," Akaran sighed.

A little bit (and some protesting) later, the four of them were back outside of the cabin, standing next to a lump of snow on the ground.

"This is it? You found snow. Look around, boy, there's plenty of it," the alchemist groused. "A man can't own the snow."

Eos'eno tilted her head and quizzically blinked a few times. "Yes a man can. A man can own and control and do much with snow. Master used to -"

"I don't want to know," Akaran interrupted, then looked her naked form over again despite his better judgment. "We are going to find you some clothes before we do much else. Looking at you is making me cold enough to hurt. Worse. Hurt worse."

"Colder? Uncomfortably so? My lord showed me how a female of your species is able to -"

"*Enough*," Steelhom finally growled. "What is it you want us to see, Akaran?"

Cautiously kneeling down, the younger priest ran his fingers through the mound and hissed in pain as he touched the debris under the snow. Carefully, slowly, he picked up a skull fragment and some bindings that had been covered up. "Makolichi knows how to craft minor spells. This was a trap he had built here. It's an aversion enchantment. I destroyed it when I came here the first time."

Hirshma blanched and even the wisp looked slightly taken aback when a latent tremor of black magic rolled off the bone. The paladin-commander wasn't far behind. "You failed to sanctify it?"

"I was busy..."

"Reckless," his instructor clarified, then grimaced when he took it out of Akaran's hands. "But to our fortune. Don't do it again, mind you. But for now, we are fortunate."

Faint as it may have been, the praise was appreciated. "If we get back to Toniki with this, we can try and attempt to scry for Makolichi there. I don't have the range but I know you do."

"Assume it works," Steelhom started to argue. "If we can't find his general proximity, we won't know if he's here or there."

"If we can't find his general position, it means he's still here on the mountain and in the fog. If he's outside of it, we should be able to get a rough idea of where he is on a map... even if we don't know exactly, or aren't sure on his heading. It might mean that the masking spell has simply gone too far to be felt but I don't think that it has."

Continuing to chew on his lip a little, slowly turning the skull fragment over in his hands again and again. "Still. That is a lot of assumptions."

The exorcist gave another shrug. "It's not a blind attempt at feeling in the ether though. Since we have a physical piece of his taint in hand, it'll allow the scrying to be much more focused. It won't just be casting a net into the water and hoping we'll get a catch."

"Yes, I know how to scry, thank you," his instructor muttered. "It's moot. I can't leave here."

"It's not moot; we're out of food," Hirshma argued.

Steelhom stared at her in disbelief. "You're a warden of Kora'thi. Grow something."

"Out of what? Slush?"

"I saw the vines that you were able to summon forth. You cannot deign to tell me that you are so feeble that you are unable to give call to lettuce or potatoes. Or berries of some kind. Feel free to entice a rabbit to the camp while you're at it."

"Ask the boy. The vines were withered pieces of tinder before I stepped in the water from that blasted fountain. I can't call on magic that I don't have. I could try to sprout more of them but I doubt the roots would taste much better than booth leather."

"Magic you once had. Go beg for forgiveness and see if you can get it back," he snapped.

"What makes you think I haven't?"

He blinked while Akaran rolled his eye again. "Because I am not of the belief that you are capable of begging anyone for anything without being held down on the ground by swordpoint. Seeing as I am happy to do just that I am offering to give you the choice of doing it willingly instead of being encouraged directly."

Standing up, the exorcist shook the snow and mud off of his fingers. "Does it sound as tiresome hearing her and I argue as it does hearing you two argue?"

Eos nodded a little too eagerly. "Tiring, yes, that is a word, a good word for it."

"How would you know?"

Giving him a faint little flicker of a smile, she placed her hand on the back of her neck roughly where she had marked him. "With the mark of home on your skin, I can hear you. Cannot always see you, but I can hear you. Tiring is, mayhaps, truly the best way to say it."

"You can... Steelhom! This *has* to come off. *Now.*"

"Don't want the thing hearing every word you have to say, do you? I bet you're going to spend less time gawking at my student, aren't you."

He shot her the foulest of foul looks. "Brother. Cut it off of my neck. And no. I'm not. She's nice to look at."

"I don't know. I rather like the idea that if you scream for help someone can hear it."

"Do not tell me you're taking her side," Hirshma quipped.

"He's taking her side."

"A side? I thought that you did not wish for me to show you how master -"

Akaran grabbed his head with both hands and sighed. "For the Love of the Goddess..."

Steelhom had to agree with the general feeling. "I can sustain myself for a time without food. That's only myself, however."

"Right. Let's get back to Toniki. Get supplies, and get what we need to try to see where Makolichi went. I'm sure we're going to need other things to get into that tower. Eos, I so sincerely hope you know what spell he used to mask it," the younger priest said as he looked into the woods towards the lake where all of their troubles hid. "Leave the font exposed for now. Load up and come back when we're ready to deal with it."

His mentor grunted in irritation. "I do not see there's a choice. Eos?"

Shifting nervously, the wisp nodded slowly. "I do, that I do, Guardian. But as with most things thus far, I do not – no, this I know – you will not like how it is he constructed it. Replicating the spell to bring it up from the water is not something that will be easy for those untrained in the ways of Ice to do."

"Oh, don't worry about that. We don't need to replicate it."

"You don't? Then how is it you seek to enter the tower?"

Akaran gave her an honest smile from ear to ear (and when Steelhom matched him, both women looked at each other nervously). "I'm an exorcist of the Order of Love. I don't care about duplicating complex spells. I'm simply supposed to break them."

IV. MARCH OF DAWN

The return to Toniki was met with minimal fanfare, although when Mariah saw that Akaran was still alive, she almost gave an uncharacteristic squeal of joy (which she would deny at length later). However, by the time they got there, the exorcist was almost frostbitten. His clothes had been completely ruined between Makolichi's attack and the surgery that he had suffered through.

What clothes that had been stored away in Usaic's cabin weren't made for someone that couldn't stand a chill. It had not made for a pleasant trip back for him. Nor had it been for the others, because they took turns giving him their cloaks as they trudged back to the village. All the while, Steelhom had kept a constant series of spells going to dissuade anything wandering the woods from getting a little too close.

Thankfully, it had worked.

All of that aside, once the party got back within the walls, Akaran was summarily marched to his room and put before the largest fire that Mariah could safely light. He was then swaddled in as many blankets that she could scrounge up, and almost immediately – despite his objections – half-drowned in the best rotgut that Yothargi had hidden away in the basement.

And Mariah simply did not give a damn what he, nor Steelhom, nor the wisp, and most assuredly not her former miss, thought about any of it. Yes, they objected. She objected at their objections, and the moment she had Akaran situated in his room, she made it very clear that her voice was louder than all of theirs combined – eliciting a remark from

Steelhom that her mentor had taught her a little too well.

Getting Hirshma's immediate needs resolved wasn't an issue at all, and Steelhom already had his own room in the inn. Mostly, they were left to fend for themselves (*after* the paladin had rechecked his wards and other spells to ensure that nothing had been disturbed). He did notice that the ones cast around the shrine felt weaker, but they still had energy left to them. He made a mental note to study them in the morning, but caved to his own exhaustion before he did much more.

Finding lodging for Eos'eno, on the other hand...

Where in the fisking pits do I stick a creature that would be just as happy floating around outside? Can't leave the damn woman out in the open like that, everyone would throw a fit, Mariah had muttered inwardly, although anyone near her could feel the thoughts radiating out of her every pore.

Getting her dressed was the first issue, one she protested every step of the way. Eventually they settled for one of Rmaci's former dresses, just to put what the bitch had owned to good use for a change. The wisp adamantly refused to put on anything heavier than the dark red cotton gown, and protested about the white lace around the bodice.

"But it is a mockery! A mockery of snow! Looks to be the most intricate of crystals as they float from the sky but it is course against the skin! Is this what humans seek to do when they seek to approach the glory of Mother?" she had complained, whining with a high-pitched keen.

Mariah's rebuke, on the other hand... "I liked it better when you were flinging Akaran across the inn. You want to be here? You dress like you should live here. Everyone is a bit on edge right now, I thank you kindly, so you can wear it or you can go curl up in a snowdrift on the other side of the wall where nobody can see you."

"Hide in snow? But snow isn't for hiding! It's for love, for wonder, for beauty! It's far more true than this fake, fake, cloth... mess!" Eos'eno looked up from the dress and tilted her head like a confused owl. "Are you well? Your face? It's so... red?"

She lost the argument soon after.

It took a while, but eventually, everyone was situated and sorted. Three of them were sent to their rooms with bellies full of stew and two full of bladders full of ale. All of them nursed wounds and headaches, even if their hearts were full of gratitude for being someplace safe and warm (except for Eos, who pouted in the Goat's basement).

Once everyone was done, that left just her.

While they rested, she went off on her own and went to work behind their backs. After Makolichi, the hounds, and Daringol? She'd barely slept for four hours in two days. She gathered her cloak and the military pick that had served her well so far, and made her bed – but not in her room. While the moon shone down on the village, she watched a steady stream of water trickle out of the ruined fountain from just inside the entrance to the shrine.

She watched and waited, fingers gripping the handle of her weapon so tight her knuckles were white. *Nobody else dies. Not on my watch. Nobody.*

It was a sentiment that was going to be echoed, at length and later, by someone else.

※ ※ ※

The crack of dawn brought along an entirely different headache. It's long been said by just about every peasant, serf, merchant (of any stripe), minor or major noble, and yes, even priests that one should always worry when an agent of the crown arrives and says 'I am from the government, and I am here to help.' It was a given.

Today was no different.

His voice woke Akaran up out of a sound sleep – the rude jerk was so loud that it simply boomed through the village. "My name is Commander Xandros Wodoria, 13th Garrison, Grand Army of the Dawn. Who speaks for the settlement?"

It took a few minutes, and when the exorcist staggered out of the Rutting Goat, he looked much the worse for wear. Ignoring the dark circles under his eye (and the darker ones under his eyepatch), he skipped a shirt and settled just for a cloak. Like it or not, he was getting used to the cold (and he didn't like it). "Me, I think."

The two of them sized each other up. Xandros didn't seem overly impressed by the bedraggled priest with bloodstained bandages wrapped around his chest and under the edge of his pantaloons. Akaran looked at the hazel-eyed and square-faced soldier with an inward groan. No question about it; this guy was a professional soldier through and through. He just had that look in his eyes, and everything about him screamed 'I serve the Queen' at the top of his lungs.

He also had another twenty men and women with him, all of them in the same garb. Half of them had horses, and the other half had weapons too big to easily carry on a mounted steed. They even had wagons laden with all manner of supplies – rations, tents, and more. All of those wonderful goodies in one place at any given time? It looked like the Feast of Ketterig had come early this year.

As the Commander took his helmet off, he made a slight show of pushing his red wool cloak open to proudly display his chainmail (dyed gold, of course) and the shortsword on his hip. "You *think* you're in charge? Tell me, man who *thinks* he is in charge, do you have a name?"

Oh Goddess, can SOMEONE not act like an asshole when they meet me? PLEASE? "Akaran DeHawk. Exorcist, Order of Love."

"Exorcist?" Xandros asked – just to be sure his ears weren't deceiving him. When the priest nodded to confirm it, the soldier quickly snapped to full attention – quickly thumping his right hand against the center of his chest. "Sir! How may we assist?"

His jaw dropped and he didn't care who saw it. "What?"

"You are an exorcist, are you not?"

"Yes..."

Giving him a smile and dropping the salute, the Commander relaxed a little. "I'm going to assume you haven't had the best experience with assistants out here, have you?"

"Not so you'd notice." He paused a moment and tilted his head. "One of your men said he was from the 5th? There aren't two garrisons stationed in this province, are there?"

"That would have been Tornias Morden, medic? Yes, he *was* from the 5th. He saw being transferred to the 13th as a punishment. Not surprised he'd claim the 5th still – not the first time. I'll *correct* him at length as soon as I see the jackass."

"Won't really be needed. So. You're willing to help? Without argument?"

"Without argument. I've brought soldiers. I've brought supplies. What happened, what needs done, and do you need anything destroyed or cleansed that we can help with?"

Mariah had slipped quietly back through the village and had ended up at Akaran's side before he even knew she was there. "Please tell me this is a good thing?"

With a slightly-unsure nod, the priest answered her and then answered the soldier while his men began to dismount and unpack. "A demon, a spy, and a lot of dead people."

"A spy? For who?"

"Empress Bimaria."

Xandros wiggled the end of his nose. "That's a twist of the balls. Thought it was just demonic dogs up here?"

"She's a bitch, if it counts," Mariah interjected.

"Well, we have ways to..." Words died in his throat as another soul made his way out of the inn and brushed past the neophyte. "You."

"Me," Steelhom answered with a half-growl.

"Exorcist, I thought you said *you* were in charge here?"

Akaran coughed a little. "I said 'I think.' I've been overruled before."

Ignoring him, his mentor crossed his arms and glared at the soldier. "*Commander* Xandros," Steelhom intoned. "Why am I not at all surprised."

"Sir Steelhom. Decided to make your way out of the Capitol for a change?"

With a half-grunt/half-mutter, the paladin kept his gaze fixed on the soldier. "When I was informed *you* were in charge of the garrison, I had to come see what happened for myself. Expected I would have to clean up whatever mess you made. Expected you to be here when you caused it though – you've learned how to delegate, I see."

Mariah scooted a little closer to Akaran and whispered in his ear. "You know anything about this?"

The exorcist shook his head and watched the two men stare each other down.

"Your *assistant* here told me what happened. Do you care to elaborate any?"

"What happened? It appears that you let the border become a tad too porous. Civan agents running amok; dogs the size of small deer charging about eating people. Two-thirds of the village has up and left, and the rest are in far too tire straits to be moved on their own."

Xandros crossed his arms and drew his shoulders up. "I see. Yet somehow, with *two* of your ilk here in this village, *both* of you seem to look as if the entirety of the Queen's Army has walked all over you. I take it that you've yet to do your damn jobs and deal with whatever it is that accounted for some of my men?"

Behind him, the Commander's men looked back and forth at each other and then at the villagers peeking from doorways and out of windows. "I'd be more concerned about the men you've actually lost, and not the wrinkles my student and I may be sporting."

"Yes, I'm well aware I've lost men. Good men. Talented soldiers. I brought more to replace them."

"I see you left your pet battlemage at home. I never thought that Evalia left your side."

The garrison commander bristled up a bit and gave Steelhom a glare that would have given even Hirshma a run for her money. "Evalia is serving the Queen, as she should. Now. My men. When word reached me that we had lost some, the courier dispatched didn't say how many. Where are the survivors?"

Before Steelhom could answer, Akaran deftly reinserted himself into the conversation. "Survivor, Commander."

The demeanor from the soldiers changed in a heartbeat. Hands went to swords, eyes narrowed to slits as each of them sized the village (and everything in it) up a second time. "Survivor? One? Of everyone I sent? What happened to them?"

"Three made it back, but there's just one left. One didn't make it through the night he came back. One died in the fight two days back. The other is still being tended to. He's awake, finally."

"Nine soldiers sent. And of them, one survivor. I suppose you think I should be happy?"

Akaran simply shrugged. "No. But the one that died the other morning saved us both the time it would take to convene a tribunal before I sent him to Maiden Piata for punishment."

"A court-martial? I don't care if you do out-rank me, exorcist. Explain."

Looking back over his shoulder to his superior officer, Akaran took a deep breath and laid it all out once Steelhom gave him a silent nod. He didn't hold anything back about anyone, and emphasized the multitude of reasons he felt that Tornias should have been hung – all-the-while keeping his dismay that the hounds got to him first.

Xandros held steady, and asked a few pertinent questions here and there. When the neophyte priest got to the part where one of the hounds had ripped Tornias to shreds, some of them looked like they were going to be sick. The Commander, however, didn't seem moved at all. When Akaran finished, the career soldier looked over at Steelhom with his brow furrowed – then let out a deep, drained sigh.

"He really is your student, isn't he?"

"What was it you said? 'May you be stuck with someone just like you?'"

"I believe I added 'you irritating tw-'"

Steelhom cut him off with a guffaw and a grin, stepping forward and giving the Commander a brotherly hug. "It's good to see you, truly, my friend."

"And you, and you. I wish circumstances could be better."

Mariah let out a breath she didn't know she had been holding while

Akaran blinked in surprise and glowered at both of them. "You two... know each other?"

With a sly grin, Akaran's mentor gave Xandros a pat on his shoulder. "Oh yes. Xandros and I were assigned to the same company when the Queen launched her last sojourn into Civan territory. The Bourshodin Occupation."

"What a miserable slog that was," Xandros added. "A year and a half in that bog of a jungle. All matter of flies and fleas and everything else."

"The everything else is why I was stuck with you, need I remind you."

"Yes, and how many of those 'everything else' was it you were stuck dealing with? The ones that did more than just suck your blood?"

Steelhom had to hide a laugh. "Just the one. Ipsil's scribe. Joline?"

Xandros didn't even bother to hide *his* laugh. "How she hated you after you left. She spent months cursing your name."

"To be fair, I cursed hers every time I had to relieve myself for just about as long."

The neophyte interrupted their trip down memory lane before more graphic details could be uttered (much to the relief of nearly everyone else present). "Commander... and Commander. Not to interrupt, but..."

"No, you fully intend to interrupt. You'll also wait your turn," Steelhom snapped, then turned his attention back to his friend. "I meant what I said about Evalia. Is she well? Safe?"

"Safer than you'll be if she ever hears you refer to her as 'my pet battlemage' again."

Off to Akaran's side, Hirshma interjected herself. "Can you two chest-thumping thugs *get on with it?* This isn't the time for levity!"

The graying-haired paladin rubbed his eyes while Xandros looked askance at her. "She's right. Unfortunately."

"Of course I am."

"Of course she is," Akaran sighed while he gave his gut a small squeeze. Mariah poked him under his ribs to that, eliciting a small yelp.

Xandros ignored all three of them. "While your student has been busy up here, there's been a disturbance to the south. I had to send Evalia and two of my men on a hunt and kill assignment."

"Disturbance?" It was Akaran's turn to tense up and focus while his instructor asked the question.

Nodding, the commander elaborated. "I hoped that this was

unrelated to the request we received from Gonta, but I'm no longer confident of that. Livestock has started to go missing, and the villagers reported strange shapes moving around at night. At first, we thought wolves, then..."

"If you say that they were larger than wolves but smaller than sheep, I'm going to quit the Order," the exorcist muttered.

That was met with a no. "I don't believe it was your hounds. But now I think it was your wraiths. Maybe other things. The reports were vague, but they concerned me enough that I felt prudent to dispatch our best, well..."

"Your best battlemage."

"My only battlemage. The rest were recalled to reinforce the army's interests in the west." Looking troubled, Xandros turned his attention fully to Akaran. "If the same creatures are haunting Gonta as the ones that are here, I am unsure that I feel confident with my wife deployed there without an escort."

Steelhom and Akaran looked at each other and reached the same conclusion at the same time. "Nesting wraiths spread, if permitted," his mentor said with a foul glower.

"They do like animals," the neophyte continued. "You found *shiriak* out in the wild. Do you think that this has gone on long enough to attract things that far away?"

"Or woke up something that's been slumbering."

"Oh I do *not* like that thought," Akaran grunted. "It wouldn't take much. I can't imagine it's Makolichi... not... no. He's been too busy up here to be known down there, unless it was in the last day... and that... timing is all wrong."

Hirshma couldn't take it any longer and barged her way into the conversation. "Do you menfolk do anything other than *talk*? People are dying, our homes are ruined, and all you three care to do is *talk* about who made who piss pus and what's going on in that rancid trading post to the south. What about *here*, what about *us*?"

"Miss, that rancid trading post is where *our people* have fled to. It *is* about us if Daringol's minions have started to flock there," Mariah interrupted. "You can't just ask for them to be ignored."

"If they were truly still our people then they would have stayed," the alchemist spat, venom in her mouth and disgust rampant in her veins.

Before anyone else could pitch in, a single voice nervously spoke up from the entrance to the Rutting Goat. "Gon...ta? Is that the settlement of men below the line of frost? In the shade of the mountain? The one you spoke of?"

Akaran cursed under his breath and moved to block her from sight of the soldiers – but it was a bit too late (and he was a bit too slow). "Shit, I told you to stay inside, you can't be -"

"Oh now I *know* he's your student," Xandros grunted. "Nothing *human* looks like *that*."

It was hard to argue with him. The wisp hadn't completely disguised herself, which meant that there were polished pieces of crystal still adorned her face and the glow in her eyes was still there for everyone to see. Then there was also the matter that she was still hovering over the ground.

It was a bit of a dead giveaway.

"Oh shit," the neophyte muttered again. "I do out-rank you, Commander, as an exorcist in the Queen's Army. You're in no position to cast judgment on me."

The commander cracked his knuckles and stepped forward, brushing past everybody to stand within inches of the priest's face. Eos'eno wrapped her pale hands around Akaran's arm and looked absolutely frightened by the stance the soldier took. "You outrank me, but I am like a brother to the man that outranks *you*. And while I cannot judge him either, he and I *both* have to answer to the Provincial Maiden, which means that *you* do too."

"Xandros, no," Steelhom cautioned. "I am no happier about her presence than you are, and yes, she is not human. She is an ally though. Strange as the situation may be."

"Allying yourself with the supernatural? I thought your job was to dispose of such things."

"Our task is to condemn the things that should not see the light of day. Not to accost the creatures that are born of it," Akaran argued. "She's a friend, and under protection of the Order."

He was less than impressed. "The Order has made poor decisions before."

"Is this Gonta the settlement in the shade of the mountain? In the valley where the tears of Tundrala now flow?" the wisp asked again, completely ignoring Akaran's efforts to push her back into the inn before any of the soldiers decided that the possibility of the Temple making a 'poor decision' outweighed the question of whom out-ranked whom.

"Xandros, no," the elder priest warned a second time. "She's of the

Heavenly Mount. She was brought here against her will and forced to serve the man responsible for this mess. She has risked her life to save the people here several times over."

Eos tilted her head and blinked in confusion. "I was forced to serve no one. Mother asked me to come to this world and aid him. I was not forced."

"Ignoring the uncomfortable fact that she refers to the Goddess of Ice as her *mother*, she has been of service to the cause. If it wasn't for her, you'd be having this conversation in a village full of corpses," Akaran argued with a tired sigh.

The apprentice alchemist ran her fingers through her hair and fidgeted a bit. "Yes, Eos... may I call you Eos? Yes, Gonta is the town to the south of here, in the valley. The one we spoke of yesterday."

The troubled look that covered her face did absolutely *nothing* for the exorcist's mood. "Then your... pet? A mage is a pet? What strange people you are. Mages are not pets, they are lords and ladies."

"Evalia would agree," Steelhom said with a short smirk.

"Evalia never is allowed to hear anyone refer to her as a *pet* anything, unless you wish to feel the skin blistered off of your face," Xandros stressed.

Hirshma growled at both of them. *"Must we?"*

The pair of them quieted while Akaran egged Eos'eno on. "Your lady may not be tasked to deal with something so simple as missing... pets?"

"What is it you called it? The city of mud. That sounds wonderful," Akaran said with a second, and entirely unrepentant, sigh.

"It is a city, is it not? And made of soggy wet dirt? This is what mud is. Did our adversary hit you in the head harder than you said? The others have called it as much, too."

The exorcist shook his head while Mariah had to hide a grin. "You really think that Makolichi is off watching the village again while he recovers?"

"Watching? Yes, watching. I fear he is not far. If the people are being accosted, then these lost souls of the underfrost may be to blame."

Akaran looked over at Steelhom and Xandros. Neither of them looked like they appreciated the revelation any more than the neophyte. "How powerful is your wife?"

"She has the fourth of the nine Scars of Balance etched into her breast. Soon she will have the fifth."

"Pretend I don't know what that means."

Steelhom interjected with an answer. "It means that she can destroy a small contingent of soldiers on her own if you give her a few minutes to prepare."

"Human or other?"

Hirshma grimaced a little. "It is an affront to the natural order that you even ask that. Are monsters like this really that common?"

"Yes. And you gave up your right to be offended for Nature, so don't interrupt. Commander, can she wipe out a contingent that's human, or can she wipe out one that's a contingent of *others?*"

His mentor looked at the career soldier and slowly answered for him. "She'd have no problems with the wraiths, given adequate warning of their nature. Makolichi... she would be a boon to aid us fighting him."

The phrasing was noted. "But she's not strong enough to take him on herself."

"She does not have our methods to deal with a thing such as him, no. Not with any permanency."

"Then we don't have time to waste. Someone has to go help her. I *have* to go now. Can't debate it."

Hirshma put her foot down (literally and figuratively). "You've nearly died once, and you can barely stand as it is. Whatever your plans are, you will not take part in anything that has you leaving my care."

Akaran ignored her completely, shifting his weight and wincing. "Xandros, I'm going to need you and your men."

Stepping back – slightly – Xandros (barely) stood down. "Convince me you haven't lost your mind."

Mariah had enough by that point, and as she shoved herself bodily between them. "Okay... stop. Everyone just... stop. Sir Steelhom, you said Akaran's still in command here, yeah?"

You could feel the reluctance coming off of him in waves. "Yes, it's his."

"Okay. Then we do this my way. We don't have time for more bickering," the younger priest said as he crossed his arms and gave nearly everyone a glower.

The garrison's commander looked at his old friend and gave a reluctant little nod of his own. "Alright then exorcist, what do you want us to do?"

"That tower is going to take some time to break into. The obscura has to go away and then any traps around it need to be broken. Then we have to figure out how to get it out of the water, unless Eos is willing to tell us."

Still hovering just inside the inn (and looking more and more nervous the longer that the men that Xandros brought with him continued to stare), Eos'eno gave a wavering acknowledgment. "I... I may know a way. But it will not be an easy thing, not without master, if we even can."

"Even if she does know a way inside, the rest will take a few days, at best. I could do more if we had assistance from the Academy or a few more from the Order..." Steelhom cautioned.

"Neither of which we have time to go get. Ok. We've got three problems then. We know that Makolichi is still around, and he's probably headed to or already at Gonta. For all we know, he manifested back there after we fought him here. We need all the firepower we can get to break into that tower, that means we need her and *if* Mako is headed that direction, Xandros's wife is gonna need me. If nothing else, just to bring her up here."

"She's capable of handling anything that comes her way," her husband obstinately argued.

"Mako has nearly killed me twice."

Steelhom quietly cleared his throat. "The one wasn't a case of 'nearly.' You died."

"Please quit bringing that up. I'm trying to forget that. I exist to *hunt* demons, and it's still sent me into the next world and back."

His hazel eyes going a little wider, the soldier tried to digest that one bit of pertinent information. "And back?"

"Are you willing to bet that your wife will come back in one piece if she finds him alone?"

Xandros shifted back and forth a little in his boots while Steelhom gave his student an incredibly disapproving stare. "You keep saying this, but I can't say that I believe it. You truly plan on leaving? I'm unsure if I can agree to that call."

"Brother, I don't see we have a choice."

"I don't want you to do this."

He placed his hand on the bandages covering his ribs, wincing slightly. "I don't either but if -"

His mentor interrupted before he could go on. "It's not an 'if.' I was able to scry for him last night. I attempted to reach the Order by way of ethereal projection to ask for someone to be dispatched to hunt for him. This... fog... has prevented me from getting through. We are, I am so very sad to say, on our own."

Akaran didn't say anything for a few long heartbeats. "You've been playing it off because you didn't want me to go after him again."

"I was."

"Brother. That isn't how we work. You can't protect me from everything."

"It's my fault that you were sent here," Steelhom said, briefly looking down at the ground. "This isn't a job for a neophyte. *You* shouldn't have been sent here to begin with."

"That's not your decision to make," the exorcist quietly argued. "The Sisters sent me. Good or ill, they sent me, which means that this is *my* responsibility to see through. If they sent me, that means She sent me. I have to have faith that it's Her will guiding me."

The paladin shook his head. "I was sent to watch you. I was not sent to watch you die or to see you throw your life away after something that already nearly did. *You* weren't strong enough to face him once. Why do you think you're strong enough now, when you can barely walk?"

Hirshma felt obliged to briefly slip into the dispute. "Twice. He got beaten by him twice."

"Not helping," Akaran muttered, then picked back up where he had left off. "If he's down there, it doesn't matter if I'm strong enough to fight him. I just need to warn the locals and then find Evalia. If you can't reach the Order, then we really are on our own, and we *can't* let him run around. I can send word for reinforcements while I'm there"

"I can go."

"No, you can't. You're needed up here to make sure that the situation up here doesn't get worse. You don't need to be an errand-boy. I spent two years doing that in the Temple." Akaran paused for a minute, biting his lip. "Literally, I did spend two years doing just that."

Steelhom couldn't argue it (any of it) and finally caved. "You are *solely* to warn the local Temple and the Guards. You are *not* to hunt for him."

"I'm to hunt for his foci," the exorcist argued. "We're going to need that, too."

Growling, the paladin took a cue from Hirshma and put his foot down (literally and figuratively). "Only if he doesn't have possession of it himself already. He may seek to hide it."

"If he's able to touch it. They can't always."

"This is true. Fine."

With a deep breath, Akaran took his win where he could get it and looked at everyone assembled. "Now... the rest of you. Hold on before you condemn my plan. I'm not done yet."

"Speak of it, Guardian of Winters," Eos'eno intoned, the agitated tone in her voice shutting down the gathering.

Akaran looked around at everyone and laid it all out. "Even once we get into the tower, we've still got Daringol to deal with. We know it has wraiths all around the woods and now we've got gutter-trash demonkin to deal with. Xandros, this is where your men come in. I need you to make sure that the walls around this village are secured. No idea what's coming out next. Might be something that decides it can try to batter past the wards. Let's put some sticks and stones in the way."

"We can do that."

"Good. You're also on pest control."

That look the priest had given everyone just came back to him. "Pardon?"

"The dogs are dead, and either Makolichi is still around here or he's headed towards Gonta, or he's in the tower. I don't know. Brother, once the village is secured and fastened up, I want you to go out and scout around and see if there's any way you can feel for Mako on your way to Teboria lake. If you find him, end him. If not, Xandros, I need your soldiers to cleanse the woods. We can't have *shiriak* and their kin running rampant. *Hopefully* nothing bigger is out there."

The protests started right away. "Spirits and demons aren't our bailiwick," he started. "We're not equipped for them. My men are mundanes. Evalia is my only spellslinger. What is it you expect us to do?"

"They're underfed goblins that need a bath. Your men can handle them. I'm more worried about the wraiths. We'll figure out the details shortly. Eos. You're staying here, and you're going to aid Xandros and Steelhom."

"I... I would wish to stay with you, Guardian of Winters. I know not these people."

"I would wish not to be going at all. I don't have a choice, so you don't either."

This time it was the paladin that had the objection. "You can't face Makolichi on your own. If you need to return quickly, we know that this wisp has the power to do that."

Akaran simply shook his head. "We don't know what else is in that tower. Could just be Daringol, could be worse. Plus... I do not like the idea of explaining her to whatever passes for the city watch down there. I don't... Eos... if they need me back here, do you have the strength to teleport down and bring me back in a hurry? For that matter, can you find me easily? I don't like being so far away from the tower but..."

"I marked you, Guardian," she answered with a slightly-smug smile. "I can find you no matter where you may be."

"That's unsettling," Mariah muttered under her breath.

The priest had to agree. "Yeah... that is. We'll need to address that later."

The wisp didn't understand his concerns and reached for the mark. "You don't wish to be marked as ice? You are the Guard-"

He brushed her hand away from his throat and glared. "*Later*. Can you do it or not?"

"It... it will be difficult. The valley is not as in tune with ice as the mountain. I will come as I can."

Steelhom wasn't so convinced. "Even if you leave her here, you have to take someone."

"I will. I need to have someone that knows the people there. Xandros, do any of your other men...? Someone to speak for me. I don't need to have to prove myself to another council of elders or the like. I don't have time."

Hirshma spoke up – and more than a little reluctantly, at that. "I might be able to help."

"That would be a first," Akaran quipped.

Ignoring the taunt, she went on. "My apprentice knows their merchant-master, and she knows the way back. She has done business in my name many times before. If you need her, I can send her."

He suddenly regretted his tone, and perked up immediately at the thought. "Mariah, you do?"

The trainee alchemist, on the other hand, didn't. "Miss! Don't make me go down there. I like it here with the soldiers. It seems safer."

"Demon hunting with a little girl?" Xandros not-so-subtly complained. "I'm not sure I can accept this."

Sighing in frustration, Akaran lost that feel-good moment and glared at both of them. "Do I *have* to keep pulling rank on you people? It won't just be her. It'll be your wife and whatever soldiers you sent with her. So. Mariah, you're with me. Please. I need you."

"Dammit I..."

"You're with me. Xandros, just to be safe, send one of your men along so the Gonta guard doesn't get all pissy when I show up. Next. Brother, Commander, both of you. About Daringol. Xandros can't go hunting little demonic rats without having something he can use to deal with those wraiths if they pop up."

While the younger girl muttered and glared daggers back at the priest, the Commander wasn't so convinced about his task. "How dangerous are they?"

Akaran rubbed his arm absentmindedly. "The scavengers aren't worth mentioning. The wraiths? If they touch you you'll either die and be resurrected as one or not die and burn so badly on the inside you wish you had."

"Pleasant."

"Not really. We also need to start siphoning essences off of that thing. Goddess knows how many souls it's absorbed and we *don't* want to take them all at once. When we move in to banish it, it'll probably call all of its bits and pieces back to defend itself. The weaker we can make it, the better."

"But Guardian, surely there cannot be so many as to be a true threat when we reclaim master's home. Their numbers assuredly must not be so large, or else we all would not be one with it?"

He looked over at her and shook his head. "There are enough that got loose that I've had my hands full of already. The dogs were carries, somehow. I can't assume that there aren't more of them around and *you* don't know how many got loose before you sealed the pass shut."

Steelhom cleared his throat and looked out towards the village wall. "What do you have in mind?"

"Well. We don't know enough about them, do we? Let's make an effort to find out."

"You're being uncomfortably vague, boy," Xandros muttered half-under his breath.

With a shrug, Akaran clarified. "They like magic, they like animals, and... Steelhom? We are known as inquisitors, aren't we?"

Steelhom's eyes narrowed into little slits. "Yes..."

"Let's go inquire."

"Let's go inquire," was quickly changed to "No, *you* go pack, *we'll* go inquire," from the elder priest. Akaran growled, at first, but this time, everyone countermanded him. Mariah herself was less than happy about the trip, so she was the first one to insist that Steelhom and Xandros would be sent exploring on their own.

Finding one of them was not as difficult as Xandros thought it might be. Once their plans were drawn up, and the garrison's soldiers were set to task to prepare their base and begin the work to shore up Toniki,

Eos'eno and Steelhom went out into the wilderness with the commander. While it did take some doing, the wisp was able to somehow use the snow that covered the mountainside to find a corrupted soul.

Her range was terrible, but the moment she picked up on one, Steelhom was able to use his abilities to home in on it. The entire thing was slightly surreal to the professional soldier – hunting people or animals was one thing. But this? Chasing after a paladin being lead by a woman that was *clearly* inhuman and *hovering* from one place to another?

The only thing that made it worse was when they found their intended prey.

It had been one of the villagers, once. Why it hadn't wandered back towards Toniki was anyone's guess, just as much as it was why it was just aimlessly pacing through the woods. It looked like one of the hounds had claimed her life; her body was more ripped to shreds than not. Whichever of the two dogs had done it had torn sick gouges out of her stomach, and completely shorn off a breast, with a deep scratch that had torn out half of her throat.

Still, that wasn't the oddest part about her.

Daringol had completely taken over this poor woman, with a number of cloudy black tentacles lazily snapping in the air through the hole in her throat and out her ribs. Worse, that wasn't the only thing a bit 'off' for the entire experience. While the fact that a corpse was up and moving around on its own was disturbing enough for Xandros, and Daringol essentially an etheric parasite nesting inside his chest, the fact that this zombie had managed to catch and hold a squirming *shiriak* against her mauled breast was an entirely new development.

The corpse turned to them when she heard them coming, but it simply stood there. She stopped trying to gnaw on it with her minced mouth hanging agape, as the *shiriak* – barely the size of a newborn – futilely bit at her remaining breast while it tried to get free. Tendrils poked and prodded at the disgusting little beast as it tried to squirm away.

Little more than flaps of yellow skin hanging off of a humanoid frame, the *shiriak* couldn't get away from the zombie that held it so tight and close. All told, Xandros was completely repulsed. Eos'eno was so disquieted that she was happy to dispatch them both. "Don't destroy the zombie. I need it."

Wrinkling her nose, the Tundrala native reluctantly agreed but then asked a pertinent question. "Do... do we need the other thing? It reeks of rot. Of an anathema to Nature."

Xandros pulled his sword out of its sheath and weighed the request. "Do we really need either? That is... that smell..."

"The smell is the *shiriak*. Yes we do, but not alive. They don't have a mind enough to speak to us. Dead is fine," the paladin answered, and began to channel light and energy down his halberd.

Dimwitted as it was, the animated corpse recognized the threat when it saw it, and the wraith within began to swell up and pull free of the body. Moving faster than Steelhom had given her credit for, Eos used one of Makolichi's favorite tricks and sent a single shard of crystal out of thin air and dead center into the *shiriak's* oddly-shaped skull. It gave a single shriek and slumped lifeless into the zombie's hands.

Then to add insult to injury to Daringol, the foul thing voided its bowels in an *utterly* horrible sound and an even worse *stench* that blossomed into the air before anybody knew it was coming. Steelhom was able to keep his stomach in check but Xandros wasn't half so lucky. He threw up while the paladin barked a Word and a shell of pale lavender light coalesced around the shambling corpse. The magic pinned the wraith inside, and stopped the zombie in its tracks.

"My student said that these things possess a sort of rudimentary intelligence. When you're done throwing up, be ready for it to try to break free."

"What exactly... ugh... what exactly do you think I'm supposed to do if it does? I'm a soldier, not a monster-killer from the Guild," the Commander half-whined half-groused.

"I expect you to stab it. Take off the head, and it should be enough to banish it."

Xandros cast a dubious stare in his direction. "Should?"

Ignoring that, the paladin waved his palm in front of the restrained body and came just short of touching it. "You don't really see things like this anymore. For a time, I have read that they were fairly common. Not constant, of course, but when Niasmis lost Her seat on the Pantheon, all manner of evil blossomed in the world. Could have been a coincidence. Could've been Archduke Belizal. Could have been the fall of the elven kingdoms. Don't know. Once the Order was re-established, we worked, we hunted."

"I know that much. Your people made damn sure that everyone knew how useful you were in a hurry," the commander noted, his eyes firmly back on the wretched corpse. "I've heard some tales that things have been heating up again. Dismissed it as unfounded rumors."

Nodding a little, Steelhom pushed his right hand into the zombie's chest. The being shook and struggled harder to break free, but Steelhom's grip was unbreakable. "The rumors are true though. Things have been getting busier. Something foul is bubbling to the surface. We are just not sure as to what. An inquisition may be in order, soon. I cannot say that there is anyone in the Temple looking forward to it, if so."

The soldier took the news with a grimace. "Word is that the border skirmishes are getting more intense day-to-day. Everyone seems to be on edge. Army command, some of the other Orders that have been marching through the area, up towards Anthor."

"And that's just here. In the west, it's worse. Much worse. The League has appointed a new Luminary, and it is understood that he is an ardent follower of Pymondis."

Eos choked out his name with her eyes going wide. "Pymondis? The Despoiler of Food? The Befouled Glutton? The Prince of Rot? The Son of Neph'kor? Such a profane Fallen has worshipers in the land of men?"

"We are equally as confused and repulsed as you, wisp," Steelhom grumbled.

"None of this is reassuring. Think this thing is involved somehow?"

With a twist and a jerk, the silver-haired paladin pulled out what was left of the zombie's heart from her chest. She made a loud, pained moan, but otherwise did nothing more than continue to struggle against the metaphysical bonds. "No... no, I do not. A symptom, maybe, of a problem on a much larger scale. This thing... this sad, sad thing? As I said, it is uncommon to see them in the wild anymore. Twenty? Twenty-five? At least that many years since we recorded the last exorcism of an *arin*."

His friend looked at the twitching tentacles that were doing their absolute best to touch either of the two men. The longer he stared, the more it looked like a face was attempting to take form in the fog inside her mouth. "I'm surprised you haven't yet banished this one. Growing slow in your old age?"

"Ruling a few things out," he answered with a small shrug. "Making sure that it's just a foul aura that's feeding this, and not something inside. This is nothing like what a necromancer or monger would summon. Interesting."

"Why do I always think 'distressing' when you say 'interesting'? It was the same way back in Bourshodin."

Steelhom took one of the twitching tentacles in his hand and held on until the pain from the toxic monster was too much to stand. "Because it usually is."

"*Dar...Daringo... seeks warmth... seeks home...*"

"Why do I doubt that?" the priest snarked back. "Damned thing: do you understand me? Can you comprehend words?"

"*Words... comprehend... know, understand, yes, Dar... Daringol knows words knows... remembers words hears words hears voices all time never ceasing so many voices so many words need home need peace need away...*"

He crossed his arms while his companion watched on. Killing people? Not an issue. Hearing a corpse talk back? That was another story entirely. "You have one chance, one opportunity, dead thing," Steelhom intoned. "Listen well – I will not repeat. You could go and be anywhere. Why are you here?"

"*No home no home,*" it rasped, the words coming from everywhere and nowhere at once. "*Set free set Daringol free...*"

"After all you've done there's little freedom to have."

"*No! No! Freedom is a must! Must be free must leave must have power to leave can feel power so hungry so need must have must stay...*" The zombie shifted to try to face him directly, but the nimbus of light still held it fast. "*Have... have to be here... cannot leave, home is so near but so cold home is not home home is compelled...*"

The admission was not expected. Even Eos'eno looked surprised when the paladin looked over at her. "Compelled? How are you compelled?"

Tentacles snapped under the nimbus, and the shifting grew more and more agitated. "*Ho... home was not here... home was.. elsewhere... man came man came removed us from home made us stay he tied us here we cannot leave here not now not yet not...*"

"Not yet? Explain, dead thing!"

"*Bound bound by shouting bound by screaming bound in rune bound cannot get free cannot make free! Can feel power! Can feel thing to make free can feed on power...! Can grow will grow must grow to be free...!*"

Steelhom looked back at the wisp with his brow furrowed and a glare plain to see. "I expect that you have some sort of explanation for this."

If anything, she looked as unnerved as he did. "Explain? No, no explain, no knowledge of this. Master said he chased it away and kept it away, was only when he was taken into the ice that this thing returned and came near his home, was only when the ice secured him that it laid siege to our tower."

"Who bound you? Was it the demon, the one in green ice?"

The zombie shook and the nimbus started to falter. "*NO! NO DEMON! Man did! Man made man found us man pulled us man shouted at us man made us cold made us stay! Daringol fight to be free, Daringol struggled! But free no power no warm no warm in cold! Must stay must stay in cold to be near warm to grow to be free!*"

"Steelhom? Does any of this make sense to you?" Xandros interrupted, all-but hovering behind the unholy creature with both hands on the hilt of his blade.

"Well, it would seem that my student's distaste for the secrets here is wearing off on me. If this beast is to be believed, apparently Usaic was keeping secrets from his own creation as well."

"*If* she is to be believed," the soldier argued.

Eos'eno didn't take it well. "Believe me? Believe or not! This thing this creature, it had no cause no call no permission to be by master! He said it came by because it craved what he sought to create, that it would attempt to return until his work was perfected! But it was perfected, it was made, and it came back regardless!"

"*Set free! Set Daringol free! Man binds us you bind us all men bind us! Men bind we wish home we wish home in any in what we can find to hold! Too cold too cold to be without a home!*"

The paladin brought his hands together and whispered another Word at it: "*Nul'mir.*" When he did, the nimbus brightened around his captive and it gave a pained screech. "It doesn't behave like others I've read about. They... how best to describe it. They exist, they grow, but they don't seek shells to become corporeal. Mostly, they stay within the ether and manifest to feed and then return back to the edges of the veil."

"So it isn't operating under typical rules and this girl doesn't know why it says it was bound here."

"Succinctly, yes."

Xandros's frown spoke volumes. "I'm starting to understand why your boy is in such a bad mood."

"As am I, to be honest." Steelhom stepped closer and planted his weapon into the ground, then dug a small white crystal out from under his cloak while the zombie continued to struggle. "No real point in attempting to chat with it more. Just as well. I need the mouth for other things."

"Free! Daringol free please free Daringol seeks home seeks warm!"

With a great deal of difficulty, his friend managed not to say anything in response. He did, however, continue to circle the zombie. "You know, no matter how many men I've slain on the battlefield, things like this always disturb me."

While the paladin began to recite a spell that made the crystal glow first white, then pink, then red, Eos'eno looked intently at Xandros. "How many you've slain? Your soul only cries for three. Maimed many, this is true, and commanded men to kill others. Yet for a soldier, you are far less than the man of the cloth."

"Only three...? How in the name of all do you know that?"

"She isn't of this world, my friend. She sees things differently than the rest. How different, I am afraid I will never know, but I would so dearly love to study her at some point. Do you have any idea how rare it is for a creature like her to be on this plane?"

Eos backed away, tilting her head as concern lit up her features. "Study? I am not an object to be weighed and measured!"

Xandros stopped walking around and looked at the wisp like he was seeing her for the first time. "I just thought she... was just... somehow abnormal..."

"Abnormal? I am *not*," Eos snapped, with a handful of jagged crystals snapping up through her arms (and ripping her dress in the process). "If you are this crass to others, I feel much sympathy for the mage of battles that you have tamed as your 'pet,' the poor human, unlucky as she is."

The exchange nearly interrupted Steelhom as he choked back a peel of laughter. Xandros was less than enthused, and tried to come up with some kind of witty comeback. Failing, he managed to at least get out "Don't call her that to her face, just don't, she won't ask questions about what you are before she blows you apart."

"She may try if she so wishes." Giving him a further indignant look, she went on. "Yet it is true. The man of Love has taken far more souls than you."

Finished with the incantation and satisfied that his crystal was glowing alternate shades of red and white, Steelhom shrugged again and pushed it into the gash in the corpse's throat. "Far more? No. I've only accounted for a few. Seven, I believe, and not all were by my hand. Four were passed to the Queen's men for punishment. Heretics, and those that consorted with demons."

"You are not the one I mean. The man, the Guardian of Winters. He, he is a killer. The ice has said it, the ice has shown the marks on his soul. More than you and you, single and combined."

"Yes well, we don't talk about that," the paladin snapped. "Not now, not ever."

Xandros blinked at him. "He's just a boy? He's killed more than what, ten? *What* did your people do to him?"

"Deny it? You deny?"

As warm light began to pulsate out of the zombie's throat, the paladin explained – marginally. "Before he came to the Order he was not... a good child."

The wisp tilted her head and blinked. "Not a good child? The ice cries his name, it knows how many have felt his hands all -"

"Yes and we *don't* talk about it," Steelhom flatly interjected. "He doesn't remember and he doesn't need to know. He knows his father was a madman. He *does not* know what his father made him do. We made sure of that. *Do not* speak of it."

The zombie wailed in pain and frustration. *"FREE! SET DARINGOL FREE! FREE OR PAIN!"*

Xandros looked back and forth at both of them. "So apparently the locals aren't the only ones to keep secrets. He seems like a nice enough kid to me. Bit rough. Didn't think I wanted on his bad side before. Wasn't entirely convinced he has a good side. Do we *have* to send him to get my wife?"

"Yes."

With a grumbled sigh, the soldier pointed back to the corpse. "Fine. Now can we please do something about this creature? The smell is making me ill."

"The smell is from the *shiriak*."

"I don't care if it's from its mother. Can we please...?"

Steelhom sighed. "Well. It asks for pain. I've gotten all from it that I think I... wait." He grabbed the creature by its jaw and looked into the hollow, vacant eyes. "Where were you bound?"

"Bound! Man bound us! Man made us stay!"

"Yes, but *where?*" he demanded again.

"Where ice chilled hearts! Where ice chilled hearts!" A single twisting arm punched through the nimbus and nearly caught the paladin by his shoulder. He whipped back and snarled, narrowly avoiding the attack. *"BOUND! Man bound us man took us from warm home man made us stay here!"*

Still snarling, he glanced over the zombie's shoulder to Xandros. "That's quite enough of that. My friend? Please put your sword through its head. Avoid the neck once I... *Enia savald et-vas folisdal anavin!*" he recited as he clenched his fist. "Now!"

The soldier didn't have to be told twice. He flipped his blade around and carved a diagonal swath through its skull, lopping half of it cleanly off. Daringol fully manifested in the cold air, screamed once, then shattered into phantom glass shards on impact. At the same time, the crystal that Steelhom had implanted flared with an inky black glow before turning dull and charcoal gray.

"Ok. So. We found one talked to one and killed one. What was the point behind all of that?"

His friend knelt down and fished the crystal out of what was left of the corpse. Once removed, he put his other hand on her chest and whispered a Word that started a small lavender fire that quickly crept over the body. A few moments later, and there was nothing but ash in its wake. "Tracking. We now have a portion of Daringol's essence. Now that we have that, finding the rest of them will be easier, even through this... fog."

"I see," he lied. "What about the other thing?" he asked while Eos picked up the broken body with one hand, daintily holding it as far from her face as she could.

Steelhom wiped his hands clean in the snow and shrugged. "The same treatment. Enough of its essence will still be in the corpse."

"Understood. This is your party; I'll follow along. Plus, we did get two of the price of one. I thought these just liked wild animals?"

"And human corpses. That it was attempting to consume a demon, even one as minor as that, is concerning. It would seem they are not as picky as we had hoped. That, or it is that they are growing stronger. This is not a pleasant development any way we can explain it. Still cannot imagine how Daringol caught it."

The wisp turned the *shiriak* upside down and shook it, then poked at it again. "A hound a spirit and a perversion of men; these I understand. This I do not. Please? What purpose is this beast? What would give such a thing life, why?"

Xandros shrugged. "One of the Fallen, I suppose. Something for Them to play with."

"Most rejoice in some manner of fear or another. They have been known to create creatures simply to terrorize and torture them. Or eat," Steelhom added.

"Or... eat?" she asked, and then she prodded it in its chest. Before either of them could stop her, she brought it to her mouth and bit down on its shoulder. As they watched in equal parts horror and nausea, she swallowed and grimaced. "Mayhaps... mayhaps better as stew," she said as she tossed it over her shoulder and turned around to walk back to Toniki.

The garrison commander watched her go and swallowed back his revulsion. "Well. She's one of the most beautiful women I've ever seen, but weird beyond what words I've got. Akaran really *is* your student, isn't he?"

When all was said and done, the arrangements were finalized.

Steelhom worked to make sure every sword of every soldier was given an appropriate blessing to aid them against the damned — it wouldn't be anything remotely strong enough to deal with Makolichi, but to hurt the wraiths and kill any *shiriak*? It would suffice. It was an exhausting effort, but one that would (hopefully) pay off in the near future, if so needed.

In the case of the guard being sent with Akaran, they gave him two.

Hirshma had her own task: preparing for the wounded with the garrison's last-remaining medic. Nobody was under any assumption that the dead roaming the woods would go quietly. While there were enough men to keep the risk of injury to a minimum, these soldiers were not trained to hunt zombies and minor demons. There would be a learning curve, and while both of the priests, Xandros, the alchemist, and Mariah tried to explain the things as best as they could (both from a professional and amateur standpoint), nobody was under any illusion that there wouldn't be some of them that would need emergency care.

The alchemist's apprentice grumbled the entire time she packed her bags. Still, part of her was eager to be as far away from Toniki as she could be, as much as she would steadfastly refuse to admit it. She hoped Gonta would be a safer place to stay (it wouldn't) but she did have hope (she shouldn't've).

Akaran was forced to sit back and watch. Like Mariah, he grumbled and muttered, though unlike her, he was openly grateful for the chance to get away from the village. Hopefully it would be warmer (it would be; it was summer everywhere else but this particular chunk of the mountainside), and hopefully they would find what they were after with a minimum of fuss (but he correctly doubted that in its entirety). So while she packed, Steelhom worked his magic, Xandros prepared his men and Hirshma readied her stores, he sat and prayed.

His mentor worked his magic in more ways than one. Late in the evening, he pulled his student aside and spoke to him at length. "Akaran? Do you know why so much of your magic is offensive in nature?"

"Can't say I've ever given it much thought."

"Most neophytes don't. But consider: *Disperse, expel, expunge.* All three Words designed to ruin a spirit or remove a shell. *Disenchant,* minor as it is, breaks magic. *Luminoso* and *luminso corsair* burn and blind the unworthy. *Bonds* entrap, and your two wards contain or warn. *Purify* and *illuminate* are the only two that truly serve no offensive purpose."

The exorcist nodded slowly. "And the sensing."

"Ah, yes," he quietly agreed. "Twelve words, out of the dozens that the Lady deigned to give us. Why do you think that is? With three purely to assist? Not even to truly defend."

Akaran rubbed his goatee and mulled it over. "Give us time to acclimate? Practice? Never gave it much thought."

Steelhom clasped his hands on his. "Because a neophyte should not be fighting things that would necessitate more than steel plate across his chest and wooden slats on his arm. Animates. Lost souls. Restless dead. There should be no reason to fight abyssian hounds or pitborn demons that cannot be stopped by a man of the Queen's Army, let alone the things you have faced here."

"I figured that out," he grumbled as he protectively rested a hand on his stomach.

"Yes. So if you are not at the rank of an exorcist-adept, you would not be taught from the next Book of Hearts. Since you are fighting these awful things, you will need to be able to defend yourself. You *don't* have the strength to learn more than one right now – but with luck, you will have time to practice along the way."

His student shrugged off his coat and pulled his sleeve up all the way. "Whatever it takes."

Steelhom smiled and drew a knife. "I hope you don't need to make use of it, but I have no doubt that you will need it. Do be careful though, I beg you: it will drain your reserves."

Akaran gave him a short nod and fought off a wince when the knife cut into his arm. "Noted. So... what's it do?"

As he listened to the explanation, Eos'eno had an entirely different concern.

Daringol's interrogation had left her with a feeling of disquiet she was not used to. The very thought that her master had somehow bound the wraith to the area for any reason confused and repulsed her. Yet the longer she thought on it, the more she realized that he had already done as much with both herself and Makolichi to begin with, and at least one of the other things he had set to guard his tower from interlopers.

The things that she hadn't been quite-so-forthcoming about just yet.

Her questions and tormented thoughts kept her from finding any semblance of rest.

Instead, while everyone slept, she left the village to find answers.

V. CLAYMAKER'S KILN

Gonta.

The second-largest city in the Waschali Province, Gonta boasted a sizable population for a city so far away from the Queen's seat of power. At nearly two-and-a-half thousand heads strong before it became overrun with refugees from Toniki, Gonta had a reputation for being a friendly, warm place to grow and live.

But, that was before the refugee problem.

Once Akaran and his companions made it down off of the mountainside, they ended up having to go right back up it. The city had been partially carved out of a valley, with emphasis on the 'carved.' Half of the city was built onto or into the rockface, with natural tunnels providing both a defining tactical advantage (not that one was needed) and a place for everyone to stay safe and dry in the spring.

Gonta happened to have a waterfall pouring down into it from far up in the mountains. Water poured freely into the center of the town, where it lazily followed a river that went deeper into the Kingdom. Farmers and fisheries and all manner of tradesmen had shops and crafting buildings that decorated the banks.

For most of the year, the waterfall posed no threat. It actually provided very well for the city – the river was wide enough for small boats to travel up and down, allowing far more trade to go through the city than almost anywhere else on this side of the Queen's Tower. And there was no shortage of tradesmen that called it home.

Gonta's sylverine mine was the largest in the region and made the one outside of Toniki look like a shoddy attempt to dig up pebbles. The land up and down-river was exceptionally fertile and home to all manner of wheat and potatoes and raizior-grass, to name a few. There was a fairly large clay pit a few short miles away from the city center and the citizens of Gonta were well-renown for their pottery.

While all those things were true, Gonta did have a problem with their water.

Specifically, with how much of it there was.

Rashio's Fall wasn't the only reason that the city had a river running through the middle of it. The waters of Ichaia's Tears (named in tribute to a pale, pink algae that grew in it) flowed out of a tunnel network that opened up about half a mile down from the waterfall's primary pool, giving birth to one of the largest waterways in the province. In the summer months, the algae would bloom along the shores, and at night, would give the entire city a soft glow that could be seen clearly from miles away.

The algae didn't typically bloom until the summer, and lasted until the middle of the fall. In the winter, the Falls slowed down to a moderate trickle – and as a direct result from the current interruption in the natural order around Teboria Lake, it hadn't been putting out as much fresh melt from the snowy mountains far above.

For some strange reason though, one which nobody had given much thought about before (and wouldn't now, either) the algae had been blooming much earlier and lasting much longer than normal as of late. It was almost like it was feeding off of magical properties from some undefined source that had somehow gotten into the water. While strangely confusing, everyone in the city enjoyed the way the river glowed at night, so nobody said anything about it.

And since nobody said anything, nobody thought to try to figure out the source. If they *had,* who knows how much faster Usaic's idiocy would have been found. Men were easily-amused creatures, after all, and a pretty distraction wasn't worth complaining about.

Algae and magical contamination aside, Gonta did have one ugly nickname that the locals hated but everyone else in the province called it. Because the Falls poured down from the mountains, what passed for summer would frequently lead to more water pouring down from above, and typically coincided with a larger volume of water flowing out of the underground.

The two combined caused a significant headache.

For roughly two months out of the year (the mountains never got all *that* warm in the summer), Gonta had a bit of a flooding... problem. The river would overflow the banks and then the farms and tradesmen and anyone and everyone else that lived near the edge would find themselves hip-deep in water. While manageable (a vast majority of the tradesmen's huts and homes and the like were built up on wooden stilts where possible), the flooding tended to be severe enough that the moniker fit year-round.

As Akaran looked up from his horse and took in the impressive work that had been done to partially carve a city into the cliff, all he could do was remember the name everyone called it whenever they weren't in earshot of any of the locals. "Gonta, City of Mud," he muttered.

Neither of his companions responded to the derisive remark.

Their feet were already caked in it from the trip.

The exorcist was not impressed. "So let me make sure I'm seeing this right. A river has cut the town in half, and about half of the people that live here actually live outside the city walls on both sides of the river. There's two gates on either side of the Tears, and if you come into the city by way of boat, there's a Port Authority office about three or four miles or so out of town that is armed with enough cannons that can sink a warship in a heartbeat should they opt to skip inspection? Not that one could actually make it this far upstream?"

"That's about right," Mariah confirmed.

"And the rest of the population lives in tunnels carved out of the inside of the mountain."

"That they do."

"So they've built it to a point where it could withstand a siege on all three possible points of entry? Why? If the Civan Empire were ever to push out of Anthor's Pass, they'd go west into the heart of the Kingdom's territory? Literally the other direction from here? Or be stopped almost immediately by reinforcements from the capitol? This isn't even where the provincial governor lives, is it?"

His other companion – a young soldier not much older than the priest himself – shrugged. "Momma told me when I was growin' up that some nobleman some fifty, sixty years back got paranoid over the thought of raiders commin' up the river somehow and layin' into the city. Spent thousands of gold an' no shortage of slaves to build the walls."

"Raiders?" Akaran asked, head titled to the side. "Seriously? This isn't the Midlands."

"Raiders," Mariah answered with a half-smirk. "He was getting ready to have a tower built out of the cliff before the Captain of the Guard back then heard him talking to himself late one night. Seems he had a habit of getting bottles of helvator smuggled in from Matheia. Guess they made him mad as a hatter, and whenever he'd run short, he'd start thinking his mirror was talking to him at night, telling him all about pirates and thugs and things that intended to rape and pillage everyone and everything here."

Private Galagrin lived up to his name with a huge smile as he listened to Mariah finish telling the story. "Cost the Queen from back then a big chunk of her taxes and stuff before anyone caught on that he was just a crazy son of a bitch dosed up on the finest brain meltin' slag in all of Waschali."

Akaran tilted his head back and forth and craned his neck to look up the mountainside, and just about hurt himself turning his head to look at the river behind them. "This had to take years to build? And nobody thought to wonder why he was doing it?"

"Made the city guard extra money to spend on new recruits and gear... gave the masons a windfall. Gave a goodly bit of work to the woodsmen and blacksmiths, too. Everyone made a lot of coin and the only one that got screwed over was the Queen. Well, the Queen's grandmother," the soldier replied. "Of course, to hear my mom tell it, the noble paid for his um, *over-planning* with a bit of sufferin' and all that."

"A bit?"

Mariah cringed and looked down at the ground. "To hear the tales about it? The Queen had his eyelids cut off, then tied him face-first to his mirror, and..."

"...and then she um, well. Had him lowered into a crucible full of molten lead, feet first an' all. She wanted to make sure he could see himself scream since he liked to talk to the damn thing so much," Galagrin finished.

The exorcist slid off of Nayli's saddle and landed a bit ungracefully on the cobblestone highway. "That is one of the worst things I've ever heard."

"Oh that ain't all of it," the private added. "She had him dunked to his knees, pulled him out, had a mage do some work, kept him awake somehow. Then did it again till it burned off his cock. She didn't let him die 'till the mirror shattered in his face."

"That *is* the worst thing I've ever heard," Akaran clarified as they made their way to the western gateway into the city.

"That ain't even the full story. To hear it said, sometimes you can hear him screamin' at night down by the smelters. When word got out, she refused to let anyone come here and try to excise him out. Said it was a fitting sentence for wasting all her time and gold."

"This whole region is full of stories like that," Mariah added with a shrug. "Further away from the capitol, the more the Queen's goons like to flex their muscles when they think she's being ignored."

Galagrin stopped and looked at her, his forehead creasing across the middle as he frowned. "Hey now, we ain't goons."

This time it was the priest that had a grin. "I'm a goon."

"See? He admits he's a goon."

That earned the priest the same dirty look. "Just cause he's a goon don't mean we're all goons. Besides. Screamin' in the night and wandering about the city when they ought to be off to the next world? Ain't that your kinda thin' an' all?"

The exorcist leaned against his horse in silence for a minute and had to give a reluctant nod. "Yes. It is."

"Sounds like you've got something to look into then, don't it?" Galagrin meant it half-jokingly, but all that the priest heard was "More work for you!"

There wasn't any more time for idle conversation. The soldiers at the gate stopped their small caravan until Akaran flashed his sigil and Galagrin declared his mission and what troop he was attached to. The guards let them through while muttering under their breath about 'more refugees' and 'more damn mouths to feed.'

It didn't go unnoticed, and the cause for their irritation was made immediately apparent the moment they passed into the city proper. You could see them everywhere – unwashed, visibly depressed and desperate people scattered up and down the streets. It was a veritable throng of the homeless and the destitute.

I guess they weren't kidding. Toniki dumped their people here, one after another. Not that I blame them.

Gonta had been crowded before the refugees hit. Cobblestone streets were covered in mud and horseshit, and with no place for Toniki's poor to go once they made it off of the mountain, they decided to call it their home. Mariah's happy mood fell into gloom of her own as she realized that too many her friends and former neighbors hadn't been able to move far beyond their homes – and that their squalid living conditions weren't much better *here* than they were back up on the mountain.

Although they were warmer – a fact that Akaran quickly (and happily) noticed in a hurry.

He couldn't do much to combat her depression, no matter how much he wished that he could. Although there was at least one thing in the sea of misery that he could get a marginal bit of enjoyment from: Trees.

Not that Toniki didn't have them, but here they were alive and vibrant and growing. There was even grass that was a shade other than drab brown, and flowers that were something other than wilted and drooping. It wasn't much of an improvement... but it was a start.

As they made their way deeper into the city, a fight erupted next to a cart with a broken wheel. Mariah apparently recognized one of the feuding parties and her dour expression lit back up with a smile. "Ralafon!"

If his head had whipped around to face her any faster, he probably would have broken his neck. "Mariah? What are you doing here?"

She charged over and gave him a huge hug that gave the priest an odd pang of jealousy. Watching her hold the stout young man – he looked to be a couple of years older than Akaran, and had another couple of inches on him – just... it irked him. For no reason that he could put his finger on. "You wouldn't believe me if I told you."

"And I don't care!" the other half of the argument snapped. "I don't care who you are or what you're doing here, but you and you can both piss off."

Ralafon gently moved Mariah behind him and took two steps towards the man giving him a hard time. "Luno, I'm not leaving until you pay me what you owe me. I agreed to escort you out. It's not my fault you suddenly can't travel."

Gesturing wildly at the broken wheel, the wrinkled merchant's voice went up a few octaves. "THE WHEEL BROKE! How do you expect me to go anywhere with a broken wheel? If I can't leave the city, I don't need your protection!"

"The wheel broke because you're too cheap to put your junk in two carts. I warned you that it wasn't sturdy enough to make it out of the city."

"And I should take the word of a filthy mountain-goat that the wheels aren't sturdy? Just who do you think you are?"

Ralafon's voice raised up to match Luno's. "I used to build wagons! That's who I think I am!"

"Maybe you should go back to it. You're a failure of a bodyguard."

"He can't fail if you never used his services!" Mariah quickly stepped up and argued. "If he says you owe him money, you owe him money. So, pay the man."

Luno straightened out his fur jacket and (ugly) caramel, ill-fitting tunic. "I'm not going to pay him on the demand of some little girl, either. Both of you can walk off a cliff before I have that guard throw you both into the dungeon!" he almost shrieked, pointing over at Galagrin (who wanted absolutely nothing to do with any of this).

Neither did the priest. However, after a week of dealing with irritating and irritable bastards in Toniki... "Pay the man. He agreed to do the job, and warned you that there might be trouble. If anything, you should be happy that your cart broke down here and not out there."

"Oh look. Someone else that thinks I should pay good money for absolutely nothing," the merchant seethed. "I'll have you arrested too, whomever you are."

Akaran's eye rolled up as he opened his coat and pulled out his sigil. Luno's eyes darkened at the sight of it, and he moved a little closer towards his broken down wagon and all of his boxes and bags. "I'm a guy that can make your day a lot worse if you want me to."

"A priest. How quaint. Why do you think I care?"

Galagrin started to speak up, but Akaran put his hand on his shoulder. "This sigil lets me tell him," he said as he patted the soldier's arm, "to look through every chest bag and crate you've got loaded on your cart to check for things you forgot to declare to the city taxmen. Do you really want me to do that?"

Luno flinched again and moved a little closer to his luggage. "I just want to get my cart fixed and then to get out of here. Away from all these... people."

"Good, and you can do that once you pay him."

"He didn't do any work! I don't owe him anything!"

The exorcist tilted his head back and growled under his breath. Before he could order their escort to start digging through Luno's wares, Mariah interjected herself again. "Hold on. Just... wait. All of you. Ralafon knows how to build wagons so he can probably fix yours. Right?"

Her friend shrugged. "I can't do it without picking up supplies. Had to sell my tools last winter, just barely scraped enough for a sword so I could get out of the province. That thing is going to need more than just a new spoke, see it? Axle is shot."

"Fine. He fixes wagons, you have a broken wagon. Pay for him to buy a new set of tools and he'll fix it. Then he's out of your hair, you can get your wares out of here, and everyone wins."

The merchant's jaw dropped. "You expect me to hire him to repair my cart after the things he called me?"

"I expect you to do it before I start calling you things," Akaran grunted. "Ralafon? You agree to this?"

With another shrug, the carpenter-turned-bodyguard made his offer. "He offered me ten gold to go from here to Anthor. Tools'll cost four. Pay up five and I'll see it done by daybreak tomorrow."

Luno's growl matched Akaran's earlier one. "Half of your pay to even get out of the city? That's outrageous. How am I to afford another guard once it's repaired?"

"Sell something on your cart. Charge more for it when you get to Anthor. Swindle someone on the way there. I'm sure you'll think of something. Now do we have a deal or do I have to start digging through your crap to see why you're in such a hurry to leave?"

He wasn't going to get a better offer, and he knew it. With an aggravated sigh, Luno reluctantly took Ralafon's hand and gave it a weak, half-hearted handshake. His employee, on the other hand, took a brief moment of delight in giving the old man a squeeze and a jerk that made his old knuckles crack. "Next time one of you refugees from the mountains gets anywhere near me, so help me, I'll piss on them."

"Be my guest," Akaran chimed. "I can give you names of some to look for."

Mariah ignored him. Completely. "Ralafon? Care to walk with us? We have to head to the Merchant-Lord's Manor. We have business there."

"You'd best pretend you've never heard of Toniki if you want to get anywhere close to it."

"I'm good with pretending I've never been there before," the priest muttered under his breath. Again, he was completely ignored. Mariah's silvery-haired friend, did, however, reply to his next observation. "I realize that they call this the City of Mud but I wasn't expecting it to be so crowded and filled with... with..."

"The unleavened and unwashed?" Galagrin offered.

"That. That works."

Ralafon sighed and looked around through the throngs of people as they made their way down the city's main street. People were stacked almost on top of each other, some working, some hawking their wares, others sitting on the ground and begging for coins. "Too many of us here. Not enough food, too little work. The city overseer has done a great deal for all of us. The people though... well, you know how it is. Times were hard before Toniki turned into a mess. You finally wise up an' leave?"

Mariah shook her head. "We're here to... well..."

Akaran interrupted and summarized the entire mess. "Toniki's problem isn't the weather. It's a demon problem. We hard one of them might have migrated south. I'm here to collect his head."

"Huh." Ralafon stopped and thought that one through. "Demons? Actual honest-to-Gods demons? Well, that explains a whole lot. I take it you've gotten rid of the ones up there then?"

"No. We have people working on it. We don't want any stragglers down here."

As luck would have it, things decided to shift slightly in their favor. At the mention of the word 'demons,' the pastry merchant that they had stopped next to perked up. When they finished giving Ralafon a brief explanation, the wrinkled old baker spoke up. "Demons? I think you need to go to the Burning Wick. Some woman wandered into town a day, two back. She didn't look none-too-well. Spouted things about a spirit and a black fog. She holed up there."

That took the exorcist's immediate attention. "A woman? From Toniki?"

"Ah-yeap. Beautiful lass. Just looked all kinds of sick. Pale skin, shaking, eyes turning dark around the edges. Ill-tempered black-haired witch."

Mariah grabbed Akaran's hand and gave it a nervous squeeze. "You don't think that's..."

His eye darkened as violent thoughts blossomed in the back of his head. "Maybe our luck is about to change."

Someone else had come up behind them, and the second that the man spoke, Ralafon unleashed a sigh with muttered profanities under it. "Oh not him, no fisking way not him."

Rudely barging into the conversation, the newest sod to take an interest in them demanded immediate recognition. "I wouldn't be sure about your luck. You there. What is your business in Gonta?"

He answered as he turned around and sized up the stranger in a heartbeat. You could just *smell* the aura of 'professional headache' rolling off of him in the way he stood, the look on his face, and the fact that in a place called the City of Mud, this prick was pretentious enough to wear a white cloak. "My name is Akaran DeHawk, exorcist, Order of Love. This is my companion, Mariah-Anne... you know, you never did tell me your last name?"

"It doesn't matter," she shrugged. "I'm from Toniki, that's all."

"Well then. Mariah-Anne, of Toniki. The man behind me is Private Yolistal Galagrin, attached to the 13th Ray of Dawn. And you...?"

"Captain Orin Paliston," the angular-faced man replied with a sneer that just dripped disgust and derision. "So. More soldiers? Here to remove the trash, are you? About time."

Ralafon was quick to complain about the comment. "We're not trash! We're citizens of the Kingdom, like you!"

Orin opened his cloak to show off the gray cotton tunic under it, trimmed with brown strips of leather and the trio of thick silver chains that decorated it from shoulder to waist. "Yes. Just like us. Which is why you cower in tents and alleys and beg for scraps instead of serving the Queen or providing for her Kingdom. We are so much alike."

"Wait! This trash, these people are my friends! Neighbors!" Mariah all-but shouted at him.

Shrugging her off without a concern, he gestured to the sea of the unwashed. "Then you are welcome to take them back with you. Now. What is your business in my city?"

"It's whatever I decide it to be," the exorcist grunted, fingering his sigil for the benefit of everyone watching.

"Decide quickly."

Akaran did. "I'm here to hunt for a wayward soul. Foul thing. One arm, skeletal. Travels in the company of noxious clouds and occasionally giant hounds that drip fire and the blood of the doomed from their maws. Seen any?"

"You say that so casually," the alchemist's apprentice quietly sighed behind him.

His declaration caught the attention of more than a few of the people standing nearby, and other hushed whispers followed. The Captain, however, didn't seem to be so moved or concerned. "The only noxious clouds about here are these... unwashed vermin."

Mariah's patience didn't last for a tenth as long as Akaran's, and she snapped. "That's quite enough! Our home is barely more than two, three days away. These people are truly no different than you, or anyone else in the province."

"These people have resorted to thuggery and vagrancy. The keep has her cells full of this rabble. I just locked another one up. Some vile bitch from your pathetic town."

Blinking, the exorcist looked back over at the merchant. "What was it you said, trader? Ill-tempered black haired bitch?"

"Witch. Though, ah-yeah, I suppose bitch works enough."

"Muttering about a black fog and wraiths?"

Captain Paliston gave a curt nod and puffed his chest out. "And things similar. She looks more dead than not. She won't trouble anyone much longer."

"Goddess. She's infected and she's right in the middle of the city? I need to see her. Now."

"Infected? Infected with what?"

Mariah squeezed Akaran's hand again and tugged at it a little. "What about Evalia?"

"The battlemage?" Orin asked, the disgust in his pale-blue eyes sharpening to concern.

"That's her. You know her?"

The Captain nodded slowly. "She is... indisposed."

"Make her disposed."

Their female companion didn't take the brushoff lightly. "Indisposed? Why?"

He didn't elaborate. "She is currently in the care of Merchant-Master Aloric Everstrand, the city Overseer. She is not receiving callers at this time, per his orders."

That caught Ralafon's attention. "Everstrand? The Marauder of Blackstone Trading Company?"

"The one and the same. Before you ask, she is relatively fine."

Akaran didn't miss qualifier. "Relatively?"

"Relatively."

That didn't reassure the young woman. "Why just relatively? She is or she isn't."

"Because she still draws breath. She took two of my men and two of hers to the north after whatever bandits have been murdering travelers on the Queen's road. She came back with half as many. The Overseer ordered her not to be disturbed when she returned."

Akaran and Mariah exchanged a look that spoke volumes. If the guardsman had noticed it, he might have softened his tone. "What did she find...?" the priest pressed, once more voicing his internal frustration about even being sent in the general direction of this accursed mountain.

"She wouldn't say," Orin replied, flipping his hand through the back of his shoulder-length hair as he did. "Only that she found 'it' and has ordered me to stop any more travel up the mountains east or down to Slag Harbor until she heard back from her husband."

"I'm inclined to agree with that order, and *I'm* the word from her husband. What's her condition?"

"You'll need to speak to the Overseer."

Mariah shrugged and looked around the street, watching people go by. "Then why are we waiting? Let's go."

Orin straightened himself and puffed his chest out again. "*I* will take the priest. You, girl, and you, Ralafon – do not get the *privilege* of entering the manor-grounds."

Speaking of looks that spoke volumes; the one that Akaran gave the captain right then should have been enough to kill the pompous twit on the spot. "You know something? I've had just about enough attitude from people lately. My rank and my allegiance mean I can go where I please with whom I please and I -"

Mariah stepped between them and put her hand on the exorcist's chest. "What Akaran means is that he would like me to check on Evalia while he goes to see about the woman in your prison."

"I didn't mean that. I meant -"

She gave him a sideways look and kicked her foot back against his shin. "Yes you did," she whispered, then to Orin, she cleared her throat. "Yes. He did. We came for a reason. We're wasting time. You'll have someone take me to her and someone take him to the she-witch, because the priest from the Order of Love – *who has authority over you* – compels you. Do you understand?"

The Captain started to issue a rebuttal, and then Akaran calmly lifted up his sigil again and let the gold flash under the sun. "What she said."

"You will promise me a thing, however," Mariah said, turning around just enough to stare the priest in the eye.

"What?"

"You *will* wait for me before you kill her. I want to watch that thundering slitch suffer."

Ralafon's jaw dropped open. "Mariah! I've never heard you use such language! And kill her? For what cause?"

Orin glared at Akaran and looked like he was going to try to argue the point. "You'll kill nobody on my watch."

"By order of the Queen, I might have to."

"By order of the Queen, if it's who we think it is, he will, and I'll help," the alchemist's apprentice clarified.

Eyes jumping from the one to the other, Orin eventually caved. "This girl? She one of yours, exorcist? She seems to have the temperament."

"Only in his dreams."

Akaran made a slightly strangled noise in the back of his throat and straightened up, squaring his shoulders. "Fine then. Let's go."

Beside them, the merchant quickly interrupted. "Well. I suppose you all have your businesses settled. There's really only one more thing to ask."

With a deep and ever-so-pained sigh, the priest walked over and set his hands down on the merchant's rough wooden table. "What?"

He held up a vaguely blue piece of fruit the size of his palm and smiled. "Belian-berry tarts, anyone?"

In some parts of the Kingdom, the Queen (in her infinite knowledge) decided that the best way to ensure that the land was as profitable as it was lawful was to put men of commerce in charge of certain territories. If a city didn't have specific tactical value, and it didn't set off the desires for men of the cloth to designate it a holy location, it was handed off to a representative from one of the merchant guilds. There were only a few different guilds left that could obtain a Contract of Governance from the crown, and every now and again there would be a dispute as one territory would try to buy out another.

Gonta was one such place, and the Blackstone Trading Company was one such guild.

Merchant-Master Aloric Everstrand, Blackstone's Marauder, was one such person. He was also the reason why the BeaST (as it was known) hadn't had any competition for those contracts in the entire Waschali Province in the last quarter-century. An older gentleman, he shared the same birthday as the Queen – and while the two had never met in person, their envoys reportedly joked as to which of them had been involved in more wars over the last fifty-seven years.

Inevitably, that sent the Queen's messengers scurrying back to the capitol looking a tad shaken and slightly paler, while Aloric's advocates were always content in the knowledge that Everstrand was the more grizzled of the two (even if not by much). That wasn't to say that Aloric was a bad guy – but you don't get titled 'the Marauder' because you spent the prime of your life *gardening*. It still quietly amazed (and disheartened) the Grandmasters of the other commerce guilds that someone with his perchance for violence would decide to settle down in this otherwise quiet corner of the Kingdom.

Every time he's said that story to me, I always wondered why nobody thought that maybe he just got tired of fighting and wanted to build lives instead of selling them, Mariah quietly mused to herself as she stood in the Overseer's foyer. Captain Orin had taken the first opportunity he could find to pass her off to the first guard that he could find, and his instructions for her care left a lot to be desired.

His manor was, for all intents and purposes, fairly simplistic on the inside – for a man of Aloric's wealth - and the foyer was not to be excluded in that. It had two lounging couches against opposite walls (trimmed in gold with sultry-red cushions), matching chairs, an oak table that could have been suited for a dining hall, assorted wrought-iron candelabras (and sconces) along with all of the other trimmings one might expect.

However, for as much wealth as she knew he had amassed, everything in the house managed to stand somewhere just at the edge of modesty. Somehow, the furnishings were understated, muted, reserved. It was a difficult balance to keep for a man of his standing, no matter how you looked at it. The entirety of it led Galagrin to make a little quip about "At least he's not bragging about where the tax money is going."

If she hadn't met him twice, she might have agreed. The reality of it was that he was a kind soul whom has seen one too many battles and had done one too many questionable things on his way up the ladder. One meeting had been brief; a casual encounter as she escorted Hirshma through the city. The other one had been at length last year at dinner when the alchemist had approached him asking for a line of credit to purchase more supplies for their beleaguered village.

He had agreed, but only on the condition that Mariah had given him a dance. While the idea of giving attention to someone more than forty years her senior had rankled her a bit, her Miss *had* encouraged it, and it *did* work, even if she felt a little used after the fact. She didn't hold it against him, and the experience was entertaining enough. If nothing else, the glares she received from his wife gave her a measure of comfort.

Still, she took a bath in the river the moment that she could get away with it.

For all of the things that Aloric was, and all the things that his manor embodied, there was one more thing that was of immediate importance: he wasn't there. His wife was, and despite what happened last year, Shalarie was as warm as always. Almost as old as the lord of the house himself, she was almost like a grandmother in tone and warmth.

It didn't take much of a discussion to convince her to lead the way to the guest quarters where they had berthed the battlemage, though it was strangely odd that she almost ran down the hallway before Mariah could knock on the door. Galagrin, sensing the danger, mumbled an excuse or two and tried to follow.

'Tried' being the operative word. The younger woman stopped him with a silent glare and took a deep breath before the wooden door. *I don't know why I volunteered to do this. This could've waited until after he checked out the dungeon. He could've done it. 'I can do it, I can help.' Every time I've even **thought** those words around him, I've gotten in trouble.*

More than a little nervously, she rapped on the door and called out to whoever was inside. "Evalia Wodoria?"

Not only was the response blunt, the voice that carried it sounded weak and tired. "Whatever you want, go away."

"Battlemage Evalia?

"Yes, now leave."

This is going well. She took a deep breath and tried to give her voice a touch of firmness that she really didn't feel. It was all she could do to stop a nervous giggle. "M'am, I can't do that. Your husband sent me."

On the other side of the door, something fell onto the floor amidst a chorus of muffled curses. "Xandros? He's here? He's supposed to be at... Toniki?"

"He's there still, m'am. He sent me for you. We need to talk."

"Oh, he did? Fisking... fisking bastard how... fisking..." Evalia pulled the door half open and leaned against the inside of the doorframe. She looked ill. *Exceedingly* ill with her close-cropped blonde hair completely disheveled and dark circles under her gray eyes. She had on a simple tan peasant's dress, and had a musty, unpleasant smell to her breath. "You're... you're not a soldier. Not even old enough to... what is it you want?"

Mariah cleared her throat a little and gave her a wary smile. "No m'am. Apprentice to an alchemist. Or... was, at least. Now I'm just... me."

"How wonderful, 'just me.' Get in here and shut the door, I'm not putting on a show for the entire house."

She slipped into the small room and looked at the messy bed, a mug of water spilled on the floor, and blankets piled up in the corner. The other thing? She could smell the stale puke radiating out of a small chamber on the other side of the room. "Oh blessed be. It just keeps getting worse. You're sick?"

Evalia crossed her arms and glared at her, making her way back to the bed and curling up on it. "I'm sorry I'm not up to your standards. Now what do you want...?"

Fidgeting and fighting the urge not to cross her own arms, Mariah started to stumble over her answer. "It's Mariah, m'am. Mariah-Anne. Xandros sent me... sent us... to stop you from hunting the monster you're after."

"Oh really? My vaunted, glory-seeking husband sends some little girl to tell his wife that she shouldn't do her job? Why?"

"Yes m'am. I'm here with an exorcist from the Order of Love. We've had... complications. The same creature you're hunting is probably the spawn of the one that's been laying siege to Toniki. Or it might be the demon itself."

None of that set well with the battlemage, and she didn't try to hide it. "*Spawn of?* It can breed? Oh now isn't that fisking fitting."

"They call it a 'nesting wraith,' whatever that means. I don't understand. It calls itself Daringol, and it can make more of itself. Then there's this other thing, Makolichi. The Order thinks it's coming here next, they chased it out of Toniki."

Evalia buried her head in the bed and growled a frustrated sigh. "So my husband sent it here for me to deal with. Wonderful man."

"Not him, the priests. Makolichi... it was gone before your husband got to the village."

"Fine. Wonderful *priests*. Not that I *can* hunt it right now, but why did they send a waif to come tell me?"

Shaking her head, Mariah explained a bit more. "It's not just me. Akaran is here. He's the exorcist. They sent him to Toniki first. He has help securing it now. But he wants to contain this thing to Toniki, so... he needs to make sure it's driven out of here so they can contain all of it."

She looked up at her with one eye peering over the bedding. "Contain? Not kill?"

"Both... but he's not sure he can kill on his own. He's not had a good run of luck so far."

"Which is why you're here and my husband and his men are at the other village. Wonderful. Just wonderful. Fisk it. Well, you're right. This does just keep getting worse, doesn't it?"

Mariah edged closer to the bed. "M'am? What... what happened? We were told you lost two of your men..."

"This is all Xandros' fault. Every last bit of it. Damn him."

"His fault? He couldn't have known, pits, *we* didn't know until... barely two days ago."

Evalia put her hands on her stomach and hugged herself again, cursing just at a bare whisper. "Well if he hadn't left me in this state then maybe that *thing* out there wouldn't have killed them while we were out there... watched it rip one of their heads clean off, couldn't do a damn thing to stop it. I tore the damn thing to bloody shreds but it took a lot out of... Now I can't even... *fisk!*"

The apprentice alchemist scooted ever closer, and looked down at the battlemage, frowning. When the realization hit her, it hit like a kick from a mule. "Oh blessed be! It *IS* his fault! Oh fisk. Ohhh *fisk.*"

"Damn... idiot... men!"

"Fisk! Well, that's not going to do anyone any good. No. You can't fight, you can't go back out there. There is no way. *Gods*, and you were supposed to be able to help." Mariah took a few steps away and then banged her head on the wall a few times to try to clear her mind enough to think. "Can't let you, won't let you. Not in your shape."

Glowering, Evalia tried to hide a scoff. "Are you an alchemist or a midwife?

"Where I live? It's the same thing."

With a grimace, the battlemage sat back up on the edge of the bed. "The cramps hit just before.. that... *thing* barreled out of a cave. I was... throwing up when it landed. It took the sod of a militiaman apart with a single swipe of its claws. It... it was a bear. I think. But it was wrong. Had things growing out of its face. Arms, tentacles. Watched it take Lieutenant Thorogoud's heart out of his chest."

"That... that sounds like what we've been facing," Mariah sighed after thinking for a minute. "Was it just the one? Are you sure it's gone?"

"I am sure that you will find pieces of it for half a mile in every direction from that cave. Took me three hours to get the smell off of me. If it isn't gone, I don't wish to stay here."

She swallowed hard. "M'am? Did you burn the corpses?"

"What?"

"Did you burn them? Akaran's been *really* insistent about that."

Evalia turned and buried her head in a pillow. "Yes, we burned them. I take it that was more important than I knew?"

"Yeah." Mariah rubbed her hands together and stared at the mage, losing herself briefly in thought. *I don't pray to the Gods but I'm starting to think I need to make an exception. Pregnant... for the sake of the Mount, she's pregnant.*

Evalia beat her to saying anything more. "Fisk. So there's a creature out there and it's killing people and I can't do a fisking thing about it because my fisking husband didn't want to pull his cock out and now I'm... I'm..." Her face started to crumble and her lip quivered just a little. "I'm a *soldier*, not a *mother!*"

"You're a woman, a wife. It is your duty to bear an heir to your husband."

"*Duty?*" she grumbled. "Maybe. But now? What little fisking good does that fisking do right now? There's a threat and I can't...! What are you and that priest you're traveling with going to do?"

She gave the only answer she could. "I'm... I'm going to hope he's having better luck."

He wasn't.

It was a dungeon. While Mariah had gotten to go into the manor, Akaran's destination went into the caves in the rear of the city and down several far-too-long corridors until he felt like he was in the center of the planet. Oil-soaked torches gave him just enough light to see the errand-boy ahead of him who was serving as his guide.

If you've seen one, you've seen them all. It had rough walls fashioned out of large stones held together by crumbling mortar. There were a handful of cells with wrought-iron bars and cots chained to the wall. The chains for the cots were also made of wrought iron, and the chains and cuffs and assorted restraints in the cells were the same.

The cells were empty, shy one, though there was fresh blood glistening in the torchlight on the floor. He didn't even want to think about what had happened to the sod that had been strapped on that particular sawhorse, and he *really* didn't spend any great length of time looking at the shining puddle under it. While he resisted the sick urge to touch it or look at it, it was nagging at him that he might – just maybe – want to take some steps to sanctify the dismal pit when this was all over.

Just to be safe.

The one cell that wasn't empty held an utterly unexpected gift: a woman sprawled out on a cot, wearing a tattered blue robe and what was probably the thinnest cotton blanket that Akaran had ever seen. Her black hair was greasy and caked with dirt, and her skin was mottled with bruises on her arms and one slowly healing on the back of her jaw. Most people wouldn't call a woman in such a state a gift, but in this case...

"You deserve every bit of this."

She raised her head up off of the cot and blinked groggily at him. "So good to see you too."

"I really doubt that."

"Not even a hello? I did give you a sword to fight that thing."

Akaran crossed his arms and just glared daggers at her. "How about a noose, Rmaci?"

The widow (and murderer) of the now-deceased innkeeper and owner of the Rutting Goat sat up and hunched over, hands pressed tight to her right side. "Would the pain stop?"

"Considering what you did? Doubt it."

"The voices?"

He didn't move an inch. "Doubt that, too. What voices?"

"You're not helping. They're not helping. Nobody is helping."

"You're a murderess and a traitor to the crown. Helping you isn't high on my to-do list. Anyone that *does* help you is just as guilty of betraying the rightful ruler of Dawnfire."

Rmaci looked up at him, pain etched on her face. "Murderess, yes, but I never betrayed my Empress. Never. Never did. Did so much in her name, did so much for the true crown, for her crown."

The smirk came unbidden. "Distinction noted. So. You couldn't have been arrested for what you did in Toniki. Why *are* you here? Why didn't you run?"

"Apparently the city guard doesn't like people begging for help and crying about the souls of the damned wailing in her ears. They don't listen. The souls expect you to listen, but they don't listen. They don't listen to me. None of them do."

He frowned and walked a little closer to her cell. He didn't see anything more than bruises and a few scrapes. "Wailing of damned souls, huh? Wouldn't a visit to the temple been more worth your time than a visit to the dungeon?"

She shook her head vehemently. "I tried. They wouldn't let me in. Said their Priestess forbade it. Someone called for the guard as I was trying to get there and they stopped me and they brought me here. I kept telling them that no, there was a demon, but they didn't listen. They said they've heard it from all of the refugees but they didn't care. They won't even send someone to... is that why you're here? Did they send for you? Please, did they?"

"I came looking for Daringol and Makolichi. Hunting demons and found a bitch."

"I missed you too. Please. Please, can you help me? I can't... it burns. I can't get it out. It needs to come out. It *burns*."

Akaran snorted. "Save the act for someone that knows better. If you're going to whine about things burning, I'd really get used to it, if I were you."

"I know, I know, you think I'm lying. I'm not. I'm not lying. I've lied to you before. Not now. *Please* help. *Please*. I know you can sense by touch. That's all I want. Just sense. Please. Touch me."

"Forgive me if I'm no longer so inclined to eagerly do that," he snarled, then reluctantly, he relented. "Dammit. Fine. Understand this: I'm fine with you right here. I'm going to humor you, then I'm going to leave and let you rot. This is a duty. Nothing more, nothing less."

"Duty. I... yes. I do understand duty."

He continued to give her a withering look. "I'm sure you do. Come here, and give me your hand."

With a half-choked laugh, Rmaci made her way across the cell and slipped her hand through the bars. "Don't deny you won't get some pleasure from touching me."

The priest turned around without giving her a second glance. "Goodbye."

"WAIT!" she shouted, at the absolute top of her lungs. The desperation behind it was the truest thing he had ever heard out of her mouth. "No, please. Please don't go. I'm not lying. I'm not. You know I'm not."

"I didn't think you're lying, I just don't think I care," he muttered, then turned to take her hand in his. "*Illuminate,*" he whispered, the Word leaving his lips with a glow that coursed down his arm and over his fingers – where it promptly leapt into her body with upsetting results. The spell made her glow inside and out just about everywhere.

It was the 'just about' that caused the problem.

Rmaci tensed up as the light hit a part of her in her core and exposed a squirming mass of tentacles coiling around her heart and stomach. Long tendrils floated inside her, some going down her legs and around her sex; others were slowly climbing up through her neck. As the light coursed into her, the tentacles began to thrash and spasm. Most of the tendrils pulled themselves back into the floating core buried deep in her chest.

She couldn't see all of it, but what she saw was enough. "OH GODDESS OH ILLIYA GET IT OUT GET IT OUT!"

Any and all doubts Akaran might have had were gone before she could even start to scream. He shouted "*EXPULSE!*" at the top of his lungs. The tainted blob in her core tensed up like someone had just thrown it into a wall. A few desperately searching tendrils pushed out from inside her body, only crack and shatter as the spell took hold. "*ILLUMINATE,*" was the next word that slipped out of his lips. It served to reinforce the effects from the prior incarnation.

Both of them could see the nesting wraith shudder and fall in on itself. Some tentacles lost cohesion; the core itself shrunk to lump half the size of a fist. It didn't fade completely though. The tighter the coils wrapped, the darker the fog became until it was nothing more than a squirming mass of inky darkness.

Shit. It's latched on. Bet it thinks her black heart is a damn fine meal. Shit, shit, shit. Trying to put on a false front of confidence, he helped guide her down to the floor. "Do you feel any different? Any better?"

"It's... quieter," she whimpered, tears trickling down her face. "Quieter. Burns, oh it burns. It's not gone. Please make it go. Please make it go. I'll confess. Anything. Everything. Everyone. I'm Civan. Reported everything I could find to my handlers. I killed Ronlin Yothargi Mowiat, stole, lied about where I was from, lied about why I moved to Toniki, lied to you, I did it, did all of it. *PLEASE* get it out of me!"

"I can't."

The pain and desperation in Rmaci's eyes flashed to anger the second he said it. "Can't? You can't? You... you excise! That's what you do! Can't or won't? Do you hate me? Hate me so much? I spared your life! Save mine!"

He stopped her with a hand on her shoulder in a sad attempt to comfort her. "Not a question of *if* I can save you. I *can* save you. But I can't right now. I don't have what I need. Daringol... it's nested in you. That's what things like it do. They nest. It's nesting in you. It's trying to take over your soul."

"My... soul? It's... it's not just killing me, it's...?!"

"It's trying to turn you into one of it." He closed his eye and inwardly ran through the list of everything he'd need to deal with it and came up with a shopping list that didn't sit well. *Blessed be the Goddess. I need quartz, I need black tourmaline, I need copper filings... can I even FIND tourmaline here? Would the local temple have it?*

The anger flashed back to raw desperation and tears. "Please. Please get it. Please, there has to be something you can do."

Akaran watched the last of the glow fade from her body and cursed under his breath. "There is," he groused as he stood up and turned to the stairs that lead out of the dungeon. "**JAILER!**"

"What...?"

About the only way you could describe the man that walked down the stairs was to call him a slob. He didn't look like he had bathed in a month, his teeth were yellow and slightly crooked, his brown hair was a greasy mess, and his uniform had more stains on it than you'd see on a battlefield surgeon. "What is it, priest?"

"By order of the Temple of Love, nobody – *nobody* – is to come down here without my, and only my, express permission. Give me your keys, then go fetch me a cask of oil, a flagon of wine, and two thick blankets, and bring them here as quickly as you can."

If he cared about the order, or that this boy was giving him one, he didn't look like it. "Fine. Whatever you do to the woman, I don't want to know about it or hear any more of her screaming. She's keeping us from enjoying our game upstairs."

"Not even going to ask?"

"Nope."

The priest didn't know how to act around someone that was being agreeable, so he just stood there, looking a little deflated. "Well... good. Thank you."

As soon as the guard shrugged and stomped back up the steps, Rmaci looked back up at the exorcist and tried to choke a question through her tears. "Promise me, promise me you'll get rid of it?"

"I'll banish it. I can't let it get a foothold outside of Toniki. It'll spread like a plague."

"You're just... you're afraid it'll spread...? Is that all you care about? Not what it's doing, done to me? After everything?"

Akaran blinked and looked at her, almost dumbfounded. "What everything? You intended to kill me, you worked against the people of Toniki, you worked against the Queen, you tried to use me for your own interests. *You played me.*"

"But I didn't kill you!"

"That doesn't get you a free pass," he shot back, exasperated. "You didn't kill me because you recognize what kind of nightmare might happen and how it could spread if that demon could get his hands on the coldstone... whatever it is... that Usaic was cooking up. Nothing more, nothing less. You didn't want to be responsible for Makolichi going on a rampage and killing any more innocents."

There wasn't much that Rmaci could say to argue that, and she knew it. "I... suppose it doesn't matter. You'll be rid of me one way or another soon enough."

He didn't give her the satisfaction of an answer right away. He slipped a knife out of his belt and began to carve runes into the floor near her cage. "We can do this one of two ways. I can excise it, and it'll hurt, and it'll take me some time to find what I need. Didn't think it would be that strong in anything infected this far away from its core. If I do, you'll talk. You'll give the Captain Orin a list of any contacts you might have in the Kingdom, anyone that works for you or whom you've paid off for more information. You'll do it without an argument."

"What's the other way?"

"I kill you, now, and try to make it as painless as I can. When you die, the wraith will either die with you or it'll be forced to manifest and I can banish it directly. It'll try to drag your soul along for the ride, but let's be honest, you're both going to end up in the same place afterwards."

She had to try not to laugh in defeat and failed. "I'm as good as dead either way."

"You've turned traitor once. I can speak for you, negotiate with the local Justiciar. You still might get out of this alive if you do."

Rmaci shook her head. "Yeah. 'Might.' Or they might make an example out of me."

"One is a certainty," he said with a shrug, then moved on to the third rune on the ground. "The other is a possibility. If nothing else, you'll get time to repent your sins for the latter."

"I've only done what I had to do in service of the Empress, in service of Illiyia."

The priest didn't buy it. "You're not a zealot, Rmaci. You know as well as I do that the Mount isn't always forgiving of murder, even in matters of defending one's country."

"I don't think any of us know that for certain. They might. They might not."

He thought about it for a minute, then slowly cut the top of his left arm open. As blood welled up, he coated his blade in it and watched it glisten in the torchlight. "They might. Right now you've got a damned soul feeding on yours. As much as it hurts now, imagine how bad it will hurt if they might not."

Rmaci went silent as he traced a very small rune on the lock to her cell door with the tip of the knife, smearing blood on the iron. "I... I can't denounce Bimaria. Can't denounce Illiya. You... you can't yours. I can't mine. Promise me you'll get me safe passage out, and I'll tell you everything about everyone."

"Only if you swear on the name of your Goddess that you will hold nothing back. I won't negotiate passage for you to Civa. Mathiea, maybe. Or Sycio. Not Civa. They won't want you back after you expose your handlers, so take that as a blessing you don't deserve."

Her mouth fell open. "You ask me to turn, and then you won't even let me go home to repent?"

"You go home and nobody's gonna know what you did or how you got out. Tell them you escaped on the way to the gallows, or that someone else ratted you out to the Queen. You'll be forgiven, and that's *after* you tell them *all* about the coldstone. That's not a punishment, and you *deserve* a punishment. Besides. Once you're in Mathiea, you might find a way to get back to your homeland. I'm just refusing to give you an easy trip. By the time you do, Bimaria won't be able to reach the stone unless she makes it down to the capitol in person."

"You're an absolute bastard."

"Wish I could say either way. Are we in agreement or not?"

"You're still a bastard. Yes. I... I don't have a choice, do I?"

Akaran shook his head. "You don't. And they say that Civans are fools. You've proved that much wrong, at least."

She seethed at him as she cursed. "A very big bastard."

He shrugged and opened her cell, leaving the door open with his back turned to her as he began drawing another diagram, a larger one, on the back and side wall. "Don't touch the runes. If you do, the shock that they give Daringol may just kill you."

"Trapping me in a prison within a prison?"

"Containment. I don't know how long it'll take it to get its strength back. Could be a few days. Could be a few hours. Could be less than that. I'm sure it doesn't think you're a safe place anymore. It might even give up on you and try to get free as soon as it can get enough strength. I can't risk it getting out."

Rmaci stared at his back and the open door. "Can't risk it and you leave my door open...? I could kill you right now and..."

135

"...and then die horribly, screaming, feeling your body burn itself into a black floating husk from the inside out, which is why I know you won't. How did you even get exposed? Yothargi came back to Toniki the morning after you knifed him, so I doubt it was him, was it?"

"It was... after... after him. Was almost at the edge of the snow, down where it was starting to warm up. Saw something come out of the dark at me. It grabbed me, caught my arm. I cut it with my knife. It didn't like the fire that it was enchanted with."

That was slightly unexpected. "Surprising. They whine so much about the cold."

She continued on with her voice at a near-whisper. "It... it flew off. I ran the other way."

"Don't know if that makes you lucky or not."

Before she could remark, the slob of a jailer returned with two other equally-slovenly guardsmen that were carrying a cask of oil. He looked at the open cell and didn't bother asking what he was doing while he held up the blankets and the flagon of wine. "Here's what you asked for. Don't even bother to explain, none of us care."

"At least you're agreeable." The jailer scoffed while Akaran came over and cracked open the top of the cask. While they watched, he walked it into Rmaci's cell and dumped half of it on the floor. The spy cursed in surprise and scrambled up onto the cot while the soldiers moved up to the safety of the stairwell.

Growling, the jailer crossed his arms and looked at the glowing torches on either side of the dungeon. "Dammit. *Now* I'm going to have to ask what the pits you think you're doing making a mess of my prison."

Akaran turned back to look at him and shrugged. "Fairly simple. If anyone walks down here they're going to leave tracks and they'll smell like oil. It'll help let me know who needs to be tossed into this dank hole next to her on charges of gross insubordination."

His charge looked down at the puddle of oil on the floor and had to give him a *little* credit. "That's... surprisingly, that's a decent idea."

"Whatever," the jailer snarked, completely unimpressed. "You made her your responsibility. I don't care. They don't care. Let her rot. No skin off of our backs."

"Good," he snapped back. He took the blankets from the guard and then tossed them, and the flagon of wine, onto Rmaci's cot before closing the door to her cell. "I'll be back for you as soon as I can find what I need and think about what exactly I'm going to do with that thing in you."

She hung her head and pleaded with him. "Please. Please hurry. I can't, I just..."

Akaran didn't feel a damn bit of pity for her. "No. You lied to everyone about serving Civa for years. You can pretend you're not dying until I get back. It'll be another few hours."

Rmaci bit her tongue and hugged the blankets close to her chest. "What are these for? Some other mystical trick up your sleeve?"

"You didn't kill me. You even saved my life. I owe you for that. This is me paying off that debt."

While she looked up – completely taken aback by the kindness after everything he had said – he shrugged and left the dungeon without giving her another thought. That, unfortunately for her, was not the end of it. The two guards that had come down with her jailer followed the priest upstairs, leaving her alone with the slob.

A multitude of long minutes later, and he finally broke the silence. "So. Civan spy bitch in our city, huh? And that pissant is gonna take some hours getting back?"

Her eyes went wide as she realized what that look on his face meant. "He said nobody is to come in here, nobody."

"Like I care what some stupid priest says," he grunted, lifting a spare key off of his belt and walking into the dungeon. "I already smell like oil. He ain't gonna know shit. Now you and me? Guess we need something to do to pass the time 'till he gets back."

He smiled wider, and slid the key into the lock.

Rmaci didn't even bother trying to cry for help.

❋ ❋ ❋

Elsewhere, another story was unfolding that would both confirm things that had been suspected, and add an extra wrinkle to the mix. In the ice tunnels between Usaic's cabin and Teboria Lake, Steelhom paced around concentric circles and runes he had both carved and burned into the floor around the central figure in the room – the giant statue dedicated to Usaic's daughter, and where waters from Tundrala trickled into the mortal world.

"I am intrigued." It was the first thing he had said out-loud in the last hour and a half.

Hirshma, on the other hand, had not been so quiet. She had been ignored, but not so quiet. "Horrified. That madman."

Hovering near one of Akaran's wards (to the irritation of the paladin), Eos'eno added her own take. Again. For the tenth time in the last hour. Steelhom had come to the decision that she could hear a gnat have intestinal gas for all the things she had commented on that he had only said just barely in a muttered whisper. "He wasn't mad. Never mad. Sad. Lost. Lonely."

"A madman that defiled the body of his daughter. There's nothing you can say to make that any different."

"No, there isn't," Steelhom agreed – then promptly brushed it off. "Putting that aside, this is... well. I am intrigued. The portal to your real home is *here*, and he's using... well, used... it to power his spell that he has in his tower. I'm not sure as to the why. It would be safer to have it where he's working, not... how far away *is* the lake from here? For that matter, how is *this* portal transferring energy to it?"

When he wanted her to respond, of course, she was quiet. Finally, she broke her silence after he watched her float nearly motionless for a solid five minutes. "The water that comes from this font comes from home. It conducts Mother's essence. It aids the magic that hides his magic that hides his tower."

"So it serves as a conduit. So it travels from here to the lake and here to the fountain in Toniki. Goddess only knows where else. So what did he do? Did he find a tunnel or something underground? Some way to... pipe the water from here to there?"

"I... I am not sure. I know that it was soon after he brought me into this world that master set the path for the ice to flow. I know that it does not go over the world, it is under. He spent many days in the bottom of our home and channeled the cold into the ground below."

Steelhom started to scratch at his chin absentmindedly, but the alchemist spoke up before he could complete his own thought. "Water expands when it gets cold, he could... Could he have carved out a pass in the ground by forcing water to ice, to expand and crack the stones, then melt it and refreeze it again and again?"

"He wouldn't have to even pick up a shovel," the paladin mused. "Water flows downhill, and it would make sense that he could easily feed it towards Toniki in a small stream. Or anywhere else he wanted. Just a single crack at a time."

Eos added a little more to confirm where his thoughts were going. "I know that for a time, master had me roam the woods and carry a rod of divining as I went. He made me tell him wherever it trembled. An odd thing, that. A rod to divine water. He should have simply asked me; it would have been so much faster."

"Then that's how. That's the only thing that makes sense. Not that much of this does, be of mind. When this is resolved I do fear that there will be a pile of Granalchi that will move into the mountains to investigate this for years. I'm not sure how I should feel about that."

Hirshma had her own thoughts on that (to the surprise of nobody). "Pity. You should feel pity. It's either going to be priests or the army or the Granalchi. Wizards or pious bastards or soldiers. Usaic and... you... you're to blame for all of this," she sighed, glaring at the wisp. "Yes. Pity us."

"I've done nothing to hurt you. Nothing, nothing to feel sad or guilt. I protected. Much as I could. I did his wishes."

"You don't feel bad for what you've done? Guilty?"

The wisp's skin bristled with crystals. "Guilty? For what cause? I am as the Mother bade me to be."

Steelhom tried to calm Hirshma's simmering temper, with about as much luck as he'd been having the last few days. "She is the direct creation of the Divine. A true child of the Goddess of Ice and no, this is not her fault. I am intrigued, not horrified. Though, I can see why you are."

"Aren't you the child of yours? Aren't all of you? The Gods gave you life each and all. Doesn't that make you children like me?" Eos asked, plain and simply not able to understand why everyone seemed so upset with her all the time.

Hirshma's response was as biting as she could be. "If that's true, then my 'Mother' only brought suffering and grief to my family."

"Surely not? Kora'thi gave you home, family, ability to better the world. To create and repair. That is a boon. That is not suffering, not grief."

"She took my daughter, my father, and let my home and brother -"

Flicking a crystal from her arm and into the faint scuffs of ice below her feet, the wisp disagreed. "You lost the latter by actions his own, and inactions yours. If the Guardian of Winters had been told years past, you'd have half of your losses. I tried, and I called, but ice is at times so slow. Men are faster. Your family was not taken by Mother. They were removed through hubris. Greed. Hate."

Steelhom looked up from the runes and measurements on the ground and tried to make sense of that. "A few years back and my student would have been learning how to swing a sword. It wasn't so much that it was slow as it was simply not his time to even take up a blade in service of Love. If you called for help then? He couldn't be this 'Guardian of Winters' you keep saying he is."

"Does it matter? Aren't you working on making that bastard's tower visible?" the alchemist groused, still refusing to take her glare off of Eos'eno.

"When the spawn of the divine gives someone a name, it is wise to find out why."

"It... she wears the skin of my daughter. That... makes... that makes her mine. Not somebody's else's. Istalla can choke for all I care."

"You'd speak ill of Mother? After all she has allowed to be done?"

"What things would that be?" Hirshma snapped.

Less and less amused by the argument the longer it went on, Steelhom snapped back at them and pressed the wisp back to his question. "Bicker later. Again, girl? His title?"

She took a deep breath and tried to calm herself. "Mother said She would send a man to protect master's works, to guard them from harm. It merely took longer than even ice should move."

"That didn't concern you?"

"Be worried? Of course, man of Love. All should know that yet for all their power, glaciers are slow. Ice is patient. I am patient. I must be so, even when I wish otherwise. It is the nature of ice."

Hirshma dimly remembered something that Akaran had told her a few days prior and added it to the mix. "Didn't he say something about a dead guy in the mine?"

The paladin gave a short nod. "Several, but yes. I know the one you mean. He said it was a Steward of Ice, yes?"

This was something that Eos'eno, apparently, had not realized. "Mother sent a Steward? How could that be, without him making contact with me...?"

"Why would the steward go to the mine to begin with? I've never heard of any man from any order visiting in years."

"I can only imagine," Steelhom answered, frowning at Hirshma. "No. Wait. I can do more than that. Alchemist, have you ever studied sylverine ore before?"

"I've studied every plant, rock, and animal in the province. What of it?"

"Then you know that the reason the Queen cherishes it is because of how it can magnify mystical energy."

It was Eos'eno's turn for a nod. "Yes. I am aware of the power, even if she is not."

He strummed his fingers on his arm again and looked her up and down. "Eos? Where was it that you were summoned?"

Hirshma frowned at the idea. "Summoned? You don't think he defiled my daughter in a *mine*, do you? Underground, in the dark?"

"I was not summoned. I was given. Born into this flesh. What... what was left of it."

Steelhom made it a point to respond before Hirshma could. The idea that there wasn't much left of her daughter made her face go pale and her mind reel in horror. "Summoned, gifted, born, created. Where?"

Then, of course, Eos confirmed it, making the horror in the alchemist's mind take an even darker turn. "Yes. Underground, in a cave. I remember it so clear. Rocks a dead brown, no moss no life to be found. But Mother's voice was there. It echoed and sang and stones inside and outside the body of the rock sang with Her in a glorious cascade of music. Amber stones adorned the walls of the cave, some in carts, some embedded in the rock still."

"Sylverine ore. So. Bolintop Mine. The steward went to where you were born, and ended up dead. And you have spent three years now waiting for help that never came because of it."

"It came! It is here, was here. The Guardian of Winters -"

"Got killed and nobody thought to tell you," the alchemist snapped. "And I used to believe that *my* mother was worthless."

Eos'eno bristled at the accusation, for the umpteenth time. "Worthless?! No! Mother brings peace, serenity, preservation! She allows for snow to fall in the mountains so that rivers may swell in spring! Her breath keeps the balance between growth too much and growth too little! Her fingers brush away swarms of the foulest insects and herds of beasts! She -"

"Might not have known," Steelhom said, a very ugly idea taking form.

Hirshma didn't buy it. "Not known? What good is a God that doesn't know what happens to Her flock?"

"If Daringol absorbed his soul, then Istalla may not have noticed..."

"What of omnipotence? She is a God, isn't She?"

Steelhom didn't dispute that – but he did offer a clarified theory. "Her magic is being corrupted and twisted on this plane. Men made this mess, men need to clean it up. The Gods tend to do that. It's one of the reasons the Order of Love is so bloody busy."

"This is just arrogance. Raw arrogance. On your part, on Theirs, on Usaic's."

"It may well be. Or it may be She knew one of Her priests is ill-equipped to win this battle, after Hers died, and so She waited for someone capable to arrive. For now, however, we need to address this in different way."

The wisp was ill-amused by any of it. "I am unsure I wish to continue to give aid to those whom disparage mother so openly. I may just wait for the Guardian to return. He knows, he knows what Mother can or cannot do. He spent time in Her home."

That was something that the priest wouldn't stomach, and he, at least, had the authority to do something about it. "No, wisp, you won't. You will, however, show me where you entered our world."

"Where I was brought will not help. Does it matter where I was brought? Does it matter the how? No. It is not me you fight against. Why are you not more in desire to find where the other was given passage to this world?"

He frowned and was slightly taken aback. "Makolichi? I assumed he would have been summoned from the same place as you. Actually, surprised your creation wasn't done in the tower, where he would have been able to control outside factors more. Equally surprised this breach into the elemental planes is this far away from it as it is..."

"Assume. You assume, when you could question? Why? Why not ask the one that would know? I am here. Why would you assume that a soul born of Tundrala would be given a door in the same place as a creature dredged out from the sea of the Brineblood?"

Steelhom walked closer to her, the frown deepening the more she evaded the question. "Then answer this: What makes you think that I would need to see where he is from, instead of you?"

She couldn't believe he was being that dense. "I was freely given out of love and desire by Mother. Master had to seek out a place of miserable agony to channel the foul stench of the Brineblood into your world. Yet, a place where none would come to further hurt nor harm, where he could stake his claim on him."

"You make it sound like he had to fight to conjure him," Hirshma said, chewing on her lower lip.

"He did."

That frown the paladin had somehow managed to get even more pronounced. "He did? Why? You've already said that Istalla wanted his work to be completed?"

Eos sighed with all the frustration of a parent teaching a child to speak. "And that is why. Mother wished it, so Zell did not. A bargain had to be made; an offering given. What it was, I do not know. I did not know where he crossed over until... recently."

"Recently? When?"

"The night that the Guardian departed. You are not the only one with questions with odd answers."

Hirshma blinked a few times in semi-surprise that the wisp would be searching for explanations too. "What did you find?"

"I found the place where that the Brineblood allowed my counterpart to surface. I found latent things that master had set to protect himself while he did his work. I... I recognize them now. I never..." She paused and suddenly looked less patronizing and more distinctly uncomfortable. "I don't... I love my lord, he is mine as I was given to him as and..."

"His touch is darker than you thought?" Steelhom suggested.

"His touch is his touch. It... it takes time for one to come to understand the strength of a touch or the things a touch can do. That is all. That is why I did not say sooner. It is because I... I..."

Toniki's last surviving elder gave a snort of derision. "Realizing he's a monster is hard for you, is it?"

The wisp pulled herself to her full height, her eyes almost flashing with anger. "Not a monster! He is not a monster!"

"He defiled his daughter's corpse and summoned a demon," Hirshma snapped back. "What do you call that?"

Steelhom looked back at the statue and took a gamble on a course of action. "I call that worth exploring. Eos, where is it?"

"This I will show you. It will take some time to get there. You will need more men with you."

"I will? Why?"

"Because I know your ways, man of Love. I simply know. I will go and check the spells above, ensure that nothing has come near. You, I believe and imagine, will need to do the same here, yes?"

He gave a nod in response and folded his arms over again while he stared at and studied the statue. The moment he felt she was comfortably out of earshot, he addressed the elephant in the room. "Hirshma?"

"Yes?"

"Take three of Xandros's men to Bolintop when we leave. I'll give you a couple of things that will show if there's a breach that my student may have missed. I doubt he would have looked for it if he thought it was just a few *corpusals*. *I* wouldn't have thought to look for one. They were there for a reason, and Eos doesn't seem enthralled with the idea of us digging around."

Hirshma had to agree. "That to me is all the more reason that we need to search it thoroughly."

"It is. Though I will not lie: I have a sinking feeling that there's much more where she's taking me that I am going to want to know."

He was right.

Oh, he was right.

VI. MUDSLIDE

After dealing with Rmaci, there was exactly one thing that Akaran wanted to do. And since he couldn't do *that*, he had to settle for getting food. He had debated if he should or not from the moment the thought popped into his head to the minute he was within range to smell the delightful odors wafting out of the first decent-looking tavern he had come across. Ultimately, he accepted that he had put down enough wards to keep Daringol contained for the time being.

And if Rmaci suffered from the wraith while she waited for him to come back?

Let the wraith torment her soul for a bit. Murderess, traitor, spy... she'll be lucky if that's all she suffers, he groused, oblivious to what was going on in her cell even now. *So if Daringol isn't able to get loose, I can take the time to get a bowl of stew.*

As luck would have it, the Golden Kiln was exactly where he needed to be at exactly the right time. The tavern was crowded with assorted rabble – everything from merchants to potters to off-duty guardsmen and everything in-between. It was a trio of the 'in-betweens' that made his visit so memorable, and so important.

All of the travel – the cold, the wet, the shit-covered streets and that musty dungeon – had done absolutely nothing for his sinuses. Every breath was starting to feel like it took twice as much effort as normal, and one nostril was completely clogged. So he consoled himself with a piping hot bowl of "Balatorb frog with abalstic-salt for seasoning," or so the bartender had claimed.

Don't know what it is, gonna pray for the best... please, please Niasmis, let it be for the best...

Truth was? It was brown, slightly oily on top, and the shredded cabbage that was there just to garnish it (because it sure as all did nothing to improve the taste). The salt gave it a bit of a hot tinge to each spoonful, and it didn't taste bad, it just... it didn't taste great. Ignoring the look of it, the steam from the bowl was helping ease a headache that was related in equal parts to both the weather and Rmaci.

Then two men slid into the booth opposite him and interrupted his meal without so much of an apology. "So, you're that priest that everyone's been talking all about. Look a bit younger than I expected."

Akaran looked up from his stew and gave a disinterested stare to his unwelcome guests. The first of the two could have blended in with any crowd in the city. In any city. He had the air of a merchant, and the body of an overweight one. There really wasn't much to say about him that would make him stand out in a crowd – his chestnut brown hair was coupled with a receding hairline, and his russet-brown eyes were bloodshot around the edges. "Who are you?"

The portly man smiled wide at him. "A friend. A friend that would like you to meet someone interesting. This is that someone."

"I don't have any friends here," he said, sizing up the other person that had slid into the booth. He, on the other hand, *did* look interesting. Or at least, interesting in the same way you would consider a still-twitching rat that a well-meaning cat would deposit next to your boots first thing in the morning. He had a square head with pronounced cheekbones and a flared nose. "And he doesn't look like he's much of a someone to be interested in."

"Ah. Judging him just because he hasn't taken a bath in an age? That's not so kind nor polite of you."

"You've interrupted my lunch. I don't feel inclined to be polite."

This drew a short laugh from the supposed merchant, who stepped his hands together and set them down on top of the table. "Not that I suppose I can blame you. But tell me, wouldn't you like a friend?"

Akaran rolled his eye and started to stand up. He hadn't seen the third man come up behind him – and *this* fine specimen looked like he should be in the army. Actually, as big as he was, he looked like he could *be* an army. "No."

"But friends are useful. If you have friends, you can sometimes meet interesting people. As I said, I'd like to introduce you to one of those people."

"Really don't care. May I finish my meal, please?"

With a short chortle, the man that now had his undivided attention (irritating as it was) flashed him an even bigger smile that had absolutely no warmth to it at all. "Oh but you will care. Priest, this is Thadius. Thadius, priest." He looked at the sad excuse for a human next to him while the merchant cleared his throat. "Hm. That reminds me. A name. I assume you have one?"

"Akaran. Akaran DeHawk. Yours?"

"At the moment, it isn't important. Just call me 'friend.' So. While my name isn't important, yours, oh, yours is. That *is* an interesting name, Akaran, Akaran DeHawk. Well. I'd like you to meet Thadius. Thadius here is what we common people like to call a moron. Isn't that right, Thadius?"

Thadius nervously looked at Akaran's new 'friend' and then at the thug behind the priest and nervously stuttered through half-clenched, yellow teeth. "Y... yes, yes that's right, a, a mor... moron."

"Morons are useful in the right circumstances," his friend began to explain. "You see, *this* moron thought it would be wise to try to liberate some imprisoned gold coins from the pocket of one my most trusted associates. That's him, behind you. He likes to break people. Not the smartest man in the province but he does know a good opportunity when someone sticks a hand in his pants, like Thadius here did."

"Ye... yes, yes that's me, moron, did a wrong thing, a bad thing, won't be doin' it again..."

The merchant calmly put his hand on Thadius's shoulder and nodded. The boy (he couldn't be more than seventeen) flinched in fear. "No, you won't, though I imagine the idea will pass through your head at some point or other if you make it through this. Because, well, you are a moron."

At war with himself to feel trapped or annoyed, the exorcist settled for feigning boredom. "Is there a point to this conversation...?"

"You're an impatient one, aren't you? I happen to like that. Shows you have things to do. I sense they're important things, and as much as I hate to burden a new friend with troubles, I must insist that you listen. You will want to listen."

"I don't think I have a choice, do I?"

His friend just continued to smile and adjusted the front of his padded wool coat that had been dyed an atrocious shade of burnt-sienna. "You see, Thadius here has now entered my employ, as a way to... apologize... for his transgressions. One of the things that I like to have him do is to go follow guard patrols just to see what might be going on and about this fair city. Sometimes they get angry and send him back with a few bumps and bruises. Sometimes not. This last time, a full patrol of Dawnfire's men went out skulking towards the mountains, and split away from a fierce little filly who went trudging into the woods down-river."

"Yes, I'm familiar with both of them."

"I am sure that you are. Now, I assume you know already, I am quite sure, that the soldiers that broke away from the pack and stayed here in Gonta went to go hunt a monster out in the wilds. The battlemage with them – her name is Evalia, though again I assume that you know it? Evalia did find a beast and promptly vanquished it to the nether-realms on her brief little sojourn through the Slag and returned back to the city proper without finding a certain thing that I believe is worth noting."

Akaran shrugged and tried to hide his surprise at the news. "You'll forgive me if I don't confirm nor deny the goings-on of the military with you." *Evalia found and killed whatever came down from Toniki? Is there ANY chance I could be so lucky that she caught Makolichi somehow...?*

"Thadius, in a sheer shocking round of brilliancy, did."

That, on the other hand, was something that he couldn't just feign surprise over. "He did? What?"

"He found a rock, as cold as Istalla's tit. Strange enough, it glows. Smells like the inside of a barrel of rotten fish. Odd, wouldn't you say?"

The foci! He couldn't have hid his reaction if he had tried. "Where is it? Do you have it on you?"

His new friend raised his hand slightly and gestured for the priest to calm down a little. "It's hidden away for the time being. Wasn't so sure what could be done with it, whom someone could trust to serve the best interests of the Queen. Just a matter of being friends with the right person, you see."

"Hand it to me and I won't care where you put it. I won't care how you found it. I just need to know where and who came into contact with it to the best of your knowledge."

"I already told you the 'how' and the 'who.' The where is... it's safe, as safe as I can make it right now. I assure you."

Akaran shook his head vehemently. "There isn't a safe place for it. That's what I'm trying to tell you."

The merchant cleared his throat while Thadius continued to look incredibly uncomfortable. "Which is why I decided to reach out to you, as a... gesture of friendship. All these soldiers mucking about, special from the local garrison? They are a bit problematic for a man of my trade. Now an exorcist is in town? Well. Now that is just simply bad for business for *everybody*. But it is business, my boy – and so I'm willing to make a little trade, if you are."

"I need that rock. You *need* to give it to me."

He nodded in open agreement. "I do, actually. Quite aware of that fact. I also need a favor. Two, in fact. The first one is easy enough; I simply need you to owe me one."

With a blink, Akaran tried to hide his slight confusion. "The favor is... that I owe you a favor?"

"Yes. A debt. To be collected at another time."

"And why would you...?"

That's when the shoe dropped. "Because you're a priest. Because you're an exorcist. Because you have the authority to make other people in authority look the other way when another way needs to be looked. Because you have de-facto permission, by right of the Queen, to do what you wish when you wish, all under the guise of serving your *well-regarded* Goddess."

"Do you really think that I'll help someone like you?"

His 'friend' tried to look offended. "Like me? I am simply just a businessman."

"Like you," Akaran grunted. "A *businessman.* You *know* that attempting to extort an agent of the Crown is enough to land you in the dungeon, I'm sure."

"Yes. Now that you mention it like that, yes. I do. Just, please don't consider this the act of corruption you're casting it as. What good are laws, if there aren't people who skirt around them? I won't ask you to murder someone or unjustly have them tortured. Maybe briefly imprisoned. Or an item returned. Or... a whatnot. That's the point of a future favor. It could be nearly anything."

That's brazen. "Why shouldn't I just call for the guards? You said I can get away with anything I want. Do you want to find out?"

The portly 'businessman' just continued to smile, like he had had this conversation a thousand times over with a thousand different people. "You could. Of course, if you did, there's no promise that that lovely little thing you walked into town would walk away safely."

"Mariah? You wouldn't -"

Akaran could feel the mound of muscle behind him tensing up. "Of course I would. I am a *businessman*, as you so impressively stressed.

This is the type of thing that I do, as a manner of course. I also know that you won't send the army after me once you leave our quaint little town."

"Give me one reason why not."

"That is easy enough to answer. You are a man of honor. A man that when he gives his word or gives a promise, he will follow through on it. You *are* that kind of man, aren't you?"

He couldn't hide the growl in his throat. "You are really testing my patience."

"Delightful. You are right. I do need to get rid of this rock. I do not think it is safe to have in this town for a wide variety of reasons and I happen to enjoy my piece of real-estate in these parts. I did say two favors – this is the second one. Moron? Show the man your hand."

Thadius couldn't hide the fear on his face. If nothing else, the nervous clatter of his yellowing teeth gave it away. "Do... do I have to?"

The so-called businessman rolled his eyes at Akaran before glaring at the boy. "I told you he was a moron. Yes, Thadius, you have to."

"F... f... fine," the moron finally stuttered. After one last pleading look at Akaran's new friend and the thug behind him, he pulled the glove off of his right hand and rested it in the middle of the table. His skin was black, like it had been badly burned, with a green shine in the multitude of cracks that were open across the skin from just behind his wrist to the ends of his fingers. "I... it... it don't hurt. Looks like... like... it should hurt. Don't hurt."

He had a feeling of revulsion just looking at it. "What did you do?"

"I did say he's a -"

Akaran glanced up at him as that revulsion slowly turned into another feeling. A darker, fouler one. "You. Shut up. Thadius, what did *you* do?"

"I... I touched the rock. Picked it up, carri... carried it back, want... wanted to give it to Riorik, he wouldn't let me, said I had to take it to -"

"Think that's enough of the story. The hand was that friendly shade by the time he managed to bring it to me. Honestly I was about to kill him and have the body burned when I heard that someone capable of addressing this inconvenience that I've been burdened with just happened to walk into my territory and thus, here we are."

"Bo... boss? Kill... killed? You were gonna have me killed?"

"He's not going to enjoy what has to be done."

"He might enjoy being set on fire even less. Unless that is what you plan to do with it. Is it?"

Thadius pulled his hand back under the table and tried to pull away from both of them. "Set on fire? B... b... b... boss, you wouldn't?!"

The priest just shrugged. "Wouldn't be so sure."

The other man thought about it for a moment and gave a bit of a nod. "That may well be true. This is the favor: simply, take care of that hand."

Akaran was trapped in this, and he knew it. "Fine. I do this, and you'll give me the stone he found?"

"I think you're going to do this even if I don't. I'll give you the stone if you agree to do me that other favor sometime in the future. Make no mistake that I will call on you to honor your end of the deal one day. Businessmen like me always have need of friends in high places."

"How do I know you won't just take the rock and run?"

Thadius's boss couldn't hide a chortle. "Me? Take it? After what it did to him? I don't think so. But I will have some other adventurous soul that happens to owe me a favor go throw it into a river somewhere, or throw it into some rocky crevasse or carry it into the heart of a rival businessman's territory and leave it under his porch. Cut my losses, hope for the best, that sort of thing. I don't think that's quite the risk you want to take for me to do, now is it?"

That growl in his throat got louder. "It's... not. Fine."

"We have an accord then, do we?"

"We do, dammit."

His 'friend' smiled all the wider. "Excellent. I had a feeling you'd be wise enough to see this my way. I do have one other... minor... request."

The growl was joined by an even bigger headache than the one Rmaci had left him with. "What now?"

"I can see it in your eyes that you're thinking about doing a deed – whatever deed it is that you're thinking – right here, and now, in this bar, to help cure Thadius and somehow put me, your new friend, in a bit of a bind."

"Is it that obvious?"

The businessman cleared his throat with a small cough. "That wouldn't be... useful. Undue attention and all that. It might create a problem that I simply don't have the time to take the time to explain. I'm quite sure you understand. It's already waited a couple days. Another five minutes shouldn't cause too much of a distress. Will it?"

Akaran stared at the hand and fought the urge to take it off of his wrist there and then. *I might be able to take the guy behind me... but that's going to cause a ruckus and Goddess only knows what'll happen if I cut that hand off in front of everyone...* "Fine."

"Then it's settled. If you take Thadius off of my hands, and that disquieting skin condition off of his, I'll have that rock he found put in yours to do... whatever it is you think you need to do with it."

Defeated, an agreement was his only option. "Fine. I give my word that I will... owe you a favor." He felt bile rise up in his throat as he said it, and promised the rest. "*And* that I won't have you hung in the street."

The specific location of the execution wasn't lost on him. "Hung anywhere, if you would be so polite."

"I suppose beheaded is out of the question."

His smile somehow got even wider. "You catch on quick. The poor sod is all yours. There's just... a little thing that I may have... inadvertently forgot to mention. You see, Thadius here... I don't quite know how to say this..."

"Th... that's not my hand," Thadius managed to eek out.

Silence reigned as Akaran sat there with a stupid look on his face. "It's what?"

The merchant finally gave up the last – and incredibly important – detail. "One of the many varied and entirely astute reasons that I call Thadius here a moron is that a few years back, he was happily attempting to steal a horse-drawn carriage. The horses didn't approve of his idea and one thing lead to another and you see, his hand ended up stuck in the spokes of a wheel. Not much to do with it after that and so, one of those wonderful priests of Melia decided that the best way to save his arm was to destroy the rest of his hand. Cut it off entirely, bit halfway down from his elbow. Told it was a spot of a mess."

"Wa... wasn't fun, not a delight not fun not..." the moron stuttered while the portly crook pulled his arm up and made him lay the hand back on the table.

"Now you see one thing that seems to be so strange about all this tale, as if any of this happened to be what anyone sane would call 'normal.' Entirely outside my comfort, if I am compelled to be honest with you. He was a one-armed man for the longest time."

Akaran looked at Thadius, looked at his new friend, and looked at the hand. "He has two hands."

"*Exactly*. I can't stay that I understand the particulars any but before four days ago, Thadius *did* only have the one hand. Made a dreadful, just dreadful sound when it pulled itself out of the rock he found. Was sound asleep myself when it, well. You can only imagine the ruckus."

"That's not his hand."

"I believe we had that covered. Do hope you're not daft, boy."

The stew in front of him, that wonderful, formerly hot, formerly passable stew, suddenly lost what little attractiveness it had as the scenario played itself out in his mind. "Forgive me. It's a little... difficult... to take in. I may have died a couple of days ago. Some things are harder to process than others right now. You know the only reason I came into this tavern was because I wanted dinner, right?"

Finally, the merchant looked as off-put as he claimed he had been. "You may have...? There's not frequently something that people can be confused about. Least of all when it happens to themselves."

"I'm having a rough week."

"Well. Then it appears I may have happened by the right person to have this chat with. I suppose that now that we're all on the same page that you'll be happy to resolve this spot of trouble? Return Thadius to his rightful state as a one-armed bandit?"

Barely resisting the urge to poke at it with his spoon, Akaran didn't even look back up at them. "I still want whatever rock this hand was hiding in when this is taken care of."

"You're welcome to it. Oh, boy. Whatever you do?"

"Yes?"

"Do it quickly. The longer that rock is in my possession, the less peacefully I sleep."

Finally getting a chance to dig in at his new friend/enemy, the priest let a smile of his own flicker. "You shouldn't. Trust me... you shouldn't. I'm not entirely sure that you'll be able to feel peaceful when you're awake for a while."

That didn't quite have the intended effect at first. "Interesting. It has a greater power than just causing limbs to unexpectedly regrow? I don't suppose you would wish to share any of that knowledge?"

"What I think is that you're going to lay in bed waiting to see if any other body parts randomly appear on your body for the next few days."

The merchant paused, and slowly stood up. "I think you delight in knowing that, don't you?"

"I do."

He laughed, and Akaran felt the goon behind him back away. "I knew I liked you. You'll hear from me as soon as you hold up your end of the bargain. Thadius? Be a good moron and go with the priest."

Looking as pained as he should have felt with that cracked and blistered abomination attached to his arm, the young thief gave his boss a pitiful look with his milky blue eyes. "I'm... I'm not a m...m...moron!"

"But you *are* coming with me," Akaran muttered while he took a sip of the stew and blanched. The merchant quietly made his way through the bar as he watched – and swatted at Thadius's other hand when the thief reached for the bread that had come with his meal. "Don't touch... anything. Just... don't touch anything at all."

The moron flinched and whined like a flogged puppy, but otherwise sat still.

Akaran caved with a sigh and passed him the bowl and bread both. "Oh, you may as well. Don't know if you're gonna... nevermind. Just eat it."

The locals called it Pauper's Row.

It was an apt description, all told. Even before the refugee crisis had hit Gonta, the street leading towards the Order of Light's shrine was nestled behind the commercial districts, and flush up against a canal that was fed by backflow from the main river that ran through the city. Fish loved to pool in it, so it even served as one of the better places to eat in the city proper. It did have an added bonus of being high enough to serve as a natural floodwall for the lower half of the town.

After the refugee crisis, the street was crowded by the sick and the hungry. Almost all of them were desperate for healers or hurting for food. Or simply just desperate and hurting. It made for a depressing walk on the best of days up the cobblestone street. *Today is not the best of days,* the priest sighed to himself, looking over at the scared witless thief he was almost dragging along behind him.

The shrine, on the other hand, did not look run down, worn out, or like it was as destitute as the rest of the Row. The street went uphill, along a lazy slope lined with marble pillars that were adorned with the busts of the Gods and Goddess of the Pantheon. At the very top of the hill, the shrine stood as a marvelous gold-trimmed edifice. Even from two blocks away he could see people working in some kind of garden, plucking fruit and harvesting who-knows-what.

At least this one tries to do something for the people. Can't say that most do. Wonder how bad what I need to do in there is going to piss off the local Priestess of Stara, he said with a twinge in the back of his eye. *Probably badly.*

"I... I don't fe... feel so good..." Thadius whined, cradling 'his' hand.

For the fiftieth time since meeting him, Akaran looked down at the blackened mess and studied it closely. This time though, he noticed that it had started to do something new. Just as they passed a very small shrine that held the bust of the Goddess of Nature, the hand began to put off a faint trail of gray smoke in the air. "Does that thing normally steam?"

With a mild whine, the thief shook his head. "No... no, not ever, never... starting... arm is starting to hurt..."

Somewhere off in the distance, the priest heard a faint whimper off in the distance that rose above the din of the crowd. *Wish these people would suffer a little quieter. I can't hear myself think.* He glanced over at the effigy and scratched at his goatee. "That's... odd. It's reacting to that bust? I mean I realize that it's holy but Makolichi practically danced on the shrine at Toniki?"

A shout over the din interrupted his questions – pleasantly, for a change. "AKARAN!"

"Mariah? MARIAH!" he shouted back, smiling at the sound of her voice in spite of himself. "Over here! I found it!"

His friend – his *actual* friend – ran through the crowd and dodged assorted vagabonds and piles of refuse on the street, waving her hands up in the air. "I got your message! You found it? Where? What is it?"

"Here's part of it," Akaran answered while the moron tried to pull away.

It didn't do him any good. Mariah stopped next to the two of them and looked at the limb, looking perplexed. "He's holding it in his hand?"

"That's not his hand."

"It's not his...? Who's is it?" The gnarled black mess of a hand twitched and a fresh crack opened from the middle finger to the wist and up under his coat. Then just as quickly, it sealed up with a sickly wet noise that popped in the air. "Wait, no, that... Oh that is just... repulsive! Is this the norm for what you people do?"

The priest grunted. "I can only pray that morons like this are not the norm anywhere."

"N... n... not a moron!"

Akaran raised his eyebrow in disbelief. "A dead hand grafted itself onto your arm after you swiped it out from under a garrison detachment and instead of taking it to a priest you took it to some local thug who was going to bury you in a ditch. You're a moron." He looked over at the alchemist's apprentice and shrugged. "Really. He's a moron."

"Maybe so," she said, then shivered a little. "He's a moron out in the cold, even if it is warmer than Toniki. You're also hurt. You shouldn't be out here either longer than you must. You're both unwise, and need to take care of yourselves."

In the distance, the earlier sound of whimpering and moaning got louder. Try as hard as he might, there wasn't a face he could put to the miserable sounds. A few heartbeats later, and he would have sworn he heard someone drop a pile of glass onto the stone street. "Unwise is... ok, that's fair. How about you? Did you find Evalia?"

"Yes, but you won't like what I found out."

He had to stop himself from sighing, and decided that right this second wasn't the ideal time to be let down even more. "That seems to be the name of the game. Tell me about it in a minute. I want to get him into the shrine."

They resumed the walk to the shrine, and the further they went, the noisier the street got. An argument ahead drowned out what Mariah tried to tell him as a merchant and one of the locals were arguing over a cask of wine. "This isn't wine! This is... *bloody piss*, what is this? Saltwater?"

The merchant in question threw his hat down indignantly and crossed his arms. "Saltwater? How dare you. It's wine! The finest in the city!"

"By the name of the Mount, this stuff is... it's foul! All of it, foul!" he shouted, kicking over the aforementioned cask and pouring it out into the street.

Akaran stepped in it as he walked by and had to fight back a retch. *Not just saltwater, but smells like week-old fish left out in the sun.*

"I think... that's a very good idea," the girl at his side agreed, stepping over the rotten swill and somehow managing to keep the bottom of her dress out of it. "What are you going to be doing about it when we get there?"

"I don't know. I mean, we need the hand, and it's not his hand so I don't... It has to come off."

Thadius heard that loud and clear and came to a complete stop. "My... my hand? Completely off? I... no, I like havin' a hand again I do it's -"

Below them and on the dock along the edge of the floodwall's embankment, a handful of fishermen were lamenting about the state of the river. "Wish I knew what's the fault with the fish today. All of 'em, dead before they even come outta the water."

"Didn't they start doin' that after that mine closed up-river?"

Grumpily, the other fishermen gave a nod. One of them agreed solemnly and hung his head. "For a bit, yah. Gods know what got dumped in when that fell apart up there. Fools."

"Well damn. Whatever it is, kids are gonna go hungry again tonight. Can't feed 'em this."

With a frustrated grumble, Akaran tried (and failed) to shut out the sounds of the crowds around them. "Regardless. I want him at the local shrine first. It's just up ahead. Hope it's an Order of Light shrine, and not a Melian temple."

"I think I saw the Melian one," Mariah hopefully added. "It's on the other side of the manor."

"Good. Their version of getting it off of him will probably involve an explosion and I don't want to destroy it just yet."

"She's the Goddess of Destruction. What else would you expect?"

The moron continued to dig in his heels and kept shaking his head 'no,' not that it was doing him any good whatsoever. "No! No don't... not them, not again! T... t... they did it the first time when I lost my hand and... no, pl... pl... please not them!"

Giving him a sympathetic look, the exorcist had to wince a little. "He's got a point. He's gonna have a bad enough day as it is, regardless of who gets their um... hands... on him."

Behind them, another one of those whimpering cries made Akaran *really* wince. "D... do you he.. hear that? That crying? All around?" Thadius babbled.

"Of course I do... we're in the middle of the unwashed and unwanted. Everyone's crying."

Mariah looked at them like they had both grown an extra head. "What crying?"

"You don't hear it?" he asked with an incredulous air. "How can you not?"

Stepping back from them slowly, the girl wrapped her hands around her mining pick. She had fastened it to her dress in a makeshift sheath/belt on the way down. "Hear what? All I hear is just you two jabbering."

"If you don't but I do... and he does..." Akaran looked down at the hand as his eye widened – realization dawning him.

Dawning on him *late*, but it did dawn on him. He let Thadius go and pulled his sword free with a shout of warning that was just a hair *too* late.

He managed to hear one of the old men talking in the lower part of the canal while people around him started to scatter. "Hey what's that down there...?" one of the fishermen asked, peering down into the water.

The world started to move in slow motion as one of the other anglers looked at the same spot. "I don't see anyth-"

Before he could finish the word, a skeletal hand punched out of the water and caught the hapless sod by his ankle. His scream was cut off as quickly as he started it, with only a scant few bubbles marking his passage into the water. The other fishermen all shouted screams and profanities and at least one blasphemy in response.

Twisted and gnarled, a bony figure launched itself out of the canal and landed on the dockside. It was a hulking monstrosity, a head taller than the average man. It was all bone with scant rags and rotten seaweed dangling from its body. Bloated and ripped lungs poured green brine through its ribs as twisting squid-like tentacles dangled from the bottom of his jaw. Chunks of green ice adorned it from head to toe; enough to offer some protection in a fight but it didn't complete encase him like it had a few days prior.

It only had one arm; the left one had lost long ago.

The left one that had been found, and was now attached to, Thadius the moron.

The other fisherman tried to turn and run, but he didn't move fast enough. The demon grabbed him by the back of his head with his only hand, and smashed his face into the wall. Blood and bone splattered everywhere before the monster threw the body up out of the canal towards Akaran and his companions.

The body tripped up Thadius and sent him sprawling to the cobblestone street. Mariah screeched in fear as other cries and calls of alarm were shouted from everywhere around them. Those screams were joined by one more de-facto shout (as if another proclamation was needed).

"DEAD MAN – RED STAIN! DEAD MAN!"

When Makolichi landed, he flung his arm out in an arc. Where his hand went, a wave of jagged barbs of black ice and yellow bone flung out. A handful of barbs tore a young man apart, and another sent an elderly panhandler to the ground with blood gushing from her thigh. The only thing that saved Mariah from the same was the priest – and he paid for it.

"LUMINAIRD!" forced a round translucent lavender and blue shield to snap into existence along his left arm. It caught three of the shards and destroyed them in a brief shower of black and silver sparks. A fourth shard sliced his right shoulder wide open.

Another cloud of freezing shrapnel left another pauper curled up in a bloody heap, and took a little girl's throat out. It was the last time that he got to do that – Akaran made damn sure of it. "GET INTO THE SHRINE, NOW, GO! EVERYONE! EVERYONE GET INSIDE, NOW!"

It kept shouting at the exorcist as it jumped up over the canal wall and landed in the middle of the street. A sickly green glow radiated out from its eyes as it screamed at the priest again and again. "**DEAD MAN RED STAIN! DEAD MAN RED STAIN!**"

Not a single soul along the streets wasted time. The rush of people charging towards the temple almost trampled the exorcist, and they did push Mariah way off to the side. She was the only other person to stand her ground – Makolichi's presence not quite as terrifying as the last time.

She refused to let it.

A flare of white energy pulsed out of Akaran's left hand and impacted almost harmlessly on the demon's side. Little bits of rotted flesh blew off in a small shower of sparks but didn't even make him flinch. "MAKOLICHI! Come to judgment, you son of a *bitch*!"

His adversary lumbered forward and caught a poor woman that attempted to run past them to get away to safety – any safety. All it did was give the demon an opening. Makolichi's clawed hand gutted her with a single swipe, and when he threw her body, Akaran couldn't move fast enough to avoid it.

Screaming in pain, the girl knocked him flat on his back, and it was a fight to get her off of him. She passed out from pain when the hilt of his sword tangled up in the mass that used to be her stomach. While he tried to get untangled, the demon had nothing else to stop him.

Thadius – poor, stupid Thadius – made it to his feet and managed to get a few steps away before Makolichi stormed past the fallen priest and closed in on him before he was forced to come to a hard stop. The moron slumped up against one of the pillars decorating the walkway while the demon's bones started to smoke and crack the closer that he got to the temple.

Roaring, the demon tried to push forward. With every step, he moved slower. Each inch he stole, the more his bones began to glow a pale white. The pillars themselves started to shine as the busts of the Gods and Goddesses of Light began to take on a brilliant golden sheen around their eyes.

Akaran saw it and had to choke out a laugh while he stood up. His shield flickered out of existence, a scorch mark burned through his cloak and into his arm to mark its passing. "Can't get too close to the hallowed ground, can you? He's out of reach you bastard... now it's just you and me..."

While the exorcist picked his sword up and started to close in on the demon from the side, Makolichi turned and lumbered away from the aura of the shrine. With a furious howl, he went for the one person that hadn't gotten away. Mariah-Anne screamed at the top of her lungs when the beast pushed through the pain and caught her by her hair and pulled her back with him.

There wasn't a damn thing that Akaran could do to stop him. "**SEEN YOU WITH THIS ONE! SPECIAL TO YOU! KILL HER THEN YOU!**"

She tried to fight back, but all she could do was kick and push at him. His claws were wrapped in her hair too tight for her to get away, and blood trickled down from her scalp and over her cheek. Thadius stayed hunkered down on the ground while men in white robes rushed out from the shrine to see what was going on.

Makolichi's voice boomed over everyone's shouts and nearly deafened his hostage. "**GIVE ME MY HAND! GIVE ME MY HAND!!**" The tentacles on his lower jaw snapped and licked at the blood on Mariah's face, electing more screams and cries from her each time they touched.

If I move for her she's dead if I try to knock him back he'll kill her if I try to pull him close he'll kill her if I if I... Time slowed to a crawl for the priest as his mind went into overdrive before an idea clicked. "The hand, huh? That's it? That's what you're after?"

"**THE HAND! NOW! OR SHE DIES! THEN YOU! THEN ALL!**"

Silver chains whirled into being along Akaran's right arm as a whispered spell took form. The silvery links whistled through the air and wrapped themselves around their target — not Makolichi or Mariah, but Thadius. The priest jerked and twisted, pulling and forcing the thief out of the immediate safety that the Temple had to offer.

Thadius tried to protest and fight away. That stopped when Akaran punched him in the face and knocked him half-loopy. With a cold, cruel smile, the priest lifted the black, blistered limb up and placed his sword against it. "Release her, or I destroy it. Then I destroy you."

From behind, a cadre of soldiers and guards rushed down the street. Pikemen, mostly, followed Evalia, limping along behind them in full Dawnfire regalia. She barely looked like she could hold the sword in her hands. Not that it mattered - her foul mood more than made up for her exhaustion.

Makolichi flinched when the cold steel touched the unholy limb, and flinched harder when Akaran shoved the tip into the bone. **"DESTROYING IT WON'T END ME! WILL NOT SAVE HER!"**

"No, you bastard, it won't," he seethed, "but it does guarantee that when I kill you after – and I *will* kill you after – you're done. There won't be a return for you. You're *done*."

"SHE'LL BE DEAD!"

Akaran pressed the sword against the hand harder, and watched as a little blue flame erupted around the tip. "So will you."

Lifting her up off of the ground, the demon dangled her between them. Dark green water puddled up underneath them, and it started to form little crystals over his feet. **"THE HAND FOR HER! NOW!"**

"Don't think so. You haven't recovered. Your armor isn't back yet. You're still hurting from our last fight," Akaran countered, slowly dragging Thadius closer to the edge of the temple grounds.

Snarling, Makolichi backed away as his foci began to smoke anew. **"DEAD! SHE'LL BE DEAD!"**

"Please please give him the hand please don't let him - !" Mariah shrieked, digging her hands into his impossibly strong fingers. None of it did any good, and the demon shook her hard. She gave another tearful, begging scream.

"LOOK AROUND, MAKOLICHI! A temple is right there, *I'm* right here, and the city guard is right behind you. Even if you somehow make it through me you are *not* going to survive all of *them*." He pushed the blade hard into the blackened, twisted hand and Thadius gave a fresh scream of his own. "You **lost** this fight before it **started**, now let the girl **go!**"

A gout of blue flames sprung to life along Makolichi's left collarbone in response to the kiss of the blade. **"TAKE HER WITH ME! WITH ME!"**

"AKARAN PLEASE PLEASE!"

With a hard shove, Akaran sent Thadius headlong into one of the pillars. "No matter what you do you don't get that hand back. The only question is if you think you can take all of us on at once or not... and we both know you can't, or she'd be dead by now. You're not that stupid."

Howling, the frost-born monster looked at the rapidly assembling group of priests, soldiers, and city guards that had taken up position behind and around both of them. **"THE END NOT THE END DEAD MAN RED STAIN NOT THE END!"**

With an unintelligible scream, the demon pitched Mariah to the ground and spun away towards the canal. He was too slow - chains whipped around Makolichi's ribs the moment he turned his back on Akaran. The beast was able to make it a few steps more before he rushed him and shoved his sword through his back and into a shriveled lung.

The demon pivoted and spun left, swinging his left arm back like a heavy club. The sword scraped free but tore a chunk of bone with it... and Akaran wasn't anywhere near where the arm lashed out at. He ducked and the swing went completely over his head, letting him punish the demon a little more. The sword flashed forward three times in a row, splitting his sternum in half as he caught Mako's wrist in his left hand.

Roaring, Makolichi tried to break free.

Tried being the operative word. "I want your other hand too," Akaran hissed, then added a short, *"Purge."*

Makolichi's roar turned into a scream. Bones cracked and shattered along his forearm while a gout of steam erupted around the exorcist's sword. His arm shattered from his wrist halfway to his elbow. A spurt of curdled black blood splashed out of the gaping hole in his chest. While the demon tried to push away, Akaran thrust his blade in and twisted as hard as he could.

With a shout of *"PURGE!"* his hand and his sword burned with a brilliant white light. With a heavy punch, he thrust his hand effortlessly into the mass of ruined flesh and brine-soaked guts beside his blade. Pure holy magic pulsed into the demon, searing skin and boiling his organs on touch. He twisted the sword again and jerked it free, crowing in victory.

Screeching and wailing, Makolichi fell down to the ground, flat on his back. Furiously glowing eyes never left Akaran's face as he tried to scramble away. "Funny. Put you down on your ass and you suddenly don't look so big anymore..."

"NOT DONE NOT END! YOU WILL NOT END THIS HERE!"

"Maybe not," he answered – and then he shoved the point of his sword through the hollow of the damned thing's throat. "But you *killed me* and a whole bunch of others. I just want to make sure this *hurts.*"

Makolichi kicked up at him and swung the stump of his arm ineffectually in the air as another charge of holy mana coursed through the blade and made brine-soaked flesh sizzle. Akaran straddled the demon and dropped down to both knees on top of him. Ignoring the burning pain in his legs from even touching the beast, he shoved both of his hands into the hole his sword had left in Mako's ribs.

Then he *pulled* with all of his might and ripped his ribcage open.

He got what he wanted: it *hurt*.

Screaming and screeching in raw agony, the tentacles along his lower face all elongated at once and sprayed a thick gray slime all over the priest's face. The gunk covered everything and sent him rolling backwards as he struggled to scrape it out of his eye and mouth.

It reeked of decaying fish and putrid brine – and tasted even worse. Reflexively, he forced more magic out of his hands and hammered Mako with it at point-blank range. The spells blew apart what passed for lungs and a blackened heart. Shards of bone rained down on everyone nearby.

Off to the side, he heard someone scream to him. "BOY - ROLL TO YOUR RIGHT! NOW!"

He did, and saw the demon start to rear back up to his feet. Cursing, he tried to wipe a handful of the gray mess out of his eye and bring another spell to bear. He didn't need to. He felt the sound of the thunderclap more than he actually heard it; the sound was so sharp and explosive that he wasn't sure he was going to be able to hear anything ever again.

For whatever discomfort that he felt, what the demon had to have gone through was so much worse. Before the sound went off, Makolichi was on his knees and lunging for him. After, the demon simply wasn't there anymore. Not as a single cohesive piece, at least.

What was left behind was a smoldering crater in the street. Through the hazy steam, Evalia began to turn an interesting (and unflattering) shade of green as the smell hit her. "You went for the hurt and not the kill... you're a violent little man, aren't you?"

He groaned and tried to wipe pieces of the demon off of his tunic. Chaos reigned around him. A handful of peasants ran down the street screaming. A young boy watched the carriage unfold from the canal edge, frozen in place by fear. A trio of white-robed priests flocked around the wounded, and more rushed down from the shrine to help.

Soldiers swarmed the causeway, a mix of gold and red cloaks from the army, matched with brown and gray tunics of the city guard. All of them looked scared shitless – though nobody could blame them. A father knelt over his daughter and wailed, and near them, the woman with the ice in her leg passed out.

Not that he could hear her over the ringing in his ears. "What?"

Evalia cleared her throat and cupped her hands around her mouth.

"I said I like you."

"You like ewe? What about ewe?"

She shook her head and gingerly strode through the debris and extended a hand to him. "You'd be the exorcist that Mariah was all on about, I wager."

Akaran scooted back and waved her hand off. "Don't, no, don't touch me," he warned as he spit out another glob of... stuff... out of his mouth. "It's burning, fisk, burning just about everywhere. Don't touch until I can... that *stench*. That's *rot*, that's *all* rot. Oh no, Mariah? Where is she?"

The battlemage pointed over to her where two soldiers were helping her to her feet. Her throat was covered in an angry red mark where Makolichi had choked her, with little blisters sprouting up all over it. "I think she's okay," she started to say.

Off to the side, Mariah cursed his name. "You fisking son of a bitch," she seethed. "How fisking dare you even..."

"You think she's gay?"

Evalia heard her retort and interrupted Akaran. "I hope that there's a *damn* good explanation for all of this."

He shook his head and plucked a piece of goo out of his ear. "There... is. Goddess."

"Good," she half-groaned as her nose wrinkled.

Mariah sneered down at him and started to walk away. "Fisking... you son of a bitch..."

Akaran couldn't hear her, and Xandros's wife didn't care. "What was that thing?"

"Demon."

"I gathered. It's gone. What do you need me to do?"

He pushed himself up off the ground and looked at Makolichi's remains and the handful of dead bodies around him. "The bodies. Burn them, right away. Take a torch to it, all of it, even the street."

"You want me to set a street on fire? That's a novel idea."

"Whomever touches the bodies, have... have them sent to the shrine after... I'll purify them after... after I get this gunk off... why did you...? He could have..."

Bemused, she grinned at him. "You look like you needed the help."

"You have no idea..." he muttered, then called out to Mariah before the battlemage could comment further. "Mariah? Mariah!"

The blisters had begun to spread all over her throat and on the palms of her hands. A few had burst, leaving streamers of yellow pus draining off of her skin. She didn't answer, but when he continued to shout at her, she affixed him with a furious glare. "You were going to let him kill me."

"Let him kill you? Goddess no..."

"You were. You could have given him the hand back and he would have -"

Akaran stopped her with his hand up. " - murdered you."

"You don't know that."

"Yeah. I do. If I gave him his hand back, he would have killed you then killed Goddess knows how many others. I couldn't let him have it," he replied. The gunk continued to burn; he just suddenly didn't care.

Unconvinced, she looked at the welts on her palms. "Miss was right about you. Have to be 'right' no matter what. You're an unhinged bastard."

That hurt. Wincing and lowering his head, he took the condemnation head on. "There wasn't anything I could have done differently... You have to know that. Don't you?"

"I'm sure that's exactly what you would've told the people at Toniki," she snapped.

Even Evalia cringed at that one. "Mariah, wait."

Rubbing her throat while tears sprung up in the corners of her eyes, the younger woman wasn't having any of it. "They were right about you. You don't care. You just want the kill. You don't care about people. Single-minded, uncaring, 'holy way or no way,' cocky wannabe priest," she seethed,

"We **have to be**. If we aren't as ruthless as they are, **we lose**. When we lose, **everyone** loses," he argued. "I wouldn't have let him kill you, there's no way, I wouldn't have, I swear I promise."

"Swear and promise all you want. Wasn't your neck he was holding."

Akaran pressed his hand on his stomach and shook his head. "You mean this time." Behind him, someone shouting out of the canal tried to get his attention, but he couldn't have cared less.

"Yeah. How lucky we are that you made it through that in one piece," she spat.

The battlemage cleared her throat. "Both of you, enough. Alchemist – you need to be seen in the temple for those injuries. Exorcist – I assume you have an explanation for what just happened, and what kind of mess you've brought here?"

"I didn't -" he started.

Evalia shut him down hard. "Maybe you did. Maybe you didn't. But you're here. That thing was here. People are dead. If you don't have answers, should I assume that it would save time if we went ahead and bent over a barrel for the unholy fisking we're about to receive from the Overseer?"

Mariah lifted her hand and started to say something, then thought better of it and shook her head at the pair of them. "I don't want to hear it. The healers. Going there now. Come find me when you're ready to go back home."

As she stomped off, Akaran tried to wipe more of the brine-soaked gore off of his armor. "I'm ready to go home *now*," he whined under his breath.

A second shout stalled his whine, and Mariah provided the exclamation point. "SHIT! AKARAN - ! MORE!"

"More? More what...?" he complained as he turned around. "Oh are you... EVALIA!"

"More - ? What in Melia's piss are *those?!*" the battlemage hissed.

He didn't answer past shouts of "LUMINOSO CORSAIR!" and "BONDS!" A brilliant ball of light popped out of his palm and arced through the air and towards the canal. When it hit, the first of the two corpses moving around moaned in pain and started to scamper away. The third turned to him as she held her stomach in her hands.

The sight drew him up short as he recognized her. Mariah retched behind him before she waded into the fray with her enchanted pick held high. He shook his shock off with a curse while his chains spun freely through the air. They wrapped around her body and pinned her arms to the side while he brought her down to her knees.

The blonde-haired firebrand did the rest. All it took was a single swing of her sword that took the woman's face clean off. Evalia stumbled backwards in undisguised horror as tentacles slid out of the inside of the woman's head before they boiled away into nothing.

Akaran strode into the mass of the dead while another of Makolichi's victims began to attack a spectator. Daringol's tentacles slithered out of the young boy's mouth and wrapped themselves around the neck of the octogenarian priest. The exorcist was ignored – and the corpse when slack when his sword punched through the back of its head and out of his nose.

The temple custodian went slack too, and passed out cold.

*If he just died, I am **not** purifying a priest of Stara. Let **them** deal with it.*

While he groused, the other corpses continued a mix of wild rampages and desperate struggles. Two of Evalia's men used their pikes to keep a thrashing body from floating downstream, and Mariah wasn't wasting any time stalking one that hadn't managed to completely reanimate itself just yet. A black fog kept pushing into and spilling out of the former fisherman's cracked and crumbled skull.

Each time it slid in, the body jerked like it was being struck by lightning. It was too broken for Daringol to take hold, though it didn't stop the wraith from trying. Akaran watched it and walked lockstep behind her before she stopped him with a "Piss off – deal with another one. This one is *mine*," she seethed.

It hit him like a slap in the face.

Not that he had any time to argue the point. Evalia had already worked her way to the canal to size up the creature in the water – she just didn't have a clue what to do about it. "That's the same damn thing that attacked me two days ago! What *are* these?!"

"If you've got any juice left, aim for the -" he shouted back.

Or started to shout back. A tentacle wrapped around his ankle and tripped him up as he made his way over to her. He couldn't catch himself on the way down and smacked his face hard on the cobblestone street with his hand tucked up to his side. The impact drove his fist into his gut, and he screamed out in pain.

It was the last indignity his stitches were willing to put up with.

Blood splashed from under his coat and pain burst through him so sharp that it felt almost as bad as when Makolichi had hurt him the first time. Blinded by pain and mud in his eye, he managed to roll to his side and call his shield up again. Even more pain burned down his arm and into his chest, but it saved his face from a lashing of tendrils and tiny hooked hands.

Yards away, the pair of soldiers dealing with the zombie in the water finally got the upper hand. A lucky blow caught it with the edge of a pike tip, and it let them drag it ashore. Evalia twirled her hands in the air – ripples of black and red energy following each gesture – and let a bolt of mana lance straight through it.

Little bits of the corpse rained down into the water while she fell to her knees with her arms wrapped around her stomach. On the other side, Mariah's victim burned with purple flames as she bludgeoned it into a thick pulpy paste. All that left behind were the screams and shouts of the other assembled guards, priest, and random citizens.

All of them, plus the bloody little girl that squatted over his head.

The disembodied voice from the hole in her neck mocked him as he struggled to get his bearings. *"Daringol seeks warmth needs warmth here warmth will come here when Daringol grows grows more grows ready for new home of homes for warmth! You have home you ARE home for warmth!"*

He caught one of the tendrils in his right hand and forced a Word from his bloodied lips. The spell coursed up the tentacle and gave the animate all the warmth it could handle. It screamed once as light flowed through and poured out of every hole in the poor girl's dead body before the child fell to the ground.

Black steam emanated off of every inch of exposed, burnt flesh. Mariah stood over the body and didn't even try to hide her disgust. "Even little girls now?"

"I can't even... I just can't," he moaned. He rolled over onto his back and groaned a fresh whine. "I want to go back home. It's good enough for that thing. It can be good for me, right? I want to go home."

"Oh I don't doubt it," Evalia quipped back as she worked her way over, using a pike for a cane. "I... I need to be excused as well. Can you stand?"

"I... ugh. Yeah. I think so. *Goddess* this hurts."

"Is that all of them?"

"Hope so," he sighed as he stood up.

"Alright. You have command of the field. Do what needs to be done, whatever that is. I can't... I can't be here anymore."

He tilted his head slightly to the side and looked at her quizzically. "From what I heard, you're far from the squeamish type."

She shrugged and covered her own belly. "From what you heard, I assume it wasn't that I'm with child."

"Ah... um, well..."

"I know a 'no' when I hear one. Stupid men. That... thing. This smell. I can't. You'll manage, I'm sure."

That should have rankled him, but at this point, it wasn't anything more than he was willing to stomach. "The bodies, the street... just going to have all of it set on fire. Throwing my armor in with the pile. Don't... want it near me anymore."

"Wonderful. I'm going upwind of all of that, if it's all the same. Check in with me tonight, sir," she finished, raising her hand to her chest in a short salute. "Not used to calling someone out of uniform 'sir.' I wouldn't get used to it."

She even managed to say all of it without a trace of sarcasm.

For a moment, he didn't quite know how to respond. "Ma'am, yes ma'am. Oh... one thing before you go."

A less-than-welcome voice cut him off. Captain Paliston had managed to get within earshot of the three of them without either of them noticing. "One thing? *One* thing? I think there's a great deal more than *one* thing that the two of you need to talk about! To start with, who in the *pits* do you two think you are to give anyone orders? This is *my* city, this is *my* town, these are *my* men!"

"We established who he is, bastard or not," Mariah snarled.

The rest of his objections didn't last. With a crack of her pike on the cobblestone street, Evalia turned to face him. "As second in command of the 13th Garrison in the Grand Army of the Dawn, *and* wife of the Garrison Commander, I outrank you."

"Fine. You do. *He* doesn't. I'm holding him personally responsable for this. **All** of this."

Akaran stopped wiping chunks of the demon off of his tunic and let his jaw fall open. "Responsible? What are you going to do? *Arrest me?*"

Orin laid his hand on the sword hanging off of his belt. "These people are dead because of you. Yes. Arresting you, and arresting everyone that traveled with you."

Evalia cleared her throat and rapped her weapon on the street again. "Excuse me. I said that I outrank you. What you didn't understand, apparently, is that this priest can give my husband orders, which means he can give me orders, which means he can give *you* orders."

"You... expect me to... follow the orders of this... *gutter trash?*" he all-but screeched.

"Yes," the alchemist-in-training answered for them.

"It'll be safer than arresting me. Be out of your hair faster, too," Akaran added. "Really, it'll be for everyone best if we don't have some big territorial fight. Really."

The captain looked at both of them incredulously. "I am going to arrest you for the deaths of... all of these people! I watched you kill them! You deserve the gallows!"

"Oh for the love of... Love," the exorcist muttered, cupping his face in both hands (and then immediately regretting that he hadn't taken his gloves off yet). Cheeks burning from getting gunk all over them a second time, he muttered another complaint to nobody in particular. "Goddess, this *stench*. It's worse than that brine-soaked piss in the water."

Evalia stepped back and turned Orin. "Fine. If you don't want to take orders from him, you don't have to. Captain, you are relieved of command of the Gonta guard."

His face turned purple. "WHAT? You CAN'T do that!"

She shrugged. "*You* are – were – the watch commander of a city. *I* am the second in command of the 13th. *I* can order you to scrub the local latrines if *I* want, and your men, I am sure, aren't going to risk *my* wrath if they refuse to do what I tell them to do."

Akaran tossed his gloves on the ground and spit out another mouthful of brine-befouled muck. "Told you that it'd be for the best if you didn't push your luck."

A soldier standing at the edge of the assembled crowd looked at his immediate superior, and then at Evalia. After a quick salute to her, he did the absolutely smartest thing he could. "Battlemage, the city guard is at your service. The sooner that this is over, the better." Two more men made similar acknowledgments while Orin stood by in a sputtering rage.

"So. It's settled. Orin, you're relieved. Exorcist, the cleanup is yours."

"Why do I feel like you just gave *me* an order, after that speech?" he grunted.

"Because you are smart enough to not challenge a pregnant woman."

He answered with a tired, bemused laugh as he sized everything up. Then, switching gears, he stopped her before she could go. "Battlemage?"

"Yes?"

"Makolichi. He'll be back. That's not the end of him. Nor the zombies. What controlled them is still loose, too."

She pondered that as he started to pull his tattered tunic up and over his head. "I presume that you intend to rectify that as soon as humanly possible?"

"Yes, ma'am."

Mariah looked down at his stomach and growled. "Tore it back open? You *tore it back open?!* You're a *damn* fool! You're going to get killed if you're not more careful!"

"Thought you weren't happy I made it back," he grunted.

Mixed emotions clouded her eyes as she worked for a reply. "I'm... not. But you did. So. Don't... damn you. Don't die again," she seethed as she turned around and stormed off. "**I DON'T WANT TO HAVE TO WORK ON YOUR IDIOT ASS AGAIN!**" she shouted at the top of her lungs.

Evalia watched her go with a raised eyebrow. "You charm everyone you meet like that?"

"Do you have to add to this too...?" he sighed.

"No. Suppose not. Oh, and one thing of my own."

He pitched the tunic next to the lump of gore that the demon had left in his passing. When he did, a chunk of bone crumbled and revealed something that glinted in the fading sunlight. Curious, he knelt down to examine it. "Yes?"

"That was a... hard decision. Risking her. You did the right thing."

Sighing, he looked down at the bloody hole in his gut. "The hand really *is* that important."

"Still. Not many would. Hard choice to make, especially for someone as young as you."

Akaran picked up something that looked like a medallion out of what was left of Makolichi's ribs. "You mean not many would be willing to throw away one life to save many."

"Not many can be that calm."

"I have a feeling she'll describe it as... something... else..." he mused as his voice trailed off.

She waited to hear the rest of it, then tried to see what he held in his hand. "What's that?"

Slowly, he turned the insignia over in his hands a couple of times and ignored the way it made his skin burn to the touch. "I'm... not sure. Answers, I think. I think this is... an answer."

"Could you be more vague?"

"Probably..." He stepped away and wrapped the amulet up in his discarded tunic with a frown. "So much for burning it. I can't believe it smells this foul. This bastard came outta Zell's ass but *damned* if it doesn't smell like it crawled out of Neph-kor's gullet. Gah. Oh, battlemage?"

Evalia lingered for a moment and shrugged. "Yes?"

"Get someone bring that moron over here."

Sitting next to the decorative pillar where he'd been so unceremoniously pitched, Thadius finally spoke up. "I'm not a moron!"

VII. FRACTURES

Traveling deeper into the mountains wasn't an easy trek. Steelhom had been joined by Commander Xandros and two of his soldiers – a fair-haired woman named Penela, and a grizzled veteran that just called himself 'Mado.' Hirshma had made good on her promise to investigate Bolintop Mine, and had left as soon as Steelhom was out of sight.

The task was, however, made slightly easier by the presence of Eos'eno. She not only knew where to go, but also an easy way to get there. Nestled an hour north into the forest was a hidden road that she took responsibility for. "Master enjoys strolls and walks through the woods whenever he can pull away from his works and his studies. Whenever I could, I spent the time to build a path wherever he may need." She smiled, looking quite smug with herself, then gave a slightly irritated look at the state of the path a few minutes after they found it. "When the ice was willing to be crafted to cobblestones, the trees had the decency to not fall on them. How rude must things of leaves and twigs grow to be when they grow tall from the land and opt to cease their grasp on life?"

None of the humans were able to give an answer; they were all too busy stepping over all of those leaves and around man-sized 'twigs' to comment. She simply floated over the rubble, oblivious to why it was taking the trio behind her so long. Even without the debris, it would have taken hours to get to their destination. But with years worth of overgrowth, mud, and fallen limbs?

It had taken nearly nine hours from the minute that the small band had left Usaic's cabin to the moment that the air had started to feel not just cold, but oppressively foul. That was even with an impromptu pair of stops along the way to start a couple of fires and attempt to warm themselves up. Fortunately, the wisp had a trick up her sleeve that kept the merry band of intrepid adventurers from freezing to death on the way.

She had been forced to admit that as much as she loved her lord and master, he was still human – and older than any of the soldiers retracing his steps (older than Mado and Penela put together, at that). While his happily conscripted concubine didn't have any concerns about flitting in the air as naked as the Goddess of Ice had made her, he had to teach her how he managed to live on his own and spend so much time in freezing temperatures without dying of hypothermia. To help him travel, she used an odd technique that allowed her to force a sphere of air around them so cold that it effectively acted as a ball of glass – keeping outside gusts of wind from cutting them to shreds. It didn't do much for the debris, but it stopped the wind.

And inside the ball?

Eos'eno had all three of them light torches that she dusted with a compound that Usaic had been working on for reasons unknown. As soon as they lit them, their torches began to put off enough heat that, trapped in the wall of air, made everything comfortably warm. It made things *so* warm that the wisp had to occasionally stop the winds from blowing so that she could cool herself off. The humans accepted it for what it was, and let her have the short breaks of freezing temperatures without much complaint.

At least, accepted it for what it was in regards to dealing with the cold. "This is the kind of hike that I thought I'd be through with taking a garrison command," Xandros muttered, stopping long enough to shake snow off of his boot.

Steelhom was quick to join in. "This is the kind of hike that I thought I'd be through with serving as an instructor."

"It is a wonderful walk through the woods," the wisp scolded them both, ignoring their discomfort. It wasn't like *they* were the ones that had been keeping a spell going on for almost nine hours straight. "I shall never understand the disinterest so many of your kind have with exploring this beautiful land."

"So many of our kind take solace in spending time with each other, more than they do living alone in the wilds," the paladin countered.

It didn't change Eos's mind in the least. "This land is not wild. This land is as nature intended it to be. Vast and open and at one with the world."

Before he could give her the tired, snarky reply that she deserved, that foul scent in the air turned into something worse. Something he could put a name to. He stopped, placed two fingers just above the bridge of his nose, shut his eyes, and began to focus on a spot somewhere directly on the path in front of them. "Xandros we -"

The Commander of the 13th Garrison was one step ahead of him. He dropped to one knee and thrust his hand up in the air. The soldiers behind him tossed their torches to the ground and quickly ducked behind cover. They had their bows pulled out of the small quivers at their sides and in hand, ready to fire at a moment's notice. Eos'eno touched down on the ground and started to say something, but Steelhom thrust his halberd across her chest, silencing her. She ended her spell at the same time as she picked up on the same taint that he had.

Mado and Penela slowly advanced forward, creeping ahead of both commanders with their bows up and eyes searching. Xandros followed behind with his sword in one hand and the other resting on the handle of his whip. There was a burnt-out, ashen glade only a few yards ahead. It was filled with badly-burnt trees and other debris; apparent remnants of an old wildfire. *The same one that Usaic had been involved with,* Steelhom realized, wishing all-the-while that Eos had told them more than the scant bit she had.

While the damage wasn't recent, the cold had kept the bulk of it from regrowing. The paladin slowly crept forward until he could see past the trees the rest of the way. "Do you see them?" Xandros whispered, a disgusted look blossoming on his face.

"I do," his friend answered, sweeping his gaze over the years-old burnt landscape. Scattered among the ruined logs and mounds of dirt, there were piles of stones that almost looked like ruined huts. Sitting on or darting around all of it? "*Shiriak.* At least seven. Maybe more. Do you see what else is up there?" he asked, pointing straight up in the air over the middle of the clearing. When the soldier shook his head no, Steelhom told him what he was missing. "Two wraiths, hovering above, center. It's Daringol."

Eos put her hand over Steelhom's and directed it to a particular fallen tree off to the right. "There are more. Do you see that fallen tree? The large one; hollow inside?"

He followed her movement and gave her a curt nod. "I see it."

"See under. I found a creek behind below it. The scavengers are not the only things residing here."

He focused on it as best as he could, but gave up after a moment and took his fingers off of his brow. "I can't quite... Usaic's fog. It's concentrated here. Seems... like it's the strongest, there."

"I found dead men there," she whispered. "Walking men, preserved, but dead. No less than four."

"I see why you wanted Steelhom to bring us along," Xandros muttered, watching the demonkin scamper about the ruins.

The wisp looked like she was suddenly about to cry. "Yes. This is where Makolichi was given a door to this world. It must be. The ice? It weeps. It cries with wailing and suffering. I feel something more than simply cold here, something painful to the skin. It is the same aura that the other possesses, only worse, older, much older and worse."

Grimly, Xandros digested her concerns. "We'll have to cull them before we can explore. Steelhom? These things are your specialty."

"She's right; this has to be the place. The only advantage they have are numbers. I don't sense a thing with any power here."

"You said that... fog?...was obscuring you. How certain are you it's just this trash?"

Steelhom tried to focus on the ether one last time, and eventually gave up entirely. "I am certain of nothing – nothing other than that they need to be put down. Mado, Penela. Go for the two closest. The rest will react as soon as you fire; you likely won't have time for a second volley. Be true with your aim. Xandros, be ready to intercept the rest as they charge. I'll deal with the wraiths."

"Disgusting rats," Mado grunted, a few beads of sweat beading on his forehead.

Just as unimpressed by the cretins, Penela's quiet voice dripped with venom. "Truly. We won't miss."

It was music to the paladin's ears. "Good. Fire when ready. I'll engage on your call, old friend."

Penela slipped off and skulked around the treeline, her coat and armor barely making a branch rustle as she slid into position. Her counterpart moved off in the other direction, very slowly, very carefully, plotting their attack. The *shiriak* had no idea that any of them were there, and continued to scamper through the ruins without a care in the world. There was a brief exchange of hushed words and hand gestures between the two of them.

The suspense, brief as it was, made Steelhom's hair stand on end. *If my student were here, this is exactly the type of situation that would have him frothing mad. He'd be demanding that they would hurry up and take their shot. I hope that he can learn patience, one of these days, and not simply further embrace his habits of procrastination met with bursts of recklessness.*

Neither of them spoke a word until Penela's arrow shot through the air and cleanly split the skull of one of the scavengers hanging off of a tree near the middle of the wreckage. Mado's bolt took another down; his arrow firmly nailing the little monster to a charred stump. The paladin was right about the response from the rest of them: as one, the remaining disgusting beasts darted to the treeline and right after the archers.

The wraiths, however, did just the opposite. They split away from each other and quickly raced to the far edges of the clearing. A ball of pale purple light shot off of the end of Steelhom's halberd and incinerated the one that was the farthest away. The second dropped low to the ground to try and avoid the same fate as it rushed towards the hollowed-out tree that Eos'eno had pointed out.

The paladin charged into the clearing as he rushed after it. A *shiriak* saw him and veered over to intercept. It was a regrettable decision on its part. The tip of his weapon caught it in mid-air and gutted it with a single swipe. With a warbled cry of pain, the little beast was flung off to the side without a further care.

Having to deal with it caused him to briefly lose sight of Daringol, giving the wraith time to shoot out of the other side of the tree. Steelhom quickly slid inside after it, a Word on his lips that forced the end of the stump to blow apart and open up. He had to use his weapon to try to catch himself as he lunged through the tree – failing to realize until the last possible moment that the ruined log was sitting over a stream several feet below.

He fell hard and slid down the embankment. The drop made him land in the muck below, flat on his ass and right in front of three of the four corpses that the wisp had warned him of. They were different than the other zombies that they had encountered so far; these wretches were simple skeletons that were barely holding their bones together through sheer force of will. The three of them lunged at him with speed that belittled their decomposed bodies.

In the field, Xandros worked with his soldiers to cut down the remaining *shiriak* with ease. One lunged for his leg, which gave him ample room to work with. His blade bit into its shoulder and carved clear through, successfully ripping part of its skull off in the process. Another jumped up at him and exposed itself to a painful strike from his whip that tied it up on the ground.

Mado was just as quick. Before it could recover – before it could even struggle to get out of the barbed chains – he calmly put his boot through its face and stomped it to death with a horrible squelching sound. Not to be outdone, Penela proved the paladin wrong and used her bow to finish the final one off.

In the creek, Steelhom's use of his halberd could have been confused with someone using a quarterstaff. As the blunt end of the stick broke ribs then shattered the skull of the closest skeleton, he just as quickly cracked an outstretched arm from the second one in half. Before he could deal with it, Daringol's wraith reappeared seemingly out of nowhere and shot through the chest of the third.

It came within a hairsbreadth of wrapping its poisonous tentacles and toxic hands around his head before Eos'eno ripped it to shreds with a cloud of crystal from overhead. Her attack made it all-but evaporate in a heartbeat. The skeletons didn't react to its destruction, nor did they have time to, had they even wanted.

Steelhom destroyed one with a Word, then quickly reduced the last one standing into little more than splinters of bone with more strikes than were actually needed. He had one brief moment to think he had won the fight. That was quickly dashed when a grime covered hand thrust out of the water and raked rotten claws down the length of his thigh. If he hadn't been wearing extra padding on his leggings, it might have gotten through to the skin.

He was.

It didn't.

When he finished it off, he stood panting, catching his breath while using what magic he could to find any more hidden surprises. Above him, Eos'eno called out to the fighters with a small shout of joy. "Done, they're done! Gone, and done! Well fought, well fought!"

A few more minutes passed while Xandros and his guards swept through the clearing. They believed her, but, they didn't *entirely* trust her yet. She wasn't human; why should they? Once they were satisfied she was correct, the three of them took a few moments to compose themselves. *That* was a task easier said than done.

If their commander had thought that killing one *shiriak* left a horrific stench behind, killing seven of them poisoned the air. Penela held the contents of her stomach in check, albeit barely. That didn't stop her from gagging and choking on the sulfuric rotten smell that promised to sink into her hair and stay there for eternity. Xandros didn't throw up either – it wouldn't do to show weakness to his subordinates.

Mado, on the other hand, had crushed one under his heel.

Tears sprung up in his eyes as the first burst of rot hit him. Eos looked at him in confusion then sympathy, but even she had her limits as he expelled everything he'd eaten on the way through the woods (and in his mind, it felt like he was losing everything he'd ingested for the last week).

That didn't stop the commander from *commenting*, of course. "GODS! Why do they have to STINK so badly? What in the name of ALL do they eat?"

"Shit," Penela answered, choking still. "They have to eat shit." That was more than Mado could do, though much to everyone's appreciation, he trundled off away from them to be sick in relative privacy.

Xandros called out to his old friend the moment he realized that he was out of sight. "Steelhom! You okay? Where are you?"

Silence reigned for too many heartbeats before the wisp answered for him. "He is fine. He is upset, but he is fine."

"What's wrong? Can't say any of us are happy at the moment." He carefully made his way to the embankment and looked down at the paladin, frowning as he took stock of the mud and gunk that covered him head-to-toe.

Saying that he was upset was an understatement of utterly epic proportions. He was holding a crest in his hand, one that had seen better days. It must have been copper at some point, though it looked positively ancient. Xandros couldn't see what was on it, but to Steelhom? There was no doubt at all what it was.

And it pissed him off *badly* not knowing why it was *here*.

"Find what you were after?"

The first answer that the paladin had wasn't worth hearing. The second part of it was cryptic. "I found a question. A very big question."

Too tired to want to play guess-the-meaning, Xandros's response was as short and blunt as possible. "What?"

Holding up the crest to try to give the commander a better look, Steelhom explained at length. "This belonged to a Templar of the Order of Love. It's from a specific caste of priests that served both the Goddess of Flame and the Goddess of Love."

"That served...? Don't the Illiyans *hate* your Goddess?"

"They do, which means that this crest dates back to before the Hardening. Or at least, when the Hardening befell the Order." He looked up at his friend and shook his head in disbelief. "These are relics. These are beholden to the Order. They are *sacred*. It's horrible history, but it is *our* history. So many of us *died* in those months and years after the people of the world turned their back on Her. There is absolutely *no* reason for this to be *here!* There's no reason for one of these to be anywhere *near* here!"

Xandros stood there confused. "That was two centuries back? Why is it in the middle of a scorched forest on the edge of civilization? Where a demon was summoned, too?"

Neither could Steelhom – and he was the one saying it. "That is a *very* big question. And it lends itself to another: *why* were these bodies not sanctified and cleansed? *Why* did I just find a long-dead follower of the Goddess defiled and walking around? Eos'eno, wisp. If you are holding back a secret about this place -"

"No, no, no secret! I aided master in clearing the path to this glade. I did not do not know anything about those souls, that crest, or the stories here. Once we arrived, he sent me back to the home; he did not wish me near here when he did his work. When he returned, Makolichi was in tow; constrained and controlled."

It was getting harder and harder to believe her the longer this went on. The only thing that worked in her favor was all the effort she had put into helping them so far. "Fine. Xandros, you, your men. Scour these ruins. If you see *anything* that could be a clue..."

"We'll shout. Do you need us down there or want us up here?"

"Eos and I will search the creek. Sort through the cinders up there. And drag those *shiriak* corpses somewhere that they can be safely incinerated." He looked down at the insignia and squeezed it tight. Little sparks burned in the air as he purified it without even uttering a word.

Well outside of Steelhom's earshot, Panela's eyes went wide and she whispered into Xandros's ear. "*He wants us to touch them?*"

"*Not the time to argue. I've never seen him this pissed.*"

Pissed was an understatement. "Get to work. It won't take me long to find out what Usaic did here."

He was right. It barely took twenty minutes of poking through the freezing, muddy creek while the sun vanished behind the tops of the trees. It was a good thing he wasn't using just his eyes. The ether vibrated in the mini-canyon. A steady spell pulsed out of his palm to help cast a glow on anything that might make a difference. Every time something started to shine even a little, Eos'eno used short gusts of wind to blow away snow and old ash.

What she *didn't* do was comment on the limp he was sporting after falling into the creek. He wasn't about to admit it, but he badly bruised everything from the back of his thighs up to his kidneys. There was only so much that chainmail would do against gravity and rocks. As he searched, the garrison commander did too.

What was interesting about the scorched woodland wasn't so much that it was a scorched woodland – forest fires happen, even this far up from the lower lands. No, the oddities were what appeared to be ancient huts and small houses scattered among the trees. Whomever had founded the hamlet had wanted to keep it hidden. The fire didn't do much to help.

"It's gotta be a town," Mado grumbled, kicking at a small pile of stones over. "Or was. Old one."

"Have to agree with him, Commander," the other added. "If these woods hadn't caught fire, we'd never see this rubble. It'd be covered in so much overgrowth that it'd be lost."

Xandros didn't hear them. Something at the far edge of the woods had caught his eye, right behind the incinerated clearing. When he realized what it was, a couple of things clicked in place for him – and *he* wasn't even magically inclined. He also wasn't the only one making an important discovery.

It took more than just wind to blow away the debris that had covered a small alcove along the canyon wall. Someone had very purposefully stacked several boulders in front of it, and nature had done the rest. Unlike the rest of the woods though, it hadn't been touched by the flames. *Must have been built after all of this was torched*, Steelhom had mused at first.

With his help, Eos forcibly pulled the rocks free. Jolts of wind, brute force, and one final storm of ice shattered the stones and sent them flying. When she saw what was behind all of it, she wished she hadn't been in such a hurry to expose it. When the paladin smelled it, he agreed. The stench that rolled out made his eyes water and even visibly effected the wisp. White blisters welled up on her hands where she had pulled the stones free, and a small wail escaped her lips as she jumped up into the air and floated a safe distance away.

A large and jagged chunk of a sea-green crystal was nestled firmly into the back of the shallow cave. The whole thing reeked of Makolichi's essence; the color, the feel of the ether around it, and the horrible smell of brine-soaked rot. *And now we know where he walked into our world.*

When he walked close to it, things in the alcove changed. A trio of hexagonal, dual-pointed pyramids detached from the walls and up from the ground. All three were attached to the central crystal by loosely-hanging silver filaments. They looked like they had been crafted meticulously out of sylverine ore, and despite being buried for Goddess-knows how many years, they all looked perfectly clean.

Scorn dripped off of his every word as he stood there staring at it. "He conjured the demon and left the fissure open. I'm not even shocked. He ripped it open and pulled the demon out right here. Conjuration magic. Not elemental. No wonder the crack didn't seal. The fool only learned half of the way to do it right."

"It is not open. Look. It is sealed," Eos whimpered, sinking back down closer to the creek. "Nothing can come out, nothing can go in."

Steelhom didn't answer her directly. Just barely above a whisper, he spat out three Words in a row. The first two made the central crystal pulse five times over. The third made each of the pylons flash twice. Leaning against his halberd, he pursed his lips and assessed the situation out-loud.

"You're... right. Sealed, and sealed well. The pylons are both emanating the fog and keeping the fissure from opening. Interesting. I wager I would find these in the tunnel under the cabin as well. They're..." Carefully, he ducked back into the mouth of the cave and touched the closest pylon. It gave him a little tingle where his fingertips brushed and felt like it was pulling at him. "They're using the ambient energy that the fissure is expelling to keep it contained. I've never seen... never heard... of a spell capable of... *this*. I may have to retract my comments: truly, this is a masterwork or the crudest cast I have ever seen."

"I said, many-a-times did I say, that my lord is a true master, a true master, of magic and all manner of spells."

"Then why did he leave a portal to Tundrala open, if he was so careful to seal this one? Or... hmm. Did he think that the world would be better off if pure magic crossed over, and failed to see the consequences? Finding a way to improve it, just by... hmm. Just by letting raw magic from the Mount seep into our realm? It cannot be that simple, that stupid, not if he was this careful to protect against Frosel. Truly, this is a crude gash, patched with brilliance."

She was as perplexed as he was. "I do not know his motives. I only know what he did with the waters of Tundrala. I did not know, he never let on or said, what he had done here. Only that he had bargained for a servant to see his work through."

"Bargained? He bargained, did he? I wonder what for, and with whom." He debated touching the horrid thing in the back of the cave and thought better of it. "Although 'Whom' is beginning to become more and more apparent."

"He never said. He returned from his trip ashen and pale. It was not long after that the fire started."

"So the fire was his doing?"

Eos wavered a little, and floated up over the edge of the creek to see where the soldiers were. "Yes, the one that sent plumes of black clouds to the sky. I think... I think that yes, it may well have been at his hand. It burned so fierce, so long. Master was able to extinguish it, but not before the damage was done and the land laid to ash as you see it now."

"If it started after he left, he could have been covering his tracks," Steelhom mused. "Leaving this fissure exposed or at least evidence of his efforts wouldn't be wise. The woods would have kept it hidden, but a fire? Scorch the land and nobody would have wanted to come explore."

"He did go back to the flames on his own. I offered aid to him, and he declined, denied my help. Bade me to watch the *thing* he returned with. So I sat on the path with the other and waited, and watched from afar."

Far from happy, the paladin did eventually back away and sighed. "Well. It's contained, at least. Not that I trust it. It will have to be destroyed, right away."

The idea openly pained her. "Destroy master's efforts? Are you sure that is a wise course? If it is causing no harm..."

"No harm?" he incredulously asked. "Look at all the things it's attracted. Leaving it as it is will only entice other things to seek it out, or manifest around it. And what if it fails? Goddess only knows what sort of trouble that will cause."

Stopping her retort before she could even make it, Xandros shouted for attention. "STEELHOM! Found something you'll want to see!"

"What is it?"

"Easier shown than said. Get up here. Need a hand?"

He rankled slightly at the remark. "I am not so old that I cannot climb out of a ravine."

"You're old enough to retire and become a teacher," the other quipped. "Now get up here."

Eos rolled her eyes in a rough approximation of how she had seen Akaran do. "You two talk too much when there is so much to be done," she huffed. With a gesture and a little gust of air, she lifted Steelhom up out of the ravine and dropped him on top of its banks. "There. Do as you must. I must study master's work before you take away even more of his genius."

Feeling strangely violated, the paladin caught his balance and nervously pressed the handle of his weapon into the ground like he was afraid his feet would never find purchase on it again. "...thank you."

The wisp just huffed at him as she sank back to the alcove. He vaguely heard her muttering about humans always seeking to destroy and never to learn. Ignoring her, he followed Xandros through the ashes to the edge of the clearing. Mado was waiting for them and guided them into the woods.

"I think we found something that might help explain that amulet."

"One can hope. I'm growing as tired as my student with all of the questions. What is...?"

The question died in his throat as he saw what *had* to have been what the fire was supposed to have hidden. While time had not been kind to it, it was obvious that it had been some kind of long hall or chapel. The roof had collapsed ages ago, although even in the rubble, you could make out pews and a few tables.

Xandros pointed down to the ground, and pushed a few loose twigs out of the way with his foot. Under it was a stone tablet that had long since fallen to the ground. It had an inscription on it, and a name etched in large letters. "A name for you, and... read what's below it."

Kneeling down, Steelhom tried to pick it up. Even though it barely budged, he could make out the lettering. "STENT. A home of and for Love."

"Mean anything to you?"

With a slow shake of his head, the paladin answered slowly. "Stent? I've never heard of such a place. "

"They've heard of you," Xandros said as he gestured over his shoulder. "There's a bust back there that looks awfully like the one you used to pray to back in Boushidan."

Confounded, he followed behind the commander as he walked over to it. "A bust...? Of Niasmis? *Here?*" There wasn't any question about it; it *was* a bust of the Goddess. Obscured by a vine that had happily taken advantage of a standing stone pillar, it was one of the few things left relatively intact.

With a half-confused shrug, his friend stated the obvious. "I'm starting to think that your involvement in this isn't as random as your student made it seem."

"I'm starting to feel as lost as he is. Stent? Truly. I've never heard of such a place."

"Well. It's old, whatever it is. I doubt that anyone has lived here for hundreds of years."

"No less than two of those hundreds, yes. And still, I sense nothing that would have sanctified this ground, made it holy, made it... anything. Not a remnant. Nothing to show that a priest of Love was ever here, except for..."

Xandros crossed his arms and looked around the rubble again. "Except for all the evidence that your people were here."

Penela cleared her throat from outside the rubble. "And more," she said, walking over to them and sounding a slight bit out of breath. "Commanders. When you two are done, I think I found where the fire started."

Giving her a shared look that was both nervous and serious, the pair followed along behind her and back into the middle of the clearing. Once they got done dodging rocks and burnt trees, she stopped and gestured at what looked like a random pile of dirt on the ground. "Take a look."

The paladin got closer and realized that the dirt wasn't just random, and after a moment, he wasn't sure it even *was* dirt. Someone or something had built a circular mound of what he presumed was clay from the creek, about eight feet in diameter. Even stranger, the mound was set on top of a perfectly flat slab of granite.

It wasn't just one circle, either, but a concentric series of them. Four triangles had been cut into the dirt at equidistant points around it. Between each circle, he could make out a long squiggly line carved into the stone. Strangest of all was in the center of the rune, where something that looked like an eye had been crafted out of onyx.

When he realized what it was, it was less of a surprise than it should have been. "This is a summoning circle."

"The demon's?" Penela asked.

"No," Steelhom answered, frowning. "I found that in the creek. This has to be something else. This is a conjuration rune for spirits."

Eos'eno added what everyone else was thinking. "The *arin-goliath*. This is where the wraith was given birth."

"Yes. Do you recognize this? Does this appear to be something your master would have ever used, ever made?"

"Master? No. I cannot see him ever using such magic, such filth."

He silenced her with a wave of his hand. "You couldn't see him leaving that crack open, either. This..." Steelhom paused and reached down, setting his hand on the onyx eye. "No. This is Makolichi's work. That demon is responsible for Daringol."

If it had been possible for color to fade from Eos'eno's face, it would have. "If the demon is then master is by... no. No! Master wouldn't let wouldn't allow...!?"

"Makolichi either did it with his knowledge or did it without. If with, then we can begin to explain it away. If without, we have more questions than answers. *Again.* I am feeling more and more sympathetic for Akaran."

Scrambling to try to make sense of it, the wisp started to talk at a mile a minute. "Do... do you think that master somehow needed, wanted the *arin*? He has no magic over the undead, none I have ever seen, no taint in his aura. If he...? If he brought forth the demon in ice and brine, did he need Makolichi to summon the *goliath*? Or was this the cost he paid, the bargain he struck? But why? WHY?"

Steelhom sat down on his haunches and pondered the question before Xandros added his opinion. "He bargains for a demon to help him with a task that he supposedly got from your Goddess. Why does there have to be a reason? It's a demon. They exist to spread misery."

The paladin shook his head. "No. That's not what wraiths of this ilk do. They collect souls and grow. They don't spread grief and misery for the sake of spreading it. But I do wonder," he mused, taking a moment to bite down on his lip as he stood back up. "This breed absorbs latent magica. They feed on it. They form under the right circumstances or right spells... an abandoned village in the woods? Surely there would have been echos of grief and misery. Humans bring that with them wherever they travel."

Eos was quick to agree. "Yes. Your kind never needs to seek out ways to suffer for the exchange of power from other creatures or beings. Your race seems to exist only to serve as an outlet for all of the suffering in the world."

The solution came from their other female companion. "It's a sponge."

"Pardon?"

Penela realized that everyone was looking at her like she had just come up with the answer to the question of 'What is the meaning of life?' "It's a sponge. The wraith, that's what it is. If it feeds on latent magica, and Usaic has been leaving doors open everywhere, what if he wanted or needed a creature or a... a... foci? That the right word? A creature, something that could travel and absorb any traces of his work whenever it got out of control or spread past his territory."

Steelhom's eyes went wide. "Blessed be. *That's it!* And if he had no ability to call on or collect the power of the damned to start with..."

"...having a demon on a leash that can *would* be a boost to his research," Xandros added. "He broke it out of the pit, used it to make his sponge."

The paladin's thoughts raced right along with him. "He likely expected to destroy both Makolichi and Daringol after his experiments were complete. He wasn't going to let them free, not if he had been going to such extents to clean up after them."

"He did speak, privately and in hushed tones when he and I were together as one, after we were together as one, that he would no longer need the other creature when he was done."

Steelhom pursed his lips and looked at the snow-covered ashes on all sides of them. "For whatever reason, it all caught fire aft... no. Not whatever reason. I am of the strong opinion that this village was once a meeting place or a gathering for followers of Love. Opening a crack to Frosel? Having his new demon pet summon the core of a nesting wraith? I am not certain but I am willing to bet that any latent magic would interact and not interact well."

The garrison's commander rubbed his freezing hands together. "That would mean that this fire was accidental, and not done to cover his tracks. The forest had this village hidden; he wouldn't need to torch it."

"Quite possibly."

Silence reigned while they pondered the revelations. Xandros broke it with an irritated sigh. "Well. That's a mess. What do you plan to do from here?"

There wasn't much else that *could* be done other than the obvious. "Destroy this, end stop that other spell, and close the portal. Yes, Eos, I know that it's your master's work. I don't care. It's *not* supposed to exist in our world. It's a threat, as much as any of these lesser demons and zombies are."

Eos landed next to them and refused to look at them. "I detest that you must, for master asked me to protect his work. Yet I must agree;

purity is to be striven to, and the world cannot be brought in tune with the natural as long as such taint stands."

Grateful that she wasn't going to put up a fight over it, the paladin started to hand out a few tasks. "Good. Xandros? Gather any relics you can find that you think we can carry back. They may have importance. Or they may not. But they are relics of the Goddess, and need to be treated as such."

"Consider it done. What else do you need?"

"Time. I need time. But I feel that it is in short supply."

※ ※ ※

By the time the sun set in Gonta, Akaran was known across the city – and detested by most.

Even with no truth to it, most people blamed him for what had happened at Pauper's Row. With five people dead by the direct hand of the demon, and then both reanimated and quickly destroyed? Fingers were pointed at him with every opportunity. (Former) Captain Orin cursing his name to everyone that got in earshot didn't help the exorcist's reputation any, either.

On the other hand, the fact that he made the city guard sweep, shovel, and otherwise pile anything that either smelled *remotely* like brine, shit, blood, or any one of another half-dozen delightful smells into the center of the street and set the entire mess on fire? *That* endeared him to half of the population of the Row. After all, a clean gutter was a happy gutter. It didn't do anything for the people downwind of it, but it briefly endeared him to the immediate residents.

Thadius was not one of those residents.

The exorcist made the removal of Makolichi's hand as painless as he could. It wasn't perfect. It wasn't pretty. The thief cried and begged and screamed. It didn't do any good. It didn't stop Akaran from having to take a few inches more off of his arm than what the moron thought was necessary.

His screaming only got louder when the priest had cauterized the stump in a bowl full of assorted rocks and a handful of herbs. It combined to make a gorgeous pale-green and yellow flame. Somehow he didn't pass out, and extra priests that had wandered down from the temple to see what aid they could provide were more than happy to take him back to give him comfort and a measure of healing. Thadius, sadly, ignored every apology that Akaran gave him through the entire experience.

The priest really did feel bad about it. About all of it.

Makolichi's foci, however, was a slightly different story. One thing that he was quick to find was a small box that he just as quickly covered in as many runes as he could think of, then blessed it with just as many incantations and invocations. *Nothing*, absolutely *nothing* that had even a *hint* of belonging to the Abyss would be able to set their hands on it.

If there wasn't so much left to do, the priest would have sat on the box personally until the end of time. Or at least, until when Evalia and Mariah were ready to travel. Instead, he found more help from the local temple (all without having to step foot inside) who were happy to take the accursed thing off of his hands and put it in temporary storage inside the shrine. He didn't even have to explain why he needed to stick around in the city for a little bit.

It was an odd feeling finding people willing to help without throwing a fit.

He could get used to it.

One thing that it did do – something he'd have to confront later – was catch the eye of a priestess standing atop the shrine where so many had rushed to. The throng of people had trampled the garden and set their efforts to provide food for the masses back a few days, though as sad as it was, that was not something that the strawberry-blonde woman held against him. She watched him work, standing quietly for almost half an hour as he questioned those that had watched the fight and counseled those that had lost loved ones.

She watched him wave away a custodian who started to examine his wounds. Then she watched him curl up into a small ball and cry bitter tears from the pain when he didn't think anyone was watching. He patched himself back up and returned to work with none the wiser.

Before Deboria went back inside, she called for her page. A few moments and a quiet whisper later, he was told that when Akaran would arrive later that night to find room and board he was to be given a room and taken to a bath without argument. She didn't say how she knew he would.

They didn't ask. It wasn't the first time that the priestess had given an instruction that didn't make sense to them – until later it would. Nobody ever had the courage to ask, and it was just as well.

Sometimes, a seer's best trick was not letting on how she did it.

Even if he wasn't going to come to the temple as soon as most people would expect.

❋ ❋ ❋

Why am I even out here? Oh no, some uncorroborated 'legend' *about some long-dead crazy city official. Nobody else confirmed it or even muttered it. It's late. Why, again, am I not in bed? Oh, right. Because dustups like what happened at the Row tend to wake up anything napping about between this world and the Veil. If Galagrin is right and the story **isn't** just legend, there's probably something malevolent hanging around here.* **Dammit.**

The other truth was that after as bad as the fight had gone earlier, he did *not* want to have another face-to-face meeting with Rmaci today. The wards hadn't sent off an alarm, nobody from the prison had sent word about her health, so, why worry? If he could put her off until morning, that would be the best for everybody involved.

Akaran quietly sighed under his breath as he stood in the middle of the city metalworks. It was set off in the back of the city, nestled in the farthest corner that the natural rockface provided. There were a handful of carts pressed together, with stalls filled with anvils and hammers and assorted end-products scattered here and there with no real rhyme and reason. Little signs showed who owned what outdoor shop.

Every inch of his body ached, but the soft popping and settling of the forges as they continued to cool from a long day's worth of work helped set him at ease. The workshops were in various stages of disarray; hastily abandoned for the night for their workers to rush back to their homes and the inns to reward themselves with dinner and pleasures after a day successful for some and miserable for others.

It reminded him of how much fun he had working as a blacksmith's apprentice, before the incident.

In the farthest reaches of the street, he could see a large smelter still smoldering from being used all day long. Someone had taken the time to carve out grooves in the rock that (he assumed) would allow the unfortunate sods that had to work the mine to push carts full of their damned unpleasant jobs. All told, the only thing that made Gonta's smithing district stand out from anywhere else in the world was the fact that half of the stores and stalls were either right again or actually inside the cliff.

He caught sight of a woman wearing far too little clothing to be comfortable in the chill fawning over some fat tradesman as they drunkenly wandered out from behind one of the stalls; a jingle of coin in her purse, and his looked a little too empty for a man wearing that much (disheveled) finery. *How wonderful. The whores and the holy are walking and working the streets at the same time.*

Doesn't that make me feel special.

Of course, very little of it mattered right now – the metalworks, the whores, the last straggling merchants going home or going to taverns. They could have been in another city. They could have been in another *kingdom*, and it wouldn't have mattered right now. *Mariah...*

The hand mattered. The rock that his new 'friend' had found mattered, wherever he was hiding it. Whomever he was. *He's going to turn up sooner than later. Goddess knows I left enough of a mess back there. If he doesn't know I took care of Thadius's extra limb by now, I'm gonna be shocked. He probably knew about it before I finished cutting it off. So help me, if he doesn't...*

Frustration brimming under his skin, Akaran raked his eye over every nook and cranny that he could see. *Suppose nothing is out of place. Not that I'd know if anything was.* As he carefully walked down the roughly-cobbled street, he realized that he was being watched. At first, he thought it was a random guardsman – no doubt wondering who this new recruit was.

How the Overseer's men can stand to wear these scratchy uniforms is beyond me, he grumbled as he scratched at his neck. The only fresh armor that was readily on hand belonged to the Watch, and when they finally found something that could fit him, he had been too grateful to complain. That was then, hours ago. *Damn leather... they boiled it. Doesn't move doesn't breathe, making my chest **itch**.*

What a difference a few hours made.

What a difference hunting something for an hour without finding it made, too. The only time that something caught his eye for longer than a stare and a smirk was when he saw a woman walking through the shadows and for a brief moment, it looked like the alchemist's apprentice. Mariah made herself scarce after he finished with Makolichi, and he assumed (correctly) that she had gone to watch over Evalia.

*All this way to find a pregnant battlemage. There is no way and no world in which her husband is going to let her help fight, when we find something that we **can** fight. If she were mine? I wouldn't let her go to the village **at all** under **any** circumstances. If one of the wraiths so much as comes close to her, the things it could do...*

Swallowing the horrible revulsion that filled his mind, he stood perfectly still and closed his eye and did all he could to calm his thoughts and cut out the world for a few moments. With a whispered Word, a soft ripple in the ether radiated out from all around him. If there was a soul out of place, there would be an echo of sorts. It was one of three different techniques that he had been taught at the Temple, and... probably the one that was going to give the best results. Probably.

Or in this case, no result at all. *Goddess. I'm so tired I'm surprised I can even get that much out of me.* His sigh was joined by a resurgence of thoughts about Mariah, Evalia, and everyone else. *If it wasn't for Rmaci... if it wasn't for that stone that thug has... I'd call for Eos'eno now, have her fetch me, and leave them all here where it's safe. Can't yet. Going to try to sneak away in the morning anyways, but I can't yet.*

Maybe things will be better by morning. He looked up at the sky and sighed again. *You know. If there was any justice in this world, the Sisters would have sent me here, and sent Steelhom or someone to Toniki. This is a simple haunting. It's something that might not even be **here**. This is the type of task they kept saying that we'd get right away, isn't it? That when needed, yes, we would come after true demons and true monsters and whatever may crawl out of the pit but... a lost soul? Isn't **this** what everyone **always** says is just... neophyte work?!*

Resigned to being here anyways, the priest looked up to the sky and tried a different technique. "**Alright. Dead thing! Lost thing! Whatever you are! If you're here, you know *I'm* here. You know what I do,**" he shouted, hand on the hilt of his sword. "**If you are confused, find me. If you are in pain, find me. If you are unsure what it is that has happened to you, find me. If you're capable of understanding this, find me. Or if you think you're stronger than I am... *please* find me. I'll be happy to test your theory.**"

Nothing responded at first. Then, out of some corner of the market, someone with a drunken slur shouted back at him. "If ya don't shut it I'll come out an' test yer theory myself! Some o' us are tryin' tae get some damn sleep!"

A woman's throaty giggle shouted out right after him. "Well, he be tryin' tae get *somethin'*, that's for sure!"

He started to shout out a reply. Before a single sound could come out of his lips, his eye went wide, his arm started to burn, and the wards in Rmaci's cell screamed across the city at him. He turned and took off running, cursing himself every single step of the way for not bringing his horse along for the trip through the district. What Akaran didn't see and didn't hear was the little voice that called out to him from far back in the shadows in the middle of one of the smoldering forges.

"{He... hello? It's... dark, so dark, so... I can't see? He... hello? Can... you hear me?}"

When the exorcist didn't answer, someone else did with a laugh that only the nervous voice could hear. "[He can't/he won't! I can/I will!]"

"{I... he... hello?}"

It was supposed to be safe in Bolintop Mine, or so Akaran had lead Hirshma to believe.

Sadly, there was only so much that his magic could do in the face of magic he didn't understand. Worse than what he didn't understand was the magic he didn't know was there. Say what you will about Usaic, his spells and enchantments had worked exactly as intended. Or at least, the spells and enchantments that he had used to hide evidence of the *other* spells and enchantments had worked as intended.

This was Hirshma's second trip to the mine in the last few weeks. Her first trip had ended with her sealing three zombies in it. Soon after, Akaran had arrived at the village and as a test of his own ability (and courage), she had sent him to go deal with it. Of course, being who he was, he was quick to make a mess of *all* of it.

She did have to admit that rummaging around through the abandoned pit probably wasn't half as fun as she had expected it would have been (although she didn't have high expectations). Not that digging through a mine on your own *could* be fun, but its condition dashed even those minor expectations. A few years back, the roof of the mine had collapsed somewhere near the central chamber – a large room that, on its own, could fit her house and two or three others without much trouble.

That chamber was home to the pumps that helped sluice the water out of the lower areas of the mine that the veins of sylverine stretched down into. Unfortunately, when the roof caved, it crushed some of the pumps. With the pumps crushed, not only did it render access to the sunken shafts impossible, it had caused the mechanisms that fed the pipes leading back to the surface to fail, a compounding it.

And to *further* make matters worse, the cause of the roof collapse was an overflowing stream. Even though it had slowed down since then, it was still draining into the chamber. The only guess she could make as for why it hadn't completely submerged the room was that it was draining into the lower shafts or to another underground river somewhere.

It was a really good guess and damn important to keep in mind later.

It wouldn't even take long for her to realize it.

Steelhom had told her to take three guards with her to the mine. When she got back to Toniki, his instructions didn't hold much weight without him actually being there to back it up. Not that she *tried* to make a fuss over it. So, she left with two, if for no other reason than to say that she had.

She hadn't bothered to learn either of their names, either. "Soldier One" and "Soldier Two" worked for her, though they would have preferred she had called them Privates Sassilo and Connel. When Sassilo had attempted to get even that much from her, the alchemist politely told them that she didn't want to get attached.

"Won't bother me so much if you two drop dead."

You could have written a book about the look the two of them gave each other.

When the exorcist arrived at Bolintop a little more than a week prior, the three zombies he had been tracking weren't alone. To even call them 'zombies' felt insulting to her, when she had known them in life. The three of them had been a small family, consumed by a vomiting sickness when she was a little girl. They weren't anyone important, but they were her people. They were important to *her*.

That was why she couldn't bring herself to try to destroy them on her own. Not because she didn't think she could. Not because she was afraid of the hounds that were stalking the woods at the time. Not because she didn't think they were abominations. It was because they were good people that she remembered and she just couldn't bring herself to killing them a second time.

Akaran, however, had no cause to show no such restraint.

When he cleared through the mine, he found the remains of a Steward of Ice – and soon after, found the three animated corpses in the central pump room. He also found the first Daringol wraith that had made a public appearance, and the young buck that it had animated. The fight was short and the deer was bloody.

When it was done, he had cremated the corpses as sanctified the cavern. His job done, he had left without exploring the lower levels. She had to admit that there truthfully hadn't been any reason for him to do so. Three corpses plus an unexpected straggler and no sign of anything else? Once all of them were accounted for, there wasn't any *reason* for him to stay.

Before she had left for the mine, Hirshma and Steelhom had a short conversation that went along the lines of: "You want *me* to go there?

And do *what?* I'm no priest! I can't banish demons! That's what you and that addle-brained fool you call your student do!"

"If you find more demons, then we will know that there's reason to explore more."

"*IF?* And if I do, *what?*"

"I would run, were I you."

She had stood there, mouth agape. "You... you're sending me somewhere to find something and that something might be demons or ghosts or whatever it is that's doing all this nastiness and the only advice you can offer is *run?* I'm not someone that *runs* anywhere! Look at me! I'm an old woman, you daft - !"

"That itself would be why I am telling you to take soldiers with you. I'm not sending you alone. You have soldiers. You have some magic of your own, whenever you can finish apologizing to Kora'thi. *Hopefully* She will let you channel Her work again into something more useful than walls of vines. Maybe the ability to slow down the loss of blood? That seems like it would be a very important, useful trick, if you could learn how to quickly regrow the damage from wounds."

"Kora'thi's magic isn't... it's not..."

Steelhom hadn't been impressed, to say the least. "No. The magic *of* the world is not magic known to easily dissuade the things that are *not* of this world. Some things yes, some ways, some things become aversions and yes, a few of you have learned how to hone and turn your energies against the unnatural. I realize that even on your best day you were not likely one of them, were you?"

"On my best day? On my *best day!?* I will have you know that -"

"- that I don't care. Go to my room at the Rutting Goat. When you're there, open the brown canvas sack with the amethyst clasp on the front. There's going to be several bundles inside. Find the one that has the *red* ribbon wrapped around it. There are going to be three copper charms with pearl insets inside it along with a sapphire-and-silver bracelet. Take all four."

"Jewelry? You want me to go to Bolintop and take... *jewelry?*"

The paladin nodded. "Yes. I do. Or go without, and risk not having them. The charms are imbued with enough of the Goddess's magic that they will dissuade Daringol from accosting you. If there is anything else Abyssian or Abyssian-tainted with more power than the wraiths, the bracelet will heat up to warn you."

"Oh."

"Yes. Oh."

And now, standing in the middle of the pump room, Hirshma looked up at the cloudy skies beyond the collapsed roof. "Well. They're not doing anything so maybe it's working. Or maybe it's not."

Dutifully standing behind her, the soldiers opted not to comment. They were just happy she had agreed to give each of them one of the copper charms instead of keeping them for herself. On the other hand, they were better armed than she was – swords eager for blood, chainmail and leather armor ready to take a hit from anything with an actual body, and Steelhom's crystals around their necks.

"Well? Are you two just going to *stand* there or *do something?*" the alchemist/harpy/old-bitch-they-all-hated snapped.

It would be a lie to say that they weren't debating doing something that would be legally and ethically questionable to her. It would *probably* be forgiven by the Gods... eventually. Since neither of them wanted to actually talk to her, they both took off without a word. While she lingered by the pile of ashes that Akaran had left behind, they started to scout the room.

While the two of them wandered through the cavern, the alchemist didn't have any idea where to begin or what to think. Steelhom had given her specific things to look for: damage to any of Akaran's wards, any odd piles of sylverine, and any evidence that Usaic had crafted any special enchantments that his student might have missed. It was a tall order, no matter how you looked at it.

Not that I'm **qualified**.

That wasn't all. The list of things further included a request to keep her eyes open for anything out of place. And, as if that wasn't going to be hard enough ("I'm not a miner!" was her argument), she was also to rule out any other outside influence. After all, there was no promise that Rmaci had been the only Civan agent sent to investigate or annihilate.

Fisking slave-driving pompous asshole.

His logic, however, had been sound. "I assume that at times, a druid of the Goddess of Nature and a specialist in magic based upon the realm of one of Her children would have had time to work spells together?"

Hirshma hated how much he stressed their interlocking abilities. "He asked for help with one thing or another. What man doesn't whine for his woman?"

Steelhom just gave her a condescending smile. "Then you have the most familiarity with his work than any of us could ever hope for. Shy the wisp, of course. As I need her with me, **you** can be spared to dredge the mine."

For some reason, the trio of zombies and the wraith had congregated here. They could have gone deeper, or could have scattered through the shafts. Instead, they opted to camp out *here,* which was oddly interesting.

More importantly, they came on their own. They hadn't been lead here. They hadn't been chased here. They came here, all the way from Toniki's graveyard, when they could have gone anywhere else at all. Maybe it was a fluke that all of them had worked their way into the chamber by the time Akaran reached them.

It was a fluke that had become exceptionally annoying over the last twenty minutes. "I know how to brew tonics that can cure a cough or a tincture for an infection! I don't know how to look for a... a... I don't even know what!" she shouted, frustrated at the cold, the questions, the fact that she was even there, and at the dampness that covered seemingly *everything* in the cave.

*Usaic's magic works on its own rules and laws but if there are rules then there is an order to it. **That** is the rule of the world. **That** is the alchemetic. I may not be some stuffy-headed know-it-all but I **know** science and I damn well remember what the **natural** order is. My spells don't change nature. They magnify it. It's **entirely** different and I am **not** going to let that bastard make a fool of me.*

If those twits from that divine bitch can figure out what he was doing, I damn well can too. "Fisk you, Usaic, hope wherever you're rotting you're forced to watch us rip everything you made to shreds!" she shouted, stopping her foot in the muddy pool that filled most of the chamber. *And I at least know how the bastard works!*

The puddle was deeper than she thought and the splash soaked her leg. Hearing her curse a second time, the two soldiers looked over at her but didn't volunteer any ideas of their own. They volunteered a pair of rolling eyes and Sassilo gave a smirk out of sight, but no ideas. That was okay: the small pool had finally given her one.

With a long look up at the small waterfall coursing into the mine, another piece fell into place. *That water. The likely source of that runoff is from Teboria Lake, where we know that that bastard wizard opened a gateway into Tundrala. Which means that this water is the same water that's laced with all that... magic.*

Usaic has been able to keep everything he's done under a mask. If Eos'eno was summoned here, then it begs to assume that he has a mask in the mine somewhere. Magic isn't self-sustainable. Whatever 'rules' *that these damn mages and wizards and abominations have, **that one** seems to be one that's immutable no matter how hard they try. So, either the mask is being charged by the latent magic in the water or there's something else... no. I bet that bastard orchestrated the roof to collapse to hide whatever it was he was working on in here.*

*We know that the wraiths are drawn to magic and that they came here before that boy-priest used his. So, if they can sense Usaic's magic and are drawn to it, that means that they can see through his concealment. Since we know that they **can**, there **is** something here, something latent, something that's a draw. Something more than the lake to coax them away.*

"Hrumph. I'm not half as bad as they think that I am. Underestimate me. Stuck-up holy men."

*Now. Why **this** room. There is something wrong here. Doesn't make sense.*

Determined not to let the priests outsmart her (she knew, she just *knew* that the two of them were solving their particular problems on their own) Hirshma took a deep breath and looked at the room, really looked at it. There was a trio of pumps opposite the path that they had followed in the lowest part of the chamber, and a waterwheel in the middle of the room. Snowdrifts from above had piled up in the corners, and icicles hung from the ceiling.

The mill had broken; half of the water wheel had shattered. One of the three pumps that should have been connected to it was nearly buried under a pile of rubble. Strangely though, there was just a little bit that made the entire system look like something was amiss.

The pumps themselves were of an ingenious design, and something about them nagged at her in the back of her mind. They were a combination of a boiler and piston with pipes that dangled into the drainage trough and other pipes that trailed from their tops and into the rusted lines that lead outside. When lit, the pumps would boil water, causing steam pressure to build up inside. When enough steam was accumulated, it would lift the piston inside the machine, which would let the steam out through the top and pull more water in from below.

It wasn't a fast process. However, with all three pumps going at once, it would have done a great job in pulling water out of the lowest places in the mine and push steam everywhere else for warmth. Since coal was abundant in the mine, it had a ready source of fuel to burn without requiring lengthy trips to bring in logs from outside.

The mill in the middle of the cavern had been built with the stream above in mind. When the mine was operational, the stream would feed the waterwheel, and that would power some additional machinery the miners had used. The pumps would handle the rest whenever water started to pool up in the wrong shaft, or in the event of a bad flood.

And in case the cave flooded completely, or they needed to prime the blowers, it would just take a couple of men to manually work the waterwheel to start things moving. While she thought about it, she looked down at the broken planks of the waterwheel and nudged it with her boot. *Yes, that's how it's supposed to work.*

Finally, it clicked for her. The small stream should have been pouring into the waterwheel. That was why it was there. That was how it worked the gears and mechanisms next to it. Except it wasn't. The stream wasn't pouring onto the wreckage.

*So I wonder... why is this **here** and not over **there**?*

She looked up at the hole in the ceiling and at the broken-down wheel while quietly working her jaw. No question about it, there was no way for the waterfall to feed the mill this far away from each other. It wouldn't have even been close when the roof was intact. The pieces were simply in the wrong place to get wet, let alone to churn the wheel.

There was only one rational answer: somebody had moved the wreckage to the middle of the room. That made it important. When she got closer to it, she was distracted by another discovery:

A little critter had made the pile of debris home.

Hirshma yelped in fright when a flicker of movement and the rustling of shifting wood caught her ear. One of the two soldiers looked over at her and drew his blade while she clutched at the dagger she had brought with her. "Whatever you are, get out of there or so help me I will show these thugs what an old lady can still do!"

The critter obliged. It was a tiny thing and looked like it had been half-starved. A small brown nose poked out of the rubble, followed quickly by a pair of round shining eyes. The ears came out next – long, floppy things that were as ratty as they were cute. Rolling his eyes again, Connel resumed looking for important clues and not just a bit of fluff that would barely make good stew.

Seeing it brought everything else to a screeching halt. All she could think when she saw it was how much her daughter had loved playing with the rabbits in the woods. They always seemed to have a way to find her, and she was never without one by her side. She had to stop a trembling tear at the memory, and smiling, she knelt down and reached for the critter.

With a wiggle of its tiny tail, the bunny jumped up into her arms before she could even reach out for it all the way. For one brief moment, the gravity of the situation vanished and a little bit of warmth crept into her heart. It nuzzled in against her chest and quietly clicked its hind feet together as it burrowed.

All she could think of was her daughter, and how much she would have loved the small ball of gray and white fur. "Why are you here, hm? What's a cute little thing like you doing down here in a hole like this?"

Just barely loud enough for Sassilo to hear, Connel answered instead. "It's being a bloody rabbit. What's it supposed to do? Bring world peace?"

His companion nearly choked in a fit of hushed laughter. Hirshma pointedly ignored both of them. "Poor thing, you look half starved. How long have you been down here, anyways?"

Rabbits weren't known to talk back. This one wasn't any kind of exception to the rule. It did wiggle a bit more though, then happily jumped out of her arms and went scampering off to another part of the cave. After she watched it go bounding off behind a snowdrift, a little sparkle of something caught her eye under the broken boards. After a moment's effort kept her from reaching it, she gave up and shouted to the guards.

Connel tried to ignore her attempts to call for him, but after the third one, he finally relented. "Ma'am, please don't call me 'soldier two.' I've served in the Queen's Army for going on seven years now and -"

"And now you can come serve that glorified hag by helping me dig through this garbage. It ain't gonna move itself."

He started to sap back a reply when the other soldier interrupted. Off on the other side of the room, Sassilo was looking down a small hallway that lead off to one of the mining shafts. "Alchemist? I think this might be worth your time." Then, over to Connel, the soldier whispered a hushed *"Can't get you out of the work but you don't have to do it with her hovering over you. Good luck."*

The other soldier grunted out a thanks and wandered over to the rubble. Hirshma passed him by without even a nod. Grumbling under his breath about his damn luck getting stuck with this detail, the guard went to work dragging bits of the wreckage off of the pile, a board at a time.

"Oh worth my time? Something in any of this soggy bog is worth my time?"

He shrugged and stepped back away while he and Connel both

flanked the doorway. She took her sweet and slow time walking over. "Never worked a mine before. Soldier, my whole life. Don't think that's right."

It was hard to admit that he was right. He was just some idiot that knew how to swing a sword. Why would he be right? Unfortunately, he was. "You're right. It's not," she grumbled. Just a few feet past the hallway, out of sight of the pumping chamber, there was a pile of coal and loose chunks of rock with little pieces of sylverine ore glistening in the middle of it. More importantly, and more than strangely, a plant was growing out of it.

A weed or moss or *something* spindly that could bloom in winter would be one thing and not worth notice.

This was something else entirely.

Hirshma knelt down to look at it closely while she tried to make sense of what she saw. It was a three-foot-tall plant that was as white as spider-silk and nearly as translucent. Long bushy leaves sprouted out from the stalk, but while the leaves were translucent the veins inside had the softest blue glow anyone in the mine had ever seen. Three large golden 'flowers' decorated the top of the plant, but they were unlike anything that she had ever seen. Each one looked like lace doilies, though while the patterns on each one were similar, they were also individually unique.

"This is... no... this is not of this world... this is not... normal..." she quietly whispered while the two soldiers waited for her next instruction. With barely a thought to them, she waved them forward to continue exploring the hallway. "Usaic you wonderful monster, what did you do..."

It was cold to her touch but far from unpleasant to hold one of the leaves in her hand. The flowers put off a quiet little musical chime sound just almost at the edge of her hearing, and the stalk vibrated just slightly whenever her breath brushed over it.

Her mind went to work in two different directions at the same time. With one hand, she reached into a pocket inside her coat and pulled out a small little vial she had debated packing for the trip. Carefully, uncorked it and poured a small pile of brown dust and bits of soil into her palm. *If it ain't of the natural world, no amount of herbal remedies is gonna tell me a thing about it. Only question now is if the land is willing to speak to me.*

The alchemist closed her eyes and recanted an ages-old prayer, one that was passed down from generations of her family. "*As fire to ash as ash to soil as soil into growth; as ice to water as water into growth; as wind to clouds and clouds to rain as rain to water into growth; as death to rot and rot to decay and decay into growth; let me reap, let me sow, let me find new places new ways for growth to take hold..."*

A small green vine sprouted from her hand as she spoke to the land. It was different than what she had done with Makolichi had attacked the town days past: those brambles wouldn't have lasted more than a few moments at best without the wellspring font that the exorcist had found. *This* spell would do more than just cause a few plants to take temporary root.

The roots wouldn't be so temporary, and they'd go searching.

The vine sprouted multiple stalks and each one crept into the pile of coal. Hirshma carefully set the small handful of soil down onto the ground and stepped slightly away from it. The vines didn't attempt to cut off or uproot the amazing flowers anchored into the seam. No, instead they coiled themselves a few inches away from the bottom of the roots.

While she waited, they turned down and sunk through the coal and into the floor. Grateful that the Goddess of Nature was kind enough to let her use the (significantly more taxing) spell, the alchemist watched the vine happily throb as it continued to grow deeper and deeper into the world. While she waited, she walked down the hallway to see if the meatshield/guard/soldier had found anything else worth noting.

He had. Apparently, the bunny decided that this was an idea worth exploring too, and it quietly hopped down the hall after them. It was so small that if she hadn't seen it out of the corner of her eye, she wouldn't have known it was there. *It's so adorable. Wish these foolish twats were half as cute as it is.*

There were more outcroppings of plants that had no business existing in this world all down the hallway. They even put off their own light; no torches required for the humans and nothing so inconsequential as 'sunlight' apparently was needed to encourage the crystalline and icy plants to grow. Walking through the shaft was akin to walking through a wonderland.

Everywhere she went, she could see clumps of phantom grass that had taken sprout on the ground. Or she'd see spots on the mine walls where sheets of reflective ice had turned rocky walls into completely flat mirrors. It was stunningly beautiful. Everywhere she went, the supernatural fauna had taken root. Even pieces of mining equipment had been turned into mystical outcroppings. A mining cart had become an over-sized flower pot for a blue and pink crystalline bush. A sledgehammer had been stood up on the flat of its head and used as a trellis for a trio of differently-colored vines.

It was all so surreal.

Out in the pump chamber, none of that beauty was being enjoyed. An offshoot of her plant had slowly snaked its way through trickling water and small pieces of sylverine. When it crept towards Connel, the end of it stood up a little bit and pointed at his face. It paused there, wiggled a moment, and then slipped itself back onto the ground.

"You're friendlier than that bitch is," the guard grunted as he struggled to pull a wooden beam out of the pile of broken wood.

The vine sprouted a few leaves in response and wiggled again.

"And you know it, too."

It sprouted three more, then pushed itself between the fallen boards. Five more stalks sprouted out and branched away, with two creeping off into another part of the cave. The other three sank into the wood and dug around. They were going after something under there. If nothing else, it encouraged him to keep digging.

Down the hallway – and ahead of Hirshma – Sassilo was on a similar journey of discovery. The ever-increasing number of odd plants and twisted tools didn't leave half the impression on him as it did the alchemist. While she was overly impressed by the nature (or at least, the lack of natural order) of the changes in the world around them, he saw it for what it was: the warping of reality.

Strangely enough, it didn't set so well with the career soldier. It sat so unwell that as he continued through passageways that felt like they were getting smaller by the minute, he pulled his shield off of his back and held it safely in front of him. Eventually, the tunnels lost their rocky texture and changed into a meandering passage that was iced over on almost every surface.

The only thing that kept him from sliding around and slipping on every inch of it was the odd texture to the bottom of the hall. It was like... was like... it had been *made* to allow someone to walk on it. *More of this freak show. Mages, exorcists, demons? Need more than the 13th up here. Need the whole damn Army. Bet Piata would have this solved in a day.*

On the other hand, a little voice in the back of his head *was* slightly impressed by all of it. It was unlike anything he had seen before. When he rounded one last bend, he caught an eyeful of a multi-tiered chamber made of the same ice as the hallway, and filled with so many of the odd plants and growths that he had seen on his trip.

In the lowest part of the cavern, in a flooded, almost completely-clear pool, there was the largest deposit of sylverine ore that he – or just about anyone else in the world – had ever seen. The amber sheen from it reflected off of every facet of the ice on the walls. A huge six-faced crystal floated over it, held in place by a six thick gold cables anchored to various parts of the room.

It was the crown jewel of the winter wonderland – no question about it.

A wonderland that suddenly turned into a nightmare.

The roar was the first sign Hirshma had that something was wrong. The screaming was the second although it seemed like it was just adding to the noise. She looked down at the bracelet and didn't even bother containing her profanity – it was doing absolutely *nothing.*

Sassilo rounded a bend and nearly ran head-long into the alchemist. Something had bloodied the side of his face, and that wasn't all. His shield was missing, he was limping, and his left arm was pulled up and tucked against his chest. "RUN MOVE GO NOW!"

Hirshma resisted for a moment while he pushed on her.

But only for a moment.

The monstrosity could barely shove its way around the support beams and through the low-hanging ceiling. It was a hulking behemoth, with a body made of nothing but snow. It had a bulky torso and gut, with legs that could have doubled as tree trunks. Its arms were just as large and thick, which made the entire thing look like some twisted mockery of a muscle-bound human. All of it, that was, except for the head.

The head could have belonged to a dragon. It had a thick long snout, and teeth that were barely contained in its jaw. Brilliant blue eyes focused on her for the longest heartbeat she had ever had in her life.

And then it roared again, and she ran. It lumbered along after them, smashing the strange plants and the support beams in the hall without thought or care. If it wasn't for the tightness of the hallway, they would have been dead. Hirshma knew it, Sassilo knew it, and the monster knew it. Halfway back to the pump room, Hirshma had one suddenly and brilliant idea.

Coming to a complete halt, she made the soldier stand in front of her to fend it off for a few moments (if you could call it that). The guard all-but shit himself in terror and held his sword with a trembling hand.

He was completely utterly and totally clueless about what to do. It was only by her barked insistence that if he didn't help, they'd all end up dead.

While he not-at-all-bravely tried to stand his ground, she focused what magic she had left into a vein of sylverine on the wall. Unlike the small vine earlier, this time she made the brambles that she had used to defend everyone in Toniki rip out of the ground. They whipped out and quickly filled the hall in front of her. As they grew, the alchemist was able to focus them to dig into the ceiling and to attack the support pillars.

Between the behemoth's rampage and her plants, the back of the hallway caved in with a roar of its own. A cloud of icy debris billowed out and blinded both of them. Her brambles absorbed as much of the spray of stones and dust as they could, and the vines closest to them kept the cave from falling on top of them as well.

The plantlife couldn't stop all of it though. They could barely see to make it out of the tunnel, and from the sound of things, the monster was suffering just as much. The two of them listened close for any sign that it was going to try to dig its way through the rubble after them. It was a miracle that it didn't — as best as they could tell, it gave up the chase and had started to work its way back in the other direction.

As soon as it was out of earshot, Hirshma grabbed the guard by his good arm and made him look at her. "*What was that!? What did you do!?*"

"I didn't do a damn thing! I found some kind of cavern. Big. Entire bottom of it is flooded and full of sylverine and there's this giant crystal floating in it and... then that thing..."

"That *thing?* Is that all you can call it?"

Sassilo carefully cradled his arm, cursing. "I don't *know* what to call it. It came out of nowhere and... it swung one of those massive fists and... almost shattered my shield... ruined it, nearly broke my arm in the process."

She didn't even keep the scorn out of her voice. "More monsters. Damn that bastard, just... *damn him.*"

"Don't know which bastard you mean. Prolly agree on the damn him though, no matter which one." With a pained groan when she pulled his arm over to look at the damage, he stated the openly obvious. "Ma'am. We have to go. Now."

With an extensive curse that matched his, Hirshma didn't argue it. Confident that his arm wasn't going to fall off anytime soon, she took off running along behind him. Truthfully, it was more of a frightened jog; age makes a difference at times.

When they reached the pump chamber, Connel was happy to see them for a few brief moments. When they shouted yelled and otherwise told him to grab his shit and run, his happiness went away. Somewhat convinced that their lives weren't in immediate danger, he almost begged the alchemist over to the broken watermill.

"Hurry up and show me. I want to get the pits out of here so I can go back and cuss out that fisking priest for sending me down here to get killed."

"Sending *you* down!?" Sassilo yelled. "*I'm* the one that went face to face with that... *thing!*"

"Yes yes, you have reason to be upset with him, too. So what is it, soldier two?"

He let the rudeness slide and pulled another board away from the pile. "That."

Behind them, the rabbit slowly hopped back up to sit beside the alchemist while she tried to make sense of what she was seeing. Someone had dug a hole in the ground, almost six feet long and two feet across. Nestled in it there was another six-sided dual pyramid tucked into the ground. Unlike the big one, there weren't any chains or cords that held it in place and it wasn't floating. It looked dull, like whatever magic had that had given the other one life had completely faded away.

Beside it there was a white silken shroud wrapped around a small lump. When she reached down to touch it, it was freezing cold to the touch – albeit not unpleasant. With the two soldiers alternatively looking back towards the shaft and down at her, Hirshma carefully unwrapped it.

A little sobbing sound bubbled out of her throat as she held a ratty little doll in her hands. It wasn't anything special to look at; just a canvas doll, stuffed with wool, with little black buttons for eyes and a small tan pebble for a nose. She ran her fingers through strands of knitted hair and tried to hold back another sob.

"Mayabille... this is... this is hers..."

Sassilo started to ask who Mayabille was, but was rudely interrupted twice over. The first interruption came when a gust of wind colder than anything any of them had ever felt rushed from the frozen cavern and into the chamber. Tendrils of silvery ice that moved in ways nothing solid ever could or should manifested briefly in the air and reached for the doll. Other little tendrils sprouted up from the small pit and tried to meet them before fading away.

A brief pillar of snow erupted around them and a small little tear in the air flashed into being briefly, just long enough for them to see a winter wonderland beyond comprehension before it slammed shut. The instant that it did, the cold winds and silvery streamers vanished along with it.

Before they could try to cope with *that* and whatever it meant, the monster roared again. Without taking the time for another thought, she grabbed all three items. And with that, everyone ran like their lives depended on it. The creature's angry shouts didn't let up until after they were out of earshot of Bolintop.

Not to be forgotten, the little bunny happily ran along behind them.

VIII. BLACK ICE

By the time that he reached the prison, there were three other city guardsmen standing in the hallway outside of it. All of them were shouting at someone in the dungeon and none of them were getting responses back. "Leave the bitch alone!" was one, "Dammit Rogerin, say something!" another, and "Get out of her cell before that crazy priest comes back!"

The rest of *that* shout died on the lips of the guard that made it when Akaran stumbled breathlessly into the stairwell. "The crazy... priest is... is here," he gasped, reaching for a wall to steady himself. "What in the name of the Goddess is going on?"

One of the others turned to him and tried to back away. Unfortunately, he backed into a wall, which did him no good whatsoever. "Rogerin, he... he missed meal call. Went looking for him. Found him here. He's in the cell with that Civan bitch. Won't answer. She's done something to him, she has."

Another guard babbled another excuse. "I went in and tried to get him out of it, but the door... wouldn't open. Tried to grab him. He wouldn't budge. Sent for help about ten minutes ago. Think they're trying to find you or Captain Orin or..."

"Orin isn't in charge of anything anymore and I thought I made it *damn* clear *nobody* was to get near her. Did you think I said that just for the sake of hearing myself *talk?*"

The one that had called him crazy added his own two copper's worth. "Don't know when he went in. Ain't none of us have seen

Rogerin since you left."

Akaran cursed – vividly – and drew his sword. "Under authority of the Queen, I am removing him from that cell. Interfere, and you'll join him in a cage hanging over the marketplace as an example of how not to live your life. Is that understood?"

The trio reluctantly murmured their consent.

It wouldn't have mattered even if they hadn't.

The second that he got a look at Rmaci's cell, anger overtook him. She was curled up in a corner on the floor, with her clothes torn to loose shreds that covered nothing. The left side of her face was covered in a deep purple bruise, her lip was split, and one eye was swollen nearly shut. There were fresh bruises on her thighs, and bigger ones on her breasts. She was conscious, barely, and crying.

Spy or not. Murderess or not. Traitor or not.

This. Of all things. *This* would *not* stand.

He didn't even realize he was walking through the dungeon before he was inside her cell. He grabbed the jailer and shoved him away from her with all of his might and into the wall. "Goddess above, Rmaci, no, I am so sorry, so so sorry, I -"

Rough hands grabbed him from behind and shoved him into the metal bars of the cell. The first blow stunned him, and the second nearly knocked him out. The impact made his arm go numb for a moment, making his sword hit the ground with a clatter. His assailant didn't get a chance for a third. Backed with righteous anger, the young priest couldn't have stopped himself even if he wanted to.

And there was absolutely no part, no inch of him, that wanted him to stop.

Akaran thrust his elbow back with all the might he could give it, planting the point into his attacker's solar-plexus. He was rewarded with a hard grunt and he was let go. He pivoted around enough to get a glimpse of where his opponent just before putting his fist into the man's mouth.

The punch made the dungeon's jailer stagger backwards. A second punch hit him right in the center of his forehead and made his neck snap back at an almost-unnatural angle. When the jailer straightened back up, there was more than an 'almost' unnatural look to him.

His mouth hung open and slack-jawed, with drool dribbling out of the corner out his mouth. His eyes had rolled back up in his head. They were bloodshot and seeping black tears down his face. More black goo seeped out of his mouth. A pair of black tentacles dangled from his nose, twitching and snapping at the air.

There was no reason that the guard should have been able to stand upright, let alone be able to fight. He fought anyways. He threw a trio of heavy, slow punches at the exorcist – the first two, he ducked. He caught the third in his hands and *twisted,* first breaking his wrist, then another twisting jerk to break his elbow.

It didn't slow the other man down at all. Akaran grabbed him by his tunic and shoved him with all of his might out of the cell. The runes erupted with sparks that front of the guard's head burst into flames that lasted for just a few short moments.

Staggering back while the exorcist trudged forward, the jailer swung his broken arm like a club, which hit him across his cheek. It sent the younger man sprawling onto a table next to the wall. Without missing a beat, the guard lumbered after him and grabbed the priest by his throat with both hands.

He vaguely heard the sound of people shouting and rushing down the stairs beside him. He *distinctly* heard a low hissing noise coming out of the guard's throat while he strangled him with an inhumanly strong grip.

Akaran couldn't get a breath enough to shout a Word, so he did the next best thing.

He reached up away from his attacker and grabbed at a smoldering sconce on the wall. After it with a sharp tug he was rewarded when it broke free in his hands. A quick move later, and he smashed the iron and wood torch into the side of the jailer's skull.

The impact broke the grip on his throat. A hard kick and shove with his foot pushed the guard into one of the cell doors. It was all of a respite that the exorcist needed. The guard didn't get a third chance to try to kill him.

Torch in hand, Akaran lunged forward and used it like a burning club. He broke his nose first, then his jaw. With raw anger blazing in his only eye, the priest bludgeoned his assailant until whatever had possessed the poor sod couldn't keep him up on his feet any longer. The blows sent the guard to his knees, hands dangling by his sides, almost in supplication.

Without any hesitation, the priest grabbed him by his throat and wrenched his head up and back. *"**ILLUMINATE**."* The Word caused a surge of light to blossom out of the guard's eyes – but black light, entirely, completely black. The result made the priest snarl in disgust. Darkness erupted everywhere under his skin, showing how deep

Daringol had spread into the guard.

While Rogerin had delighted in raping Rmaci, Daringol had fed off of the heinousness of the act. It wasn't going to be the last thing that the wraith was going to swallow – he was going to make *damn* sure of that.

In the stairwell, he saw more people finally arrive. One of them he didn't want to see; the other, he didn't care. Mariah shouted at him from the doorway, her voice almost at a shriek. "AKARAN! WHAT ARE YO DOING?! STOP!"

Akaran paid her no heed. "When I told you bastards that I was going to make you choke on me, *I fisking meant it,*" he seethed. While the girl watched, he jerked the guard's head back to force him to look straight up.

And then, smiling, he calmly flipped the torch in his hand right-side up, right before he shoved it, point first, into the guard's mouth as hard as he could. His attacker spat blood and loose teeth around the handle, bloodshot eyes as wide as they could be. With another, harder thrust, he twisted the torch until it was well and firmly lodged in the jailer's throat. Snarling, he stepped away and jerked his victim forward, letting Mariah, the other guards, and the battlemage get a nice long look at the corrupted rapist.

After a handful of heartbeats, he was confident that everyone had seen enough.

The jailer had a sword in a sheath on his side; within a moment, it was in Akaran's hands. While the apprentice alchemist watched in horror, the priest took four rough swings with the blade. It took that many before the guard's head hit the cold stone floor with a meaty thunk. Wet and bloody bits of wood stumbled out of his neck while the rest of his body slumped to the ground.

Red blood and black tendrils gushed from the stump. The blood went everywhere; mostly on the priest, but some even splashed on Mariah's feet. The tendrils were quickly joined by a cloud that morphed into a face screaming in agony. With the host destroyed, the wraith would have vanished on its own in a few moments on its own.

A shouted Word blew it apart instead – an exclamation point handed down for emphasis.

Standing still, breathing hard, rage radiating off of him so forcefully that it was almost palatable, Akaran looked up the stairs and seethed out a question that felt more like an order. "Who. Touched. Either. Of. Them."

Nobody spoke up.

He raised the sword and pointed at one that looked like he was trying to hide behind Mariah. "You. Was it you?" One of the others gave a nervous nod to confirm it. "Get over here. **Now**." Unsurprisingly, the jailer didn't budge.

"Akaran! What did you...?! You can't just - !"

"Get over here or I will have someone bring you to me. Your choice. One of the options has a chance that this ends well for you. One doesn't. For anyone."

With a slightly helpful shove, Evalia pushed him down the steps. Once the choice had been taken away from him, the guard slid up to the priest while staring at him with wide and utterly terrified eyes. Akaran didn't bother explaining anything. He just grabbed him by his wrist, looked down, grumbled "*Illuminate*," one more time, and waited.

Light glimmered and danced across him. After a moment, he was shoved back towards the stairway. "He's clean. Did *anyone* else at all? Did *anyone* else come into this cell?"

The guard answered him with a tremble in his voice. "No, no, nobody, we've been asking. If, if we hear of anyone, we will tell you, tell someone and anything else you want, anything at all. Just please, please don't let that thing get inside us, please!"

"If another one of the has gotten free, you'll find out soon enough. I can promise it."

The threats, the bravado, and everything else ended when Maria barged her way into the room. She had changed her clothes at some point, and was wearing a pretty blue peasant's dress with a tan sash around her waist. "AKARAN! WHAT DID YOU DO?"

"Daringol."

"Daringol didn't kill that man!"

He wiped a spot of blood off of his cheek as he looked at her. "He wasn't a man anymore. He was defiled. I didn't have a choice."

She didn't buy it. "He was defenseless! On his knees!"

"I didn't have a choice."

Evalia, on the other hand, had a slightly different opinion. She was wearing the same style of dress as Mariah, though she had a rank insignia dangling on a silver chain on her neck. "You had a choice. You made one. It's done. What about the prisoner?"

Somehow, he had forgotten all about her. He started to turn around to check on Rmaci, but the battlemage beat him to it. "I don't -"

"You don't know because you're too busy arguing and leaving your back exposed. Is that the one from Civa?"

For one brief moment, he felt the weight of a judgment pressing on his shoulders. "It is," he answered, and started to walk into her cell.

He didn't make it to the door before Evalia stopped him and stepped inside. "He did a number on you, didn't he?"

It would be a lie to say that Rmaci hadn't enjoyed watching the fight (and execution) take place. However, that didn't mean she trusted Evalia to be any better. She pulled at the blanket on her cot and used it to cover herself up with shaking hands. "Bastard fisking... fisking bastard... I..."

Speaking softly, Evalia gave her a reassuring smile. "He won't do it again."

"Again? What does it matter if he does it again? He did it," she scoffed, then looked over Evalia's shoulder with a hateful sneer. "You. Akaran. I trusted you, you said I'd get a trial and -"

"Even if you didn't trust him, that wouldn't have stopped that asshole, would it have?" Xandros's wife calmly interrupted. "No. You know, some would say you deserved this."

Mariah was only too happy to comment. "Some would say the bitch deserves a lot more than that."

It was not a thought shared by everyone. "And others would say *nobody* deserves it," Akaran countered, refusing to meet Rmaci's stare.

"Not your people she killed. Not your friends, not people that were like *family* to you."

"That guard had a family, too," Evalia interjected. "He died. They're going to suffer grief because he died. It's a cycle. Death begets death."

"I'm seeing two murderers in here right now...," the apprentice grumbled, stepping backwards away from the priest (and the ever-growing pool of blood in the middle of the room).

Their prisoner gave a throaty, tired chuckle. "Little baby alchemist. Grown up have we? See the man hiding behind the boy? The killer behind the priest? I saw it, knew it was there."

Evalia let a small smile flicker across her lips. "I can see it too," she said, and reached for the flagon laying nearby. Slowly reaching over to her, she offered it to the Civan spy.

Rmaci blanched and pulled her blanket tighter around her. "N... no. That bastard, he... he drank it, then pissed in it. He made... made *me* drink from it. Bastard! Hope Gormith makes you suck on HIS cock!"

"I'm surprised he even risked coming close to your mouth, with all the things I've heard about you," the battlemage whispered. "I would've expected poison to be in your fangs. Or is that how you did it? Demons running rampant in your blood, and you gave him a little bite between beatings?"

Her change in tone brought a fresh bout of anger to the Civan's voice. "I didn't... you're a sick bitch... no, when he was... was in me, I felt it move, felt it leave me when he... he..."

"When he used you like the Civan whore you are?" Mariah asked.

Akaran didn't let her continue. "Mariah! That's enough!"

"Sticking up for her? After everything she did?" she seethed, glaring daggers at the spy.

Shaking his head, he stepped between them and made her look at him. "She was abused and assaulted and it was under my watch. That is ENOUGH."

Even Evalia had to agree. "He's right. Mariah, go upstairs. There's a matter of security to be discussed. Everyone else, go with her."

"You want me to what? You can't be serious!"

"I can, I am, I do. **Leave us.**"

The apprentice couldn't believe it. "And you're letting him stay."

"I am. Be as angry with him as you wish, but the matter of security concerns him as well. Go back to my room. You *do not* need to hear this."

With her shoulders tight and fists balled up, she spat on the floor. "Fisking... fine. You two fawn all over her. Rmaci? I hope you rot for a very long time you murdering sack of shit." She didn't even address the priest as she stomped off, with the other jailers in tow behind her.

"I suppose this means... means you two aren't gonna honor the deal he made with me?" the Civan croaked.

Evalia blinked in surprise and looked over at the exorcist. "A deal? He made a deal? What deal did you make, Akaran?"

"Safe travel outside of Dawnfire if she gives up the name of her handlers."

"Oh, is that all? Rewarding her with a way out? Maybe Mariah was right about how you felt about the bitch. She and I talked about this woman for a long time today."

Rmaci's chuckle returned, but it wasn't full of mirth. "The baby... baby alchemist didn't really like me. Guess I got one too many cocks in me she wanted for herself. Guess... guess she finds this fitting..."

"I'm sure she does. What about you, Akaran? Do you find it fitting?"

He didn't delay his answer. "No I... no. No, I don't. She hasn't been taken to trial. She hasn't been turned over to the Queen's justice."

"What if the Queen's Justiciars had ordered this? What if some lieutenant in her army caught a spy and ordered her tortured until she made a full confession? What would you do then?"

That was a harder question to answer. When he did, his voice lacked total conviction. "Not have offered my personal protection."

She smirked. "Good dodge. No, I know your type. That isn't true, and you know it. You would have stepped in and ordered it stopped."

"You're right, I would."

Nodding, Evalia looked back over at Rmaci. "What do you think, Civan? What would you do if your Empress ordered a citizen of Dawnfire held and raped?"

"We don't rape prisoners."

"Yes you do," the battlemage whispered. "I *know* you do. You just don't say it's state-sanctioned when it happens. You make all the right little excuses when you had the prisoners back over," she said with a slight shake of her head. "So. Not much I'm able to do about you right now, I suppose. Exorcist? Is she clean?"

Akaran slipped into the cell and touched Rmaci on her shoulder. She flinched back, eyes going wide. He whispered *"Illuminate,"* quietly, then looked back to Evalia. "Yeah. Daringol left. The one in the guard was the one that was in her."

"Not much of a relief, but a relief. Can she be turned over to the Overseer for trial?"

That was an even harder question. He looked down at the murderess and slowly came to a decision. "In her shape...? No. I'll need time to make sure that Daringol is gone for good. I'm certain it is but..."

The second-in-command of the 13th pressed him for details. "Time? How much time?"

"I might know by morning, if I work through the night. There's also the matter of the rapist. I'll need to dispose of him properly, as well."

She frowned. "You don't look like you can work through the next hour."

"I... it has to be done," he sighed.

"Does it?"

Akaran couldn't even believe she asked. "Does it? Daringol is like a disease, like a plague. If we don't make sure that it's completely expunged, it could spread."

The battlemage's frown deepened as she looked between the guard and the spy. "It could already be everywhere, couldn't it? The city could be drenched in it."

He rubbed his hands together and then focused on something just above and behind both of them, like he was staring through the wall. After a long drawn out minute of silence (that felt like a year), he reached into one of the pouches at his waist and pulled out one of the small crystals Steelhom had crafted just for this type of situation. "No. No, I can say that for sure. The air is... clear now. Except for here. That could be from that guard, could be from her, could be from me. Goddess knows I'm covered in it."

"The joys of the job. So that corpse and that woman are the last vestiges?"

"Yes. We'll leave when she's been cleansed. Steelhom is more than capable of handling Toniki until we're done here."

She gave a quick nod, content with his answer. "Fine. Then we'll leave in the morning."

"I just said that I don't know if I'll be sure she's no longer carrying any more of that wraith left inside her," he replied, completely confused on how she managed to misunderstand him.

"There's not going to be any doubt."

"I didn't realize you'd joined the priesthood."

Evalia smirked and stood up, turning to face him. "Oh, I haven't. I just learn quickly. Civan? I apologize for your rough treatment. If the boy here hadn't killed your rapist, I give my word, I would have. An awful lot slower, too. Might've even let you help. Course, you gave him your wraith, so maybe you *did* help."

It didn't have any effect on her. "Platitudes... don't mean anything now. What if I'm with child now? What are you going to do about that?"

Akaran blanched, but Evalia beat him to a retort. "I'm going to be happy that I won't have to be concerned with it," she said as she took Akaran by his hand and walked out of Rmaci's cell. Then, without a word, she suddenly reached for the half-empty barrel of torch-oil and shoved it over. Black gunk spilled out and flooded her cell before anything could be done to stop it.

The Civan's eyes went wide and fresh terror exploded across her face. "What are you...!? Akaran what is she doing...?!"

He didn't have a clue. "Battlemage, what are...?"

"What must be done," Evalia answered. Horrified, all he could do was watch as she picked up a torch and threw it on the ground.

Akaran and Rmaci screamed out the same thing at the same time. "WAIT NO!"

All the screaming in the world didn't do a damn bit of good. The oil ignited with a roar and bright red flames raced through the dungeon while the battlemage pulled Akaran out of the room. Helpless, all he could do was watch.

Rmaci got out one more coherent scream before the flames raced up her blanket. "AKARAN NO YOU - !" The next scream was of pure agony. Fire blossomed on her skin. What was left of her clothes had soaked up some of the oil, and even more had gotten in her hair. She was immolated within moments, screaming and slapping at the flames as they coursed over her skin.

While she thrashed on the cot, the priest grabbed Evalia by her dress and shook her hard. "WHAT DID...! WHY? WE MADE A DEAL! I MADE A DEAL!"

"You did. I didn't. "

"DAMMIT! I OUTRANK YOU! MY WORD IS LAW!"

Seemingly immune to the last strangled screams that came from the dungeon-turned-furnace, Evalia calmly brushed his hands off of her dress. "She murdered three people and conspired against the crown. She might still pose an imminent threat to the good citizens of the kingdom. Like you said, Daringol is a plague. She's a carrier. She isn't anymore."

That wasn't enough to mollify him. That wasn't even *remotely* enough. "I gave my word, I told her if she cooperated. I didn't consign her to death by fire!"

"Did you think she was going to tell us the truth now? About any of it? That fisking rapist *ruined* any chance we had of getting *any* information. She'd lie. She'd lie through her teeth. She was probably going to lie anyways but there wouldn't be a damn bit of actionable information we could use to root out her network. The tree's been poisoned."

"There could have been something! We don't know, she won't get the chance to tell us now!"

They were forced to walk up the stairs and away from the flames. Thick black smoke poured through the chambers. The sole window in the dungeon wasn't enough to keep it from choking the pair of them. "Complain to the Overseer. Complain to my husband. The threat she posed is real. The threat that Daringol poses is real. The threat that this city is under the longer you have Makolichi's hand in the temple is real. The threat your decision to let her loose, or waste any more time here, is real. It doesn't matter if you like it, it had to be done."

"You still... but I promised... and like that, *she was just fisking victimized!* That *alone* is punishment enough, isn't it? *More* than enough?!"

Evalia rolled her eyes. "Say she didn't cooperate. We hold her for trial, and she'd be executed. Say she didn't cooperate, and the Capitol decided it wanted to make an example of her. How well do you *really* think she was going to be treated? This isn't some quaint 'everything is perfect' world we live in here, boy, and you should only *pray* that you're never looked at the same way a woman in prison is if someone ever takes *you* captive."

Akaran couldn't choke back his fury. "Saying that it would happen somewhere else doesn't make it right that it happened here!"

"I didn't say it did. I am dead serious, exorcist, if you hadn't killed that man I would have, and I would have made it last a *very* long time. However, to hear you say it, time is of the essence. We got all we could from her. Burning her body now just speeds it up."

"For the sake of the Goddess, did you have to burn her alive?!"

The battlemage just shrugged. "I burn people alive on the battlefield. Make them blow apart, too. Once I even found a way to dissolve a man's face clean off. It's not much different doing it here than it is out there." She looked over her shoulder. "Easier to clean up when they're outside, but, it's not much different."

He covered his mouth and fought back a horrific wave of nausea. "That's..."

"You don't get to play the 'I'm better than you card,' boy, so don't try. I know *exactly* what you do, and you know *exactly* what happens when your ilk do your jobs. That roasting lasted just a handful of minutes. What do you think happens next?"

"That's for the Gods to decide, not us."

"Traitor, murderess, spy? Don't be daft about as to what They will decide. I need sleep. You do too. You'll realize I'm right in the morning. Besides. Her people prefer to be cremated. This way solves every problem at once."

Speechless, he couldn't answer. She walked away with her head held high. Shaken to his core, he started to walk away when a mage – and several of the Overseer's men – rushed down the hallway with shouts and demands of their own. He didn't answer (he couldn't answer) at first.

Then, quietly, he simply whispered for them to let it burn until everything was ash. There was nothing left to do at that point, other than just to cry. Cry, and pray.

The way that the Order of Light shrines were constructed – nearly universally – was deceiving to the naked eye, if you were on the outside looking in. Most people would never see anything past the top two or three levels in your average city (smaller in outlying towns, larger in major locations). That was what most people saw. In Toniki, the ground floor was it. In any shrine that was built in a city the size of, say, Gonta? There were basements hidden below.

Earlier in the day, they had been gruff, borderline nasty. The Priestess had been a no-show to his request to an audience. She had delegated his requests to the Lower Adjunct, who in turn delegated them to someone that barely had standing enough in the Order to push a broom. Some of that changed when he threatened to drop Makolichi's hand in the Pool of Blessings right inside their front door.

Some, but not all. They liked it less that he had asked for a room. Again, they agreed, if for no other reason than because they didn't feel any safer leaving the hand outside of their sight than he did. The *only* reason that any of them seemed to trust that he wasn't *completely* insane was that enough of them had watched him fight the demon. It earned him a measure of trust. A very small measure. But a measure.

Maybe we should quit trying to be subtle about the things we do. If we were more open about our work, maybe people would take us more seriously? It can't be worth trying to keep it silent, can it? Telling people that we're here now go away then doing what we do and leaving without any excuse other than 'We were sent' hasn't won over hearts and minds in two centuries. And if the other Orders opt to lead the charge against the damned? That can only work out for everyone, right?

Those thoughts aside, Akaran couldn't even begin to say why an Order neophyte welcomed him with a smile and a hot mug of spiced tea when he finally wandered back to the shrine, nor why he was offered a fresh robe and an escort to the lower levels. Then again, it could have been that they were afraid that the horrid odors permeating his clothes would ruin the shrine. If that was the case, they were right.

Between that nameless jailer and then... her... the smell wasn't getting out of his clothes.

Maybe not even off of his skin.

Ever.

A different neophyte lead him from his temporary room into an unexpected chamber that he had only seen once before, in passing, at the Grand Sanctum of the Pantheon in the Dawnfire capitol. It was a large square underground pool, in a large, square room. If you were ever lucky enough to sit in it, you'd discover that the water was constantly heated by recurring enchantments cast on rocks below the waves every day, without fail, by some priest who apparently had nothing better to do than cast spells to warm rocks in the bottom of a pool all day every day. *Just think. All of Usaic's work could just be to spare a Steward of Istalla from trying to make a pool just like this one cold in a desert.*

There was a moment of mortified laughter in the back of his mind at the idea. The woman that lead him into the pool must have thought the bemused-yet-terrified look was about the idea of getting into the water, and quietly whispered that "It is a great honor to be given permission to rest in the Pool of Harmony's Warmth."

"Oh, oh nothing of... I'm sorry. It's just..."

A flicker of a smile flicked across her lips. "A long day?"

He nodded and looked around the room, the eyes of every God and Goddess of the Pantheon staring down from the alcoves above. *Except for Her, of... course...?* The thought died in his throat when he realized that in the spot typically empty in any other display of Their Holiness, there was a small statuette of Her, standing in (diminished) glory.

But it was standing there in Her glory.

While the neophyte slowly walked around and behind him, she gently pulled the robe off of his shoulders. He was too stunned to even blush as his mind raced as to *why* any of the stuffy egotistical *pricks* that followed under the Order of Light would even have one of Her icons *anywhere*. Even attempts to form words to ask the question came out as half-thoughts and tongue-twisted utterances. "What is... how, why are...?"

"Her symbols were never destroyed by the Order. Not in the temples and shrines outside of Civa, that is. She was punished, but She was never banished. Many of the eldest of the Order hope that one day, She will find a way back to Her true place among the ranks of the Upper Pantheon," she answered, smiling as she took him by the arm and guided him into the warm, soothing pool.

"You keep them where? In storage?"

She nodded with a slight smile. "Yes, in a manner of speaking. Clean, safe. Waiting."

Akaran settled in and slowly sank down on the steps of the bath. There wasn't a way on the planet he could have held back the groan that slipped out of his mouth as the warmth infused his aching, battered, and chilled bones. "But not up there," he said as he bobbed his head in its general direction.

"No, not up there. This is the first time in a generation Her spot has been filled," she answered, her tone quiet and soft-spoken. "Before you ask; you earned it for Her today."

"I... what?"

The priestess dipped a small ewer into the pool and poured it over the back of his head. The water smelled like lilies and honey as it drifted up his nose. "Do you know the second-most oft-repeated question today?"

Wordlessly, he shook his head and tried to look up at her. "I barely know my name right now."

"That was the third-most. The second was 'Which of the Pantheon struck down the demon?' They did not believe the answers at first, not until those that heard the name you called when you did your works spoke up."

"That explains the looks I got..."

"No, the looks you got came from the way that you did the works after. Brash, rude, demanding. It was not comforting to those that were terrified." She poured another jug of the perfumed water down his back, and rubbed away soot off of his shoulders. "For a man of Love, comfort is not what you do."

He ignored that but went back a few comments. "You haven't -"

Her fingers touched the edge of his neck and loitered there, slightly puzzled. "Istalla? You bear the marking of the Goddess of Ice, and proclaim Love. Interesting."

"It's been -"

"Yes, yes, a long week for you. It has been, you poor man. Too long, for a man of your age. You have lessons to learn still. I wish you did not, for your sake," she sighed. "They did not believe the answers they received because none of them believed that your Goddess held such power. That not only does She have such power, but that She would risk one of Her few followers for the sake of so many that hate Her."

Akaran pulled away and sank lower into the pool, then turned to face her without caring about his nakedness. "And what, exactly, did you tell them?"

"The truth," she said, smiling and dipping the urn back into the pool. "That your Order is maligned, for reasons. That your brothers and sisters are what you are because of your Goddess." She stood, and waded into the pool with him, her gray-green eyes sparkling in the torchlight. "And because of what you are, the work you do in Her name *is* good and *is* of the Light and *is* strong. Even if the work you do is worked in silence."

He continued to back up away from her – but she continued to move along with him. "You can't be a priestess of the Pantheon and expect me to believe that." He blinked for a heartbeat and looked at her again. "Wait... I was just -"

"Just thinking that? Yes. You were. I know. I know many things about you."

With what felt like all of the eyes of the Gods upon him, peering through the statues that adorned the edges of the pool, the exorcist tensed up – every inch of him expecting yet one more fight today. "Who are you."

With a tilt of her head, the woman brought her strawberry-blonde braids from behind her back and ran her hand through them. He *finally* got a clear look at her face. She had soft features, but was older than he had first thought. Little crows-feet radiated out around the corners of her eyes, and a set of deep pockmarks decorated her right cheek up to and under her hair. "I would have thought it would have been obvious. Has it truly been so long since you have stepped into one of our shrines?"

"Lady, I'm -"

"- in no mood for games? Life is a game, Sir Exorcist. Be what it is, be all that it is in the wonder and warmth we show each other in the Light, and the things that we do in the Dark. You've not learned that yet. I know you will. I know many things about you."

It didn't soothe him in the least. "Who are you."

Her smile faltered for a heartbeat. "I mean no harm to you. I could not, not here, not even if I wished. This pool, this place, it is harmony. You feel it, don't you? The call of the water?"

Akaran stood his ground in the center of it, fists balled up. "I feel like I'm being played. Again. Again and again and again," he hissed, seething, days of pent-up frustration beading up just under the surface of his skin.

"How... odd," she mused as the tension in the air boiled. "It doesn't call to you. You don't feel it. You don't... the water doesn't call you. I... don't call to you. So, so *odd*."

"Odd? You act like you're -"

"- reading your thoughts?"

He punched his hand into the water and didn't even try to hide it anymore. "QUIT THAT."

The woman took a step back and giggled at him, in a soft and innocent way. Any other time, and it would have been endearing. "You truly don't know who I am. You don't feel the call of peace, you don't feel the harmony of the water, Their touch do you? You *are* one of the Gods but you don't *feel* it. Who am I? Who are *you?*"

"I am *leaving*," he snarled, stepping further away and raking his eyes around the room as he looked for anyone that might be listening in or waiting to strike. "I am an exorcist of the Order of Love and I am *leaving*."

Her smile faltered again, but this time, it didn't come back. "Wait. Please, I ask you to wait. I... I am sorry. I am so, so truly sorry. If you don't feel you wouldn't know and if you can't feel then... there is a weight upon your soul. Oh, child."

"You don't know me as well as you think if you think that's a surprise."

"Of course, no. No, no I had... I assumed, I've met... I've met angry men, I've met murders and thieves. I've consoled soldiers and punishers of the Queen's very own court, and I've never... Child. My name is Deboria Ult. I am the Priestess of Stara of this sanctuary."

That didn't help much, though it did slow his departure. "The Priestess of Stara? You're -"

"Yes, child. I speak for the Gods here, the full Pantheon. I am here, for Them, to be Their voice, to be the guiding light for those that follow and honor the Pantheon. This is my sanctuary, this is my shrine."

Slowly, ever so slowly, he relaxed his shoulders and unclenched his fists and slightly bowed his head. "Then... Priestess. Forgive me."

"You? Forgive you? No, child. I am humbled, and it is my apology to give. Please, sit? I truly do mean no harm to you. I am just simply as I am, a servant, just as you."

Warring with the thought (and a lack of trust), he finally caved and sat down on the closest edges of the pool. The fatigue of the day's events caught up with him all at once, and he leaned back against the pillar that the bust of Hircanton, Demi-God of Storms, sat upon. "Why are you doing this?"

Carefully, slowly, she glided through the pool like a bird in the wind. Her robe flowed out behind her while her fingers trailed in the water. "Because it is what you have earned, and what you need. I am not a woman that has ever held Niasmis in esteem. I will not lie about this to you. Yet I am one that sees the good in even the worst, that sees the glimmer of Light in the lost. You are not the worst, though you may be lost. You have fought hard today, and brought great honor about your Matron. I cannot - will not - ever turn my back from a warrior that bears light on his blade."

"People died today."

"People die every day."

"You don't understand. People died today because of me. Because of my choices and my decisions and..."

Deboria's smile slowly returned. "Yes, I see. You blame yourself, even when you should not."

He closed his eye and sank into the pool until the water was over his shoulders. "A prisoner... a woman. She... you say you can hear my thoughts. You know what happened."

"I see the guilt over the fate of your charge on your face; I need not listen to your soul." She stood still and closed her eyes for a long minute. When she opened them, the priestess knelt down so her eyes were level with his. "Yes, I see what it was that transpired. You did not sin against her. You could have done no different. Had you done different, far more would have passed, had you stayed with her."

"And the jailer? I didn't even try."

"Why would you, should you have? He sinned, sinned gravely, and the darkness in the pit came for him and claimed him before you ever returned. If not by your hand, another would have. Even if the darkness that had overtaken him could have been banished and left the man standing, his punishment would have been swift. Perhaps not done with a torch, but, it would have been swift," she had to add.

Akaran looked up at her, his anger cracking while tears began to form in the corner of his eye. "I *enjoyed* it. It felt *good*. It felt *right*. I executed him without even attempting to banish Daringol... the wraith in him, I mean."

She touched him, cupping his cheek. "Your shock is not over in that you enjoyed it. You are no different from any soldier, any warrior. You would not fight, you would not weird a sword, if you did not relish your work on some level. An animal level, an instinctual one."

"I am a priest. I condemn the damned. I shouldn't... the living, I..."

"The shock is not that you enjoyed. It is that you don't feel guilt for taking a life you *think* you might have been able to save. Yes? Even if you did not wish to, you could maybe have, had banal rage not consumed you?"

There weren't words that could answer her. Instead, he just whispered a question. "How can a man claim to be holy when he relished bludgeoning a man to death, and didn't stop someone from burning a woman alive?"

"Because you must kill, to balance the natural order. The Goddess of Nature served the Goddess of Love, or did at one time. Kora'thi establishes the balance between growth and decay. The natural order. Love Herself has taken it upon Herself to re-establish the balance between the living and the dead; returning the lost to the peace they belong to, and the damned where they should go. That is the order of the supernatural, the order of the eternal."

He buried his head in the water for a few moments before replying. "Why are you doing this?"

"I am a Priestess of Stara. *All* of Their children who serve the light deserve comfort in times of suffering. You... you need to feel comfort. There... there is another reason too; I should not lie."

"The real reason," he sighed. "What is it?"

"*A* reason. No less and no more real of my reason to try to soothe your mind. It is a reason that will do the same, albeit in a differing way."

"Planning on telling me or making me guess?"

Deboria slipped beside him, and lowered his head to the top of her chest, cradling him like a mother with her child. "This monster you faced today. It was not your first time?"

"It wasn't."

"And the one that took the jailer, took the murderess. It is not the first time you have fought it either? It is one of many of the same as one?"

"Yes."

Her smile faded into a grim frown. "This thing, that demon. It is the one that has driven so many from their homes on the mountain? Toniki, and those that live near? So close, and so far?"

The exorcist sighed his response. "Yes. I came here to stop it before it could do any harm. I failed."

Shaking her head, she had a slightly different take. "You did, and you did not. You did more good than you know, and more than you would admit. Tell me. This village, town, whatever it is that they call it. It is not a town where the Gods are given much mind, is it?"

"If they didn't have a Light shrine there, I wouldn't believe they knew them at all."

"That is what I feared, and what I felt and heard from those that I spoke to. Is it through choice or through an eventual slipping, a slow walking away?"

Akaran gave it a thought – though not a long one – and answered as earnestly as he could. "Both. Town elders were Kor'athi worshipers. Shit happened to them. Rest of the people gave up after."

There wasn't any way she could have hid the giggle if she wanted. "Shit happened? That is a summation in two words that I feel covers a great many things. Still, it does feel appropriate. Tenders of Growth. Always finding ways to dig up the flowers with the weeds."

He managed not to choke on her reply (barely). "You can't speak like that about them, can you?"

"I am a *Priestess of Stara*, my child. One must understand that even in the heavens, some stars hang lower than others. This shrine we speak of. Is there a priest there to tend it? A lantern in the dark?"

"None I've seen."

"Is it your thought that it is the lack of this light that has given rise to these shadows?"

It was another one of those 'easy' questions to answer. "It didn't help."

Deboria knew it before he said it, of course. "I think then that I shall deign to visit this shrine. Bring word of a path to the lost."

With a snort, he cupped some of the pool's water and let it run down his face. "They don't like the light up there."

"They do not like your spark, my child," she chided. "Sometimes it is the lights that burn the brightest that burn those that need to bathe in them."

"I don't think -"

"- that it is a good idea? No, I can imagine you would not. They've not greeted you so kindly, why would they greet me so?" Shaking her head again and ran her fingers through his ponytail. "There is the fear of this monster that perverts and pervades the landscape in the mountains. Your duty is to protect the innocent, and the holy. You have many reasons to not wish I to return. I, or the girl that you traveled with to here; the girl you wish to leave behind?"

Akaran tried to slow her down some. "I hadn't said that. I hadn't implied that."

"But you did think it, on the trip down; and in the fights you had with her today. You would be happier if she didn't return to the village with you."

Looking rather wounded and indignant, he shrugged. "Can you

blame me? That thing *killed me*. I'm pretty sure *I died*."

Again, that didn't help either. "If you will not let death stop you, and she knows of the wounds you suffered, why will you let fear of it stop her? You can only protect the people that wish you to protect them. Otherwise, it is they that need protection from you."

"Forgive me, Priestess, but that's wrong. Sometimes, people act against their best interests for no other reason but to have something to act against. Because they feel the need to fight against themselves just to have something to fight against. When they cannot see reason, those that *can* need to step in to hold them back."

The introspection wasn't lost on her, although it did surprise her that he actually tried to broach the subject with thoughtfulness. "Perhaps. But were that the case, we would need to grant power to people to let them take such power over us. We are not so quick to grant it, and some of us have that power regardless. Do you always trust the queen to do what is right, or only what is right for herself? Do you trust the Gods to do what is always right, or what is right for Themselves? Of course you do not."

"Well, no, because what They always think is right doesn't always better everyone else around them."

"*Your* perception, and not necessarily *Theirs*. Nor even necessarily correct. So if you cannot trust the Gods – you, a priest, a man who battles the dark for the light – and you, a soldier – a man who fights for the safety of the loyal subjects of the queen – if you cannot trust the voices that have power over you, why should you expect Mariah to trust you, when you serve those you do not trust absolutely?"

"Because... that's... the way of it. We trust our families, or we don't. We trust our friends, or we don't. We trust the people close to us, or we don't. Until we have reason not to trust, then shouldn't people trust?"

"Do you trust the Lady of Love absolutely, in all things, at all times?"

Slowly, he nodded. "Well, yes."

"So you do trust in one absolutely, just not in the rest." Her eyes twinkled in the torchlight. "Your reasons to trust or not trust are your reasons, hers are hers, mine are mine. Trust is built upon experience. When you have more experience, others will trust in you more. Until you do, they will not, until you can convince them to do so. As now must I, convince you, to trust me. Trust that I have all the faith in the Gods that I believe have need of me to take my light to that shrine, if for no other reason, than to better illuminate your path."

Akaran didn't even try to hide his sigh. Why bother? "I'm not going to win this, am I?"

"I think that you knew the answer to that question before even I did. I do have an answer for the last one you have. Well, one last one, of two."

"You're not going to let me sleep in here, are you," he lamented.

Again, she gave a laugh with a smile. "It's not in here that you wish to sleep, and even if it were, I dare say that the image of all of these Gods you have so much contempt for in your heart would cause you more gas than rest. And no, you may not sleep in the other place you are considering either, and *no*, one does not need to be a mind reader to know that you are a young man under much stress that could use an older lady with... the skills of an older lady."

There was no way he could do anything other than blush and try to curl up around himself in response. "Well um, no, just, it's... long... day and all and..."

Her laugh continued on with a firmer, more serious edge. "The other, more pertinent question. The people that asked about your order? Your Goddess? You worry that whomever speaks for me tomorrow and takes the light of the shrine while I ascend into the mountains with you come morning, you worry that that person will turn them away or berate them for even inquiring about your Lady, will you not?"

"I do. I'm still not sure why you did it, and damn sure not convinced that others will."

"They will not need to. I have already sent those that have asked to a home in the city that I know lets others of Love's flock to congregate. I have sent urgent word to the Capitol, to the Grand Temple of Love, asking them to send one of the Brothers to come preach to the masses, or to educate those that wish to hear. They will be offered room and a berth here – and a place to teach, should it be wished. You may not make a convert, but you have earned Her a chance to find followers by way of a priest far better equipped for such things than you."

And just like that, *any* thought of getting her to sleep with him or sleeping near him or him even sleeping suddenly went far far away. "You... sent word? To the Temple? To... *the* Temple?"

"Yes, and with your name featured prominently for the why and the how and what work you have done. Be proud. Your instructors will know of your work, and how it has brought honor to your Goddess's name."

Akaran looked up at her, and suddenly felt like he was going to be -

"Please do not be ill in the Pool of Harmony. Your fear betrays you. Surely, they will be pleased to know how your efforts have given glory to the Goddess, and even glory to the Queen?" His discomfort wasn't appeased by that, nor was it with what she said next. "And... child? The clarity of the pool *also* betrayed you. I am honored, but for some things, a woman doesn't need to be able to read thoughts to know when her eyes are perfectly capable of seeing."

He went *completely* crimson, head to toe, and tried to sink under the water to hide from her.

All she did was just to laugh while he debated his options. "And no, you may not drown yourself in it either!"

Morning hit everyone at once, even if not equally.

Some of those that it did hit gave plenty of thought to hitting back.

Only a couple of them would have the opportunity to do it before long, though the bulk of them wished to. Eos'eno had aided them with building a shelter that fit everyone comfortably and well out of the chill. Unfortunately, that did nothing for soothing aching muscles or grumbling bellies. The *shiriak* and the rest had done a wonderful job of clearing out the wildlife.

It was just another reason to hate the foul-smelling vermin.

With food out of the question (and their rations barely making a dent), the only thing that Steelhom wanted to do was close the breach and return to the village. Everyone else just wanted to know what exactly he intended to do. It wasn't until the soldiers found the paladin down by the crystalline structure that Xandros found the courage to ask. "So. What's the plan? You weren't overly talkative last night."

His friend didn't bother to look away when he answered. "I was preparing myself for this. This is not the kind of risk to be taken lightly."

"It's a crystal."

"It's a crack."

Xandros frowned and gave his sword-hilt a tight squeeze on his waist. "It's a crystal with a crack in it?"

"Eloquently put," Steelhom sighed. When he realized that the 13th's Commander wanted a more detailed response, the priest sighed a second time and elaborated. "He sealed the breach, but he didn't seal it well. I have to applaud him for trying, even if he's the reason why it's here to start with. Wherever it goes, it will not be pleasant to close."

"From what you said... I imagine it goes into the Abyss. Though... that's not... an easy thought."

"A hole opened directly into the place of eternal torment and torture? No. An easy thought it is not. Cracks like these, they... circumvent... the way that eternity is ordered. There are many layers to what lay beyond the mortal world. A breach cuts through them like a knife through freshly-churned butter."

Xandros had already begun to regret even asking. "So you're saying that this is literally a passageway into the underworld. A doorway to let things out, or to throw things in."

"Simply said. Yes."

Unnerved, the commander chewed on his lip for a minute. "You make it sound like this is... common."

Nor did what Steelhom say next make him feel any better. "The Abyss is an old prison, my friend. Old prisons have cracks."

"That may be the single-most terrifying thing I've ever heard," he muttered. "Made worse by how nonchalantly you said it. So while I debate what I'm going to be doing to cleanse my soul when this is all over, what are you going to be doing about that... crack?"

"Destroy the crystal, then attempt to seal the entrance."

Penela looked over at Mado and quietly mouthed an "Attempt?" just out of earshot.

Xandros pushed his luck just a little. "If I ask how you intend to do that, will you be able to give a straight answer that I can understand?"

"Probably not, my friend," he sighed before looking up at them from the bottom of the creek. "The four of you: when I do this, something may try to come out. Just because the hole has been sealed doesn't mean that there haven't been things attempting to exit. *If* something does, *and* I cannot destroy it? Run, and make sure word gets out as quickly as you can. Where one thing walks out, others will undoubtedly be soon to follow."

Whispering beside him, Eos's voice managed to carry in the still air. "Do not fear what may be released. I will not tolerate another of the defiled to rise from master's machinations. I have failed him many times over; I will *not* fail him again."

"Well, two spellslingers are always better than one," Xandros quipped back. "Unless they're aimed at you. Still, I think that her being on our side evens up the odds. Penela. Mado. You heard the old man. Get ready to run. I'm staying right here."

The two of them answered jointly with an immediate "Sir, yessir," but it was Mado that cleared his throat to try and come to terms with things on his own. "What should we expect?"

Steelhom just shrugged. "Whatever the Abyss deigns to send. Eos'eno? Do you know where it goes? I presume Frosel?"

"I would assume the same," she said with a nod. It was an irritating quirksome habit she had learned from Akaran, and now she answered everything with a dip of her chin. "Do... do be careful. Do not touch anything that drains into this realm. Destroying this shard may cause a flood of damnation and misery."

"Right, no touch. Steelhom? It's your show now," Xandros replied as he slowly drew his sword. The other two soldiers did the same, and you could feel the tension radiating off of them.

Almost mimicking the wisp, the paladin gave a nod and took a deep breath. Without saying anything, he flicked his staff out and connected with the pyramid on his left. The construct broke into three chunks and bounced off of the alcove's wall. The second one pulsed with a strange yellow light for a moment before reverting to its normal sheen. If it was going to react to half the spell being destroyed, he wasn't going to give it a chance.

Steelhom's next strike shattered it as easily as it had taken out the first. The ground began to rumble a little, and the central crystal started to pulse with the same yellow color. Off in the distance, something made a cry; something inhuman, something tormented. It took a moment to realize that it wasn't in the distance, it was from the crack — it just sounded like it was from far away.

Metaphysically, it was.

His final strike went right to the center of the brackish stone. The impact put a massive crack straight down its center. The gold chains from the pyramids caught fire on the ground, and the flames raced up and into the crystal. The sickly glow erupted with a brilliant flash just before the stone shattered.

Shards peppered Steelhom and Eos'eno both and forced the two of them to turn away. The cry ramped up exponentially around them, drowning out all thought and their own voices shouting in pained shock. When they turned back to it, the top of the crystal was gone from their waist-up. A thick fluid — something that was water, but somehow not — boiled and gushed forth from it with a sulfurous stench rushing into their senses.

Disgusting clods of *stuff* began to float up from the center, and then down the side of it. "It is as you feared!" Eos wailed. "That... those waters... that is from Frosel...! Zell's home!"

Stifling a gag (which was more than Xandros could do above), the warrior-priest concurred. "It would appear so. That... odor..."

"*Whatever* it is you opened up, for the sake of the Pantheon, *close it* before the stench kills us all!" his friend shouted down.

Steelhom didn't answer him. Instead, he knelt down and placed his hand on the first of several runes he had spent the wee hours of the night before carving into the ground and the sides of the alcove. A simple circle of golden light tricked through the rune and then followed thin lines that he had chiseled out to connect the written Words together.

The containment ward fully in place, he stood and started a prayer with as much reverence as he could fit into his heart. "Goddess: Matron, Mother, Lover, I call on You, Your glory, Your might, Your sight. Cast Your gaze to me, and see what it is I ask You for..."

In direct response, the light pulsed three times over – gold, then purple, then white – and began to shrink around the stone and the breach within it. As soon as it started, the frothing mess boiled higher as a groan echoed in the small chamber. While they watched, his concerns proved to be completely justified.

A creature screeched just under the surface of the water as desperate hands lunged out of the mess. The cacophony was nearly unbearable as more of it pulled free of the frothing churning sludge. It was human – or more aptly, had been once. Now? Whatever it was was just a ruined, blackened mass of open sores and charred skin. "*HELP RELEASE HELP RELEASE HELP RELEASE!*"

Xandros couldn't help himself when he caught sight of it. "What in the name of the Pantheon is THAT?!"

"*PLEASE LET ME OUT PLEASE HELP ME PLEASE AWAY FROM HIM AWAY FROM HIM!*" it pleaded, almost halfway out of the hole.

The rune circle continued to constrict around the breach, but when the froth started to splash against it, the light began to fluctuate and waiver. "GODDESS I CALL ON YOU – GRANT ME THE STRENGTH TO CLOSE THIS DOOR! GRANT ME THE STRENGTH TO CONDEMN THE DAMNED!"

"*PLEASE NO PLEASE DON'T!*" it pleaded, desperate for help, desperate for anything. Each time it pulled at the crystal, his blooded and broken fingers slipped and failed to give it purchase. "*WILL DO ANYTHING WILL ATONE EVERYTHING WILL DO ANYTHING PLEASE!*"

Steelhom leveled his staff to point directly at it, and with a Word, forced a burst of light to shoot right against the soul's shredded face. The blast knocked it back for a moment, but it surged back out of the froth again almost immediately. "Stay where you belong!"

"ANYTHING ANYTHING PLEASE DON'T! I'M SORRY I'M SO SORRY PLEASE DON'T PLEASE ANOTHER CHANCE!"

The circle of light constricted suddenly, and the froth began to well up in a quickly filling puddle. "The Gods have condemned you. By command of the Goddess of Love, *I* am ensuring you *stay* condemned."

It gave one more desperate lurch, and managed to pull all but its right leg free. *"IT'S NOT LOVE TO LEAVE NOT LOVE TO STOP NOT LOVE TO CONDEM! I'LL DO BETTER AGAIN DO BETTER! EVERYTHING BETTER!"*

Eos'eno darted in before it could escape any further. She placed a lone fingertip on the soul's head with a pained, nearly heartbroken smile. It looked up at her as her body shifted to her pure, inhuman form. Holding her finger on its brow, she floated in place with the froth of the portal splashing onto her legs. Yet somehow, she hung there unfazed.

This time, only Steelhom could hear the whisper she made. "No, you will not." A single spear of ice pulsed from her fingertip and pierced it through its face.

There was a small little pitiful wail that came from it, and just as quickly, its head fell back and broke off of the body. The rest of it crumbled and vanished back into the boiling waves. Almost gingerly, she pushed herself back and away from the fissure while Steelhom finished the spell.

The light coalesced around the portal. The froth boiled away into black steam, and when the spell tightened around the crystal, it constricted one last time. The stone – and the horrid muck within it – imploded with nothing more than a few scattered pieces of melting rock and embers left behind.

Everything went silent and the air calmed and stayed still. The only thing you could hear was the priest's ragged breaths as he knelt down and let the remainder of his magic trickle out of his hands, where it dispersed safely into the ground. Eos'eno said nothing, but like him, she began to relax and let her body shift back into a more 'normal' form.

Finally, Xandros spoke up. "Steelhom I have seen you do some seriously fisked up shit but this... that... that thing, that was a person? It was a person that could... I mean we all die I'm a soldier I know that better than anyone else but you how could... it was begging for help and you... how could you just..."

Shaking slightly, he looked up and over at his friend. "How could I send it back?"

"Yeah... how could... I never saw one that looked so... alive..."

"It wasn't alive. It was dead," he argued. "It was damned. I didn't condemn it. I enforced the will of the Gods."

That wasn't enough for him. "It couldn't have found a way to repent? What if Their will was to let it find peace? You don't even know who that was, or what he had done!"

"Then it will have another opportunity," Steelhom countered. "One where and when I am not on hand to usher it back to the life it earned after it left this one. Now. We're done here. We need to return to Toniki."

Eos didn't need him to ask for her help. With a wave of her hand, air spiraled under his feet and lifted him up and over the lip of the creek. Panela was on her knees, head bowed, desperately making a fevered prayer to any Godling that would listen. Mado, on the other hand, was almost halfway across the ruins when he saw them start to make way from the exorcism and condemnation. "What happened? Everyone okay?"

The paladin didn't answer, but Xandros did. "Mado... don't ask... and... you a religious man?"

"Nope, never."

"Become one. And quit fisking Yadin's wife. Act like your soul depends on it." His underling started to comment on the accusation, but shut up when his commander waved him silent with one hand while the other pulled a flask free from his belt. It was the first and only time that anyone ever had seen him drink on the job - which was enough to convince him to shut up.

Several long and quiet minutes later, the paladin reached for the wisp and touched her hand. "Do you know who that was?"

She pondered her answer for another long moment, then nodded. "It does not matter. It is what it is, and what it always will be, and what it is is that I see your true name, man of Love. That has been made clear in the ice. Now. Your student calls. Travel quickly and safely, Curator of Souls. We all are to be needed soon."

He couldn't get his question out before she vanished in a small cloud of fog, ice, and snow. It didn't stop him from asking it anyways. "Curator of Souls?"

IX. PREPARATIONS FOR PENANCE

Morning came for Akaran just as early as it did for his mentor.

Thankfully, it came with less bloodshed and soul-wrenching confrontations.

That wasn't to say that daylight hit his eye *happily*, although considering what was at the end of his bed, it could have been worse. Deboria had taken steps to make sure that his belongings had been removed from the inn he had set up shop in, and not longer after she left the pool, a soft-spoken page escorted him to relatively spartan quarters for him to spend the night.

He stretched with a yawn, and the yawn turned to a curse as he kicked something hard at the end of his bed. When he had gone to sleep, there hadn't been anything there. That had changed overnight.

How the box, and the note in it, ended up at his feet, opened up an entirely different and distinctly unsettling round of questions. Inside the wooden box was a chunk of nearly obsidian crystal with a green tint and a hand-shaped imprint on top of it. He could *smell* Makolichi on it even without having to touch it.

It was just as hard to imagine how it had survived the trip into his room – until he saw that a few choice spells had been carved on top the lid. Whomever had brought it in knew a mage with enough wherewithal to know how to secure a relic box (the same way he'd worked over the box holding the foci). *Mages. I am getting tired of this many mages.*

Of course, touching it became a necessity. The only saving grace was that it boiled away into nothingness with a simple whisper of

"Expunge." After everything else? He truthfully expected it to float up of its own accord and attempt to bash his face in.

When he read the note, he almost wished that it had.

"Yes, you're someone that's worth being owed a future favor from. See you then."

And then there was the matter of the signature. While it was good to know who he was dealing with, and while the name meant little to him (now), there wasn't a speck of doubt that he'd see him again. Only a certain *type* of businessman carried a title like this one.

"With all due regards and well wishes, Riorik, the Hobbler."

At least it didn't take him long to get dressed and ready to leave. He was entertained by one darkly-amused thought while he packed. *Of all the people I intended to impress... a Priestess of Stara and... yeah. It's safe to say that this is the head of the local Guild of Thieves. If not the Provincial. Wonderful. My life is... weird. Even by Temple standards.*

Even still, with all of his belongings packed and ready to travel, it took nearly an hour to make his way out of the sanctuary and to be on his way out of the city. Another half-candlemark later, and he felt confident enough to duck into a copse of trees for privacy. Not that he was going to have any. He had been too focused on the road ahead (and lost in his own argumentative thoughts) that he didn't notice his pursuers until one of them spoke up and broke him from his reverie.

Mariah chimed in with a quaint, yet irritated, question. "What are you doing?"

Dammit. "Leaving."

"I assume without us?"

He nodded at her and realized she was still wearing the same peasant robe she had been given last night. This time though, she had her cloak on with it, and her own bags packed and over her shoulder. "That's the plan. How did you know I was going to be here?"

Shrugging, she blew off the question. "I met someone last night, late. She said to expect this."

"That priestess is going to be a pain in my ass," he muttered. "Listen, Mariah. Stay here. All of you should. Just turn around, tell everyone to stay put."

"There is something seriously wrong with you if you think that I'm not going home," she scoffed.

Akaran rubbed his temples as his headache returned in full force. "It isn't your home. They're not your people. You yourself said that. You're there because you've been stuck there. Stay here, and you'll find other passage to Ameressa."

"If I really wanted to do *that* I could have done it years ago," she argued, stamping her foot to make a point. "I'm going back to Toniki, and that means I am going with you."

"Mariah."

That was when he realized she wasn't alone. Behind her, the battlemage cleared her throat and demanded his full attention. "She isn't the only one that's going up there."

Deboria, beside her, had her own thoughts on the matter, too. "I did say that there was no sense in arguing about it."

"Goddess dammit," he grumbled, then saw the soldier that had accompanied them down hanging as far back as he could while still being in the trees. "Galagrin. *You* talk them out of it."

"Can't do that."

"You can try; I *can* give you orders to do so."

With a sympathetic smile, the soldier shrugged his shoulders so high it made his neck almost disappear. "Yessir you can, but she can tell me to shove them up my ass an' she might actually do it herself. Ain't no way I am going to get in the middle of a contested command."

Evalia smiled at him, absolutely delighted. "Keep using your head like that and you're going to earn yourself a promotion, private." Then to the exorcist, her voice took on an *entirely* different tone. "And *you* can shove the attempted orders up *your* ass for all the good it's going to do if you even try. Don't think about countermanding me because there isn't a guard in this city that's going to listen to you."

"You'd have thought that he would have figured out that there's no sense in trying to exert power when there's nobody around to help enforce it," the apprentice alchemist added.

"GAH!" he shouted, thrusting his hands up in the air. "What is *wrong* with you people!? Haven't you been paying attention? *Any* attention to what's going on?"

"Attention to what?" she pressed. "The fact that you're deranged? That you're a borderline maniac? You executed a man last night, you offered a traitor safe passage, and you almost got me killed. How, in any world, does that make you qualified to warn us away from anything?"

Akaran couldn't believe what he was hearing. "You don't care about the Queen any more than I do so drop the pretense about being pissed that she was a spy."

"Fine. A murderess. Or did you forget about that part?"

It wasn't the reply he was expecting and he had to admit she was right. "No I... fine, okay. So say I'm deranged. What does that make you for wanting to follow me?"

She was ready for it. "I *don't* want to follow you. I don't want to be *near* you."

Feeling briefly vindicated, he tried to win the argument with a shout. "Then fisking - !"

Tried, but failed. "She may not wish to follow you, but she does wish to help you pick up the pieces when you next fight. She does care for you, even if not for your methods." Her voice was so soft, it was a miracle that he could see her lips moving. "Do not seek to deny her what her heart wishes; it is possible to have a fondness for a soul even when there is disgust and anger that is there only because of age and a lack of reason. There are others she still cares for in the village too; do not forget that. Lives that matter to her as much as yours does."

"Age and lack of reason?" Mariah grumbled. "What kind of insult is *that?*"

"Mariah, you won't be safe," Akaran tried to argue (again). "There's no way I can say that you won't get killed when we end this."

Evalia cleared her throat and added her own opinion. "She won't get killed. I think I happen to like this little spitfire. I will have her under my protection."

"Under yours?" he groused. "How wonderful. *You're pregnant.* If Makolichi breaks containment or... no. Worse. So much worse. If *Daringol* finds you, do you know what will happen to that child? You saw what happened to that fisking pile of rat shit guard last night! Do you *really* think that it's worth the risk to your babe?"

"One would hope that you would try to excise it before it got to that point."

That, at least, he had a good answer to. "Not if I'm dead. You folk tend to forget that I was once already. It's a bit of a big deal for me and really drove the point home that this isn't a normal hunt and banish job."

"Yet you came back from being dead," Deboria interrupted. "It is a safe thing to say that in this world that does not oft happen – not and leave you the delightful soul you are. One could argue that it is safer to be around a man that did not let a trifling difficulty as a still heart slow him down for long."

Evalia rubbed her hands together while she sized up the priestess. "I think -"

"- that you like me as well, and not just the girl? I appreciate your kindness, lady battlemage."

"Don't push it."

Deboria just smiled at her. Akaran tried to confront Xandros's wife head-on. "Evalia, please, don't go with us. Stay here. Protect yourself."

"And leave my husband in your care? I need that man alive to be a father to our child, thank you very much. I can't be assured of that unless I'm there standing right next to him."

"Dammit," he seethed. "Please would you three listen to reason!"

The priestess tried to fix him with a comforting smile that did about as much good as his arguments. "They listened. Their reasons are greater than yours. Now. Would you care to attempt to try to argue my decision to travel, or can we simply say that you will not come out the victor in that battle and spare me the breath and you the further damage to your dwindling credibility in their eyes?"

Even Mariah cringed at that while Galagrin whispered a pained, "Ouch."

His hands went right back to his throbbing temples. "I really think I hate you all."

"You do not hate us; if you did, you wouldn't try so hard to dissuade us from going to where you think it is not safe. Us, you love – some more than others," she added with a wink and a nod to Mariah. The angry blonde girl's cheeks went as crimson as Akaran's. "But what you hate is the uncertainty around what will happen next."

Galagrin quietly interjected a little bit of support. "In his defense, that's not an unreasonable opinion."

"**Thank you.** *Someone* at least listens to me."

"Oh no, I'm not taking your side," he quickly shot back. "If I do, the Commander may well have me scrubbing latrines."

Evalia gave him another encouraging look. "That promotion looks more and more in the cards for you."

Contented with the fact that they had come to an agreement (no matter *what* Akaran said), Deboria cleared her throat and silenced everyone's grumbling. "We have spoken enough. Though, exorcist, I am not sure that I understand your thoughts on how it is you intend to return us to the village? You did not bring your horses or carriages."

"I made arrangements for my horse to be kept here until I returned."

That was unexpected, even by a woman that could feel certain thoughts. "You intend for us to walk...?"

"No," he answered, then shrugged with a roll of his eye. "Just remember, you three *asked* for this. And *you* didn't try to stop them," he said, pointing towards the soldier in the rear.

"After how well they handled you? No sir, not a chance."

Akaran just sighed. "Fine," he muttered, then he gently pressed his fingertips on the back of his neck. With a small pulse of magic, he triggered the contact. "Eos. We're ready."

This was even a little more confusing for the priestess. "Mariah said that it would be some kind of mage? I expected someone to be here already. Who is it you're speaking to that we cannot see?"

The young girl gave a slightly sheepish smile. "I said it would be a spell. Not a... mage... exactly."

"Then what...?"

A thick cloud of snowflakes and white crystals blossomed up from the ground in the middle of all of them. When Eos'eno stepped out of the vortex, both Evalia and Deboria stepped back in surprise. She had been kind enough, at least, to keep her human form. "Priest. You... you've been fighting again, you have, I can see it on your face. And... your bandages. Split your stomach anew? After all it is we did to repair it?"

He glared at her and rested his hand on his side again. "I've been busy..."

"Were you able to find the foci?"

"Found the foci, found Makolichi."

The wisp couldn't hide her surprise. "Is he gone? Did you...? Tell me!"

He shook his head and gave up any pretense of pleasing anyone. "He's been dispersed again. We hit him hard this time."

"But he is not destroyed?"

"No."

It took her a moment of quiet thought before she spoke again. "I believe then, as your kind has so oft said, the word is 'shit.' Yet, I see. It is no matter. The Ice is patient. It is Her nature. Though, at times, it is useful for a sudden avalanche to move obstacles out of the way for good."

"Can't say I disagree. How are things up there?"

Neither the priestess, the battlemage, or the mundane soldier had yet found a way to explain her otherworldly essence to their personal satisfaction. "They have been better. Your mentor has found much, and it is not findings that are good. He is returning to Toniki as we speak."

His frown deepened tremendously. "Like you said. Shit. How not good were his findings?"

She struggled with an answer. "I... I think that it may be best if you speak to him. We found the place where both Makolichi and the wraith were created, and found evidence of how. Steelhom is most angry."

"Wonderful!" he crowed. "I so wanted everyone pissed off, and lucky me, here we are."

"A... Akaran?" Deboria interrupted, finally finding the courage to speak up. "What is this... woman? She is not human? I cannot feel her, as I do others?"

The wisp quickly whipped around to size up the priestess. "A question I could ask of you. Human, yes, you are, but you are unlike any I have seen. You... how odd. You glow, glow around your eyes and ears. You see and hear much more than what a simple woman ever could."

Evalia, on the other hand... "How nice, the two of them are fascinated by each other. I'm assuming that you know what she is and that you're sure she won't kill us? Are you going to tell me that this thing is our ride home...?"

"If I do, will it convince you to stay?"

"She glows, too," Eos interrupted just as suddenly as Deboria had. "Not in her ears but in her eyes and... her womb? And to think that you are all so worried about where it is that I and Makolichi come from, when you so haphazardly bring your own new life into the world at inopportune times. So careless and in-artfully."

Both of the men present flinched at that. "Haphazardly?! It wasn't a planned decision but I like to think that I am perfectly skilled at bringing life to this world."

"You haven't answered the question. What is this... thing? I cannot hear into her."

The exorcist looked at all of them and quietly shrugged again. "Well, at least she's spared your digging. Eos'eno, meet Evalia, Battlemage of the 13th Garrison and irritated wife of Commander Xandros. Also meet Deboria Ult, Priestess of Stara, who wants to come with us for reasons I'm neither sure I understand nor care about all that much."

"I thought I had explained those reasons at length. I thought you smart enough to listen."

He ignored her. "Ladies. Meet Eos'eno. She is a wisp that was summoned out of Tundrala and placed in the body of the dead daughter of the cryo-kineticist that caused this shit storm. Oh, and the body's mother is the druid-turned-alchemist elder of the village, Hirshma, who is also Mariah's mentor. Small town problems, eh?"

"Mother of... the *body?*" Evalia interrupted.

Deboria swallowed back the butterflies that suddenly swelled into her throat. "That is... a disturbing claim. She isn't of this world and you've let her live?"

"Why do all people think that it is his wish to end all things that are not of this world?" the wisp asked with a grumbled pout. "It is the duty of an exorcist to banish the damned, not punish the divine."

Quietly, the priestess had to agree. "Yes, this is true. Forgive me, veil-walker, for I mean no disrespect. This is... simply not what I expected. The Order of Light does welcome you to this world, as it does seem that the Order of Love has given you their approval. We do live in odd times, I think you will agree."

"She means that the Order of Light doesn't really trust us, and they're nervous that my Order has lost its collective mind and while there's plenty of reason to second-guess us at every opportunity, they have had to admit that it may not be wise for anyone to get in our way when it comes to dead things and extra-planar entities."

While Galagrin stifled a snicker, Deboria tried to clear her throat. "This, he says, and yet he complains about my ability to see the things that others may think. Succinctly said, of course."

Akaran looked over at the battlemage and waited for her to add her own two coppers to the chat again. "I suppose you have something to say, Evalia?"

"I helped blow up a demon yesterday, and watched you execute a man by shoving a torch down his throat last night before cutting his head off. I may as well believe you that she's friendly and hope that you *haven't* totally lost your mind. Don't have any other choice."

Eos'eno managed a far-too-human scoff. "A soul that speaks sensically. A trait that more of your kind should aspire to reach. Are we all now ready to depart?"

"Well. I can't get any of them to stay behind," Akaran answered. "Hope you can handle taking all of us at once."

"I am too far from the waters of Tundrala to do so, and too taxed after the last day to serve as transport more than once more. To return with five of you? I do not think that I can. Four? Four... it will be difficult, and I will not have strength much in the next few days."

Galagrin spoke up before anyone else could. "I'll stay."

The exorcist disagreed without a moment's hesitation. "No, you come. One of you four stays behind. At least I can protect *one* of you."

He couldn't agree with that either. "You're not going to get any of them to stick around. We just had that argument. I can get back. For that matter, I can get your horse and take it up with me."

"Not helping, Galagrin."

Evalia grinned at him. "Not helping you, you mean. He's right, we're going."

"*Fine*," he sighed. "No. Wait. Not fine. Galagrin?"

The soldier cocked his head to the side and gave Akaran a quizzical look. "Yessir?"

"Do me a favor, please. Evalia, you said you ran into a bear with things coming out of it, right? Tentacles and hands and things?"

She gave a quick nod. "Yes. There's more of them in Toniki, I presume?"

"Lots more," he grumbled. "Galagrin, got a job for you if you're hanging back."

He stopped looking interested, and started looking worried. "Won't like it, will I?"

"Afraid not. I don't want to leave here without giving things a full sweep, but let's be careful. Take the stuff Steelhom gave you and go out where Evalia went hunting." Akaran flicked a look over to Evalia and cleared his throat. "Battlemage, give him directions, quickly, please."

She quickly rattled off the directions while Galagrin contemplated his fate. "You're asking me to go hunt more of your monsters? By myself, sir?"

"No. Evalia, you still have another couple of people here, right?"

"Yes. They'll be leaving soon to head up to the village. Galagrin, they're stationed at the river barracks."

Even Akaran looked a little relived. "Go get them, and... Evalia, they have any more battlemages stationed there?"

"One. Bit of an ass."

"Get that one too, just to be safe."

Deboria quietly lifted her hand for attention. "Speak with Totoro at the Sanctuary, as well. Ask him for Inniat - while not an exorcist, he is able to bring light to the dark. I sense an ally of the Heavens may aid you in this search."

"Do it. Just make sure that there's nothing else down in that cave. And leave the gems with them when you come back. Oh. And, take Mariah's. She won't need it back at the village. Leave it with whoever is running the city guard. Let them deal with things when you're done. Just to be safe."

Galagrin took the order in stride (the promise of backup helped).

"Yessir. I'll get on it right away."

"Thank you. I hate to ask you to do this."

"Duty of the army to ensure the safety of the Queen's people. No different than yours, sir."

Akaran couldn't help but respect him a bit more for that. "No, suppose it isn't. Good luck," he offered. "Eos... let's get this over with."

Eos smiled and wrapped a new cloud of snow around her body. "It is as you wish, Guardian of Winters. We leave. Come together, touch me, one and all."

Everyone took a cautious step forward and carefully laid their hands on hers and her shoulders. Deboria finally started to realize how far in over her head she was and nervously asked one simple, yet pertinent, question. "I... I have never traveled before by spellcraft. Will this be unpleasant?"

"Probably."

She just blinked and tried to calm herself for what was to come. "Oh. I... see."

Before anyone else could waste time with idle chatter, the wisp pulled everyone in as tight as she could. One final wave of snow erupted on the ground under her feet and nearly instantaneously enveloped all of them. Then, just as suddenly, they all vanished at once.

One would think that after the last snowflake fell that there wouldn't be anything less to comment on in this tiny, out of the way outcropping of trees well past the supposedly all-seeing eyes of the city guard. With all of the interesting people gone, there shouldn't have been anyone but an idle squirrel wondering why the ground had gotten so cold. Although when Ralafon slipped out of hiding and stood in the middle the clearing, he should have wondered why everything turned so suddenly *frosty*.

"Ah. There you are. I've spent too much of my day looking for you, old friend."

The craftsman turned slightly and gave the other watcher a sneer of disgust. "Oh, you. What do you want?"

The man walked closer, his smile never fading, and his gruff voice never changing in tone. "Oh, you? That's no way to greet an old friend, is it?"

"You're not a friend. Not an old one, either."

He tugged a little at the corners of his orange-ish jacket and his smile only grew. "Not a friend? Oh, oh my. You wound me. Straight to the heart, cuts quick, cuts deep. I suppose then that you aren't inclined to do me a favor, are you?"

"I don't *do* favors for you, Riorik. You do them for me. Or did you forget the arrangement?"

"Ah. Yes, that arrangement," he replied with a little cough. "It's time for us to *re-negotiate* the terms."

Ralafon's head tilted as he tried to make sense of whatever fresh madness was standing in front of him. "Re-negotiate? Have you been huffing fumes from the kilns? There's nothing to -"

His smile didn't change in the least as he sucker-punched Ralafon hard in his solar plexus. "Since we're not friends I suppose you're not going to feel half as betrayed as I wish you would. I have to be truthful, that takes away some of the enjoyment I had from that. Not all of it, be of mind, but... it's a little disappointing."

Bent double and gagging, the response was as strangled as it was hateful. "You... you're a dead man, you're dead now. It's off, it's over, we'll find -"

"You'll find someone else, I'm sure," Riorik replied as he gave the other man a comforting pat on the shoulder. "Another smuggler, another businessman who can bribe the guards to look the other way. That someone else won't be in my territory, however. As I said: we're re-negotiating, and part of the new deal is that you and your handlers take a long walk and go somewhere else. Trefagur, maybe. Mont, possibly. Or, you can all go walk into the river and stay at the bottom. I do not care."

"We're going nowhere. We're not gonna do a thing. Do you think I go anywhere by myself? There's eyes on you, eyes, Riorik, and they're gonna make sure that you pay for this, pay for anything you might do to me and -"

The threats were completely and utterly ignored. "Oh, do please quit your petty mewling. It's *me* you're talking to, Ralafon. *Me*. Do you think those eyes are doing anything other than *bleeding* right now? I'm not called the hobbler because I'm the type of man that sends hugs and kisses and roses to people. Though Riorik the Kisser sounds like a fun title."

"Riorik the Cockless when we're done."

His petulance earned him another punch to the gut that knocked him to his knees. "Would have thought that first punch would have gotten the message across. Let me speak in a different way," he muttered. "You are going to pass along a message to your handlers for me. You'll do it today, and then, you will leave. You will have until midnight to make your exit from my lovely city, *or*, come dawn, people will see you hanging at *both* gates on *both* sides of the river. The only question is which side is going to have which piece of you."

"Are you *insane?!* Did you forget who I answer to?!"

"No, not at all. That's what we're having this conversation. That man that just left? The one that burned your agent alive in her prison cell? That man now owes me a favor. He's my new friend. He and I are going to be *great* friends."

The silvery-haired 'craftsman' spit up a mouthful of bile and spittle. "He's as dead as you are."

Riorik, for whatever reason, disagreed. "Maybe. Maybe in time. This is not that time. What I think you fail to understand is that the boy is now under my protection, even if he doesn't know it yet. Granted men in his profession don't have long lives, but... the people and things that tend to hunt men like him don't tend to be agents of other governments. If *anything* happens to him that looks like it may have been at the end of a Civan knife, there *will* be a reckoning."

"That's it? That's your message? You're risking your life to protect some *priest?*"

"Ah, no. Not entirely," he quickly clarified. "That's *part* of the message. The other part is that after your people leave Gonta, if anything happens to *me* that can get traced back to *you*, then I have people who now have very explicit instructions to make sure that every name of every traitorous little rat in this city and the territories around it are delivered right to my new friend's bedside. And not just his," he added, "but half a dozen other men and women of various points of power that would be happy to advance their lot in life over my dead body."

Looking up from the ground in absolutely bewildered shock, Rmaci's handler still couldn't believe what he was hearing. "You wouldn't... you... we'd kill you. We'd kill everyone you've ever held dear."

"That's just the nature of the business we're in, isn't it? I know things about you, you know things about me, and we operate in good faith that the other won't do something that would be irreparable to a respectful working arrangement."

"There's no coming back from this, Riorik. There's no chance. You just started a war. You won't win it. The Empress has people everywhere. You don't know all of them. You can't. They'll have your head."

The Hobbler gave a little nonchalant shrug. "And if they have my head, then they *will* find yours somewhere *far* away from your shoulders. I'm quite sure you feel that the new terms are one-sided, and I have to agree that they are. Yet, all good deals have their end, and our existing arrangement is over now. You are leaving my city. You will do so without a fuss, and without making me regret not calling in my favor that the exorcist owes me."

"In bed with a priest. You're in bed with a priest. Never thought you'd sink so low," he seethed.

Riorik shrugged, then kicked the spymaster between his legs. The retching sound that filled his ears was almost as fine as any bard's tune. "Oh Ralafon, my old friend. Your problem is that *you* never actually bother to *think*. Now. I meant what I said. By the time the moon crests, you'll be well on your way far away. That's the deal. Your payment is that you get to live," he went on, adding, "Choice is of course ultimately yours, but for now, I have things that I need to do."

"Won't... forget this, you fisking mule-fisking... fisker!"

The Hobbler looked down and finally frowned. "I might add in a dictionary to help teach you new words, broaden your vocabulary. It looks like you could use the help with so much swearing and so little content. Well. Pleasure doing business with you," he concluded, just before kicking the spy in his ribs one last time. "As always."

EPILOGUE

He had died and fallen into the Abyss.

All about were black waves frothing with blood and insufferable cold. Souls wailed in the distance as an all-consuming darkness roiled in the water just below his neck. All he could do was struggle to hang on to the shattered husks of damned souls sent to drown before him.

He screamed and shouted and wailed alongside them. There wasn't any escape, there was no place to go. He was trapped, hopeless, and knew it was only a matter of time before his essence was condemned to an eternity of drowning alive in the unfathomable deep, and the demonic legions within.

An errant wave flung him into a sickly green chunk of ice. He screamed in raw agony as a dozen mouths all opened at once and began to chew on him with teeth made of frozen brine. They gnashed at his flesh, swallowed, and bit harder again as his skin grew back for the thousandth time. Pushing against the ice only made his hands freeze to the surface the moment he touched it; then a mouth opened and ripped his left hand off of his arm.

More screaming. More pain. More suffering.

His arm grew back. It hurt as it did. But it always grew back. His arms, his head. His stomach. Every part that was bit off, torn out, or ripped open grew back. The only part that hadn't was the icicle-sized hole in his forehead.

All under the watchful eye of the horrific eternal storm that churned through eternity, and hungrily consumed all. When another condemned sod slammed into the voracious iceberg, it spit him out back into the waves where he floated, and screamed, and begged more and louder until he thought that the Pantheon itself could have heard him.

In a way, it did.

"Ah. There you are."

Her voice cut through his suffering like a knife. He thrashed and looked around wildly, looking for the new threat. That's all there was in this place; threats. Nobody ever came to look for people here. Nobody ever came to find someone here – not for any reason that you would wish to experience.

"Oh, look. You're scared. Isn't that helpful," she muttered.

It sounded like she was all around him but no matter how quickly he thrashed in the water, he couldn't tell who or where she was. "Whatever you are please no please no more please no!"

"If you don't even know who I am, how do you know you don't want more of what I have? Hm?" she mocked.

A wave filled with more acid than water washed over him and pushed him deeper into the ocean, cutting off his words with agonized screams from his boiling lungs. When he crested the water again, he saw her sitting on one of the floes with her legs daintily dangling over the side. "Please stop it please help me please I'm sorry I'm so sorry I -"

The little girl flicked the ends of her curly blonde hair over her shoulders. "No doubt how sorry you are. You've got plenty of reasons to be sorry, too."

"I didn't mean I didn't mean I just wanted to - !"

"Yes, we all know what you just wanted to do," she chirped as she reached down and grabbed him by the back of his neck. "And you deserve every bit of this for all the damn trouble you caused."

The broken soul twisted and tried to fight out of her hands as she effortlessly pulled him up to drop him onto the ice. Remarkably, nothing happened – nothing lunged to bite at him, nothing tried to grab him and rip him to shreds.

It was simply the irritated little girl glaring at him with her arms crossed over her clean white dress. "I didn't cause trouble! I just wanted to work!"

"Oh, yes, your precious work. Your *precious work* is why I'm down here in this festering shit dragging your rotting corpse out of here."

"What? I don't understand! I didn't cause any harm to my work!" he cried as he scrambled back away from her – albeit not too far back.

Scoffing she rolled her eyes. "Ignore the fact that you murdered a man, for starters. Ignore the fact that you opened the door to this Gods-forsaken pisspot and pulled out a demon to do your dirty work. There's the *other* shit you did."

"I controlled him! He couldn't do anything I didn't let him!"

"And then you died, you idiot," she growled. "You died, and your little pet ran free. He ran free and made other little pets and they've killed a whole lot of people."

He shook his head desperately and curled up with his arms around his legs. "Not my fault, not my fault. What they do is their fault, they were just to help with my work and should have gone away when the work was done! I finished my work!"

She reached over and slapped him across a blistered cheek. "Oh you idiot, you haven't even begun to finish your work. The Lady has a job for you, and She's gone to a great deal of trouble *negotiating* your release."

"Re... release? I'm... you're letting me go?"

"No, *She's* letting you go. *I'm* perfectly content with letting you rot – but funny story. *Your* shitty work got someone very close to Her badly hurt, and *She* doesn't like seeing Her so-called man get hurt. Boys can't be men. Boys can't be anything."

He started to sob in joy while winged monstrosities started to circle overhead. "Anything you want! Anything, just make this all stop, make this pain stop!"

"The pain isn't going to stop anytime soon, wizard. Your next stop is back to the Sands. Can't have you dragging the taint of this place along behind you; you need to get all cleaned up," she replied with a cold, nasty smile. "Scoured. Bet that's gonna rub right through your soul. Kinda hoping She lets me watch."

Sobbing and trembling again, he looked up at her. "And... and after? What comes after?"

"After that? After, you're going to help him destroy your precious work, and every damn thing you summoned to help you make it."

"Destroy it? NO! Not after I've suffered HERE for it! NO!"

The little girl grabbed him by his throat and leaned in so close he could feel the breath leave her mouth. "Either you help him destroy your work, or She's gonna let him destroy you. I hope She will. I wanna watch."

He cried out in anguish – though if it was from the grip she had on his throat or the thought of losing his work, she couldn't tell. Nor did she care. "Why are you doing this to me? Why set me free then torture me more?!"

"Because of what you did to Her people. Because of what you did to the souls you stole to make that sad bundle of shadows that calls itself a wraith. Because you took liberties with Gods that you had no belief in to make your work and because that's the price you're going to pay to get out of here." She thrust him over the ocean of brine with one hand and shrugged while he dangled and tried to climb up her arm. "Or I can drop you right back in there and tell Her you wasted Her time. *Be happy* Zell got you, you old fool, and that She didn't meet out punishment Herself. Rumor is, She's a bitch when She's pissed."

"NO! NOT BACK IN NO PLEASE DON'T! DON'T DROP ME BACK IN!"

"Good choice, I suppose," she said with another shrug. "Hope you reconsider when you get back up there. I really, *really* want to watch him take you to task for all you've done."

He shook his head vehemently and tried to get back on the ice. "I won't I won't I'll do it I'll do anything!"

"Pity," she sighed. "Usaic? I really, really want to watch."

End: Saga of the Dead Men Walking
Dead Men in Winter

Next: Saga of the Dead Men Walking
Favorite Things

THE COMPENDIUM OF THE DAMNED, THE DIVINE, AND ALL THINGS IN-BETWEEN

Adelian Empire (Agromah)
The former Empire that ruled the continent of Agromah for hundreds upon hundreds of years, before their last Emperor made the wrong deal at the wrong time.

Alenic Ocean / Ocean of Tears
One of the three oceans of the world, the Alenic Ocean is more 'sea' than an Ocean, but the fifth Queen of Dawnfire ordered her cartographers to name it as such – because she's the queen. While on the map as the Alenic Ocean, most people know it for its unglamorous nickname: the Ocean of Tears. That title was given due to the slave trade, piracy, and general tales of suffering that have plagued the waters south of Dawnfire between Sycio, Mathiea, the K'pina Isles, and Ogibus Bay.

Anthor's Pass
An easily-traversed path that leads from the edge of Dawnfire and underground through the first half of the Equalin Mountains before ending along the edges of the Midland Wastes. Controlling the Pass can give you a door – or a wall – into either the Civan Empire or the Kingdom of Dawnfire.

Basion City
Located in the Kettering Provincial Region, Basion City is heralded as "The safest place in Dawnfire," due to being far from anywhere the Kingdom borders. It's home to a hospital, of sorts, for those exposed to unnatural rigors that have left the mind weary.

Belian-berry tarts
Sweet tarts made from red belian berries. Considered a delicacy around most of Dawnfire, they are fairly common in cities throughout the eastern part of the Kingdom. It was said that the biggest regret held by Empress Bimaria of Civa was that in her failure to win the last Imperium War, she was unable to safely secure enough belian bushes to plant them in Civa Prime.

Blackstone Trading Company
The largest trading company in the entire western hemisphere, the BeaST is owned and run by Master Aidenchal, a dedicated follower of Uoom, and it has holdings that stretch from Civa to Mathiea and everywhere – literally everywhere – else.

Book of Hearts
The holy scriptures of the Order of Love, revised (extensively) after the Hardening, and handed directly down to Mother Adrianne (who really, really hated that title).

Bourshodin Occupation
An ugly part of Dawnfire's history. The Occupation was the result of a perfect storm of events: The Imperium Wars waging around it, Bourshodin was a city on the northern edge of the Missian League, firmly in the middle of Gulil's Jungle. Unfortunately for the inhabitants of Bourshodin, the city was of strategic importance to both Dawnfire and Civa, and the two sides traded blood over and for it for five years. When the war was over, little was left of Bourshodin except for broken walls and drying tears.

Cavisian Ocean / Ocean of Nightmares
The Cavisian Ocean starts where the northern border of the Civan Empire ends, and continues around the upper half of the globe. The only two places known to mankind of any note in the waters is the snowy continent of Crys, and the cursed lands of Agromah (the latter being

where the ocean earned its current nickname).

Collector
With great power comes great responsibility, and the Granalchi understand this. So when one of their men of 'great power' ceases the safe practice of magic, Collectors are sent to collect them and their work for future study... and sometimes dissection. Although the dissection sometimes happens before any talk of studying can be done.

Contract of Governance
Offered by the Kingdom to various merchant guilds, a Contract of Governance grants a Guild the right to govern a village or a city where military access isn't a critical component. The crown has long found it easier to tax those that earn money than it is to learn how to effectively learn to manage trade – which, while allowing for a goodly bit of corruption to take hold, keeps it somewhat honest.

Crys
A frozen continental island to the far north, past Agromah, and towards the top of the world.

Disciples of the Grand Inferno
Priests and priestesses that carry Illiya's words, tend Her shrines, and serve her people.

Emperor Podera (Adelian Empire)
During a bitter civil war, Emperor Podera grew desperate to keep power over his territory, and struck a deal with Arch Duke Belizal, a Daemon lord of immense power. The deal was ill-advised, and eventually, did not work out in his favor. Rumor is, there's a special place in the pit with his name on it...

Empress Bimaria
Ruler of the Civan Empire.

Feast of Ketterig
A yearly celebration held at the end of every winter in Dawnfire, as it rings in summer months, warmer temperatures, and a new dawn.

Goblin

Shit-and-piss soaked creatures, goblins tend to run no taller than two feet high and around fifty to sixty pounds. They are sentient, barely, and you can find occasional outcroppings of them in parts of the Equalin Mountains or in the lands around Matheia.

Granalchi
Masters of the Arcane. They bow to no God as a whole, but simply seek to control and use elemental magic in any and all forms. They are the top-licensed guild of mages throughout most of the known world, and they like it like that.

Grand Sanctum of the Pantheon
The largest shrine to the Order of Light – and all the Gods and Goddesses that the Order honors – in the Kingdom of Dawnfire, and some wonder, if not the entire world. It's located in the Dawnfire Capitol, and most are welcome to visit.

Helvator
A white wine from Mathiea, it has numerous psychotropic effects and is banned from trade inside the kingdom of Dawnfire.

Ichaia's Tears
An underground river that starts somewhere deep in the middle of the Equalin Mountains, and is known for the softly glowing pink algae in it that coats the riverbanks along Gonta every year.

Justiciar
Judges in the Kingdom of Dawnfire. While larger cities have ones that are assigned to them directly, smaller villages have to rely on traveling Justiciars to settle matters of legal dispute (or criminal proceedings of critical nature).

Knights of Flame
Paladins of the Goddess of Fire, Illiya.

Lady Olessa Roseorn
An influential member of the Fellowship of the Alchemetic, located in Ameressa.

Luminary

The ruler of the Missian League, a loose collection of cities, villages, and territory on the western side of Dawnfire. They're recognized as an independent region, though lately, they have begun to make decisions questionable enough to concern the Queen.

Maiden
A Maiden is a title granted to a select few leaders in the Kingdom. Their words are law, and are often placed in charge of the Queen's primary interests, notably her armed forces. Most armies would call them "Generals" or "Admirals," but they are both more than that and less. Military-minded Maidens answer directly to the Holy General Johasta Fire-eyes, while any other Maiden (few as they are) speak directly to the Queen herself. Each military Company is assigned a Maiden as a matter of course.

Maiden's Consort
A Maiden's Consort is comprised of her Consort-Blade (bodyguard, assassin, executioner), her Paladin-Commander (to lead any detachment of holy soldiers the Maiden requires), her Knight-Commander (whom leads mundane soldiers), her Arch-Templar (whom oversees medical needs of the Consort), the Consort Brother (often a high-grade mage, or at the very least, a historian with a bent toward magical arts), and her Betrothed (whom oversees governance and administrative functions).

Merchant-Master Aloric Everstrand, Blackstone's Marauder
Aloric is a mercenary-turned-merchant, and carried his warlike ways on the battlefield into the negotiating chambers. He is currently (and happily) installed as the overseer to the city of Gonta (though his reach spreads throughout much of the province).

Mother Adrianne, the First Exorcist
After the Hardening, thousands of worshipers of Niasmis were cast out of their homes and hounded by Illiyans until well after they escaped the Civan Empire. Adrianne was a simple woman – wife to a blacksmith, mother to two children. As time and fate turned, the Goddess picked her (against her wishes) to guide the lost to a new home in the south. Granted the honorific of 'Mother' of the Order (also against her wishes) as her legacy grew, Adrianne was the first person that Niasmis entrusted with the knowledge of how to combat the dead and damned head on.

Northern Tribe of the Snowy Peaks of Crys
Considered the seat of power for the continent, it's often said that the Ouinzhee Maidens hold sway over every aspect of the Tribal life from shore to shore. Few people can confirm, as most find it too cold to make the trip worth their while.

Old Veritas
The last city of the Adelian Empire to fall before the might of Arch Duke Belizal. Nisamis's personal Archangel, Li'Orla, had been sent on a mission of mercy from the Heavens themselves to stop Belizal from razing it to the ground. When she went missing, Veritas came to an end. One hundred and eighty-six years later, a new settlement was built on the ruins, a place lovingly referred to as the Port city of Fritan. Why anyone would do such a stupid thing is up for debate.

Maiden Piata, the Madwoman
Maiden Piata heads Nova Company, assigned to protect Anthor's Passageway on the Dawnfire side. She is known to openly practice death magic, is widely believed to be among the most sadistic of all of the Queen's citizens, and is not one to cross. She is served by Paladin-Commander Hitrio and Consort-Blade Brandolin.

Pool of Harmony's Warmth
The pool is a safe place within the safe place of an Order of Light shrine. To be allowed to bathe in one is a high honor, and most people go their lives without ever seeing one.

Precipice
The last place you go when you've got nothing left. The Precipice is the wrong side of whatever purgatory that a sinner may aspire to. The region of the Abyss where the Dragon-God Gormith holds sway to cast final sentence upon all souls that fall into the pit, it oversees the eternal torment below.

Priestess of Stara
Separate from the individual priests and priestesses that serve the Gods of their respective Orders, a Priestess of Stara serves all the Gods by caring for the Shrines of the Order of Light and providing care for pilgrims or worshipers in need.

Rashio's Fall
A beautiful waterfall that is fed by waters from Temboria lake and a few small streams. It flows directly into the City of Gonta.

Sands of Time
Once a soul passes on from the mortal world, the first stop is the Veil, and the sandscape within. It's a timeless region with no real beginning or end – it begins where you enter, and ends where you leave. On one end is the pathway to the Mount of Heaven and the Pantheon beyond. On the other is... the other place. The rule of thumb (not that there's anyone that can ever recite this rule to you) is to never look back over your shoulder if you can already see the light...

Scars of Balance
A ranking system for Melian priests. As the surest way to celebrate destruction is to destroy, the devout followers of Melia learn how to channel the will of their Goddess into varied acts of, well... destruction. The Scars serve as an outward sign of how proficient a priest is in using that magic – both as a way to brag, and as a warning for others to know to stay away. The more Scars, the deadlier the follower.

Sephilal
Otherworldly dragons that fly between the Worlds after the World beyond the Veil. They care little for the Gods and less for mortals, and the feeling is mutual.

Sister Catherine Prostil
The last Sister of Niasmis before the fall of Agromah, and the Grand Temple of Love. Maiden-Templar Catherine Prostil in Basion City is a direct descendant.

(The) Stewards of Blizzards
Priests of Istalla that dedicate their lives to preserving artifacts, antiques, and other works of art or amazement, to safeguard them against the ravages of time.

Usaic
The ice elementalist at the heart of the misery that's befallen Toniki.

Waschali Province
The easternmost provincial region of the Kingdom of Dawnfire. It holds immense strategic value to the Kingdom, as the primary passageway through the Equalin Mountains between the Kingdom of Dawnfire and the Civan Empire. Among other villages and cities, it encompasses Anthor's Pass, Triefragur, Gonta, and Toniki. It is under the direct oversight of Maiden Piata and her Consort.

Defiled
The 'defiled' are mortal/natural creatures that have been exposed to or twisted by Abyssian magic/auras to the point that they have become monsters in their own right. Corpses that have arisen from the dead on their own volition are lumped into this category, as are animals (or even people) that have been corrupted past the point of the Laws of Normality. Creatures, and even inanimate objects, that have been turned pose as much of a threat to the living world as demons... and some demons have been known to start out this way.

The Defiled can also be considered a broad category for various breeds of creatures that can fit on either side of the 'formerly alive' and 'entirely demonic' spectrum. Wraiths, for example, are often purely the souls of the dearly departed; dogs and wolves, given the right nudging, can grow into Abyssian hounds.

At the Battles of Coldstone's Summit, the notable Defiled included:

Abogin
Revenants. Damn near impossible to completely put down, these undead are bound to the mortal world by a foci of some kind – be it part of their body from death, or an object they were fond of in life... or an anchor by someone that summons them. Until the foci is destroyed, revenants will keep coming, and coming, and coming.

Arin-Goliaths
Nesting wraiths. Spirits that have gained the power to absorb other spirits and latent magic. The more they absorb, the stronger they become. Often mad, and rarely able to control themselves with any sense of individuality, they are not a common sight. When they do manifest, they often evolve out of loose spirits in larger cities where

magic and energetic auras are naturally present.

Corpusal
Zombies. Animated corpses, frequently mindless, usually utterly worthless. While fairly easy to kill, if they swarm in a pack it becomes an issue; or if they're one of their stronger cousins, it can be a completely different ballgame.

Giata
Abyssian Hounds. They can't be reasoned with, they can't be bargained with. They often are found serving as guards for stronger demons or are summoned by wizards, warlocks and more... but these are truly wild, unfriendly, and unforgiving beasts.

Shiriak
Vile, baby-like creatures that reek of sulfur and rot and bile and worse. These scavenger-demonkin are attracted to places of rot, decay, or mass slaughter. They can sniff out a massacre a hundred miles away, and can zero in on a plague just as easily. Servants of Neph-kor and His minions, they pose little threat.

Gods and Godlings
The World beyond the World is full of an infinite number of creatures and beings of immense power that dwarf anything mortal men can use. Some of those things are easier to cope with than others, and others still... are a different story entirely.

Archangel Li'Orla
The firstborn angel in service to Niasmis, she was last seen at the Fall of Agromah, and her current whereabouts are unknown (even by the Goddess of Love). Or at least, that's what they say. Rumor has it that a man in a blood-red robe knows a little more than that...

Episturine
Guardians of Tundrala. Nothing escapes their gaze for long, and they will bring the full wrath of the frozen realm down on the heads of any that dare challenge Istalla.

Hircanton, Demi-God of Storms

One of the many Demi-Gods until the gaze of Kora'thi, Hircanton is responsible for managing the weather. Depicted as having two faces, His nature can either bring life or death. As even the worst of his storms is purely neutral and done entirely without malice, He does have a home on the Pantheon.

Isamiael, Demi-God of Health
The Lady of Medicine draws Her power from Kora'thi and Pristi both, She is the patron deity of Templars, Clerics, Medics, and even the random soldier who needs a little extra help to stop some bleeding.

Pymondis
Even by the standards of the Abyss, Pymondis is a vile thing. The son of the God of Disease, Pymondis is a gluttonous monstrosity that wallows in the fruit of the world, and gorges Himself on the spoiled remnants. Known otherwise as the Despoiler of Food, the Befouled Glutton, and the Prince of Rot, His influence can be felt with every wasted crumb, every piece of spoiled game, and every piece of fruit consumed by worms...

THE MAGE'S HANDBOOK OF SPELLS, INVOCATIONS, AND OTHER FLASHY EFFECTS

The Exorcist's Book of Words

'Words,' as used by the magically-inclined members of the Order of Love, are specific spells used for a variety of effects. They are the bread and butter of many a priest, and while they're supposed to be used as sparingly as possible... not everyone follows that particular set of instructions. Sometimes Words are etched onto the skin of the caster – this is done to amplify them, or to enhance the connection to the spell. Others are simply spoken with no need for runemarks.

Allay (Word)

Establishes a feeling of warmth, peace, and eases doubts and suspicions of those that hear it said, when invoked in the name of the Goddess by a Priest of Love.

Bonds (Word)

A spell that manifests streamers of holy light that wrap themselves around the target of the spell, either to capture it or to move it. It's not a spell that works well on etheric subjects, but it does have a fairly strong measure of success against physical entities. There's one priest in the Order that the bonds behave a little differently with, appearing as silvery chains instead of lavender tendrils...

Desist (Word)

A short-range stun and pushback Word that can be used to quickly quell a fight or hostile act. The stun effect doesn't last long enough to allow it to be suitable for active combat.

Disenchant (Word)

Breaks any spells or enchantments on a person or item, and can destroy non-sentient magical constructs (although it doesn't do them any favors).

Disperse (Word)

Breaks apart focused concentrations of magic that don't have physical forms, such as spirits, befouled auras, or unfocused clouds of wild magic.

Enlighten (Word/Ward)

Enlighten causes anyone within hearing of the Word to suddenly gain a deeper sense of understanding of and interest in a conversation, concept, or lesson. If used as a Ward, Enlighten causes an aura of peace and fascination with any objects within the ward circle.

Expel (Word)

Expel evaporates lesser undead and deals critical damage to lesser Abyssians. It can be used at a distance, only requiring that the intended target is at the forefront of the caster's mind. While typically used at-range, it can be channeled down through a weapon or other object that an exorcist may be holding at any given time.

Expulse (Word)

Expulse serves the same duty as Expel, but it hits harder – and can only be used up close and in person (touch required). Also like Expel, it can be channeled into a weapon or another object, as long as the spellcaster is holding it.

Expunge (Word)

Like Expel and Expulse, Expunge can banish an unholy spirit or destroy a demonkin. Unlike the two, Expunge is designed to break apart any anchors that an entity may have in the physical world (such as in cases where a spirit has taken over an inanimate object). It provides a much stronger force than either Expel or Expulse, and uses more of the spellcaster's energy.

Illuminate (Word)
Forces light to coalesce around anything with a dark aura, giving away location – if not necessarily type or intent.

Luminaird (Word)
This Word manifests a translucent shield on the caster's arm with a limited lifespan. While it can't absorb many attacks before it fades, it is better to absorb 'some' than 'none'...

Luminoso (Word)
Summons an aura of light around the caster.

Luminoso Corsair (Word)
Allows the projection of a circle of light on a target object or general location at a distance.

Nul'mir
This Word is a type of binding spell that completely immobilizes an entity, but can only be done at very close range. It's used for entrapment or interrogation purposes, primarily, or as a step in an active exorcism.

Purify (Word)
A point-blank infusion of holy magic into a person, item, object, or area within two-three feet of the spellcaster, with the intention of safely cleansing the area.

Purge (Word)
As Purify is used when the well-being of the intended target of the infusion of holy magic is important, Purge is the brute-force "I don't have time to wait to see if this can be done gently" way to call upon a cleansing effect.

Unmask (Word)
A step-up from Illuminate, Unmask completely exposes the true nature of a spell, supernatural object/creature, enchantment, or magic-imbued item to the priest that utters the Word.

Invocations

While Words get the point across, they're mostly just simple spells with relatively simple effects. The Order of Love is a unique outlier, too; most Orders don't use single Words as much as they do full-blown invocations. Niasmis's priests have been known to use longer, more convoluted requests for divine aid when the situation absolutely requires it, preferring instead to get the point across as quickly as possible.

Call of Questing Growth (Order of Nature)
"As fire to ash as ash to soil as soil into growth; as ice to water as water into growth; as wind to clouds and clouds to rain as rain to water into growth; as death to rot and rot to decay and decay into growth; let me reap, let me sow, let me find new places new ways for growth to take hold."

*This invocation to Kora'thi spreads roots through almost any terrain, searching for any desire that was present in the mind of the petitioner when the spell is cast. The vines that sprout act oddly sentient, lending credence to the argument from druids world-over that plants are as conscious as any other living thing. (As this has never been shown to be true when studied by anyone **not** of their Order, most simply assume that Her druids spend too much time with the wrong leaves in their mouths.)*

"Celiouso et-vas balintin lumin." (Order of Love)
"Circle of warding, provide a bastion of light." This invocation not only *activates and recharges any existing Wards set in the immediate area, it overlays radiant light to chase away the dark.*

"Enia savald et-vas folisdal anavin." (Order of Love)
"Worldly stone of warding, become this soul." This invocation causes a *crystal in the possession of the priest using the invocation to take on a facet of the aura it is being exposed to. This aura will grow stronger when in the presence of other things like it; ie: it can be used to track wraiths of the same breed, zombies raised by a specific necromancer, or demons that share a magical or physical bond.*

Generic Spells/Invocations
Sometimes, you don't need to seek the favor of a God, or devote yourself to fancy spells and complicated abilities. And other times, the

magic is either so rudimentary that anyone with so much as a sliver of affinity could cast the spell – albeit with the details slightly different from mage to mage and priest to priest.

Obscura (Spell – Generic)

An obscura enchantment is a spell that is specifically designed to hide, mask, or otherwise place a metaphysical fog around an area to keep it from being discovered by prying eyes.

Manabolt/Manabomb

Not everyone uses magic for reasons holy (or un-). Some users simply need it to make things blow up without bothering to manifest their magic as bolts of fire or ice or even blasts of lightning. These spells don't take any special words or invocations. For those mages (and some followers of Melia), they're content in using raw force-of-will to create and launch unstable bursts of ether.

Ideally, launched from a great distance.

ABOUT THE AUTHOR

Hailing from the Parkersburg area in West Virginia, USA, Joshua is a stay at home adoptive father to his furry demonic overlords, or as other people call them, cats. A geek, a gamer, and a cosplayer for charity, he's spent far too much time thinking about geopolitics and societal norms, so trying his hand at being a writer seemed like a good idea... it's less scary than the real world.

Usually.

Got a question?

Want to learn more about the Saga?

Check out his website or send him an email!

www.sagadmw.com
sagadmw@gmail.com

The Saga of the Dead Men Walking
Where good things happen to bad people,
and the good people are questionable at best.

Year 512 of the Queen's Rule
The Snowflakes Trilogy
Snowflakes in Summer
Dead Men in Winter
Favorite Things

Origins of the Dead Men Walking:
Year 512 of the Queen's Rule
Slag Harbor (An Interruption in the Snowflakes Trilogy)
After battling Makolichi in Gonta – and before facing him down for the final time in Toniki - Akaran decides to leave Private Galagrin behind in the City of Mud to make sure that nothing got missed in his sweep. What he finds is more than just a stray shiriak; it's an answer to an unasked question...

Year 513 Q.R.
Claw Unsheathed (release date: Fall 2018)
Who's to blame when a young girl is accused of murder? Did she do it, or did her father? And when she's cornered and the claws come out... does it matter?

Year 516 Q.R.
Fearmonger
Years after Toniki, a grizzled Akaran serves as a peacekeeper to the Queen – and nothing wants the peace to be kept.

Year 517 Q.R.
Blindsided
Stannoth and Elrok couldn't be any more different. Trained mercenaries in the Hunter's Guild, they absolutely hate each other – but they don't have a choice but to work together.